FACE TO FACE WITH A KILLER

"Come along little lady," he said. "The show starts soon. You may not be the star, but you could win an Oscar for a supporting role."

The gun pulled away a couple of feet, and she exhaled. PJ stood at her full height, even though it was painful, bending her left arm and pressing it tightly against her ribs to immobilize them. She could see the face of her attacker, and recognized him as the man who had murdered Rick. PJ swiped at her bloody chin with her right hand and then wiped her hand clean on her jeans.

He gestured toward the rear door. She didn't move fast enough. He placed his hand between her shoulder blades and pushed. Stumbling, she moved out of the door he had opened for her and into the backyard.

"Scream, and it'll be the last thing you do," he said softly.

BOOK YOUR PLACE ON OUR WEBSITE AND MAKE THE READING CONNECTION!

We've created a customized website just for our very special readers, where you can get the inside scoop on everything that's going on with Zebra, Pinnacle and Kensington books.

When you come online, you'll have the exciting opportunity to:

- View covers of upcoming books
- Read sample chapters
- Learn about our future publishing schedule (listed by publication month *and author*)
- Find out when your favorite authors will be visiting a city near you
- Search for and order backlist books from our online catalog
- Check out author bios and background information
- Send e-mail to your favorite authors
- Meet the Kensington staff online
- Join us in weekly chats with authors, readers and other guests
- Get writing guidelines
- AND MUCH MORE!

**Visit our website at
http://www.pinnaclebooks.com**

ACT OF BETRAYAL

Morgan Avery

Pinnacle Books
Kensington Publishing Corp.
http://www.pinnaclebooks.com

* On *Chameleon*
** On *Chameleon*
*** On *Fire Cracker*

PINNACLE BOOKS are published by

Kensington Publishing Corp.
850 Third Avenue
New York, NY 10022

Pinnacle and the P logo Reg. U.S. Pat. & TM Off.

First Printing: June, 2000
10 9 8 7 6 5 4 3 2 1

Printed in the United States of America

To my son Timothy,
whose spirit is as large and beautiful
as the Ethiopian sky under which he was born

Revenge is a wild kind of justice,
which the more a man's nature runs to,
the more ought law to weed it out.

—Francis Bacon, 1561-1626

One

Cut didn't have the connections to pull off the murder inside the prison, but now his target was on the outside. The timing couldn't be better. He always associated the summer heat with the day that his boy died.

It was hot in the apartment, but Cut was used to the heat. His lean body sweated freely, and the undershirt he wore was soaked under the arms and down his back. The last week of July in St. Louis was bad enough when a person could lie in the deep shade of a tree and let the breeze take away the sweat. In his long years he'd spent many an hour enjoying such breezes, the kind that left behind a salty taste on the skin and a hope for more than distant thunder from heavy clouds in the west. Compared to an afternoon under a shade tree, the apartment was a little slice of hell.

It would have been nice to open the window.

Though he had rented the apartment months ago, he had only furnished it with two rickety wooden chairs he'd picked up at Goodwill. That was back in February, and he hadn't noticed that the apartment didn't have air-conditioning then. No wonder the rent was so cheap. Even in something as important as deciding where the target would die, Cut was a practical man. No need to part with more money than he had to.

The linings of the leather gloves he wore were soaked with sweat. He'd worn the gloves every time he was in the apartment.

As the weather turned hotter, his palms, encased in winter gloves, responded like the tongues of eager puppies. Smelled like a wet puppy, too, one that had been rolling to pick up odors that were only attractive to another dog. After being sweated in and dried a few times, the gloves had lost most of their flexibility. He was planning to throw them out afterward, which was a shame because they had cost him fifteen bucks.

Last week he had brought in all the supplies he needed. Securing the chemicals had been an interesting challenge, something he'd never had occasion to do. Cut spent some time putting the weather stripping on the door and sealing the heat vents with plastic bags. He'd found a dead mouse in one of them, dried and stiff, and taken it as a good omen.

On the Big Day, he got to the apartment at seven in the morning, after treating himself to a biscuit breakfast and a cup of coffee at a fast-food place. It was a good thing he remembered to bring the insulated picnic jug of water. He took a sip, the cool water mingling with the sweat on his lips and trickling down his throat. He tilted his head back to enjoy the water, like a bird drinking. He pictured himself carousing in a birdbath, fluffing his feathers and shaking the water down to his skin. It helped some, took his mind off the heat. He wasn't an imaginative man, but when he did get a good mental image he held onto it.

A couple of years in Vietnam had taught him that heat was a relative thing. An enlistee at the age of thirty-four, Cut was almost rendered helpless by the heat when he stepped off the plane and into the jungle. Then he put it behind him in his practical way and got on with the business of surviving. He stayed in one country's service or another's for fourteen years, moving into covert activities after the evacuation. He wasn't in the US Army after Vietnam, but the action was rewarding and the paychecks were regular. His only complaint was that it seemed that every place he was sent was blazing hot or so cold he began to think that blue was the normal color of his fingertips. He found he had a talent and a love for knife work, both close-in and with throwing knives that flitted like black wings of death, and he earned his nickname time and again. When he started to slow down, he told himself that it was a young man's work and he should get his bony carcass out of the way and let them carry on. But he kept the name because he liked it.

It was four in the afternoon. Cut's stomach was empty, but his determination was fueled by thoughts of his only son, who had been so cruelly taken from him. He pulled off one glove and fished into his pocket for a peppermint candy. He popped it into his mouth, then carefully placed the wrapper back in his pocket and tugged the sweaty glove back on.

Released from prison that morning, Cut's target was on his way to the apartment. It had to be so. When a man got out of prison, he got himself a few drinks and then he got himself a woman. For the past several months, the target had corresponded with a woman, Ginger Miller, who lived in the hot-as-hell apartment on the third floor of an apartment building in south St. Louis. Cut knew all about that, because he wrote the letters himself. Ginger was the name of a teacher he'd had a crush on in sixth grade, and when the opportunity came to choose a woman's name, he indulged himself. She didn't really live in the apartment, but the target didn't know that. Ginger's letters had started out friendly, then grown hot and encouraging, and the last few had been open invitations to sex.

The young man on the receiving end of those letters would be coming to Ginger's apartment, as surely as a raccoon to an open garbage can.

He sucked in the heated air, held it in his lungs, and thought that he could open the window for a little while and close it after the target arrived. No good. He'd already used the petroleum jelly, sealing the window glass and the frame as best he could. That hadn't done his gloves any good, either.

Just when he was berating himself for having weak thoughts of cool breezes and bathing like a bird, he heard the stairs creak-ing. Exhaling deeply but silently, his lips pursed into an o, Cut flexed his fingers and fought the stiff gloves. It was time.

Perched on one of the chairs near the door of the apartment, he waited for the knock. When it came, he pressed the button on the tape player on the floor next to him.

"Come on in," the sexy female voice said. "The door's open."

He had recorded it from a porno movie.

The door opened and the target stood there with a silly grin on his face and a swelling below the belt that probably wasn't a wad of money in his pocket. Cut rose and swung his fist in one smooth motion. As he'd guessed, one punch was enough to knock the unsuspecting man out. Even though Cut was sixty-six, he knew he was strong. He kept up his arm strength with push-ups every morning, and the morning of the Big Day had been no exception.

It paid off. The target landed flat on his back in the hall. Cut dragged the unconscious man inside the apartment and over to the other chair, parting the sheets of plastic that he'd thumbtacked to the ceiling. Grasping him under the arms, he lifted the man easily to the chair that stood there. He stripped him of his clothes, thinking that added a nice touch of humiliation, then secured him with leather arm, leg, and chest restraints. He had decided against restraining the head. If his target thrashed around and convulsed, so much the better. Then Cut taped the man's mouth. No sense taking the chance that anyone would hear him scream. The young woman on the first floor was home with her baby, but as far as he knew the residents of the other apartments weren't home. He had watched the building, and on other Wednesday mornings the place had been deserted except for 1B, the woman and baby.

Cut had eliminated lethal injection first thing. Too gentle, although if he left off the anesthetic part of the process, it had possibilities. It would have been interesting to try electrocution, but Cut had feared electricity since the time he had nearly died of a bad shock as a child. He couldn't set up an electric chair himself, and he couldn't very well hire an electrician. Too many questions, and not a clue to what he could answer that didn't sound bad. Bringing lumber up the three flights of stairs to build a gallows held no appeal at all. He couldn't do a firing squad properly with only himself to hold a gun, and besides, he didn't want to be thought of as some kind of cheap-thrills Charles Bronson in the *Death Wish* movies.

He picked up the jug of water and doused his captive. As soon as the man got through sputtering and became fully alert, his eyes showed fear.

Good.

After taking a last look at the man's pleading eyes, and watching him struggle against the restraints, Cut closed the flaps of the tent, walked over to door, and yanked the cord he had strung. He picked up the water jug and tape recorder. No sense wasting perfectly good things.

He would like to stay and watch, but he was worried that gas would escape the makeshift tent and make staying inside the apartment dangerous. He had a fleeting thought for the woman and the baby in 1B, but knew he had sealed up the apartment pretty well, including the windows and vents. They should be okay.

He heard the fizz of the cyanide tablets as they hit the acid, and moments later saw very faint tendrils of vapor rising from the bucket. Standing at the door, watching through the clear plastic, he saw Rick Schultz, Detective Leo Schultz's son, hold his breath as long as he could, holding onto life. Inevitably, the young man released the pent-up air through his nostrils, and took in his first breath of deadly gas. Cut closed the door tightly and left him to die.

A son for a son.

Two

PJ Gray smashed the buzzing alarm clock with a righteous-ness worthy of a pulpit-pounding preacher. It was 6:00 A.M. Monday morning, and it seemed as if her head had just hit the pillow. In fact, she had gotten three hours of sleep, but her body was slow to admit even that. She turned over onto her side, closed her eyes, and indulged in wishful thinking.

Her cheek was lightly brushed by something that registered as spider legs. Popping her eyes wide open, she found herself with a close-up view of honey-colored feline eyes. Megabite, responding to the sound of the alarm and the expectation of the meal to follow, was on PJ's pillow to make sure the human did her part in the morning routine. PJ, grateful that she had felt the cat's whiskers and not real spider legs, blinked at the sunshine that was brash enough to come in her window. Still inert, she was bumped on the nose by Megabite, who clearly wasn't satisfied with progress made.

She had just about convinced herself to sit up, promising herself a long shower and a leisurely breakfast, when the phone rang. Fumbling for it, she sent Megabite tumbling to the floor, and earned an indignant stare from the cat.

"What?" she barked into the phone. It was all of Monday morning pared down to a single word.

"Take it easy, Doc. After all, I waited until the alarm went off."

"Just how do you know when my alarm goes off?"

"Deduction. I'm a dee-tective."

"Not so anyone would notice."

"Christ. Okay, I'll call back after you have your coffee. You can explain the delay to Lieutenant Wall."

A defensive Detective Leo Schultz was like a porcupine rolled into a ball. She squeezed the bridge of her nose and regretted every drop of wine that had passed her lips the night before. Mike Wolf hadn't left until nearly 3:00 A.M., so that made it this morning rather than last night that she had done her unaccustomed drinking. Fine way to start the day.

"Let's start over, detective," she said in the best apologetic tone she could manage.

There was a pause as Schultz unrolled himself and flattened his quills.

"Got a call from Dave," he said. "Tenant complained of a bad smell from an apartment next door. Dave didn't get too excited, since this time of year we get a fair number of those calls. People go on vacation, leave the family pooch in a locked-up apartment. 'But I left plenty of food and water out,' they whine when King the Wonder Dog turns up looking like a well-done roast. Those places are like ovens, especially the ones on the top floor."

"Could you get to the point?" PJ was thinking of cool water splashing on her face and Tylenol going down her throat.

"What, have to go to the bathroom? I always have to take a piss as soon as the alarm goes off. Got my bladder trained that way."

"Schultz."

"Yeah, anyway, this call turns out to be a corpse of the human variety. Male Caucasian. Weird setup in the room, plastic, bondage, must have been something kinky. Dave wasn't too specific."

"Good for him. He has excellent judgment."

Schultz gave her the address and she wrote it down. It was

on the way in to work, so she'd stop there without going to her office first. It looked as if a shower and breakfast had moved farther away—in fact, over the horizon. She told Schultz she'd be there before him, and to let Dave know to expect her.

PJ slipped on a pair of linen trousers that were draped over a chair. They were supposed to go to the dry cleaner's that afternoon, but would have to get another wearing. Remembering with a groan that she had intended to do the laundry yesterday, she knew there wasn't much hope of finding any clean clothes in her closet. She had spent time with her friend Mike instead.

Mike's wife, confined to a long-term care facility after a botched suicide attempt that left her with a devastating head injury, had died suddenly. A brain aneurysm accomplished what Sally Wolf hadn't been able to do with a bullet. Mike had appeared at her door with the news, and there was nothing to do except invite him in and let him stay as long as he wished. Mike had become like a brother to her, so that meant the death of his wife, even though PJ had never met the woman, was treated like a death in the family.

The price of her compassion—one of them, anyway—was opening her closet door and seeing that the only summer blouse left had large orange and red flowers and a deep V neck. It was that or go with long sleeves on a day that promised nearly a hundred degrees by noon. She slipped the blouse over her head, figuring that she had been possessed by the Demon of Poor Fashion Sense when she purchased it.

PJ made her way down the hallway to her son's bedroom. Sitting on the edge of Thomas's bed, she admired his unlined forehead and angular tan cheeks, and couldn't resist running her fingers over the soft, barely there mustache on his upper lip. At thirteen, Thomas was looking more like his father every day. It was eerie, the way that she could catch a sideways glimpse of Thomas and think it was Steven, come back into her life.

No chance of that, even if she had wanted it. Steven had remarried the day after the divorce was final, and was happily cooing to his new wife and baby back in Denver.

Impulsively she bent over and tickled Thomas's nose with the tip of her shoulder-length hair. He snorted, wiped his nose with the back of his hand, and looked sleepily up at her.

"Mike gone yet?" he said.

"Hours ago." She refused to think of how few. "I got a call from Schultz and I need to go to work. What's on your schedule, T-man?"

He yawned. "Winston and I are going to bum around the house and then ride our bikes over to the rec center after lunch."

"Swimming?"

"Yeah."

She was glad the two boys were back together again, close companions as they had been since shortly after she and Thomas had moved to St. Louis. There had been a brief period when Winston believed that Thomas had started vicious rumors about him. It wasn't true, but it had driven the boys apart.

"Tough life," she said, thinking about how she had savored her own childhood summers in Newton, Iowa. "Be home by four. I don't want you out during rush hour on your bike."

"Geez, Mom, it's not like we're riding on the interstate."

"By four." She kissed him on the forehead. He was almost back to sleep. She noticed that his alarm was set for nine-thirty.

Envy swept over her.

In the kitchen, PJ poured Megabite a dish of dry food. The cat sniffed it and decided to wait and see what Thomas would offer.

* * *

PJ was surprised to find a trio of HazMat vans parked in front of the apartment building on Lake, and a crowd of people who must have been tenants clustered in small groups. Some were hastily dressed, some still in nightwear. A few men stood on the sidewalk in their boxer shorts. They had been rousted out of the building.

The HazMat teams were packing up to leave. When PJ got out of her car, a faint smell of ammonia wafted over to her. She had a short wait at the door of the building as her ID was checked and her name entered onto the log of people entering and leaving the scene. The walls of the tiny entry vestibule were dark dirty green, and seemed to press in on her. It would have been depressing to come and go through the spot every day. There was no one in sight, so she started up the stairs.

Climbing the flights of stairs to the third floor of the building where the murder had occurred, PJ was reminded in the clearest way that she had recently celebrated her forty-first birthday. The twenty extra pounds she carried weren't defying the law of gravity, either, and by the time she reached the top she was breathing hard. The ammonia smell grew stronger as she climbed. It lightly stung her nose and throat, and there were tears poised in the corners of her eyes by the time she got to the third floor.

The door with the yellow tape was down at the end of the hall. There were three doors on each side, painted the same shade of green as the entry hallway, and a run of patterned blue carpet down the center. Decals were used to number the apartments, and the lettering was comically crooked, as if put on by a drunk. The yellowed wallpaper of mismatched patterns seemed appropriate for the place. There was a small window that hadn't seen a washrag and a spritz of glass cleaner in years at the end of the hallway, but it wasn't open. The overhead lighting consisted of two bare bulbs. The heat was stifling, a physical thing that crawled up her body. She closed her eyes and tried to pick up the bad odor reported by the tenant, but the ammonia overrode everything else, even the smell of the ashtray at her feet, crammed with butts. Evidently a smoker in 3A was exiled from the living quarters and used the hall as a smoking lounge.

It could be worse, she thought. *If the toilets aren't working, tenants in these places go out in the hall rather than foul their own nests.*

There was an officer planted in the center of the hallway, controlling access to the apartment. The young woman looked as if she had been dipped in starch and blow-dried. Every hair was in place, her uniform was neat, and not a drop of sweat was in sight. PJ shook her head. It was criminal to look that competent before seven in the morning. The only concession to humanity was the fact that she had edged her way down the hall, presumably to escape the source of the odor—the end apartment, where the door was standing open. The officer's eyes were locked onto PJ and narrowed in disapproval.

It must have been the orange-and-red flowered blouse.

PJ strode purposefully down the hall and identified herself again. Officer Erica Schaffer informed her that there had been cyanide gas in the end apartment which had condensed, evaporated, and left a film of acid. The HazMat team had washed down everything with an ammonia mixture and then sucked up the liquid with powerful vacuums. A few minutes ago, the place had been declared safe for entry, and the tenants would be let back into the building soon. It was obvious, though, that none of the curious stood a chance of getting past Officer Schaffer.

At the sound of their voices, Dave Whitmore's head popped around the corner of the doorway. He came out, wiping his brow, pushing back the shock of brown hair that spent more time blocking the vision of his left eye than staying neatly in place. One look at his face and she knew that he was seriously upset. Dave had a reputation for squeamishness, but what he was feeling must have been far beyond that. It set off alarms in every part of PJ's body. She was close enough so that the smell of decay from the end apartment slammed into her, floating out on top of the ammonia like roadkill layered on hot asphalt. She felt her legs grow weak, as if she were trying to stand on columns of water rather than muscle and bone.

"What is it?"

"Boss, the victim is . . ." Dave said. "My God, it's Schultz's son."

PJ exhaled, and tried to draw shallow breaths instead of gulping the foul air. "Can't be. He's in prison."

"He was released last Wednesday. The Assistant ME says the decomposition is accelerated because of the heat, but she estimates the body's been there four days or more. Probably won't be able to be more precise than that, but the general time frame fits."

"How do you know it's him?"

"He had the release papers in his pocket, along with some letters addressed to Rick Schultz. His clothing was searched by the HazMat team before they bagged it. You might find a dead guy with somebody else's wallet, but not his prison release, for God's sake. He looks bad, real bad. He was tied up and gassed. There's no positive ID yet. That'll come later. But it's him, all right."

She could read the certainty in his voice, and a numbness settled over her like a cold fog descending from somewhere much chillier than the ceiling of the hallway.

"Schultz is on his way here," she said flatly.

"Go on back down and see if you can intercept him. He shouldn't be up here."

PJ pivoted and headed for the stairs. She hoped to catch Schultz outside the building, but she was too late. She heard his booming voice in the front hall, stepped up her pace, and met him on the second-floor landing. She put her arms out, her hands touching the walls on each side, forming a barrier to block his way. He towered over her five-foot-three height, and was still a powerful man although the years and poor habits had taken their toll. He could easily charge right past her. He stopped and melodramatically shielded his eyes.

"Christ, Doc, you ought to hand out sunglasses when you wear a blouse like that."

"Schultz . . ."

He came up close to her and dipped his eyes toward her neckline.

"Nice view, though."

He swiveled his head around, and when he was sure there was no one else in sight he kissed her lightly on the forehead. She remembered doing the same with her own living, vibrant son, not thirty minutes ago, and she trembled at the thought of what waited for Schultz in the apartment on the third floor.

"Leo, there's something I have to tell you."

He nodded his head toward the stairs. "Let's go on up, and we'll talk. You have some ideas already? This place smells like the world's biggest cat litter box."

She was silent. He studied her face and took a step back. "Tell."

There was no way to sugarcoat it, and Schultz wouldn't want that, anyway. She put her hands on his shoulders, feeling the warm skin beneath his light shirt. There was a slight dampness under her fingers. The Pacer he'd driven over in didn't have air-conditioning.

"The victim is Rick."

His eyes went wide. "He's in—"

"No, he's not. He was released last Wednesday."

"The asshole didn't call me."

PJ wasn't sure if Schultz was referring to his son or to some prison official. She knew that Schultz had used his law enforcement connections to keep an eye on his son in prison.

His body slumped, and he leaned against the wall. She

watched his face carefully, and saw waves of emotion pass over it like an earthquake and its aftershocks.

"I've got to see him," he said. "Move, Doc."

"Dave thinks it would be better if you weren't involved right now," she said. Her words sounded hollow. "So do I."

"Shit," he shouted. He shoved her aside roughly, and she banged her shoulder into the wall. "Get out of my fucking way!"

He barreled up the stairs and disappeared into the hallway. PJ turned and went after him, her heart leaping out to him in his pain. She wished she hadn't been the one to give him the news.

Schultz had taken a lightning bolt through the heart. Looking at PJ, hearing her words, he was transfixed. Then everything seemed to come loose inside him, whirling out as though chunks of his body were flying away into space. His knees gave way, and he sagged against the wall. He couldn't seem to find the center of himself, and his vision faded around the edges.

The victim is Rick.

He pushed PJ aside angrily. Why would she try to keep him from his son? He had to see his boy, no matter what. At the top of the steps, he saw an officer in the hallway. She put her arms out toward him, then backed off as he showed no sign of stopping. Toward the end of the hall he was met by the unmistakable smell of death, ripened by heat.

Christ, that stink has nothing to do with Rick. Nothing.

He blundered into someone at the doorway, and pulled together enough focus in his eyes and mind to recognize Dave.

"Tell me what happened," Schultz said hoarsely. It seemed as though he hadn't used his voice in a long time. "It's not Rick, is it?"

Schultz held Dave's gaze and saw his own agony reflected there.

"Boss, you should wait downstairs. You don't want to remember Rick like this."

Schultz lowered his head and lunged forward. Catching Dave off guard, he rammed his junior detective in the center of the chest, sending him staggering backward. Dave was a big bear of a man, tall and broad, but Schultz had desperation on his side.

There was a photographer in the room snapping away, and the Assistant ME was off to one side. They looked over in surprise at the commotion at the door and assessed the situation rapidly. Deciding they were suddenly needed out in the hall, the two nearly tripped over themselves, and then over the recovering Dave, trying to get out in a hurry.

Schultz took a few steps toward the center of the room. There was a chair, an old wooden one that had been painted green at one time.

A man's body was fastened in a sitting position in the chair with leather straps at the wrists, ankles, and around the chest. He was naked. Someone had draped an opaque piece of plastic sheet across his groin as a modesty cloth. Not approved investigative practice, but they had probably guessed Schultz was on his way. It was a small kindness, and he was grateful for it.

The tissues of the man's body were swollen, and the bands of leather dug in so tightly they were practically buried. His mouth was taped, and there was crusty dried blood on his chin that had dribbled out from underneath the tape. His eyes were open, and there were so many broken blood vessels in them that the whites looked red. Patches of skin had begun to slide off, as the skin of a ripe tomato can be neatly removed after immersing it in hot water.

Schultz noted objectively that there were no maggots, and that meant the place had been tightly closed off indeed.

Rick Schultz had been slowly suffocated from the inside, his flesh and heart and brain starving, as hemoglobin carried the cyanide through his blood vessels in place of oxygen.

In a gas chamber, it could take ten minutes to squeeze the life from a convict. In the uncontrolled amateur horror show in apartment 3F, there was no telling how long it had taken for his son to die.

After the initial viewing, Schultz's eyes could only take in a little at a time. His gaze rested on a foot, then flitted to the window, then to a shoulder, then to the peeling paint on the leg of the chair. Schultz wondered if it was lead paint.

Hazardous. Have to warn somebody about that.

He couldn't draw breath, and his heart felt as though it had split apart in his chest. His roving eyes landed on the right hand. There was a silver ring deeply embedded in the flesh—a ring that Schultz recognized. It had been given to Rick by his mother. There were initials RWS on the face of the ring, and on the inner band, Schultz knew, was the inscription *Love from Mom and Dad.*

Schultz was struck down by the sight of the ring, like a giant redwood felled by a saw. He dropped to his knees, covered his face with his hands, and sobbed.

Three

PJ came up behind Schultz, placed her hands on his shoulders as he knelt, and let her tears flow hotly down her cheeks. After sharing Mike Wolf's grief for his wife just hours earlier, she didn't think she had any tears left, but she proved herself wrong.

She hadn't known Rick personally, but she knew with utmost certainty that Schultz was facing what no parent should ever have to see.

His sobbing subsided as abruptly as it had begun, like a storm over the Sahara. She put an arm under his elbow as he clumsily got to his feet. His arthritic knees must have been screaming while he was kneeling, but sensory information connected with things other than what was in front of him just wasn't being processed.

PJ found her voice. It came out strong and sure, and she was glad of that.

"Leo, come with me. Let the others work in here now. We'll wait downstairs."

She got him as far as the second floor, but he couldn't seem to go any farther, as if he were tethered to his son's body and the cord only allowed him to travel that far. Folding chairs materialized, brought by a considerate officer from outside the building. Schultz sat, his large hands on his thighs and his eyes focused on the stairs. She waited next to him, one of her hands resting on his, refusing to let her thoughts stray into the dangerous territory of imagining what she would do in his place, if Thomas had been the one in the chair.

The thing in the chair.

The Assistant ME, Dr. Georgia Morton, came down the stairs, and Schultz stood to meet her.

"Tattoo?" he said. He had no room for civility, for extra words.

"An apple with a worm, and the word 'rotten,' in blue letters, I think, on the left buttock," she said. "It's hard to tell! the color." Her voice was low and sympathetic, and didn't carry beyond the three of them.

Some time later, the body was brought down on a gurney, impersonal in its zippered black bag.

Schultz sighed as the gurney was maneuvered down the stairs, past the two of them on the landing, and out the front door.

"We can go now," he said.

Out on the sidewalk, PJ winced at the sun and heat. At ten in the morning on the third of August, the humid air sat on St. Louis like an unwelcome crowd of houseguests who refused to get off the couch and leave. Already the sidewalk felt warm under her soles, and the sunshine was an oppressive weight on her shoulders.

Schultz seemed oblivious to the heat. His eyes followed the van bearing his son's body as it made its way down the street.

"Let's go to Millie's," PJ said. "We can get some breakfast and figure out what to do next. We'll both do better if we get a little distance."

She knew neither of them would ever forget those images in the hot building, but she was offering comfort and companionship, holding them out like a menu, for him to pick and choose whatever would do him the most good.

His head turned toward her, and she saw something frightening in his eyes, something primitive that evoked rending and bloody revenge—justice of a wild and very personal kind. He blinked, and it was gone.

"Okay," he said. "You buy."

Four

The expansive windows of Millie's Diner were fogged over. Millie hated the heat, and she must have had the air-conditioner dialed down to sixty-eight degrees. The hot air outside pressed against the window glass like a dog at a butcher shop. PJ could practically hear it panting to get in.

Inside, she let the cool air, the familiar sounds, and the forthright sanity of the diner envelop her. The aromas of coffee, bacon, and even greasy hamburgers were welcome, and pushed away the odors of ammonia and death that hung around her face, in her hair and clothing. Ignoring the half-dozen empty tables, PJ and Schultz seated themselves at their usual stools at the end of the counter, leaving one place between them. Millie didn't mind them taking up three places, because the middle stool was the one that wobbled, and all the regulars avoided it anyway.

The utensils were cold to the touch, and the steam rising from other customers' coffee cups actually looked appealing.

The news had preceded them, probably in the form of a phone call from Dave, because Millie didn't approach right away for her usual banter. Schultz had been coming to Millie's Diner for more years than either he or the proprietress cared to remember, and the two of them had an established routine of insults.

Millie eyed them from the safety of the kitchen, peering

around the edge of the food pass-through, her halo of frizzy gray hair visible even though she thought she was hiding. When she couldn't avoid it any longer, she brought out a cup of coffee for each of them.

"Nice blouse," Millie said.

PJ mumbled her thanks.

"I'm real sorry about what happened," Millie said, finally making eye contact with Schultz. "He was a real pain in the ass, but he was family."

PJ held her breath. She wasn't sure how Schultz would react to that description of his son, no matter how closely it sliced to the bone of truth. Rick had been serving time for selling marijuana to school kids, which was not exactly the occupation that a cop would choose for his only offspring. PJ knew that there had been arguments over behavior, money, getting a job, petty thievery, and minor vandalism. It was an escalating pattern. Rick had been sliding into career criminal status, and Schultz had been belatedly trying to apply the brakes and slow his descent—belatedly, because he hadn't been much of a presence in his son's life until his wife, Julia, abruptly washed her hands of him. Schultz's tough stance and his refusal to get his son off easy on a drug peddling charge had led to a physical confrontation between father and son.

Nevertheless, he was Schultz's son, and she knew that Schultz hadn't given up on the young man. In fact, Schultz had been planning to work with Rick to turn the situation around after he'd served his time.

"You really know how to cheer a guy up, you old bat," Schultz said. "You ought to work for a greeting card company."

Millie started to get her hackles up. PJ could see her forcing herself to be nice.

"I'm not going to mess with that," Millie said. "I figure we have a truce, at least for a while. It's early for lunch. You still want your usual?"

"Hell, why not? My bowels can use a load of grease."

She pinched her lips together, but kept her silence.

"I'll have a biscuit to go with my coffee, please," PJ said. "Or a roll. Whatever you have today."

"Coming up," Millie said. She headed for the kitchen. "Someone could learn a few things about being polite," she said, just loud enough for the two of them to hear.

So much for the truce, PJ thought.

PJ's sweet roll, a huge creation that could have filled a generous soup bowl, arrived in just a couple of minutes. She held her hand over it for a moment, enjoying the warmth. It was freshly baked. She sliced it in half, unwrapped two foil-covered pats of butter, and started one pat melting on each half. Her dad used to enjoy a sweet roll that way nearly every morning, and her mom teased him about adding butter to an already fat-laden item. "Like sprinkling sugar on Frosted Flakes," she'd complain. PJ tried to lose herself in the sensations, the routine motions, and the memory as a way of avoiding what came next.

She had no idea what to say to Schultz.

A man she cared deeply for, respected, and trusted was . . . what? Angry? Numb? Sad? There had been that terrifying glimpse of what was going on inside him that she had gotten on the street outside the apartment building, that moment when his eyes had shown her things she didn't want to see.

She was a professional, a psychologist with years of clinical experience before she turned away from her practice and moved into the corporate world. There she had used her computer skills to develop virtual marketplaces, where buyers strolled aisles that existed only in a computer, buying this item, leaving that one on the shelf, every preference noted and analyzed. Then came the divorce, the move to St. Louis from Denver, and her work with the St. Louis Police Department. She had been Schultz's boss for over a year, and in that time their relationship had gone from outright hostility to acceptance of the value of each other's approach to the job.

And possibly to something more.

She put that last distracting thought away quickly. It wasn't the time to examine her feelings for Schultz. She should be thinking only of how she could comfort him, help him to make some sense of his loss. As soon as the thought entered her mind, she knew that trying to make sense of things was the wrong approach. Even if she came to an objective understanding of why Schultz's son died, she wouldn't be able to make emotional sense of it. There was nothing to do but cling like a bubble on the surface of Schultz's emotions.

It would have been nice if she could have plucked some magic product from those virtual grocery shelves in her former job and make everything all right for Schultz. In spite of her training in grief management, she wanted a quick fix for him.

PJ started on her roll, and let her thoughts slide into a black pit she'd been skirting.

What if it had been Thomas? How could I bear it?

Just the thought made her chest tighten and a spasm travel up her spine. "Fairies dancing on your back with cold feet," her mom used to say.

Millie came out of the kitchen carrying a white china plate loaded down with a burger and fries. Stuck in the top of the bun was the diner's trademark, a toothpick with a little American flag at the top. As Millie placed the plate in front of Schultz, PJ noticed that the flag had been moved down the toothpick.

It was flying at half-mast.

Schultz spotted the flag. He put his elbows on the counter and rested his head in his hands. "Christ," he said. "Jesus fucking Christ."

"Hey," Millie said. "You got no call to talk like that. I was only trying to show you I was sorry for Rick, you old fossil."

Resolve solidified in PJ. Her feelings had been shifting like the continents over molten magma, but now they had formed a crust and taken a new shape. If the victim had been her son, she wouldn't rest until justice was done. She would see to it that the killer never took another life. And that's exactly what she would do for Schultz.

She reached over and snatched the toothpick from his hamburger bun and slipped it into the pocket of her trousers. Out of sight. Then she leaned over the stool between them and spoke softly close to his ear.

"We're in this together, Leo. Every step of the way."

Halfway through his meal he announced that someone had to tell Julia. As soon as he said it, PJ was mortified that she hadn't thought of notifying Rick's mother and quietly taken care of it herself. But studying his face, she knew how important it was that he be the one to do it. At least she could be next to him.

"The phone's right over there," said PJ. "I've got some change, I think."

"I have to make the phone call," he said. It sounded as though he was trying to convince himself. "Before she finds out some other way."

He dumped his change on the counter and pawed through it. Unbidden, Millie coasted by and emptied her pockets of the tips she had held out that morning, adding to the pile for the pay phone. Evidently she was thinking way ahead of both of them.

PJ tried to rise from her stool and follow him to the phone, thinking she would be quietly supportive as he talked, but some deep, surprising reluctance kept her rooted in place.

Schultz's fingers were steady as he punched in the phone number. He felt he was holding up very well, once the body was taken away from the kill site. There had been that ridiculous flag on a toothpick gimmick that Millie pulled, but he wouldn't let anything like that take him by surprise again. He knew Millie's heart was in the right place, but the sight of that tiny flag had been unbearable.

He made a pact with himself that when he was with others, and there was work to be done, he would hold together. He couldn't help the fact that his son's death was a public display—a police matter, too—but from now on he could control when and how he would do his grieving.

A man answered. Schultz had never spoken to or even seen Julia's live-in partner. When she had suddenly left Schultz, it was to move in with her sister in Chicago, but that hadn't lasted long. Within a few weeks, she had another man in her life. The only thing he'd done on the home front during that time was grow mildew in his shower stall.

Glassup. James Glassup, that was his name. Schultz couldn't bring himself to call the man by his first name. It was too comradely. Too understanding.

"Mr. Glassup, this is Leo Schultz. Is Julia there?"

"Hold on a sec. She's just out of the shower."

It's ten-thirty on a Monday morning. Doesn't anybody there work for a living, or is it just a perpetual love fest?

He heard mumbling in the background, and he pictured Julia standing there, hair dripping, a towel loosely draped around her, smiling as the phone was held out to her, then changing expression when she learned who it was.

"What's wrong, Leo?"

No *How are you?* or even a simple *Hello.* She knew that he wouldn't call unexpectedly unless it was an emergency. She'd been a cop's wife too long.

PJ and Millie were huddled at the counter, trying not to watch him. He saw his own pain reflected in their faces, especially in PJ's. He squeezed his eyes shut.

"Rick's dead."

There was a thump. He hoped she hadn't fallen down, but

then he heard the bedsprings squeaking. She had sat down heavily on the bed, dripping hair forgotten. He waited a few moments. There was a sharp intake of breath.

"You there, Julia? I'm so sorry to have to tell you this."

He wasn't there to put his arms around her. Just like all the other times in their marriage that she'd needed him.

"God, no . . . how?" Her voice was small, and tugged at him.

"He died several days ago, probably the same day he got out of prison. The body was found this morning."

"Oh God, oh God . . . he wasn't killed in prison? It was an accident, then?"

"It was a homicide."

There was a silence so long that he thought she had hung up.

"Are you sure it's him? You haven't seen him for months. Prison could have changed him." There was the smallest lilt of hope in her voice.

"He had his release papers and his initial ring, which aren't conclusive by themselves. But he also had the tattoo."

A vivid memory: Rick on his twenty-first birthday, the ring new and shiny on his finger, suddenly dropping his trousers for the two of them, showing off the tattoo he'd gotten as a rite of passage. Schultz's own face forming a reluctant smile, Julia's eyes opening wide and her hand flying up to her mouth . . .

She dropped the receiver and fumbled for it. "Leo, you have to tell me. You have to. How did he die? Did he suffer?"

They always ask that, he thought. And most of the time he told parents what they wanted to hear, which was some variation of the truth that didn't sound so bad. Eventually they would find out the real details, as they should, but on the first contact he tried to find some way to soften the blow. No one ever faulted him for it. He wasn't sure if that was the right thing to do in this case. It didn't feel right keeping things from her. She was his wife, or had been. There was no use trying to hide things from her and have her find out from somebody else. Schultz cleared his throat, shoved the images of the third-floor apartment away, and settled for a compromise.

"He was killed with poison gas. He probably never knew what happened."

He was batting .500, and that wasn't a bad percentage for the truth.

Five

"It's CHIP's case, and as long as I'm on this project I get to work it." Schultz stood with his hands on his hips, his words hanging in the air in front of PJ like the odor of yesterday's fish fry.

PJ, Schultz, Dave Whitmore, and Anita Collings were all in PJ's small office in the downtown St. Louis headquarters building. In the office's former life as a utility closet, it had never seen so much excitement. When all the members of the Computerized Homicide Investigations Project were present, there was barely enough room to breathe.

PJ tapped a pencil on her worn wooden desk. The fluorescent light in the ceiling was turned off because of the loud buzz it produced. She had a bright desk lamp, and at the angle it was shining on Schultz he looked like a bad flash picture. There was a large and sinister shadow on the wall behind him. He would be dismayed to realize that his shadow gave the impression that he was bald. PJ knew that Schultz was sensitive about the U-shaped ring of hair that left the top of his head bare, and especially about the few long strands he combed over the bare spot. She had an impulse to reach out and muss up the long hairs, but managed to keep her fingers occupied with the pencil. It was not the time for sentimentality, and she wasn't even sure what the sentiments were that made her want to reach out to him.

The office door was closed to keep out the noise from the men's room across the hall, and in the confined space Schultz's physical and emotional presence took up more than his fair share of space. Feeling as though she was being pressed against the wall and suffocated, PJ reached over to a side table and switched the fan on high speed. The moving air helped restore some of the balance in the room.

Dave and Anita were doing a good imitation of wallpaper.

"This isn't negotiable," PJ said. "You're not working on this case. Surely you see that you couldn't do an objective investigation."

"Objective, hell. I'm motivated, and that's all that counts."

The door opened and Lieutenant Howard Wall stuck his head in. The room went silent at his entrance, words and emotions ricocheting off the walls and coming to rest at their feet.

"Schultz, I need to talk to you," Wall said.

"So talk," Schultz answered. He didn't bother to swivel to face the man who was his boss's boss.

"In the hall."

"Yeah, coming."

Schultz levered himself out of his chair with a heavy hand on the corner of PJ's desk and left the office, slamming the door so hard the pencils danced in their cup on her desk. The three of them strained to hear the low, muffled voices outside. At one point the wooden door rattled in its frame. Schultz had smashed it with his fist. In less than a minute, Wall opened the door again.

"Schultz is taking the rest of the day off," he said. "He's going directly home. It might be nice if one of you spent some time with him this evening."

So that was that. PJ wondered what Wall had said to him. It must not have been the reasonable approach she had tried. Schultz might report to PJ on the computer project, but Lieutenant Wall held the administrative strings, and he had apparently jerked them. Hard.

"Let's see what we've got," PJ said, drawing the group back to the investigation.

Dave spoke up first. "Not a whole lot. Zip on the fingerprints. The killer must have been wearing gloves. It would have taken several trips up to that place to get all the supplies in, so we're talking about a careful person who planned over a period of time. Not to mention one who didn't mind sweaty hands."

"Speaking of supplies, where do you buy those chemicals? There couldn't be too many sources," PJ said.

"Au contraire, Boss," Anita said. Normally Anita exuded cheerfulness, so much so that PJ expected the air around her to sparkle. Since the events of the morning, the sparkle had gone internal, a little fire of determination warming her eyes and giving off heat with every toss of her head. "There are hundreds of chemical supply houses," Anita continued, "and the quantities we're talking about here wouldn't ring any bells, especially if the order was split."

PJ sighed. It was going to be a frustrating case, compounded by the personal aspect for Schultz. She had a feeling that he wasn't going to keep his fingers out, no matter what Lieutenant Wall said.

Was that a bad thing? Should a father seek justice personally? In Schultz's case, she wasn't one hundred percent sure he was intent on bringing in the criminal to face trial. That wasn't a kind thing to think about a coworker and friend, she realized, but it somehow rang true to her.

"Let's assume the killer wouldn't store this stuff for a long time, so the purchase would be recent," PJ said. "We'll have to start canvassing those chemical supply companies, looking for purchases in the last couple of months. For now, we'll look only in Missouri and across the river in Illinois. If the killer is that careful, he—or she—wouldn't take chances with long-distance transportation."

Dave grinned. "I'm just picturing the jerk hitting a pothole on Interstate 40, having the chemicals bounce around in the back seat, and giving himself a fatal whiff."

"Too bad that didn't happen," Anita said.

"Since he lived to make use of them, he must have had some safe method of transport," PJ said. "Maybe he made one trip for the cyanide and one for the acid. That might be something to check for—not just combined purchases."

"How about the restraints?" Anita asked. "Anything unusual?"

"Leather belts from discount stores," Dave answered. "So far, we know Wal-Mart carries them, and most likely others. Probably hundreds of thousands of belts sold all over the country. They were all men's belts, so that's a vague indication that the killer is male. Doesn't have to be, though. A lot of women shop for their men."

PJ opened her mouth to ask another question. Dave raised a finger to forestall her.

"The plastic that was tacked up to form the tent seems to be the kind used by painters. Held up with masking tape, a brand that's widely sold." Dave made spray-painting motions with his hands and accompanied them with sound effects.

"Again, common items with many sources," PJ said. "At least we can learn one thing from that: the killer didn't go at this casually. Careful planning went into it. We'd be better off focusing on the chemicals than on belts, tape, or plastic, I think. I'll talk to Wall about getting help assigned. We're going to need more than the three of us."

As if he had been outside the door listening for his name, Wall came into the office. He flopped into the chair vacated by Schultz, his arms and legs akimbo, like a doll set down by a giant.

"I just heard back from the chief. You've got half a dozen officers to help out with the grunt work. We've had to beat off other volunteers with sticks, just to keep other cases staffed."

PJ couldn't help wondering where those officers had been when she and her small team were overwhelmed with work on other investigations. The murder of a member of a law enforcement officer's family brought the other officers running like soldier ants when the nest is threatened. A flash of bitterness surfaced, but she dismissed it. She was grateful for the help, and knew that more would materialize if she could justify it.

"Thanks, Lieutenant," she said. "We can sure use the help."

"Any leads?" he said.

She shook her head and summarized the discussion for him.

"Somebody had to see something," Anita said. "I can't believe nobody noticed the new tenant carrying weird stuff up the steps to the third floor. Don't people wonder about those things? What about the landlord? Didn't he ever see the person who rented the apartment?"

"I've already checked that out," Dave said. "The owner himself lives in the building, kind of unusual these days. Most times there's a manager on site and the owner is some guy who's been in the building maybe once or twice, or lives out of state and has never even seen the place in person. It's just a line on a tax form. Anyway, the apartment was rented entirely by mail in response to a sign on the lawn, in the name of Ginger Miller. Didn't even ask to see the place first. No signed lease, just month to month. The payments came in cash at the first of every month since February. The owner doesn't have the envelope from any of the payments. When I asked him if all that wasn't a little strange, he said he didn't care as long as the tenant was quiet and paid the rent on time. Doesn't even know for sure that his tenant was a woman. Or that there was only one person involved."

"Okay, so the owner's not a fountain of information," Anita said. "What about the other tenants? I'd at least say hello to Ginger on the stairs, you know, offer to carry strange packages."

Dave raised his eyebrows. "Obviously, the rest of the world isn't like you, Miss Congeniality. Tenants saw no evil, heard no evil, spoke no evil. Most of them look like monkeys, too. Except for that really nice woman in 1B. She's a looker."

Anita poked him in the arm. "Hey, I thought you were spoken for. You're not supposed to be looking at other women."

"A guy always looks. Anyway, she's got baggage."

"Baggage?" PJ said.

"A six-month-old baby. That's not my scene."

"Melissa know about that?" Anita said. "I thought she came from a big family. Seems like she'd want kids."

"Yeah, but not yet. We want a few carefree years before getting those little ankle weights. Not that I dislike kids. But I figure when I'm forty or so, I'll be ready for the dull life." He glanced sideways at PJ. "Uh, no offense, Boss."

"None taken. But you'll find that life with kids is hardly dull." PJ thought about the challenge of raising a teenage son as a single mother. Just when she thought she had a good handle on things, Thomas would come up with something new that required creative parenting. She knew from recent experience that her son wasn't immune to bad influences. A case she'd worked on provided her with ample evidence that evil could take root in her own family, right under her nose. She was more watchful of her son as a result, just at the time in his life when he was pulling away to become his own person.

"So we have a man or a woman that nobody saw," PJ said. "Or any combination or multiple thereof. I don't suppose Ginger Miller is a real name, anyway."

"Phone company has two Ginger Millers," Dave said. "Motor Vehicles has one more who doesn't have a phone. We'll check those out this afternoon. No record at the post office of Ginger Miller at that address, so there was no mail delivered there except to Occupant. The mail slot in the front hall was cleaned out regularly, though."

Anita perked up. "No fingerprints on the mail slot?"

"One set. The postman's."

PJ was a trifle embarrassed that Dave and Anita had been so productive while she had been chowing down on buttered sweet rolls at Millie's. Then she reminded herself that it had been necessary to get Schultz away from the scene, and she was the best one to do it.

She thought of the look on Schultz's face when he got up from the counter to phone Julia. She had wanted to accompany him to the phone, hold his hand, lean her head against his shoulder while he made the most difficult phone call of his life. But she'd done none of that.

Am I so afraid of committing myself to the man that I can't let him lean on me when he needs me the most? Or am I afraid it isn't me he needs?

"The owner lives there and never saw the person?" Anita said. "How'd she pick up the key the first time?"

"The owner lives in a basement apartment with an entrance around the back of the building. He can't keep tabs on anybody from there. The tenants go in and out of the building using the front entrance. The key was mailed to a post office box, and he doesn't remember the address. It was months ago."

Wall grunted. "A little sloppy on his record-keeping, wouldn't you say? Maybe we should ask the IRS to drop in on him. Might jog his memory."

"Couldn't hurt," PJ said. "I'd like Dave and Anita back in that building talking to the other tenants again. Hit the neighboring buildings, too. Someone may have seen something. Make sure you touch base with the new officers first, and get them going on the chemicals and the various Gingers. Let me hear from you by seven at the latest. I'll be at Schultz's by then."

The two young investigators gathered up their notebooks and left. Wall seemed reluctant to go. PJ refilled her coffee cup from the machine on a table squeezed into the corner of her office, and offered him some. He declined, which turned out to be a good thing because she remembered that Schultz had made off with her spare coffee mug last Friday.

His son was already dead then, but no one knew about it. Except the murderer.

"Lieutenant, I'd like to ask you something," she said.

"Shoot."

Something had been on PJ's mind, and it looked as if Howard Wall would be her best source of information. She knew he had kids, four of them in fact, the oldest being about Thomas's age.

"I know this is way out of line, but I need someone to stay with Thomas tonight when I go to visit Schultz. Do you have a regular baby-sitter I could call? Someone . . . mature? I'll call Thomas and tell him I don't know when I'll be home, but I hate to leave him alone for a possible all-nighter. A few hours he can certainly handle, but I don't feel right about all night. I'm almost sure he'll be able to stay at his friend Winston's house for a few days, but I want to talk to Winston's dad about it first and not just spring it on him. I can get it set up by tomorrow."

Lieutenant Wall nodded. "You call Thomas and tell him to expect Al Baker. He's a young officer, but he's very reliable. Works in public relations, and he's great with kids. Given the circumstances, I'm sure he'd be happy to volunteer his time. Don't let his appearance fool you either. He's under thirty and looks like a surfer, but he's all class."

PJ was relieved. She had been reluctant to ask, but she didn't have any advance plans for overnight care for Thomas. While she had been in the hospital after an encounter with a killer who marked her with a knife, Thomas had moved in with Schultz. She didn't have a large circle of friends in St. Louis, as she had in Denver. Her work didn't lend itself to meeting new people and socializing. One friend of hers, Helen

Boxwood, would respond to an urgent request, but she was a nurse who worked nights and couldn't rearrange her schedule at a moment's notice. Bill Lakeland, Winston's father, was the type who planned ahead, having never mastered the flexibility that parenthood entailed. Impromptu requests put him into a tizzy. Her other close friend, Mike Wolf, was out of consideration, also, since his wife had just died, and he was in no condition to take on extra responsibility. He needed time with his own teenage daughters.

It seemed a long time since PJ had sat commiserating with Mike, yet it was only twelve hours ago. No wonder her head was throbbing. She'd had only three hours sleep, and twice that many glasses of wine.

When PJ first became a single mother, she was very sensitive about being self-sufficient in caring for Thomas. She had to prove to herself and to all the imagined critics out there that she could handle it alone before she was willing to reach out for help at difficult times. On her first day on the job as head of CHIP, she never would have guessed that she'd be secure enough as a single person, a parent, and a professional months later to ask her boss for a recommendation for a baby-sitter.

"Thanks," PJ said. "That's a load off my mind." Wall didn't get up to leave. "Something else?"

Wall cleared his throat. "Something you should know about Schultz, and I doubt if anyone's told you. Especially Schultz himself."

She waited as he ordered his thoughts and selected his words. Wall rarely spoke hastily.

"Years ago Schultz had a problem with binge drinking. Not that he was a regular, an alcoholic or anything. It only happened when something went bad at work. He'd get really drunk, and it lasted three or four days. He would do that maybe once a year. Then he'd be back on the job, and nobody ever talked about it. As far as I know, he quit it over ten years ago. He got through his entire divorce and didn't let himself go like that. But with what he saw today, I just don't know."

"I appreciate the warning. Maybe I'd better not wait until this evening to get over to his place as I'd planned."

"Nah, he'll be fine. It won't hit him until later tonight."

PJ thought that he spoke with the certainty of experience. She wondered if Wall had been the one to coax Schultz from his earlier retreats from reality, and if he'd had anything to do with putting a stop to them ten years ago. She wasn't even sure it was a good idea to stop. As a psychologist, she realized the value of the safety valve in situations where the pressure could be overwhelming. If sitting at home getting stone drunk once a year was Schultz's safety valve, why mess with it? Then she realized that maybe he didn't drink just at home. An inebriated law enforcement officer would be a community concern, a danger to himself and others.

Wall walked out, and she was left alone with her thoughts. Everyone else was out doing the field work they'd been trained to do. As a civilian, she began her work on a case right at her desk. Later on she might join the others, but her first task was to develop a computer simulation of the crime scene.

She opened the slim homicide file. There wasn't much in it yet, but it would grow in thickness almost by the hour. It was identified by a case number only, not with a name, until the ME's office provided the official positive ID based on a combination of dental records and the tattoo. But it might as well have been emblazoned *Schultz, Richard William* in neon-bright colors.

She flipped open the case file and paged through until she found the sketches Dave had made of the apartment. Those plus the Polaroid photos would allow her to re-create the scene in the computer. Using customized software, she began the lengthy process of building the apartment, and the victim, in virtual reality.

The CHIP team had come into existence as a result of a federal grant to investigate the use of computers as crime-solving tools. The grant arrived in the form of a powerful Silicon Graphics workstation and limited cash for salaries. The St. Louis Police Department, unwilling to let the grant money slip away and the computer equipment sit idle, advertised for a computer expert to undertake criminology research. The ad appeared in the *Denver Post* just as PJ was scanning the classifieds looking for a way out of the city. Her husband Steven had just left her to move in with his lover, Carla. PJ couldn't stand to stay in the same city with the two of them. Among the nearly half a million other residents of the city of Denver, she felt their presence acutely.

Taking her son and a few possessions that predated her marriage to Steven, she took a pay cut and moved to St. Louis to begin her new career. She had envisioned herself as an desk-bound researcher, spending her days quietly developing virtual reality simulations and generally fiddling around with a high-end computer she couldn't afford on her own. Instead, she was the head of a dynamic team of homicide investigators who challenged her skills, her professionalism, her commitment, and from the very first day, her composure.

And she didn't regret it for a moment.

PJ entered the diagram of the apartment into the computer, using the sketches and measurements Dave had made. Her software would take it from two dimensions to a three-dimensional wire-frame rendering; then she would work to fill in surfaces, textures, and shading, extrapolating what the back sides of objects looked like. She was creating a world in the computer, one that she could manipulate and control.

It was an artificial world she created, but the more detail she added to it the more it seemed to take on a substance of its own. Eventually, her virtual world became so real that it was a meaningful investigative tool. She could enter that world, fooling her senses, immersing herself totally in a space that existed only in a computer's memory and storage. She could be right on the scene of the crime and watch it committed, or put herself in the terrifying situation of becoming the victim of a homicide. Or, if she had the stomach for it, play the role of the killer. By doing so, she hoped to reach a better understanding not only of the physical facts of the crime but the behavior of the criminal. It was behavioral profiling elevated to the next step.

And she could do it repeatedly, trying out variations, using a combination of guidance from the computer, her training as a psychologist, and her intuition to come closer and closer to what she hoped were the actual detailed circumstances of the killing. Details that, without the use of virtual reality to portray them vividly, might be locked irretrievably in the mind of one person—the killer. Her groundbreaking software made use of artificial intelligence, or AI, to help the computer fill in missing information by making a series of best guesses.

She scanned in a photo of Rick, not one of the crime scene photos but the one taken at the time of his arrest for selling drugs. In a process she had developed that she called scanimation, her program would take a scanned image and animate it, bringing it to life within the computer's memory. Facial expressions and realistic body movements added greatly to the believability of the people who populated her virtual world.

She started with the premise that there were two killers, a man and a woman, just because she had to have a starting point. It seemed logical to her that Ginger Miller had an accomplice, perhaps a man to help subdue young strong Rick Schultz in case an amorous approach didn't work. For those figures, she had to rely on generic images of an adult male and female, characters she called Genman and Genfem. If necessary, she also had a Genkid available, a child about six years old that she hoped she'd never have to use. In a previous case she'd needed an adolescent, so she had modified Genman for the purpose. She'd saved the model and dubbed it Genteen.

After a few years at this job, she figured, she'd have a stable of generic creations to call upon as needed.

Genman and Genfem were as nondescript as she could get them: less than middle aged but not young, average height and weight, forgettable facial features, Caucasian but with adjustable racial characteristics if needed, dressed in jeans and plain T-shirts. She inserted them into the simulation and, on a whim, named them Bonnie and Clyde.

PJ outlined the action of the simulation briefly. She didn't provide too much information, because she wanted the computer to draw upon AI to fill in some of the details. Seeing what the computer could come up with when it used its own "imagination" sometimes led to startling insights. And sometimes it led to utterly ridiculous conclusions, much to the amusement of the rest of the CHIP team. Her computer drew upon a large encyclopedia of information to help in decision-making, but didn't interpret that information with the full range of human experience. She was still trying to live down the time her program needed a way to get a Genfem out of a building without being seen. The computer, which had the Bible to draw on in its reference database, had created an angel who clasped the Genfem firmly under the arms and flew her out a window, along with PJ's credibility.

A quick run-through yielded a rough view of her idea of how things happened. For her first effort, she watched the playback as if it were a computer game, with the figures three inches high on the screen. Everything happened in real time, although she could speed through slow sections if she wished. Later on, when she had the simulation more refined, she would immerse herself in it. That meant using a special Head-Mounted Display (HMD) to enter the virtual world so that everything appeared life-size to her. She put the playback on automatic and turned the computer loose.

The simulation started in the third-floor hallway. The three-inch-high Rick on her monitor approached the door of apart-

ment 3F and knocked. Bonnie opened the door, smiling, and
invited him in. He went without hesitation. There had been
some letters found with Rick's body, in the pockets of clothing
left on the floor. PJ didn't have the text of the letters. They
had gone straight to the lab, but supposedly Ginger was pretty
explicit about her plans for Rick. Toxicology results weren't
available yet, but PJ thought it likely that Rick had stopped
for a beer after getting out of prison, tossing back a quick
three or four, loosening his inhibitions and impairing his judgment. Maybe he had intended to contact his father after taking
care of priorities one and two: beer and sex.

Bonnie closed the door behind him, and Rick looked con-
fused at the lack of furniture in the room. At least that's how
PJ interpreted the odd look the computer had slapped onto
Rick's face: his eyes were round as an owl's, and his mouth
looked like a Cheerio.

Bonnie approached and hugged him—actually her arms
went right through him in this early, crude version of the simulation—and apparently reassured him. She kissed him,
stripped his clothes away, and then invited Rick to sit in the
one chair in the center of the room. Bonnie opened a sack on
the floor and took out one leather belt after another, restraining
Rick in the chair. PJ flushed as she imagined how Schultz
would react to her idea that Rick was a willing participant in
the bondage. Worldly as he might be, she couldn't imagine
him cheerfully accepting such speculation about his own son.
She resolved that Schultz would never see the simulation of
his son's death. Whether it reflected reality or not, it might
be too hard for him to take.

When Rick was secured, and evidently expecting things to
proceed in a pleasurable manner, another figure entered the
room. Clyde had been hiding in the bathroom. The two con-
spirators began bringing sheets of plastic from the bathroom
and fastening them to the ceiling to make a tent. Rick
squirmed, but was unable to get free. Unfortunately in the

first run-through, they were building the tent across the room from the spot where Rick sat in the chair. PJ sighed. There was a lot of work left to do on her simulation.

A bucket was brought from the bathroom and carefully filled with acid. Cyanide tablets were tossed in, and the plastic tent filled with red smoke. Wrong. The vapor was supposed to be colorless, or nearly so. Bonnie and Clyde beat a hasty retreat. Rick sat in his chair across the room. A minute later, with no sign of a struggle, his eyes closed like those of a baby doll laid on her back, a much gentler death than the one Rick had suffered in real life.

PJ assessed her simulation. Not too bad for a first attempt, but definitely not ready for prime time.

She glanced at the Mickey Mouse clock on her desk and was surprised to see that it was ten minutes after four. Schultz had been sent home about eleven. She'd been working in a concentrated fashion for over five hours. She called Thomas at home, relieved that he picked up the phone on the third ring. He had gotten home at four, as she had requested. Assorted beeps in the background indicated that he was playing games on the computer. Winston was with him.

She wasn't sure how the news of the death of Schultz's son would affect Thomas, and she hadn't thought out how to tell him before dialing. He and Schultz had grown close over the past few months, and she was sure Thomas was beginning to think of Schultz as a father figure. Thomas knew about Rick, but had never met him.

PJ gave him the news matter-of-factly. She didn't want him to hear from some other source, and besides, Officer Baker was supposed to come around at five o'clock, and Thomas had to know the reason by then. Thomas was silent, then said that he would like to see Schultz.

"I don't think that would be a good idea now. Maybe in a day or two."

"He must feel terrible, Mom. He shouldn't be by himself."

PJ acknowledged her son's compassion, and it stirred her own. She felt a stab of pain at what Schultz was going through and would be facing in the days and months to come.

"I know, sweetie. That's why I'm going over to his house. I don't know when I'll be home. He might want to talk a long time, maybe all night."

She explained about the officer coming to stay with him and Winston.

"You and Winston use the security chain and ask for ID before you let him in. He's about twenty-seven years old and blond, so you know what to expect. Have him phone me when he arrives. I hate to admit it, but I haven't even talked to the guy. That's not something I'd ordinarily do. I'd at least like to speak to him and tell him all the bad tricks you play."

"Hey. No fair."

"Actually, I just want to know he got there okay. You guys can order a pizza for the three of you. There's money in the desk drawer."

"All right! I get to choose something good since you're not here to vote for all those veggies."

She smiled. A conversation with Thomas could fly off in any direction, but sooner or later came down to food. "I'll phone later tonight. Take care, T-man."

"You too, Mom. And tell Schultz . . . well, you'll think of something."

Six

Laden with sacks of roast beef sandwiches and fries, and with a two-liter plastic bottle of Coke tucked awkwardly under her arm, PJ made her way up the front walkway leading to Schultz's home. The lawn looked neglected, burned out in the August heat and ragged from lack of mowing. She doubted that its condition was going to improve over the rest of the summer. She climbed half a dozen steps and stood on a four-by-four concrete landing that served as the entry porch. It wasn't covered by a roof, and PJ felt exposed as she stood there. The century-old home painted in shades of gray and trimmed with white had seemed welcoming on previous visits, but on this trip it seemed dour and disapproving. She could swear that the third-floor dormers were frowning down at her. A curtain moved in a window next door, and she wondered if the neighbors all had the news.

She had no free hand to press the doorbell, so she leaned her elbow on it.

The door opened almost immediately, as though Schultz had been watching her coming up the sidewalk. One look at his face, and she was glad she had come.

"Is that Diet Coke?" he said.

"Nope. The real stuff."

"You said the magic words. Come on in."

She stepped in and Schultz closed the door behind her, cutting off the sunlight and heat. It was after six o'clock, but the heat and humidity outside showed no sign of letting up for the night. All the curtains on the first floor were drawn shut, and no lights were turned on. He had cranked the air-conditioner way down. It was cold.

"You expecting penguins any minute?" PJ said. "It's freezing in here."

"Oh? I didn't notice," he said. "When I got home, it was hot, so I turned down the dial. I guess I set it too low. Here, I'll take those bags."

He took two bags in one hand, clamped the two-liter bottle in the other, and walked off, leaving her standing in the entry hall. She sought out the thermostat, locating it down the main hall outside the bathroom. It was set on sixty degrees. She bumped it up to seventy-four, then joined him in the kitchen.

He had dumped fries out on a napkin and unwrapped one of the sandwiches, but then had gotten stalled. He sat at the table staring in the direction of the food, but not seeing it. She opened kitchen cabinets until she found some glasses. The ice cube trays in the refrigerator were empty, so she poured them each a glass of Coke without ice. Luckily it was cold already—she had gotten it from a refrigerated case at the store. When she sat down opposite him at the kitchen table, he began to eat without waiting for her to unpack her food.

"Thanks for bringing this stuff," he said between bites. "I owe you one."

The rest of the meal passed in silence, except for the sounds of eating, which seemed magnified in Schultz's small kitchen. The high ceilings added to the situation, but Schultz didn't seem to notice. PJ imagined her chewing noises and slurps coming back around like an echo long after she had left.

She was sitting close to Schultz, but the two of them seemed to be in different worlds.

* * *

"Sshh," he said. "You talk too much." And he closed her mouth with a kiss.

PJ responded, leaning into Schultz's warm, reassuring presence, and let herself be enclosed in his arms. For the first time in many days she could close her eyes and not be haunted by terrible images of death. A draining and emotional homicide case had just concluded, and Schultz had driven her home. They were alone in her kitchen.

For a moment she forgot her battered and stitched body and rested her head on his chest. It was awkward at the kitchen table, so they moved to the couch in the living room. His hands gently roamed her body, avoiding the painful spots from her ordeal. It was soothing, so soothing, to relax and let Schultz's strength serve for the two of them.

Fatigue and painkillers did their work, and she faded to sleep. In the morning, she woke with Schultz beside her. He must have carried her upstairs to bed. She nestled against him, smiling at the way his erection tented the blanket. His hands and his kisses were more insistent than on the night before, and she felt his fingers leaving trails of fire on her skin.

She sat up on the edge of the bed, naked, her back to him.

"We shouldn't be doing this," she said. "I don't know if this is what I want. What either of us really wants."

He said nothing. She could feel her own heart beating, and there was a roaring in her ears.

"We've got to think more about this," she said. "This is complicated. We work together."

And you're bouncing around from one woman to another since you got divorced, she'd thought. Maybe I'm just the next in line.

She heard him get up and dress, but didn't turn around. She was afraid of meeting his eyes, afraid that the insubstantial barrier she had built with her words would collapse if she looked in his eyes right then.

She got up and went into the bathroom. When she came out after a long shower, he was gone.

The note read: Take as much time as you want. I love you. We can work it out.

The phone in Schultz's kitchen rang, but he didn't make a move to answer it. After a few rings, PJ answered it herself. It was Dave checking in, with the news that eighteen chemical supply houses had been placed on their contact list, and that not a single one of them had anyone to answer the phone past 5:00 P.M. except security guards. Short of tracking down the owners at home and persuading them to go back into the office, there was nothing to do but wait until business hours resumed the next morning. Dave inquired tentatively about Schultz, and got a report that food had been offered to the gods and all was well for the moment.

When they finished eating, Schultz cleared the wrappers and glasses, then stood facing away from her at the kitchen counter longer than necessary. She thought he might be crying. She rose and walked toward him, intending to lay a hand on his shoulder.

"Schultz, I—"

He rounded on her, and she saw that his eyes were dry and hot.

"Don't try any of that shrink bullshit about grief on me, Doc," he said. "You have no idea how I'm feeling, so don't say that you do. I'll handle this in my own way."

PJ shut her mouth, suppressing the unspoken words of sympathy.

"I'm going out," he said. "You can go home or come along or sit here at my table by yourself, for all I care. But I'm leaving."

He left the house, walking with long strides. Worried, she scurried after him. He got into his car, which was parked at the curb in front of hers. She barely had time to make it to her car and keep him in sight as he drove off.

She couldn't get her thoughts to straighten out as she pursued Schultz. Why couldn't he accept any comfort from her? Weren't they close enough so that he could turn to her when trouble came along? If there was such emotional distance between them, surely there couldn't be anything other than a professional relationship. Yet, she reminded herself, people grieved in individual ways, and maybe his was solitary.

PJ raised her hand to her lips, feeling the pressure of Schultz's kiss months after it was placed there, on a night when she was the one who needed comfort.

God, the man isn't easy. Nothing about him is easy.

He was heading downtown, and she thought with relief that he was going back to work. It was a controlled environment, and she could talk some sense into him there.

Instead of going to the headquarters building, he wound his way through unfamiliar downtown streets she hadn't had reason to travel, and pulled up in front of a bar on Broadway, south of the main commercial district. As soon as she realized the destination, she knew that he was about to go on a drinking binge, as Howard had described. Should she try to stop him, or let him grieve in whatever way he wanted?

Stopping him didn't appear to be an option, because while she had spent indecisive moments in her car at the curb, he had gotten out of his and was already pushing open the door of the bar. Setting aside her deeper concerns to deal with the moment, PJ hurried after him. At least she could be some sort of stabilizing influence, and make sure he got home safely.

At 10:00 P.M., PJ finished up her third glass of orange juice. She had stayed away from alcohol entirely, determined not to repeat her wine-drinking fiasco of the night before. Schultz was drinking Scotch, and she thought he'd had a couple of refills, but didn't really pay attention because she was so distracted by his behavior. He had gone through several stages from surly to glad-handing everyone who got within reach. He talked about everything but his family.

A dark cloud had settled over him in the last hour, and his glass stood untouched on the bar. She felt that he was ready to leave. When he came out of the bathroom and wove his way back to the stool next to her, she suggested that he go home. She was prepared to stay until they got kicked out of the bar, but if she could get him home at an early hour, so much the better. She could send Officer Baker home and stay with Thomas herself, and Schultz would have a long time to rest. If the way he looked was any indication, he was going to need some recovery time.

To her surprise, he agreed. He offered to drive her home and spend the night in her bed. It wasn't the first suggestive remark he'd made while they were at the bar, but it was the mildest of them. She hoped he wouldn't remember his behavior in the morning—especially the times she'd had to remove his hands from various portions of her anatomy.

"You're not driving, Leo. Give me your keys."

"Why should I? You afraid I'll pick up some hot little thing and fuck 'er brains out?"

"Something like that. Just give me the keys."

"Come'n get 'em."

So she did. She searched his pockets, eliciting more crude comments, until she extracted a set of keys. One of them was marked with a police department number, which made it the car key. He'd need his house keys. She removed the car key and handed him the rest, then asked the bartender to call a taxi. When the taxi arrived, she hustled Schultz in and gave the driver the address. Schultz had given up protesting, evidently seeing that it was useless to argue with her. The driver's attitude improved when PJ gave him twenty-five dollars, which was all she had left after paying the bar bill for the two of them. Schultz had left home with two dollars in his wallet.

* * *

Schultz tapped on the glass that separated him from the taxi driver.

"Just pull around the block until she leaves," he said. "Women think they can run your life." The last part he added to make the driver think they were on the same wavelength, two beleaguered and worldly men. It worked. The man nodded and took off.

The taxi took a slow turn around the block and by the time they got back to the bar, PJ's Escort was gone. Schultz opened the door and got out.

"Keep the fare," he said. The driver nodded happily and took off.

Schultz dug into his pocket for his wallet and removed the spare car key he always kept there, right next to the folded fifty-dollar bill for emergencies. He patted the roof of the reddish-orange Pacer affectionately. It wasn't the greatest car he'd ever gotten assigned by Vehicles, but it had proven to be reliable, even if the steering did pull sharply to the right. Tonight it would take him exactly where he wanted to go, and that was the nearest liquor store. The time in the bar with PJ was merely a prelude to the real thing. He'd actually had little to drink, and nothing in the last hour.

It was time to get down to the business of forgetting, and that required a lot more than a few hours with a well-meaning impediment named PJ Gray.

PJ quietly shut the rear door of her home and walked into the living room, announcing herself as she did so. Al Baker rose from the couch, where he had been watching an opera on PBS. He was in his late twenties, blond, tan, muscular, wearing cutoff shorts and a tank top. A bit of California transplanted to south St. Louis.

"Hi," he said. "I didn't expect you until after midnight, at least."

"We broke up early. Tired, I guess," PJ said.

"How's Detective Schultz?"

"As well as can be expected." She didn't add that she thought Schultz was a saturated sponge as far as alcohol was concerned. "Thanks for coming over tonight."

"No problem. I love kids. Thomas really whipped me on that X-Wing game. He's good on the computer. Good kid, too. We hopped in my car and drove Winston home about an hour ago."

"You guys got pizza, didn't you?"

"Yeah. We argued over that," Al said with a grin. "I'm a vegetarian, and that boy's a hopeless carnivore."

Al collected a magazine he'd propped open on the couch. *Scientific American.* So he watched opera and read science articles in his spare time. PJ found herself admiring his trim waist and the firm contents of the cutoffs as Al walked away from her. She wondered if he was married. Or if that made any difference.

"Dr. Gray?"

"Hmm? What?"

"I said goodnight, Dr. Gray. Give Detective Schultz my sympathies."

"Oh, of course. Goodnight."

PJ closed the door behind him, feeling what could only be described as horny, a response out of sync with the day's events. She wondered if the bartender had spiked her orange juice or if Schultz's persistently roaming hands had sparked her sex drive.

Upstairs, PJ changed into her pajamas and splashed water on her face at the bathroom sink. Finally, she was tired—drained—and no remnant of her earlier response to Al Baker remained.

She went into Thomas's room and let her eyes adjust to the

low level of light provided by a night-light next to his bed. He was sleeping on his stomach, with one leg completely off the bed and his face turned away from her. He had surrendered his pillow to Megabite, who curled there like the Queen of All Cats, paid her due by her humans. Megabite's eyes opened slightly, showing little slices of the cat life within that never slept deeply.

All she could see above the blanket was Thomas's hair, disarrayed and blacker than the moonlit night sky outside his window. In the dim light she could make out the cluttered top of his dresser, and a photo frame standing there. She couldn't see the picture in the frame, but she knew it was of Schultz with his arm on Thomas's shoulder, the day they had all gone to a baseball game together. Schultz had bought her son a Cardinals cap. The picture had caught the moment, a half-smile on Schultz's face and lines pinched between his eyebrows, Thomas grinning and giving a thumbs-up, black eyes full of life, the red hat barely containing his exuberant hair.

The image of Schultz's son appeared in front of her, and the remembered smell of death filled her nostrils. She was glad it wasn't her son. She turned and left the room in which Thomas slept, thankfully alive, and felt guilty for the selfish thought.

When Schultz arrived home he climbed the stairs to the front door accompanied by the satisfying clinks of three fifths of Scotch bumping together inside their sturdy brown bag. The house was dark, and he left it that way. He went into the kitchen to get a glass for the Scotch, having decided to be civilized and not drink directly from the bottle.

He was alone, and it was time to give that pact that he'd made with himself a rest, the one where he'd promised not to fall apart. There was no one around. He could drop the pretense of holding up in public and dig himself a hole in the ground for a while.

Schultz knew that in a couple of days when the haze wore off and he couldn't justify the binge anymore, nothing would have changed. Rick would still be dead. Schultz would still be a shitty father whose intervention in the downward spiral of his son's life had come too late. And he would still be the asshole who had given the boy's mother—his own son's mother, his wife of many years, for Christ's sake—the news over the phone. He should have gone to her in person, like the time he went to see her to find out if their marriage was really over.

He wondered if he would actually have been crass enough to leave a message on her answering machine if she hadn't been home.

Schultz fumbled for a glass in the cabinet next to the sink. There was enough moonlight coming in the window over the sink so that he could see to pour himself three fingers, not bothering with ice. Lifting the glass, he peered through the Scotch as if it were a window to his heart. If he squinted hard enough, he might find a shred of decency there.

He didn't deserve PJ, that was certain. After this was over, he'd lay off trying to get her to admit she loved him.

Through the murky darkness of the liquid in the raised glass, a small light shimmered. It reminded him of when he was a kid, still living on the farm before his parents were killed. He'd sneak out to the swimming hole when there was a full summer moon. He wasn't supposed to, and he didn't take his little brother because even with a child's reasoning he knew it was dangerous, and he didn't want anything to happen to George.

Naked in the night, the sounds of the country around him, Schultz had plunged into water that looked black. He knew it was clear as glass, since he could see the bottom during the day. Ten feet down, at the bottom of his dive, he'd open his eyes and look through the heavy smothering water, searching for the sky. And there would be the moon, glorious and beckoning, up in the life-giving air. He'd flex his young arms and push himself to the surface, using the round, shimmering white ball of the moon to keep him oriented. Otherwise, he might lose his way in the uniform blackness.

The light in the glass he held was red, not white, and it certainly wasn't the moon. It was the message light on his answering machine, probably PJ checking to see that he made it home. If he didn't respond, she might come around to his house, and he didn't want that to happen. He didn't want her to see the bottles lined up like obedient little soldiers on the counter.

He sighed, put the glass down, and checked the machine. There were two messages. Punching the PLAY button, he was prepared for PJ's voice—concerned, angry, or both. But the voice on the machine was neither. It was mechanical and flat, altered by a device made just for that purpose.

"He didn't die fast, you know," said the voice. "You think about that, Detective Schultz. You think about him tied up helpless like that, and gasping for air. Then think about what I'm going to do next. Oh, and have a nice day."

There was a second message, and that one was from PJ, trying not to sound like she was checking up on him. He barely heard her words.

Stunned, Schultz replayed the messages. The time stamp placed the first call two hours ago, when he was with PJ. He plucked the tape from the machine and slipped it into his pocket. Then he emptied the whiskey bottles down the drain.

Suddenly there was too much to do to waste time on self-pity.

Seven

PJ got to Headquarters early Tuesday morning to work on the computer simulation of Rick's murder. Deep in thought in front of her monitor, she almost dropped her cup of coffee when her office door was flung open, startling her.

"When's the last time you saw Schultz?" Lieutenant Wall demanded.

Whatever happened to small talk?

PJ hesitated. She didn't want to tell Wall that her last view of Schultz had been his backside as she shoved him into a taxi outside a bar.

"I went over to his house last night," she said. "We talked for a while."

Wall closed his eyes. She counted to ten mentally right along with him. Exactly at "ten" he opened them.

"When and where, specifically, did you last see Detective Schultz? And the car he was assigned?"

PJ tapped her pencil on the desk. "Want to tell me what this is about?"

"You first."

PJ was cornered. "I went to his house a little after six. You suggested that someone spend the evening with him, so I volunteered myself."

What PJ didn't say was that as a psychologist and a friend—a very close friend—she had thought that she might be able to help Schultz begin to deal with his grief. That was the logical explanation. There was also the feeling that she was drawn to him.

"And?"

"I stopped after work for sandwiches. We ate in his kitchen. Then we went out."

"Out?"

"Can't you speak more than one word at a time?" PJ said, irritated. "We went to a bar. Schultz had . . . a couple of drinks, I think. I had orange juice. About ten o'clock, we went home."

"What bar?"

Progress. Two words. "Brandy's, on South Broadway."

"I know the place. You were in the Pacer? Did you go into his house with him then?"

This is getting downright personal.

PJ clamped her lips around a remark that she would definitely regret later. She knew that feelings were running high after the murder of a member of a detective's family, but the way things were going Wall's next question would be one she definitely didn't want to hear, or even think about.

"We had driven there separately. We went home separately. What's this all about, Lieutenant?" PJ fixed a look on her face that said, *I showed you mine, now show me yours.*

Wall settled heavily into one of her chairs and propped his elbows on the desk across from her. "There was a hit-and-run this morning about seven," he said. "A couple of blocks from Schultz's house. Four-year-old girl, and she's not expected to live. A couple of people saw it, and they say the car ran up on the curb, like the driver was going after the girl."

"I'm sorry to hear that," PJ said. She was puzzled, but waiting to hear Wall out.

"The car was described as a reddish-orange Pacer. Two witnesses on the street reported the license number. One got only a partial, the first three letters as MBF. The second witness reported MBF 181. That's the vehicle signed out to Schultz."

PJ sat back in her chair, stunned into silence. Wall shook his head.

"There's more. The driver wasn't seen clearly enough for a confident ID, one of the reasons being that he was wearing a hat. But the general description matches Schultz."

"Schultz doesn't wear a hat. I've never seen him in a hat," PJ said.

"He has one that he only wears to funerals. You haven't been around long enough to see him in it."

"Eyewitness accounts are notoriously unreliable."

"I know that. But I also know they can't be completely ignored."

PJ closed her eyes. She tried to imagine a bitter Schultz depriving some other parent of a child. Wearing his funeral clothes and running a four year old over on the sidewalk out of spite, so others would feel the way he did.

"He wouldn't do that. He wouldn't." She shook her head. "Okay, he might have been a little inebriated and depressed when I last saw him. But he was on his way home, and he didn't have alcohol at home. He had to leave his house last night to get drinks. I think if he'd had a bottle in the house, he would have parked himself at the kitchen table rather than have me tag along after him like a chaperone. You're saying he deliberately went out this morning and ran down some child while he was sober?"

Wall shrugged. "He could've gone out for booze after the two of you parted, and stocked up at home. I've known Schultz a lot longer than you have, and I can't imagine him doing anything like that. But then he's never seen his only son murdered and plumped up like a hot dog, either."

"Oh God, Howard, do you think he did it?"

Wall shook his head. "I don't know. I hope not, but things look bad. His car was found parked right in front of his house.

It's got a broken headlight and blood that's the same type as the girl's. Probably the DNA testing will confirm it."

"Did he lend his car to someone? What does he say about it?"

"I'd sure like to hear his side of things, if I could just find him."

PJ realized that he was hinting that Schultz was at her place. "I haven't seen him or heard from him since I put him in the cab last night," she said. She said it with enough conviction so that Wall was evidently satisfied, at least for the moment. He rose and walked toward the office door.

"Wait, I've got an idea," PJ said. "He phoned his ex-wife yesterday. I know he felt bad because he wasn't there to tell her in person. Maybe he's at her home in Chicago."

"Yeah, we've thought of that. No one answers there, and the Chicago PD says nobody's home. They're looking for Julia and her boyfriend. God Almighty, PJ, it looks like they might be hiding him. I didn't think I'd ever be saying anything like this, but he's wanted for questioning for vehicular assault. If that little girl dies, it's manslaughter, at least."

Eight

News trickled in to PJ in her office, brought by Dave, Anita, and Howard Wall, concerning the murder of Schultz's son, the status of the little girl, and Schultz's disappearance. She felt as though she were a spider sitting at the center of a great web of information gatherers. Every knock on her office door was a twitch on one of the strands of the web, bringing the spider to full alert.

Rick Schultz's toxicology results, the first few quick tests, showed a .08 blood alcohol content, right at the state's legal limit. He had stopped off for a few drinks between his release from prison and his fatal encounter in the nearly vacant apartment. Police officers were trying to trace his steps, visiting bars and liquor stores, displaying Rick's picture. It was possible that he had hooked up with someone and gone with that person, so that the death was opportunistic and not planned.

Remotely possible, PJ thought. *About one chance in a zillion.*

The notes that he had received in prison from Ginger seemed to indicate a plan that had been in place for months. A cellmate claimed that Rick had started getting the notes about five months ago, only a month into his short sentence. That was also about the time that Ginger Miller, whoever she really was, rented the apartment on Lake. The notes came every couple of weeks and Rick was secretive about their contents. He only bragged that he had a girlfriend on the outside and she was hot for him.

In the middle of the morning, Anita made her way to PJ's office with something PJ had been waiting for: copies of the two notes found on Rick's body. He had folded them into tight strips and put them into his back pocket. The HazMat team had removed them from Rick's contaminated clothing and bagged them for analysis. Because of their sheltered position inside his pocket, they had not been exposed to the acid condensation.

"All those lines are crease marks," Anita said as she handed the copies to PJ. "The originals had been folded and refolded so many times it was a wonder they hadn't fallen apart. 'Course, one was practically glued together. When the lab techs soaked it to spread it open, they probably could have filled a sperm bank."

"Geez, Anita, don't mention that to Schultz."

Anita sniffed. "I know when to keep my mouth shut. Besides, he's a big boy. I don't think Schultz'd be shocked to find out that his twenty-six-year-old son got his rocks off occasionally."

PJ bent over the note. There was no date or return address on it.

Ricky,
   It's almost time now. I'm lying here naked thinking about what I'm going to do to you. The first thing is take your clothes off so I can get a good look at what you've been saving up for me. I figure we'll take a shower together and I'll wash that prison stink off you. I want you to soap me up real slow. I hope you're getting hard just thinking about running your hands all over my body, but wait until you get out, Ricky. Don't you go sticking that cock of yours any place that isn't my hot slit, baby. You come straight to Mama.

                    Love and kisses you-know-where,
                                        Ginger

"That's it?" PJ said. She was disappointed that the note didn't offer more to go on.

"The other note's just like it," Anita said. "Just the basics. I guess that's what a guy who's been in prison for a few months wants to hear."

PJ considered. "Besides the obvious imagery, there is something here that I'm sure Rick picked up on whether he realized it or not. A feeling that he's really special, that this woman is waiting just for him."

"There's a little bit of a threat there, too, don't you think?" Anita said. "Maybe he enjoyed being told what to do. Dominated."

PJ thought back to her simulation, in which Rick didn't object when he was tied into the chair. She quickly scanned the copy of the other note Anita had brought, but there was no overt reference to bondage.

"Were any other notes recovered?" PJ said. "I'd like to know if Rick expected to be tied up when he entered the apartment. Was he being intentionally submissive, and that's the way Ginger got control of the situation? I've been wondering how she managed to overpower him."

PJ thought back to the Bonnie and Clyde of her simulation. She had assumed that there were two people waiting in the apartment for Rick, one of them the enticing female who wrote the letters and the other, most likely a strong man, as backup in case the enticement didn't work. Perhaps two perpetrators weren't necessary if it was known to the killer that Rick would go along willingly with a bondage scenario.

"Do we even know for sure whether or not Rick knew Ginger before he went into prison?" PJ asked. "If they didn't know each other, why would she suddenly start writing to him?"

Anita shrugged. "We've been through Rick's apartment, and spoken to a couple of buddies of his. He had an off and on roommate, off when Schultz ran him out, I think. Anyway, the roommate kept the apartment, and stored Rick's stuff since he was expected back in just a few months. No mention of Ginger, no photos or notes in the apartment. As far as his friends know, he wasn't seeing anybody right before the arrest, although there was a girl named Kathee Kollins about six months prior to that. Two k's, two e's. As for why Ginger started writing to him in prison, women do crazy things like that. I read it in Ann Landers."

"I'd like to talk to Ms. Kollins. Anybody know her whereabouts?"

"Dave's looking her up. Although I'd like to be the one there with you when you ask her if she likes to tie up her guys."

"Maybe it'll be obvious, and I won't have to ask."

Anita's brows knit. "Obvious? Like she answers the door in leathers, with a whip in each hand?"

"That's not quite the same thing. You're thinking of sadism. There's usually a bondage component to sadism, but bondage can be used without inflicting any pain. It can be all about power."

"You sound like you know entirely too much about this kinky stuff," Anita said. "Is this the shrink talking or the practitioner?"

"The psychologist, of course. Back in Newton, Iowa, where I grew up, everybody thought S&M meant spaghetti and meatballs."

Anita laughed. "Good one, Doc. Too bad Schultz isn't around to appreciate it."

Anita drifted out, leaving PJ with her thoughts. PJ reread the notes, finding that they didn't reveal much about Ginger from a psychological viewpoint. She had the sense that the writer was older than Rick, but that was just a hunch. The words seemed too blunt and confident for a person the same age as Rick, and there was that reference to Mama. That could be just a phrase in common use or there could be something to it, that the woman was old enough to be his mother.

On the other hand, the cutesy signoff indicated a younger woman, maybe even a teenager. Ginger was shaping up to be quite a puzzle.

Lieutenant Wall stopped in at about twelve-thirty and uncharacteristically asked PJ to lunch. She accepted, and found herself sitting across from her boss in a Subway a few blocks from Headquarters. It wasn't the best place for conversation because of the noise level of the lunch crowd, but at least their words didn't travel beyond their own tiny table.

She told him about her first simulation effort, which she had been working on refining all morning, in between news bulletins on the two cases. He nodded approval, but seemed distracted.

"I have a couple of items of bad news," he said, brandishing a potato chip in her direction as if he were scolding a child. She hadn't gotten over the feeling that he was somehow holding her accountable for Schultz's actions. Schultz was, after all, a member of her team, and she had been the last one to see him. She couldn't escape her own recriminations, thinking that she should have stayed the night at Schultz's, sleeping on his couch. Looking back on it, she thought she had been looking for the easy way out. Had she been too eager to get home to Thomas, to fall into her own bed and put the horrible events of the day out of her thoughts, at least for a few hours? She'd called Schultz on the phone when she got home, but gotten only his answering machine. She had planned to call back in a few minutes, giving the taxi a little longer to deliver him, but her pillow had beckoned and she'd never gotten around to it. Things could have been radically different if she'd just stayed with him. For one thing, he wouldn't be missing.

Wall kept his eyes on the table. It was uncharacteristic of him, and she braced herself for bad news.

"Caroline Bussman died at eleven forty-two this morning.

We're not just looking for a hit-and-run driver now. We're looking for a murderer."

"You said manslaughter earlier."

"I said manslaughter at least. With witnesses claiming that it was deliberate, the prosecutor will go for murder."

PJ closed her eyes and let the anger she had felt when she first heard about the girl bubble to the surface. The Bussmans' lives were forever changed when an orange Pacer veered onto the sidewalk and struck their daughter. Justice seemed a hollow concept when measured against the taking of a young girl's life and a lifetime of agony and guilt for her parents. Yet justice was all the St. Louis Police Department had to offer, and even that might mean the painful stripping away of the defenses of one of their own.

"I'm sorry to hear that," PJ said. "Her family must be devastated."

Pain showed in Wall's face, and in the eyes he turned up to meet her own. She knew he had four children, including a little girl Caroline's age. He was taking the death of the four year old hard.

"She never regained consciousness," he said, his voice barely carrying across the small table. "They never got to say good-bye."

PJ nibbled at her sandwich in silence. Her appetite was gone, but the mechanics of moving the food up to her mouth and chewing it gave her something to concentrate on while both of them regained their objectivity.

A noisy slurp alerted her that Wall was ready to continue the conversation. "Next item. Schultz didn't take the taxi home," he said. "We found the driver and he says he let Schultz out after you left. Apparently our man Leo drove home in his own car. If he even went home."

PJ narrowed her eyes. "That rat," she said. "He certainly fooled me. And I paid that driver twenty-five dollars, too." She felt her cheeks flush. She, the experienced psychologist, had been blatantly fooled. She had been too close to events to see what Schultz was planning.

"He was humoring me, and I fell for the whole thing," she said. "He was just looking for a way to ditch me and go off and do whatever it is he really wanted to do."

She thought again about the way the evening had gone, about pushing away his hands that had persistently taken liberties, and wondered if that had been an act, too. Burning with indignation, she pushed her feelings down like a jack-in-the-box being pressed back into its brightly painted box, and snapped the lid closed on them. The crank immediately started turning and the music was playing, though, and sooner or later those emotions were going to be right back in her face.

When they were nearly finished with lunch, PJ excused herself to visit the rest room. She had just seated herself in the cramped stall when her cell phone rang. Fumbling with her purse, she removed the phone and answered the call.

"Gray. CHIP," she said automatically, responding as if she were in her office.

"My, aren't we formal?" Schultz said. "I happen to know you're not at Headquarters."

PJ's head swiveled around, shocked to hear his voice, and even more shocked to think that he was watching her and knew where she was at that exact moment.

"Schultz," she hissed. She was hunched over on the toilet with the phone pressed to her ear so that his voice couldn't be overheard even in the ladies' room, ignoring the fact that she was perfectly alone. "Where the hell are you? What's the idea of fooling me with that taxi?" She lowered her voice until she was almost growling into the phone. "And if you ever put your filthy hands on me again, drunk or not, I'll slice off your balls and fry them for breakfast, you, you faker!"

"That's my girl," he said. "I knew you'd be happy to hear from me."

She was mute with a fury that overrode any consideration of Schultz's situation or recent events. She pressed her lips together and glared at the back of the stall door. Her gaze should have melted a hole through it in moments, but evidently the door was hardier than most.

"Where are you?" she demanded in a whisper, when the wave of anger had crested.

"In the train station in Chicago," Schultz said. "Didn't Julia tell you? I told her to call."

So he had gone to visit Julia, after all. "How did you know I wasn't in my office? Do you have somebody watching me right now?"

"No, but I know your habits. You're eating lunch at the Chinese place, Subway, or Pizza Hut. Got to be one of those three."

"You're right, Mr. Know-It-All. And did you also know that Lieutenant Wall is with me?"

"Christ, I'll hang up. Don't tell him it was me. I'm going AWOL for a few days. You said my name aloud, didn't you? Shit."

"Idiot. Even I'm not that stupid. I have privacy at the moment."

"Oh, you're in the john. Well, take your time, then. Just tell him you were freshening up. Men are trained not to question that."

PJ, elbows on her knees, left hand holding the phone to her ear, squeezed the bridge of her nose with the fingers of her right hand. She couldn't believe she was sitting in the bathroom having a ridiculous conversation with a man wanted for questioning in a murder—a man who had shared her bed, no less, although to her knowledge nothing had come of it beyond adolescent groping.

"Do you have any idea what's been happening here," she said, "while you've been gallivanting off to Chicago?"

"No, but I'm sure you'll tell me in your own sweet way."

PJ reined in her anger, and all of her many questions for him, and summarized in a few sentences the hit-and-run and the fact that he was a wanted man. She kept her voice low, imagining Wall with his ear pressed against the ladies' room door.

"Jesus Christ," he said. "A girl dead. I'm so sorry to hear that. You've got to believe me. I had nothing to do with that girl's death. I wasn't even in St. Louis at the time. You believe me, don't you?"

The pain in his voice was like slivers of glass twisting in her stomach.

"I want to, Leo. Why don't you turn yourself in and explain everything?"

"I can't do that, Doc. First he took my son, and now he's framing me, and goddamn it, that girl died for it. I won't let him get away with it. I swear I won't."

"Who? Who's framing you? Do you know a Ginger Miller?"

"I shouldn't have said that. Forget about that. Who's Ginger Miller?"

She told him about the notes in Rick's pocket, omitting their glued-together condition. There was no verbal reaction, but she could practically hear his brain ticking.

"I'll be in touch," he said. "Don't tell Wall I called you. Give me three more days before you tell Wall anything. You can do that for me, can't you? Three days?"

"Schultz! Give me something to go on," PJ frantically whispered into the phone. "I can't help you unless—"

"You stay out of this, Doc. This is way, way over your head. I didn't kill that girl. I swear it. You gotta trust me. Three days, you hear me?"

The connection was broken.

PJ silently cried a few tears of frustration and helplessness, then splashed water on her face and went out to finish her lunch and somehow not blurt everything out to Howard Wall.

* * *

Schultz hung up the pay phone and sat in the booth for a couple of minutes, immobilized with grief and anger. It hadn't occurred to him that the strike would be a triple whammy, even though the voice on the phone had warned of more to come. His son dead, an innocent girl's life taken, and he himself framed for a cold-blooded murder. Rick's horrible death was bad enough by itself.

If I was meant to be devastated, all right, you can stop already.

And he'd lied to PJ, probably just the first of many lies before this was over, one way or another. He had been in St. Louis at the time the girl was killed, not three hundred miles away in Chicago, as he had claimed. He'd been at the St. Louis airport, waiting for his flight to Dallas. He couldn't tell PJ that, because he was afraid that doing so might put her life in danger from the asshole who was after him. The less she knew about his whereabouts the better.

It had been a busy night. From home he had driven to a place called Secure Archives, where he kept a rental box. Secure Archives offered private storage, like safe-deposit boxes for those who wanted access outside banking hours. The company offered a range of sizes, from something the right size to hold a few canceled checks or letters from a lover to room-size storage for businesses that wanted to keep their old records, or backups of critical computer files, off-site.

There was no night attendant at Secure Archives, but that didn't matter. They had an elaborate security system that required a retinal scan plus an actual key. It wasn't a cheap service.

Schultz carried the key in his wallet at all times.

Inside his rental box there were a hundred gold coins, shiny mint condition American Eagles. He loaded the coins into a small carry-on bag that he kept in the trunk of the Pacer. It had taken him years, with his limited financial resources, to accumulate the coins. Another reason for the length of time was so that the funds were never missed by his wife, Julia. She probably would have gotten the wrong impression. When a man saves up money and hides it from his wife, it usually means hanky-panky.

Fanny Obermeier, a first-class fence for gold and gems, didn't even grouse too much when she was awakened at midnight by a phone call from Schultz. Late-night phone calls were not unheard of in her business. In consideration of their long-term friendship, she gave him seventy-five cents on the dollar for the coins, on the condition that he not spread that outrageous fact around or her other clients would want the same deal. Fat chance of that.

Getting three sets of false identification wasn't quite as easy. It took him five hours and used up not only ten thousand dollars of his cash fund (he got the bulk discount for purchasing more than two) but a couple of favors called in as well.

He had dropped his car off in front of his house, resisting the temptation to go inside and pack a few things, even personal mementos, all the little things that defined his home life. What was the point? If he made it back, they'd be there waiting for him. If he didn't, well, it wasn't as if he had anybody to inherit them. It dawned on him that he was a dead branch on the family tree now, with no one to carry on to the next generation.

Schultz walked a couple of blocks and got on a bus. He rode from place to place, transferring often and checking for a tail. As he rode, he began the process of compacting his grief and anger and fear into a tight little ball that took up residence in his gut. There would be time for all that later, assuming there was a later. When he was sure he wasn't being followed, he took the public rail system, the MetroLink, to the airport. He chose his first destination by looking at the monitors that listed departure times. It turned out to be Dallas.

What had started out last night as a random thought when he sat in the bar with PJ—that someone was after him and had used his son's death as the opening shot in a vicious game—had turned into the stomach-churning truth. He had dismissed that thought as paranoia until he heard the message on his answering machine, and the thought had sprung out like a hunting cat lying in wait. He was being targeted, indirectly at first, through his son and a girl who was a stranger, but that was bound to change. Whoever was after him wouldn't hesitate to use his loved ones against him. They already had, in fact. That meant Julia was in certain danger. He had dealt with that with a phone call to her, setting in motion a plan they had discussed years ago. She had poked fun at the time, only five years into their marriage, and he had grown increasingly annoyed at her reluctance to take the possibility seriously.

In his many years of detective work, Schultz had encountered some of the vilest misfits of society, and put a lot of them away in prison. But prison terms didn't last forever, and inevitably some of those criminals walked the streets again. In most cases, long prison sentences had turned them into ineffectual old men with no fire in their bellies for revenge. But all it took was one. One son of a bitch who blamed Schultz for having the audacity to throw a kink into his criminal doings, and who carefully tended thoughts of vengeance over the years.

As far as PJ was concerned, he thought he could keep her out of harm's way, if she would just listen to him for a change.

He wondered if he could do the same for himself.

Schultz went to the departure gate, getting there just in time for boarding. He was on the second leg of his trip to anonymity, flying from Dallas to Philadelphia.

His small carry-on bag seemed to pull at his arm. The

weight of a child-size coffin and a family's grief were packed inside, ever since his phone call with PJ when he learned about the death of Caroline Bussman.

The flight attendant glanced at his boarding pass as he entered the airplane, smiled, and said, "Have a nice flight, Mr. Anderson."

He had a window seat. Trying to keep his breathing even and steady, he watched Dallas grow small beneath him. His chest hurt, and he thought he knew why.

A hand had reached out from his past and was trying to squeeze the life from his heart.

Nine

The afternoon crawled by for PJ. She sat at her desk, enhancing her simulation and waiting for news, her mind busily constructing scenarios that would explain the conversation with Schultz. She had gotten through the remainder of lunch with Wall by hurriedly finishing her sandwich and then telling him that she was upset over the death of the girl and would appreciate being left alone for a few hours—things were moving too fast, she said, and she needed some time to catch up. He gave her an odd look, but accepted what she told him at face value. It was, as far as her memory served, the only time in her life that she had trotted out her "fragile feminine nature"—a fiction that some women keep on tap for situations they'd rather avoid. It probably wouldn't have worked with anyone at the department except Wall, and she wasn't even sure it had actually worked on him. He was probably just humoring her.

The copies of the notes from Ginger were tacked on the corkboard on the wall directly in front of her. PJ wondered what the forensic handwriting analyst would have to say. She knew that the report might include insights into the personality of the writer, and even her state of mind at the time the notes were written. Interesting, and certainly a contribution to the psychological profile PJ would attempt to develop for Ginger, but not the crucial items she wanted to know. Age couldn't be accurately determined by graphology, or left-handedness, or even, with absolute certainty, the sex of the writer. Nor could it snap a picture, which is what PJ really wanted: something solid to hold in her hands.

PJ made a note to herself to check on the possibility of boyfriends for Rick. They had been going on the assumption that Ginger was a woman, but the handwriting couldn't prove that conclusively, and the assumption could blind them to other possibilities. Maybe there were homosexual contacts before or during Rick's prison stay.

PJ wished she could talk it over with Schultz. Since he had come blazing back into his son's life after years of opting out of parental responsibilities, Schultz had been watching the young man closely. He might know about homosexual inclinations, even if he had pushed those observations under the rug and she had to pry them out of him. He might even know Ginger, or at least point them in the right direction. But he was off on some inexplicable adventure of his own, and she had no way to communicate with him until he initiated the contact.

His conversation with her had been disturbing in a number of ways. She didn't mind him running to Julia's—in fact, it seemed a compassionate thing to do—but he could have let her or someone else know what was up. Notifying someone seemed so basic that it was hard to believe Schultz hadn't done it.

But I've never seen him in these circumstances. Not even close.

She thought it was totally wrong of him not to face up to the hit-and-run charge. If he had been with Julia in Chicago, then there was a simple explanation for the crime that had occurred in St. Louis, one that didn't involve him. His car had been stolen and the thief, maybe drunk or high on drugs, had accidentally struck the child. Everything could be cleared up. But disappearing made him look guilty.

Could he have done it? PJ wanted to trust him, but she remembered that Wall had told her about drinking binges when things went sour for him. He could have run the girl down after a full night of drinking, and be in denial about it.

When her phone rang, she jumped. Schultz? Would he call her at the office?

"Dr. Gray, it's Julia Schultz."

"Mrs. Schultz," PJ said. Her mind was clicking fast, trying to make the best of the opportunity to speak to anyone named Schultz. "I'm so glad to hear from you. Have you spoken to Leo lately?" She slipped the question in innocently, she thought.

"No, not since noon, when I drove him to the train station."

"The police haven't contacted you yet?"

"I already know about my son's death," she said, her voice cracking slightly. "Leo told me, and then he came up here. We talked all night. I was so glad to see him."

"So you haven't heard the latest? Where are you now?"

"I'm at the lakefront with my friend James. We've been watching the sailboats. I wanted to get away from the house." There was a pause. "Heard what latest?"

"Why are you calling me now?" PJ countered.

"Leo asked me to call you this afternoon and tell you he was on his way back to St. Louis. His train left at one-thirty. I don't know how long it takes for the trip."

"Mrs. Schultz, I have some more news. I hate to spring this on you, but it's vital that you know. A little girl died this morning after being struck by a car. The police are fairly sure it was Schultz's car."

There was a longer pause. "That's not possible. He wasn't there. I got a call at three A.M. to pick him up at the train station. He was with me until noon. He wasn't even in St. Louis this morning." Her voice had gotten shriller with each sentence.

"Take it easy, Mrs. Schultz. I'm sure there's a good explanation, but right now it appears that Schultz's car was the vehicle involved. And he was tentatively identified as the driver."

"That can't be!"

"It's important for you to know that the Chicago police are looking for you for questioning about him. You need to tell your story. I want you to get off the phone now, and call the police. Tell them where you are. You'll be picked up in a few minutes, I'm sure. The best thing you can do for Leo is tell the police—"

She heard the click of the phone disconnecting. Julia had hung up on her.

"Exactly what you've just told me," PJ finished lamely.

PJ hung up the phone, her thoughts spinning. Schultz had asked for a three-day grace period before she said anything about the fact that he had contacted her. He hadn't known about the hit-and-run when he called, or he probably wouldn't have gotten her involved in the first place. Undoubtedly the purpose of his phone call had been to pump her for information about his son's case. The way he had reacted when he found out he was a suspect seemed far too extreme. Grace period? Telling her she was in way over her head?

He knew the workings of the law. Even if things looked bad on the surface, there could be ways to corroborate Julia's story. A train ticket stub, for instance. Someone who could identify Schultz at the station in Chicago. Maybe they stopped at a favorite restaurant after Julia picked him up. If he knew he was innocent, and Julia and her friend backed up his story of spending the night in Chicago, then why was he so leery of turning himself in? What was he running from?

There were only two explanations that came to mind. Either Julia was lying about his alibi, or he feared for his life if he turned himself in.

Or both.

Ten

The next target would be taken down Tuesday night, possibly on a crowded street and almost certainly with some show of security around him. It would be hard to get up close. Cut reviewed his choices, and settled on throwing knives from about twenty feet, which would be outside any circle of security men. It was silent, no gunshot to give away his position, and no retained weapon to pose a disposal problem. Even if he was somehow picked out of the crowd, how could anyone prove that the knives originated in his practiced hands? He would be wearing gloves, of course, leather ones that gave him an excellent grip, so there would be no fingerprints. The temperature after dark wouldn't be low enough to justify even unlined gloves, so he would have to remember to get the gloves off in a hurry.

Cut needed money. He considered making a phone call to get it, then decided that it would be better if he obtained it himself with a couple of quick daylight muggings. His first netted him only fourteen dollars. On the second he was lucky: two hundred and eighty-three. He never did understand why people carried around so much. He never did, except of course when he had to buy something out of the ordinary. He didn't trust credit cards. They led the weak-willed into trouble. Not that he was weak-willed when it came to spending money, but there was no sense taking any chances. Although Cut was an eminently practical man, he also believed in the temptation of the spirit, and he didn't want his spirit tempted by any little scraps of plastic.

He cruised North County in his rental car, a nondescript tan Chevy Cavalier, popping peppermint hard candies into his mouth, chomping them, and watching the stores and houses stream by outside his car window. While he was driving around, he heard on the radio that the victim of an early morning hit-and-run had died, and that police were looking for a suspect for questioning.

It was one of the harder things he'd had to do, run down that little girl. He felt bad for her mother. He knew how hard it was to lose a child. In his case, first a daughter and then a son. That wasn't right. Children were supposed to go to the cemetery and take flowers to their parents' graves, not the other way around. But the hit-and-run was over in an instant, and it was part of the plan, so he stuck to it. He wouldn't hesitate to change a plan for a good reason—it had saved his hide before—but shying away because it wasn't a pleasant thing wasn't sufficient.

Cut found what he was looking for, a camera store. He paid cash for a serious-looking but inexpensive camera, an equipment bag with a shoulder strap, and a couple of rolls of film. He still had a satisfying chunk of money left from his earlier fund-raising activities, so he let one of the pizza places on Lindbergh seduce him. Hunger satisfied, and with a slight buzz from the two beers he had downed, Cut headed to his hotel room for an afternoon of contented sleep. He hadn't gotten a lot of it the night before, and he wanted to be at his peak physically for the night's work.

The hotel, the latest in a string of them he'd used, was one of those instantly recognizable places where he had known no questions would be asked if cash was paid in advance for a few nights' stay. It had the laughable name of The Executive Palace, and its benefits besides the lack of curiosity of the staff were the bus stop nearby and the presence of a Steak 'n Shake a block away. He was a hard, strong man, with all the fat burned off by work, and ordinarily had little interest in luxuries of the mind or body. But these weren't ordinary times for him, and lately he'd discovered Steakburgers. He laughed at himself. If he stayed at The Executive Palace too long, he might have to loosen his belt buckle a notch.

His full bladder woke him at 7:00 P.M. He spent a half hour thoroughly familiarizing himself with the camera, which turned out to be simpler than it looked. Packing the equipment bag carefully, Cut added a bundle from his suitcase. He showered, decided to pass up dinner as a small atonement for the pizza and burgers he'd been eating lately, and then took the bus downtown. He got off a few blocks from the Grand Mississippi Hotel, which was located in Laclede's Landing, a stretch a few blocks long on the Mississippi waterfront crammed with nightspots.

Victor Rheinhardt, his target, was attending a charity fundraising dinner at the hotel, along with three hundred of the city's socially privileged. Cut found a good place to wait, at the rear of the hotel, near a loading dock. There were no guards, no activity of any kind. The strong scent of garbage, especially spoiled food, told him that the large trash receptacle near the dock hadn't been emptied in a while. In August, the smell didn't just get a little bit worse every day between pickups—it doubled. There was a dusk-to-dawn light, but Cut slipped into a shadowy niche that shielded him from the limited reach of the light. His dark T-shirt and dark pants made him nearly invisible against the wall.

Checking his watch, Cut figured that he had a couple of hours to wait before the dinner broke up. Then, as the crowd of dinner guests was leaving the hotel, he would walk around the front and take a few pictures. Hopefully he wouldn't be the only one doing so. If things went awry at that point, he was just an admiring citizen photographing a St. Louis hero.

Cut planned to get as close as he could to Rheinhardt, re-move the two throwing knives from his camera bag, and send them on their way. He would mill around with the rest of the crowd, a shocked and fearful look plastered on his face, and then ease himself away into the night during the precious min-utes of disorientation that followed the attack. He knew all about that brief disorientation—he'd used it to good advantage before.

It was an ambitious plan, but a solid one.

Forty-five minutes went by uneventfully except for the fact that Cut was getting hot in the long-sleeved black T-shirt he had chosen to blend in with the night, and his nose was run-ning a little from his usual summer allergies. The combination of long sleeves and a runny nose had led him to indulge in a furtive bit of nose-wiping, and he found it ironic that he was more worried about being discovered with snotty sleeves than with throwing knives concealed in his camera bag.

Cut was startled in midwipe by a noise. Very close. A creak-ing noise, like a door opening reluctantly. He slipped as far back in the shadows as he could.

The loading dock door was opening. Not the big one that rolled up like a garage door, but the ordinary entry door next to it. A man stepped out under the dusk-to-dawn light. He was wearing a tuxedo. One of the dinner guests, then, probably out sneaking a smoke. Cut drew in his breath slowly, tried to let it out slowly. He was only thirty feet from the man, who was looking down, fumbling in his pocket. Cut couldn't make out his features clearly. A cigarette lighter flashed a tiny de-fiant flame. Then the man tilted his head back, the tip of the cigarette glowing brightly, inhaling deeply. The orange glow of the dusk-to-dawn light fell on his face.

It was Rheinhardt.

Cut hesitated, not quite believing his luck. Rheinhardt was alone and exquisitely vulnerable, puffing away, probably hop-ing no one would miss him inside the hotel while he sucked in a few puffs. Cut slipped the pair of throwing knives from his camera bag. They were eight inches long and double-edged, with a dull black finish so they wouldn't catch the light. He hefted them in his left hand, admiring their weight and balance. It would be a shame to lose them.

He ran forward, light on his feet, and passed one knife from his left hand to his right as he darted toward Rheinhardt, coming in on the man's left side. When he had closed the distance to ten feet, he saw Rheinhardt's head swivel toward him; the man had picked up the motion. The blade flew from Cut's hand, turning end over end, barely visible in the muggy night because of its nonreflective black surface. It caught Rheinhardt in the neck, burying itself half of its length, transfixing the man as he turned toward Cut, wide-eyed, cigarette hanging loosely from his lips. The second blade, not wanting its twin to have all the fun, tumbled silently through the space between the two men and landed with a muted thump to the left of the sternum.

Cut saw the man drop. He looked around; no witnesses. He approached the body to be certain of the killing. Bending over Rheinhardt, he pulled off his gloves and shoved them in his pockets. If the man had a faint pulse, Cut might not have been able to feel it through his gloves. He pressed a couple of fingers of his right hand against the bloody throat of the man lying on the ground. There was no pulse. Life had fled quickly. It was a clean easy death compared to what Cut's son had endured, but setting up a homemade gas chamber and luring a victim was too elaborate and risky a thing to do every day. After the harsh statement delivered by the first target's death, expediency ruled for the follow-ups.

He was tempted to retrieve his lovely and useful knives, but he knew that would create a disposal problem. Better to leave them in place. Cut wiped his bloody hand on his victim's shirt, being careful to leave nothing but smears, no recognizable finger or palm prints. He moved away rapidly, relieved to be out of the revealing cone of brightness from the dusk-to-dawn light. Back out on the street, he strolled through Laclede's Landing, his hands jammed into his pockets to conceal the slight bulge of the crumpled gloves that also rode within them. The sidewalk was busy with people barhopping, and none of them gave him a second glance.

He hadn't needed the camera, after all. It had been a waste of money, and that was a small blot on an otherwise gratifying mission.

Eleven

St. Louis awoke on a steamy Wednesday, the fifth day of August, to news of the slaying the previous evening of a fixture in the city, the popular Prosecuting Attorney Victor Rheinhardt. He had held the elective office for almost twenty years. Although PJ hadn't lived in the city that long herself, some of those in the law enforcement and judicial structures of the city wouldn't remember a time in their careers when Rheinhardt hadn't held the reins of the prosecutor's office.

Most likely a few of the up-and-coming were secretly glad to see an opening at the top, although she thought that only the most hard-hearted of the law-abiding citizens of St. Louis—plus several thousand convicts—would have wished that manner of death on the man. By 8:00 A.M., when PJ arrived at work, it was clear that the jockeying for position and advantage was under way, as assistant prosecutors strutted their stuff.

It wasn't CHIP's case, as was made amply clear by the defection of most of the officers who had been assisting on the Rick Schultz homicide. She understood the pressure on Lieutenant Wall and his superiors. She could close her eyes and hear his excuses. Rick Schultz was the son of one of their own, but the inescapable fact was that he had also been an ex-con.

The fact that an ex-con died an unnatural death was only news so long as nothing overshadowed it.

Victor Rheinhardt was not only a local celebrity, but the city's chief prosecutor. It was imperative to the reputation of the department to have a quick arrest, and Chief Wharton would not only be watching the case with a magnifying lens, but meddling in it himself.

PJ found it hard to be sympathetic with Wall when he appeared midmorning, harried and hurried, and announced that he could spare only her core team, Dave and Anita, to continue working on the Rick Schultz case.

The three CHIP members sat glumly in PJ's office.

Anita looked like a pixie on downers. Dave had the sleepy detached look that had earned him the nickname Witless, a play on his last name of Whitmore. If he were a bear, he'd be about to go into hibernation.

"Any helpful news on the chemical sources?" PJ asked.

"News, yes, helpful, no," Anita said. "Two companies, Brenner Chemical Supplies in Springfield and Overton Chemicals in Peoria, have records of purchases by a G. Miller. Small quantities over three months. Nothing alarming. Always paid with a postal service money order. The orders were picked up directly at the loading dock, but no one remembers anything out of the ordinary. They tell me it isn't unusual for chemistry teachers to do that."

"During the summer?" Dave asked.

"I suppose so. Restocking for the next school year, and have to be ready by the time the fall semester starts. Or it could be summer school at a college. G. Miller must not be too memorable. Both companies claimed that about a quarter of the direct pickups are by women, but none of the loading guys remember anything unusual, and can't put a face to the name."

"Our gal Ginger may not have gone in person. Or maybe Ginger looks more like a George," Dave said.

"Anything on the money orders?" PJ had perked up. She tapped a pencil rapidly on the desktop.

"Purchased at the main post office for cash. The receipts show the address on Lake where Rick's body was found. No ID recorded, such as a driver's license number. I sent copies of the receipts over to handwriting."

"Good work," PJ said. "At least we have something moving along. So Ginger could be a chemistry teacher."

"Or live next door to a chemistry teacher, or have at one time ten years ago known a chemistry teacher, or passed a chemistry teacher in the aisle of the supermarket within the past six months," Dave said.

PJ frowned at him. "That's not a positive attitude."

"Yeah, well, since Schultz isn't here I figured I'd take over for him as resident curmudgeon."

"You're not old enough to be a curmudgeon," Anita said.

"Age has nothing to do with it," PJ said. "Or gender. I once knew a girl—"

"From Nantucket," Dave said, "who kept all her cherries in a bucket. Not one did she spill, till along came old Bill, who peeked at her cherry, then fucked it."

Anita guffawed and slapped her knee. It was a very un-pixieish action.

PJ struggled to keep a straight boss-lady face, and then gave up. She laughed with the others.

"All right, I get the point," PJ said when order was restored. "Geez, I miss that man around here. I never thought I'd say that."

Or feel it.

"On with the case. Forensic handwriting analysis didn't give us much to go on," PJ said. "There's a strong indication Ginger was in conflict over what she was writing—that the notes weren't written in a state of high sexual excitement as the content would lead you to believe, but in a calculated manner."

Anita sniffed. "I could have told you that," she said.

Wall phoned to let PJ know that Julia Schultz had walked into a police station in Chicago and said that Leo had spent the night with her, but that she didn't know his present whereabouts. PJ wondered what level of knowledge Julia had. She tried not to be hurt that Julia might have an insider's seat while she was frozen out. Leo and Julia had been married for decades and only divorced a few months, which certainly put PJ's own claim to his affection and trust in perspective. Purely on the basis of time served, Julia deserved to be taken into his confidence.

PJ brought herself up abruptly from those thoughts. She was starting to sound like a jealous wife. What claim did she have on Schultz, after all? He had made some advances during a vulnerable moment. He was on the rebound from a divorce and a failed relationship with Helen Boxwood, a nurse they had met on a previous case. In fact, the relationship with Helen couldn't even be called failed. It hadn't gotten off the ground. And Schultz had been so eager, so pathetically sure that Helen was the right woman for him. Perhaps she was. But without giving that effort half a chance, he had somehow switched around and focused on PJ. What did that make her— the second rebound woman? Was there anything lower than that? The whole thing would make a good article for *Cosmopolitan*.

If he didn't have a good handle on his own private life, how could he think that he was ready for a relationship with PJ? With his boss, of all people?

I love you, his note had said. *We can work it out.*

PJ had avoided examining her feelings, and she knew it wasn't the time. But she couldn't pull herself away from thinking about how she felt toward him. Physical attraction, yes. She could acknowledge that much, although it surprised her. He certainly wasn't a conventional sex object.

Friendship and a respect for his professional abilities, definitely.

What else was lurking in the lesser-traveled pathways of her heart? Perhaps she could sort things out during a leisurely bath, with a puffy inflated pillow to rest her weary head on and cucumber slices working magic on the shadowy wrinkles under her eyes. But right then the voice of her deeper emotions was drowned out by the stress and jangled nerves resulting from multiple deaths impacting her life.

Bam! Mike Wolf's wife dies. She was practically a vegetable, but it counts anyway. Whack! Rick meets a horrible end. Pow! A little girl crushed by Schultz's car. Her parents stolid for the cameras, despairing in private. And then Rheinhardt. The cold-blooded assassination of a man I'd only met twice but was part of the law enforcement family. Deaths in the family, all of them.

PJ shook her head to get her spinning thoughts in order. Then she noticed that Dave and Anita were staring at her expectantly. She must have missed something, a joke perhaps. She decided to bluff it out.

"Enough of that," she said, as much to herself as to them, tapping the pencil on the desk with what she hoped was authority. "What do you think of the possibility of two killers? Or that Ginger was a man, and Rick Schultz went to the apartment for a homosexual contact?"

"Whoa, boss," said David. "Where's that coming from?"

She explained her theory that Rick would have to be overpowered in some fashion—by his sexual urge, or by force. He was—had been—tall and muscular, a formidable man, as Schultz had been in his youth. In Schultz's case, there was a soft roundness where there used to be well-developed muscle, but Rick had gotten himself in shape in prison. It had been confirmed that he had been on a serious fitness and weight lifting regimen. If Ginger was a woman, she'd have to be specially trained, carry a weapon, be lucky, or all three.

Dave shook his head. "I just can't see that," he said. "You're forgetting that Rick was already impaired by alcohol. Wouldn't that make him an easier target? What about the good old-fashioned method of taking someone by surprise? He could have been jumped the minute he opened the door, when he was busy thinking about doing some jumping of his own."

PJ scowled, but she knew he was right. They just didn't have enough information to go on. "Damn!" she said. "Everything on this case seems so slippery. We could sit here all day and jabber about it. I don't know about you two, but I need to get out and do something."

"I'd like to go over the simulation you're working on," Anita said.

"It's got two bad guys in it," PJ said. "Bonnie and Clyde, I called them. I don't even know if it's relevant. I'm getting frustrated with this."

Anita stared her down.

"Okay, I'll start it up for you. Don't expect much."

PJ busied herself with her computer, bringing up the simulation. "Just press F1 to start it. F2 will give you a replay as many times as you want." Then she got up from her desk, intent on getting out of the office and attacking the case physically.

Got to get my hands on something.

"I'll be back," she said.

"Doctor Penelope Jennifer Gray," Dave said, "aka The Terminator."

She aimed a kick at his shin as she went by, but he was surprisingly fast for a sleepy bear.

Out in the hallway, she was unsure of exactly what prompted her to make an exit. She wanted to take some kind of action, but what? She wound her way through the busy halls until she stood outside Lieutenant Wall's office, waiting for inspiration. Others brushed by her with a greeting or a puzzled frown at her immobility.

She realized it wasn't Wall she wanted to see. Having finally made up her mind, she left the building and drove over to Schultz's house. She knew that officers had already been there, and even gone inside to make sure the fugitive wasn't hiding, dead drunk, or just dead. A locksmith had opened the rear door and then replaced the lock. But her key would still work on the front. She fished it out of the bottom of her purse, remembering the time Schultz had insisted they exchange keys. For emergencies, he said. So far the only emergency seemed to be one of his own making.

Schultz's mailbox was overflowing, so she emptied it. She'd have to remember to stop his mail so it wouldn't be so obvious that no one was home.

She stepped inside, cutting off the heat and brightness of a St. Louis August afternoon that was bent on living up to its reputation for excess. By comparison, Schultz's house was a dark cool cave. She stood in the front hallway for a minute, letting her eyes get adjusted to the dimness.

Only the front half of the house was actually darkened. Looking down the hallway, she could see that curtains and blinds were set to let in filtered sunlight in the rooms that looked onto the backyard. Drapes in the front living room were tightly pulled. Impulsively she climbed the stairs and checked the situation on the second floor. Same thing: front closed, rear open. Schultz's bedroom overlooked the rear yard, and afternoon sun streamed cheerfully in. On the third floor, which was set up to be a separate apartment, the window coverings were arranged the same way, even though by all other signs the third floor was closed off and unused.

The house was split down the middle, light and dark. It puzzled her, but she couldn't think what the significance could be. It wasn't energy conservation—the sun was shining deeply into the interior of the house through the lightly shielded rear windows. She returned to the first floor and went into the living room. She pulled the cord to open the traverse drapes and looked out at Lafayette Avenue. Could Schultz be hiding from something outside?

A flash caught her eye across the street, a round shiny spot in the second-story window of a house across from Schultz's. In a moment it was gone, and there was a slight movement of the curtains in that window. She replayed it in her mind, rechecking her impression. She was almost certain she had seen the end of a small telescope, like a bird-watcher's scope, poking through the curtains. The lens had caught the sun, and then it vanished. Whoever was over there had seen the drapes in Schultz's front room suddenly and unexpectedly yanked open, and retreated. It triggered a memory: her mother complaining that a neighbor always watched her when she went out in the yard to work in the garden or hang up laundry on a clothesline. Of course, where her mother lived, on the edge of the small town, it was assumed that neighbors casually watched out for each other. But one particular neighbor, Mrs. Dollins, apparently had taken it as her sworn duty.

PJ smiled. So a Mrs. Dollins lived across the street. Schultz was the kind of person who would hate to be spied upon, so the front of his house was tightly buttoned up.

Then it occurred to her that Mrs. Dollins, or whatever this individual's name was, might have seen Schultz's comings and goings. She might know if his car was stolen or if he had been behind the wheel at the time of the hit-and-run.

Excited, PJ headed for the nearest phone, in the kitchen. It was a real contribution to the hit-and-run case, she thought, and exactly why she had felt she needed to get out and do something instead of remaining cooped up in her office.

In the kitchen, she stacked Schultz's mail on the counter. Then, just as she passed the sink, she stopped abruptly. She had picked up the faint smell of alcohol, and it disturbed her immensely. When she had brought Schultz sandwiches the night of the discovery of his son's body—*only two days ago, can that be?*—there had been no alcohol smell, and she had rooted through his kitchen cabinets looking for clean glasses for the two-liter bottle of Coke she'd brought. She was sure there hadn't been any liquor bottles in the cabinets then. Yet the smell, although old and fading, was undeniable. She forced herself to check the logical spot, the trash can under the sink.

She opened the cabinet door, and the odor got a little stronger. There were three bottles, each with a small amount of liquid residue in the bottom, stuffed hastily into the trash can. Her heart plummeted to her feet.

So he had stopped for booze after slipping away from her at the bar. The evidence couldn't be ignored and she couldn't think of any other explanation. Surely the officers who had been in the house had noticed the bottles also. There was only one conclusion: Schultz had gone on one of the drinking binges Wall had told her about.

Sloshed to the gills and angry at the world, he might very well have run down the little girl. Or just been blind drunk and not even aware of the collision with her small body until he'd seen the damage to his car later. Then he'd run away, put distance between himself and the awful responsibility.

Everything he had told her could be a lie. Probably *was* a lie.

She sank down on one of the kitchen chairs and let the feeling of betrayal soak in. It was several minutes later that she remembered why she'd come into the kitchen in the first place. That had been way back when she was still looking for ways to prove Schultz innocent.

Should she tell anyone about the possible busybody across the street? If the person behind the telescope had seen anything, most likely it would be incriminating. That would just hasten the confirmation that Schultz had deprived a child of life and her family of seeing that child reach her potential. If PJ kept quiet about it, maybe no one would discover that source of information. If the person had already been interviewed, it was likely that he or she hadn't revealed anything to the police. No one likes to be caught spying, especially if that spying is a pathologically important part of one's life.

But keeping silent didn't feel right for PJ either.

That man isn't easy, she thought. *I'd be better off doing shampoo market studies.*

Finally she decided that she had, by not actively disagreeing to it on the phone, given Schultz a three-day grace period. That grace period wasn't up yet. The moment it was, she would tell. Friday morning, she decided. She'd give him until Friday. Out of respect for the work they'd done together, and that's all.

Not from love. No.

She stood up from the table, wondering if there were any more revelations to be found in the kitchen. Noticing a light on the answering machine blinking, she went over to check it. It wasn't the message light. It was a warning to replace the missing tape or messages would be lost.

Her brow furrowed. She had left a message for him Monday night, after going home from the bar. It had been a thinly disguised attempt to check up on him, and at the time she thought he deliberately hadn't picked up the phone or returned her call because her attempt was so transparent. So the tape was in place Monday night—she had made use of it. What reason could he have to remove it? Or had the police taken it?

Doubt rose, like a balloon floating up through her emotions. The tape might be important. There could have been something on it, something more sinister or fascinating than her own lame message that had sent Schultz streaking away into the night.

PJ's cell phone rang, and she pulled it out of her purse. It was Dave.

"Rick's old girlfriend has been tracked down," he said. "She's moved twice in the last year, and doesn't have a steady

job, so it's taken a little while. I'm on my way over to talk
to her. Wanna tag along?"

"You bet. Drop by Schultz's house and pick me up, would
you?"

Dave cleared his throat. "So you know about the bottles."

"Yeah. Nice of you guys to keep me informed."

"You didn't mess anything up, did you?" Dave said, ignoring her barb. "Wall didn't want the house disturbed, in case
Schultz comes back."

"Why didn't you seize the bottles?"

"There's no arrest warrant issued. Officially we went into
his house on the report of a neighbor that Schultz hasn't been
seen in some time and might be the victim of foul play inside.
Once we verified that wasn't true, we had to leave. Officially."

"I see. And which of you planted the idea in the neighbor's
head?"

"Um, I did."

"Well, come on by. I'll be outside the front door."

Fifteen minutes later, Dave picked her up. They drove in
silence for a time, as Dave negotiated the streets, heading for
the area north of downtown.

"We're going across the river," he said. "She lives in an
apartment in Granite City."

"Don't we need to get the Granite City Police involved?"

"We've given them a heads up about it," he said. "If we
wanted her picked up and brought in for questioning, then the
coordination would be more formal. But we're just stopping
by to ask her a few questions, which we hope she'll answer
without fuss, and we'll be on our way."

"How do we know she's home? It's a weekday afternoon.
She could be at work."

"Granite City PD cruised by and heard the TV on. There's
a good chance she's there."

"I thought you said she lived in an apartment. How exactly
did they cruise by and hear the TV?"

Dave shrugged. "I guess they cruised on foot."

The haze hanging over the city was worse at the riverfront. The Mississippi River flowing under the McKinley Bridge was a flat shade of gray that blended into the haze, so that in the distance it was hard to see where the river ended and the sky began.

Granite City was a maze of unfamiliar streets to PJ, but Dave drove confidently. She questioned him about it, and found that his parents had lived there for a few years before moving to the West Coast.

They pulled up in front of an apartment complex where the buildings were in a U-shape around common ground. Dave parked the car and they walked into the U. All of the upper apartments had identical balconies, and all the lower ones had small patios. A tiny swimming pool took up one end of the green space. A group of women, seated in folding chairs under umbrellas around a separate kiddie pool, looked up and stopped their chatter. The toddlers in the wading pool continued their antics. PJ thought it strange that there was no one at the main pool. It was summer vacation. It seemed as if every school kid in the complex should be in the pool. As they got closer, she noticed a lot of water splashed out on the pool surround. It looked as though a large boisterous group had just left. It restored her confidence that pools were still attractive enough to lure kids out of their air-conditioned rooms.

"First building on the right," Dave said.

"And straight on 'til morning."

When they got to the door, they could hear the TV playing loudly. Either the soundproofing was a farce or Kathee Kollins had poor hearing. PJ knocked politely, then pounded on the door when she got no response.

The door opened slightly, held in place by a security chain.

"Go away," a voice said from the height of PJ's waist. The words were a little slurred. The door slammed.

PJ and Dave looked at each other. "Is Kathee in a wheel-chair, or very short?" PJ asked.

"Unknown."

PJ stepped up to the door again and knocked loudly. After several minutes, the noise level of the TV went down, and the door opened again. PJ slid her foot into the narrow open-ing, wincing in advance. She thought it would be squashed.

"Go away."

"Wait! We're from the police department, here on official business. Is this the home of Kathee Kollins?"

"Who?"

PJ slipped her arm into the slot, dangling her civilian de-partmental ID from her hand. She squatted down and spoke loudly at doorknob level.

"I said, we're police—" Her ID was snatched from her hand. Startled, she drew back her arm, and the door closed.

Dave laughed at the frown on her face. "It's not funny," she said. "And it's your turn to knock."

Before he could take his place at the door, it opened. A woman stood there, and hiding behind her was a young girl about seven years old.

"Come in, Dr. Gray. I'm Kathee Kollins. I wondered when someone would come to talk to me."

PJ stepped into the apartment. Dave lingered, keeping the door open in case a quick exit was needed.

"Sorry about the confusion," Kathee said. "That was my daughter Kyla. She doesn't hear well, although she's usually a lot better off than she is today. Her hearing aid happens to be in for repair. It's kind of specialized, and she doesn't have a spare."

Kyla's face appeared around her mother's right hip. PJ signed "hello" to her. The girl's eyes opened wider, and she stepped out from behind her mother. PJ saw that both sides of the girl's face were scarred, the skin stretched taughtly over her cheekbones. There wasn't much of an external ear on either side. Kyla rapidly signed an apology for her cautious behavior to PJ, explaining that her mother had been asleep, and she was not allowed to let anyone in. PJ conveyed her acceptance, and told Kyla that she did the right thing.

As PJ and Dave followed the woman into the apartment, Dave tapped PJ on the shoulder.

"That was neat. When'd you learn to sign?"

"In the early part of my clinical practice, I had a couple of patients who taught me."

"Well, you made a hit here," Dave said. Kyla was shadowing PJ, her eyes attentive.

"Mrs. Kollins," PJ said, "as you guessed, we'd like to ask you a few questions about Rick Schultz. Is there someplace we can talk alone?"

Kathee signed rapidly to her daughter, who went back and turned the sound on the TV up again. The three grown-ups went into the kitchen.

"Please have a seat," Kathee said. "She can't hear us in here, as long as we don't shout."

They sat around a small table. Dave took out a notebook and pen.

"It's Ms. Kathee Kollins," she said. "I'm not married. Haven't ever been. So you can get it right. Two e's, two k's."

Dave smiled as he wrote the name.

PJ, who was sitting opposite Kathee, searched the woman's face. She was about twenty-five, with hair the color of candy apples and a smile that lifted her out of the average category in looks.

"Kyla mentioned that you were asleep," PJ said. "Do you work nights?"

"Yes. I'm an admissions clerk at a hospital. I just landed the job a week ago, and I'm having trouble getting adjusted to the night shift. I'm a morning person. Can I get you something to drink, coffee maybe?"

"No, thanks. Ms. Kollins, when's the last time you saw Rick?"

"About a month ago."

PJ blinked and Dave sat up straighter. Neither of them had been expecting her answer to indicate such recent contact.

"I visited him in prison. I wanted to make sure everything was really over for us. You see, I met somebody."

PJ nodded. "And was it? Over for you?"

"Oh, yes," Kathee said. "I thought I'd be sad about it, but I guess it was for the best."

"I hate to bring this up," Dave said, "but we checked the prison visitation log. You weren't on it."

"I used a fake name," Kathee said, lowering her eyes. "I thought Rick would refuse to see me if I was announced as the real me."

"So he was angry with you," PJ said.

"He was, but he didn't have any right to be. He was the one who broke it off."

PJ thought she didn't exactly sound full of grief about her ex-boyfriend's death. It flashed into her mind that Kathee might have learned about Ginger during her prison visit, and become jealous. Maybe Rick had flaunted his sexy correspondent.

"Let's start at the beginning," PJ said cautiously. Dave had picked up the same train of thought, and was watching Kathee intently. "When and how did you meet Rick?"

Kathee folded her hands on the table. "I guess it was about three years ago. Yes, that's about right. Kyla was only four then. I was taking classes at a community college. Rick was in one my classes." She laughed. "Neither of us was very enthusiastic. I dropped out because my child care arrangements fell through, and Rick—well, he just fooled around too much to be a serious student."

Dave asked the name of the college and the dates attended. He jotted them down.

"What attracted you to Rick?" PJ asked.

"He was handsome, well, nice-looking at least. I like big guys. He looked a lot like Kyla's father. He was fun to be with, and helped me take my mind off my problems."

"What kind of problems?"

"Kyla's medical bills, mostly. She's already had a couple of surgeries, and there are several more on the horizon. We're both very hopeful."

The hope and concern sounded genuine.

"Do you mind if I ask what happened to her?"

"Not at all. People ask all the time anyway, and most of them are a lot ruder than you. We were in a car accident. Kyla had a head injury and some bad burns. She's lucky to be alive. My own injuries were minor." Kathee pulled up her right pants leg to expose a terrible scar that started about mid-calf and climbed up beyond her knee. "It keeps on going up. All I have is the scar and a slight limp. And the memories, of course. Kyla lost her hearing and most of the skin on her face and neck."

"I'm so sorry for you both."

"Yes, well . . . we're survivors. We're getting along, and we've got each other."

"How did Rick fit into that picture? Had the accident already happened by the time you met him?"

"No. It amazes me, looking back on it, that he stood by us right after the accident."

Knowing what she did about Rick, PJ thought that was amazing too, but she kept quiet about it.

"I think it was Kyla's condition that wore him down. He had this image of a perfect little family, and Kyla didn't fit in. She needed a lot of special care, and several hospital stays. He wasn't mature enough to handle it." Kathee nodded in the direction of the living room, where the TV blared away.

"So Rick wasn't ready to settle down? Was he seeing other women?"

"No, it wasn't that. It was something else." Her face darkened. "He was using drugs. He was bringing them into my house—marijuana, cocaine sometimes, some pills I couldn't identify. I had a feeling he was selling, because of the quantity that turned up sometimes. I couldn't have that. I told him to get rid of the drugs or get rid of himself. It was a hard thing to do. I loved him, I think."

"It was brave of you," PJ said. "You were thinking of Kyla."

Kathee gave her a grateful look. The two women were talking as single mothers, and had practically forgotten Dave's presence. Dave was busy scribbling down the conversation.

"He didn't take it too well. He stormed around and smashed stuff. But secretly I think he was glad to be given a way out."

"I thought you said he was the one who broke up your relationship," PJ said.

"He did," Kathee said. "He had a choice, and he chose drugs over me. I'm not responsible for that."

"Why'd you go see him in prison then?" Dave said. "Doesn't make sense."

Both women rounded on him with identical expressions. "Of course it does," PJ said. "She loved him. She wanted to give him one last chance before going out with someone new."

Dave rolled his eyes. "Shall I play the violin music now?"

"Ignore him," PJ said frostily.

"Hey, we all have our burdens," Kathee said. "And I see he's one of yours."

Dave gave an exasperated sigh and put his nose back into his notebook.

"I have some really direct questions to ask you," PJ said. "And they're rather sensitive."

"Just a minute," Kathee said. She got up and checked on Kyla, then sat back down. "Fire away."

"Did Rick date other women while he was seeing you?"

"Not as far as I know. But he did have a lot of evenings

unaccounted for, particularly when the drugs entered the picture."

"You did have a sexual relationship, didn't you? Did you ever have the impression he was bisexual or homosexual?"

"If he preferred men, that would be a big shock to me. Our relationship started out with a bang and kept going from there, if you get my drift."

"Did he like to be tied up?"

"He asked me once to tie his hands behind his back with his belt. Neither of us got off on it, so that was the end of that."

"When you visited Rick in prison, did he say anything about a new girlfriend?"

"Hmm . . . not directly. He said he didn't need me anymore. I didn't know how to take that at the time, but looking back on it, it could have meant he had somebody waiting for him when he got out."

"Does the name Ginger Miller mean anything to you?"

"Ginger? Sure. I can't vouch for the Miller part, though. I don't know for sure that I've ever heard her last name."

PJ felt her hopes zoom upward.

"You know her?" Dave said, sitting forward eagerly. "Who is she?"

"Ginger is my daughter's imaginary playmate."

Twelve

Schultz aimed a kick at the flat tire, knowing it wouldn't do any good but needing the action anyway. He was on Interstate 94 outside Bismark, North Dakota, heading west. He had a car he'd rented under the name of James Richfield, and one thing after another had gone wrong with it.

Apparently no one at the rental company ever bothered to check the car's radiator, because he hadn't gotten twenty miles out of the city before his engine overheated. A truck driver who carried a couple of five-gallon containers of water stopped and filled up the nearly dry radiator for him, commiserating and sharing the news that he was on his way home to see his new grandson for the first time. Forty miles down the road the engine started to sputter. He pulled over onto the shoulder. It sounded as if he was out of gas, but the gauge said a quarter of a tank. He tapped the plastic on the front of the gauge and the needle slid down to empty. It had been stuck.

Once again rescued by an over-the-road driver, Schultz was delivered to a well-equipped truck stop fifteen miles farther on, where he paid for the driver's lunch, not stopping to get anything to eat himself, then bought a gas can and filled it. A few words with the man behind the counter resulted in an announcement over the PA system that a good buddy—that was him, Schultz had to remind himself—needed an eastbound hitch, and in minutes he was on his way. The driver bent Schultz's ear about gun control, but that was a small price to pay to get moving again.

Schultz chafed at all the contacts he was making—people who could later place him in certain locations at certain times, if anyone was following him asking questions—but it was unavoidable. If he wanted to switch rental cars, he'd have to turn back to Bismark, and he didn't want to double back on his own path. Car rental agencies were widely spaced in North Dakota, along with everything else.

He had gotten a whole seventy-five miles farther when the right front tire blew with a sudden pop and pull on the steering wheel that caught him in deep thought. He corrected without incident and pulled over on the shoulder.

To his amazement, the trunk yielded an inflated spare, a workable jack, and a beat-up tire iron with a stain on one end that jangled his cop sense, but he refused to allow himself to examine it closely. Changing the tire took only a few minutes, but it was hard work for a man in his mid-fifties who already carried a spare tire of his own twenty-four hours a day. It didn't help that he discovered that the lug nuts were so loose. He felt obligated to pop the hubcaps on the other three wheels and check those out, too. Having a wheel fly off at seventy mph and causing an accident wasn't his idea of maintaining a low profile.

He stowed the blown tire and the tools in the trunk and headed out again, wondering what else the car had in store for him. At 6:00 P.M. hunger drew him off the interstate, and he made an impromptu decision that Billings, Montana, was his destination for the day. All of his decisions were spontaneous. The more he planned his future actions, the more likely it was that anyone chasing him would pick up a pattern in his movements and get ahead of him.

Whoever it is seems to be ahead of me already, at every turn.

It was just fifty hours since Rick's body had been discovered, and in that time Schultz had gone, in the eyes of the police, from grieving parent to a man wanted for vehicular manslaughter. It was as though he had been picked up by the heels, held upside down, and shaken—cut loose from everything that anchored his life. He had barely slept, and emotionally and physically he was on shifting sands, liable to make a misstep any minute. That stuff he'd blurted out to PJ about being framed was an example. He knew he needed rest, and he needed to get his thoughts together.

Schultz checked into a Motel 6 and foraged in the convenience store across the street for dinner. The store had a selection of sandwiches and a microwave, so he carried back a sack of heated roast beef sandwiches, a bag of corn chips, a six-pack of root beer from the cooler section, and a couple of stale doughnuts bypassed by the morning crowd and left sitting forlornly in the display case. Nutritional it was not, but by the time he got the items back into his motel room he was ravenous from the smell of the roast beef. He flicked on the TV and put it on CNN. Then he spread out a towel on the bed to serve as a tablecloth and tore into the food. He ate in the manner he always did when he was alone, which was to get the food in fast and worry about cleanup, not to mention social graces, later.

After wolfing down the first sandwich, the edge taken off his hunger, he started to consider the situation. He was worried about Julia. She was an obvious target for anyone out to get him. Julia and he had made plans for her to get out of state, but that was before Caroline Bussman was run down with Schultz's car.

He didn't know what Julia would do when she got that news. Most likely she would go to the police and establish an alibi for him. Then what? After she told her story, there was no reason for the Chicago police to keep her in protective custody. So she'd be on her own, as she had been through the latter part of their marriage, he thought. He pushed down the guilt. All he could do was hope that she had sense enough to get out of town, to use the plan they had discussed for her to go to Florida to stay with her friend Cassie Wilkins.

Julia and Cassie had been friends for decades. Two years ago Cassie and her husband had retired to a senior community in Florida, but shortly afterward her husband had died. Julia had a standing invitation to visit anytime, but had never taken Cassie up on it, due to one thing or another. Schultz thought she'd be safe there, because if someone was after him it was undoubtedly due to a connection with his work with the department, and Cassie had no link to him or his work.

He licked his lips, cleaning off the glaze from the doughnuts. Surely Julia knew enough not to hop in her car and drive directly to Cassie's.

Surely.

He thought back over the events of the last two days, trying to pin down exactly why he felt such a great sense of danger. At first, there had been only the numbing shock of his son's death, and the manner of it.

The way Rick looked . . . No, don't bring that up. Doesn't do any good.

It had been during the evening he spent with PJ at Brandy's Bar that the feeling that he was being pursued first came upon him. Between one drink and the next, he had suddenly acquired a feeling of terrible naked vulnerability.

It was something PJ had said, something about Rick's past coming back to haunt him, and that his past was probably responsible for his violent death.

Not Rick's past, but mine. Mine.

The extra sense that Schultz had when it came to crime-solving, that link he was able to develop with the killer, had set up a clanging in his mind that was impossible to ignore. The answering machine message had simply been the icing on the cake.

Rick's killing was an execution, pure and simple. Although Rick was doing time for selling drugs, he was only a small building block, one of many at the bottom of the pyramid; Schultz was sure of that. His son had been caught selling marijuana to schoolchildren. That looked bad for a cop's kid, but it was the level of drug crime that a sixteen year old would be involved in, not someone ten years deeper into the business. Rick was lazy. He had been trying to find a way to pick up some cash to avoid holding down a legitimate job. No big-time drug deals gone bad, no Colombian drug lords snapping at his heels.

Who would possibly hate Rick enough to go to that much trouble to kill him? A stranger killing, a psycho picking an opportunistic victim? Not likely. It had been set up in advance. Ginger was proof of that. Ginger wrote the come-on letters. He died in an apartment rented by Ginger.

Ginger Miller. Ever since PJ had mentioned the name to him, he had thought there was something significant about it, something he should recognize.

His eyes were heavy with the need to sleep, and he knew he had to be on the road early tomorrow. He switched off the TV, barely aware that there had been something on the national news about St. Louis, something about a politician, maybe. Fleetingly he remembered seeing Chief Wharton's ugly puss on the screen. Must be a high-profile case. Schultz couldn't work up any interest in checking into it. He seemed completely disconnected from the concerns of ordinary homicides.

In the bathroom he unwrapped the soap, put down the bath mat, and took a hot shower. As he breathed in the steam and scrubbed, he suddenly straightened up. The shower spray hit him in the face like hot needles, but he didn't notice.

He had an idea what the whole thing was about. It was something that happened thirteen years ago. He started piecing things together in his head as he stood under the shower, washcloth dangling from his hand.

It all fit. He felt a thrill of elation at having figured it out and put a name to it. And then fear, somewhere in his gut.

A man with Ginger Miller's initials was after him, and the worst thing about it was that the man was a cop, a retired cop now. After thirty-three years with the department, Schultz was finally up against one of his own.

Thirteen

When Schultz reached his twenty-year anniversary with the St. Louis Police Department he was given a gold pin and a new partner.

That was thirteen years ago, but Schultz remembered that particular new partner as if it had all happened yesterday. At that time Schultz had a reputation for being good with the new detectives, showing them the ropes and keeping them in one piece until they could fend for themselves. He wasn't gentle with them, and at one time or another all of them hated him. He had gone through five partners in the last eight years, all of them better off for their stint at driving Schultz around town.

Vince Mandoleras was Schultz's new apprentice, twenty-eight years young and in awe of his senior partner. They were working burglaries. Three weeks into the partnership, Vince made a good collar and recovered a couple hundred thousand dollars' worth of stolen electronic equipment. It was actually Schultz who led him to the scene, maneuvered him into making the arrest, and made sure Vince's fly was zipped when it was time to talk to the lady reporter.

A month later, an informant told Schultz about a guy who was selling computers out of the back of his pickup truck. It seemed that when Lemont Clark got four or five beers in him, he'd yap to anyone who'd listen that he had enough hot shit to stock him a warehouse, and maybe he'd just rent one of those storefronts on Gravois, open up a deep-discount computer store, and put in a waiting room for the customers. Cash only, and don't expect no receipt.

Schultz and Vince sat across the street in an unmarked car and watched Clark's apartment. They saw him lug boxes out in a steady flow, pile them in his truck, and return a couple of hours later with the truck empty. A couple of times they followed him and witnessed the transactions. Vince leaned out the window and brazenly took pictures. But they weren't interested in the marks who bought the stuff. They wanted Lemont's supplier, the one who was pilfering from manufacturers' shipments. They couldn't decide if Lemont was the one doing the pilfering or if he was just the salesman. In two weeks of surveillance, they didn't turn up any deliveries to the apartment.

"Must have shit stacked from floor to ceiling in there," Vince said. "We could get him on fire code violations alone."

"Could be running a mail-order business or something," Schultz said.

"Yeah," Vince said, spreading that little-boy grin on his face like jam on toast, "or something. When we gonna bust this asshole?"

"Patience isn't your strong suit, is it?"

"I got plenty of patience. I even got slow hands. You just ask my girl."

Vince had a relationship with a single mother of twin baby girls that loosely qualified as an engagement to be married. Talk was the babies were his, but he hadn't owned up to it yet. He said he was waiting for a salary increase before making the leap, but Schultz had a feeling that after he got a raise there would be some other excuse on the horizon. The Mandoleras men had always been slow to commit. Glen Mandoleras, Vince's father, was a detective in narcotics. Schultz had known him for a few years. Glen hadn't married Vince's mother until Vince was long out of diapers.

After a few days of being bugged about holding back, Schultz got a warrant to search Lemont's place, based on the photos Vince had taken. Schultz had a feeling that they were rushing things, but there was nothing he could put his finger on during their surveillance, so in they went.

Schultz figured Lemont would bolt toward the rear when the cops showed up at his door, so Schultz took the fire escape around back himself. He sent Vince to the front to deliver the bad news.

Schultz kept telling himself to ignore that little buzz at the back of his skull that warned him when things weren't right. It was a simple arrest. They had a warrant to go in, backed up with Vince's photos of goods being sold on the street. And if anything went wrong, it was Schultz who would take the brunt of it when the guy ran straight into his arms.

He climbed the fire escape and approached the window they'd scoped out earlier—the one he expected Lemont to come bursting through as if his pants were on fire, with all that hot electronic equipment burning his ass.

On the way to the escape window, Schultz came to a frosted window that he supposed was the bathroom. He ducked down to pass under it, but then noticed that it was large enough for him to crawl through, and it was open about four inches. He could raise the window, duck inside, and grab the guy before he had a chance to hide anything—like the record books he must be keeping somewhere if he was accountable to some-body higher up. It was Lemont's records, not Lemont himself, that Schultz considered the catch of the day.

Schultz put his fingertips on the bathroom window sill to steady himself, and then slowly lifted his head up until his eyes cleared the sill and he could see into the room.

He found himself staring at Lemont's naked butt. The man was standing at the sink, shaving. The room was steamy. He'd just taken a shower. Most of the mirror was fogged up, but Schultz could see Lemont's face reflected there as he lifted his chin and ran the razor down his throat.

Heart thudding in his chest, Schultz froze in place. Lemont hadn't reacted at all, hadn't seen him. The man calmly rinsed the razor under the faucet. Feeling like a Peeping Tom, Schultz quickly scanned the interior of the bathroom. It looked as though the window was easily accessible from where Lemont stood, and it would be his logical bolt-hole as soon as Vince pounded on the front door and announced himself.

Schultz slowly lowered his head until he was clear of the window, then positioned himself next to it on the fire escape, pressing against the wall of the building. He drew his gun and waited for all hell to break loose.

A shotgun blast jolted him, and he almost pulled the trigger on a wild shot himself. A heartbeat later, the first sound still in his ears, the shotgun was fired again.

His partner didn't have a shotgun. Something was terribly wrong.

He looked in the window. Lemont was nowhere to be seen. Schultz realized the man must have seen him after all, and had just kept his cool, pretended that he didn't see an extra set of eyes in the mirror.

Schultz had spooked the man toward Vince, just the opposite of what he intended to do.

He shoved the window up hard and dove in head first. Schultz found his cheek mashed up against the porcelain base of the toilet and his left leg twisted painfully. He righted himself and dashed for the door. It had been only seconds since the second blast.

He raced through the door and down a short hall, his breath coming fast and his chest heaving. There wasn't time to give in to the sickness that churned in his gut. He rounded the end of the hall, and there was Lemont, framed in the open front doorway.

Lemont hadn't stopped to get dressed. In his left hand he held a bulging briefcase with papers shoved hastily into the side pockets. His right hand was hooked around a shotgun, the butt shoved up in his armpit and the barrel lowered. He was prodding something with his foot, something that had to be Vince's body. A glance at his partner lying there, face and chest splattered with blood and opened up like ripe fruit in a compost pile, sent a bolt of rage through Schultz's body—rage at this lowlife shithead for blowing Vince away, and rage at himself for letting it happen.

Lemont started to step over the body. In a moment he'd be gone, a naked animal running with the others in the street, maybe never trapped and made to pay for the life he'd taken.

Schultz took his stance and pumped several bullets into Lemont Clark. The first went into the back of his shoulder, and the rest into his chest when he turned.

The heat of the rage left Schultz almost immediately, and the blackness receded from the edges of his vision. He looked down at the carnage and shivered. Coldness crept up through his feet, where he stood in the mingled blood of his partner and the coldhearted bastard who'd killed him. He wondered if he was any different from Lemont, and he thought about Vince's girlfriend and her twin babies, and he thought about the news Detective Glen Mandoleras was going to get about his son.

He lifted his own gun toward his face and looked down the barrel for as long as it took his breathing to return to normal, trying to remember how many shots he'd fired and whether there was one bullet left to deal with his overwhelming failure. The three of them would make a nice pile on the floor, however untidy.

On some subconscious level, Schultz decided that he'd have to live with the events of the last few minutes. The urge to pull the trigger slipped away, and reason returned. He bent over, fumbled around in the mess, and came up with Vince's belt radio. Schultz hardly ever had his own handy when he needed one. He pressed the talk button.

"Officer down. Repeat, officer down."

Fourteen

Schultz went through the motions of getting ready for bed in the motel in Billings, but his thoughts were focused on Glen Mandoleras. He tried to dredge up every last bit of information about the man that he could remember.

Glen had joined the St. Louis Police Department sometime around 1980, Schultz thought. He remembered that because it seemed to him that father and son came on board within a few months of each other, an oddity in a world where age generally corresponded to number of years on the job. A man Glen's age would normally have a couple of decades of seniority. Glen had been a Vietnam vet, lean and muscled and still with a military bearing even though his time in-country was long past. He never talked about what he did after the war and before he moved into law enforcement, and eventually his fellow officers stopped asking. Glen moved up fast, and seemed to have an affinity for narcotics work on the street. Schultz knew him well enough to trade cop talk, but their paths didn't cross much.

Vince Mandoleras died at Schultz's feet in 1985, and after that Vince's father's work never did recover. Glen was broken by his son's death, but after some initial anger didn't seem to hold it against Schultz, who had been cleared by Internal Affairs. Schultz had claimed self-defense, and IA had gone for it, although they'd raked him over the coals for a few months about that shot in the rear shoulder. After that, Schultz found that green detectives weren't exactly lining up to be partnered with him, and over the next few years his own field assignments had tapered off. Glen took early retirement around 1990 and moved out of state. He moved somewhere warm, but Schultz couldn't remember exactly where. By now, Glen would be in his mid-sixties—old enough to be retired for real.

The years could change a person, Schultz knew. Bitterness could grow and take over a person's whole outlook until it became the only reason for living. Schultz's actions had planted a seed of bitterness in Glen's heart thirteen years ago. Had it withered over time, or was it mature, ready to be reaped in a vengeful harvest?

Schultz felt good to have a direction for his investigation. He had some phone calls to make if he was going to track down Glen Mandoleras, the man he suspected had awakened one day filled with blackness and hate. The man who had taken a son for a son, and then some.

Giving up on the prospect of getting to sleep, Schultz decided he might as well get started. There was a lot of work to be done, and lying around pretending to sleep wouldn't accomplish anything except mussing the sheets. He needed help, and Anita Collings was the person he turned to. She had an intense sense of loyalty, the ability to keep her mouth shut, and a true cop's feel for the brotherhood of law enforcement, even if she was a sister. He dialed her phone number.

"Collings," she answered groggily. Belatedly, he remembered it was past midnight. He didn't apologize for calling late, though.

"Anita, it's Schultz," he said.

"I'm listening." Her voice was suddenly alert and intense.

"I want you to do some things for me, outside channels and no questions asked. Can you do that?"

There was a moment's hesitation, and he thought perhaps he'd misjudged her.

"Sure, boss," she said.

"First is find out if my ex-wife is at the home of Cassandra Wilkins in Spring Creek, Florida. It's on the Gulf side, south of Tallahassee." He heard her rooting for paper and pen, and gave her a minute to get it down.

"I'm not sure if she's made it there yet. You might have to check back in a couple of days. Tell Cassie that Burpy wants to know, so Julia'll be sure that it's really me you're making the call for."

"Burpy?"

"Yeah, Burpy. Got a problem with that?"

"That's not one of the Seven Dwarfs, is it?"

"None of your business. You ready for the next one?"

"Fire way, boss. Things can only go up from Burpy."

Fifteen

Cut slept part of the day Wednesday. After Tuesday night's exhilarating knife work, he was too keyed up to do anything but channel surf in his motel room for hours. It was that or walk the streets, and he didn't want to take any chances with being picked up. He finally fell asleep, still sitting up in bed, sometime around dawn. He woke a few hours later with a stiff neck and a ravenous hunger.

A hot bath and a couple of steakburgers improved his attitude until he could laugh at himself for even noticing the discomforts. He was getting decadent in his old age. He resolved to double his morning workout, at least until he got back to his old environment.

Things were going well, except that there had been no public announcement of Schultz's arrest for the little girl's death. In fact, there was very little in the news at all about the hit-and-run—a couple of paragraphs on page six of the *Post,* and no detailed description of the vehicle or driver. Peculiar. He had circled the block until there were a couple of witnesses handy before aiming the car at the girl. Didn't those witnesses come forward?

That's the problem with people nowadays, he thought. *No one wants to get involved.*

Then it occurred to him that Schultz's fellow police officers were covering for him. He should have foreseen that. Loyalty was important. Hell, he'd do it himself.

It would have been nice if Schultz spent some time in prison before Cut killed him. That way the misery would have been spread out over time, and Cut would have gladly waited five or ten years and then gone after him when he was on the outside again. That was the original plan, but if Cut had learned anything in his military and post-military activities, it was to keep his options open.

The next step was to scope out a venue for the job. Cut thought about brazenly walking into police headquarters and blowing Schultz away. He let himself run with it for a few minutes, enjoying the images, playing around with different body sites he'd aim at, then tossed it aside. He was a practical man. He knew he wouldn't accomplish his goal with a plan like that, and even if he did, he wouldn't come out of it alive. That wasn't good. He wanted to live. He had a reason to live.

As long as Cut was alive, he could keep the memory of his son alive inside him, and somehow that made his son a little less dead.

No, it wasn't a suicide mission.

Cut took the bus over to Lafayette Avenue to take a look at Schultz's house. He got off a few blocks away and strolled down the sidewalk. It was afternoon, and a fine day for August at that, but there was minimal activity in the neighborhood. The yuppies who lived in the rehabbed houses were all at work, and many of the houses that hadn't undergone an internal remodeling and an external face-lift belonged to people too old or sick to be outside. There were a few stay-at-home moms. He could tell by the minivans.

It was summertime, and the yards should have contained at least a few kids playing. But the kids were inside soaking up the air-conditioning and probably playing Nintendo, useless hunt-and-strike games that were no substitute for the real thing.

He walked past Schultz's house and continued on to Lafayette Park. There he did find evidence of life. Preschoolers fed the ducks and skinned their knees on the playground. Mothers talked about whose kid did what first. He didn't linger. A lone man earned sharp glances from protective mothers, and he didn't want to draw attention to himself. Cut left the park, crossed Lafayette, and walked back toward Schultz's house on the opposite side of the street. He found what he was looking for a few houses past his target.

It was a house that looked as if no one was home, and there was a garden hose hanging next to an outdoor faucet. He walked around the back of the house, acting as if he had every right to do so, and found a treasure trove: garden tools in an unlocked outdoor storage shed. He put on the owner's cap and gloves, picked up the hedge shears, and went around the front of the house. There he trimmed the bushes under the front windows. He worked slowly, spending most of his time watching Schultz's house. When he ran out of trimming work, he bundled the cuttings and left them around the back of the house. Then he got the hose out and watered the front lawn. It was a hot afternoon for outdoor work. No one paid any attention to him, possibly because they didn't want to imagine themselves out there sweating.

He watched a woman park in front of Schultz's house and go in. Not long afterward, the front drapes suddenly opened and the woman stood there, staring out. Worried that she would spot him and remember his face, he bent over and weeded out some crabgrass, giving her a rear view. She came out later with a grim look on her face. He didn't recognize her. It wasn't Schultz's ex-wife—he knew what Julia Schultz looked like.

He made up his mind that he could easily break into the house. He'd do it when Schultz wasn't home, and then wait for him inside. If all went well, he'd have enough time for a slow kill.

That was for later, though. Cut methodically put the tools back, putting in the effort to clean the hedge shears and wondering whether the owners would even notice that the lawn fairy had visited while they were away.

It was time to go back to the motel, get something cool to drink, and build the bomb.

Sixteen

PJ sat at the desk in her small office in the headquarters building. Thomas was staying with Winston for the next few days, so she didn't have to be home at any particular time. She had gotten back to her office Wednesday evening to find Anita gone. Anita had been through the simulations and hadn't even been impressed enough to leave a note.

There had been some excitement that afternoon when Kathee Kollins had recognized Ginger's name. Kyla was called back into the room, and Kathee, PJ, and Kyla signed intently while Dave sat impatiently, frustrated by not following the conversation. PJ then explained to him that yes, the imaginary playmate's name was Ginger Miller, but the name came from a woman who'd been a volunteer in the hospital during one of Kyla's surgeries. She was "about two hundred years old," according to Kyla, had been a schoolteacher for at least a hundred of those, and had been very nice to Kyla during her stay.

Dave promptly checked with the hospital and found that the woman did exist. She had been a volunteer for a decade, and had died last spring at the age of ninety.

Dead end.

Whether the name had any significance or was just a co-incidence was impossible to say. PJ and Dave both leaned toward it being a coincidence.

PJ worked on her VR simulation of Rick's murder for several hours, then set it aside in frustration. Dialing up a private bulletin board, she made contact with her longtime mentor, Merlin, and the two of them moved into a private chat room. It was as close to talking face-to-face as she had ever gotten with Merlin.

Merlin's nickname for her, Keypunch, came from her college days, when computers only accepted data and programs on punch cards. PJ had excelled at keypunching the cards, and was the envy of her less dexterous fellow students.

She had known Merlin since college, although she had never met him in person. He communicated with her only in dial-up connections, starting from the time when bulletin boards weren't in wide use yet. Merlin had seen her through high points and lows in her life, while revealing little about himself. She was aware from long association with him that he had global connections, and he chatted with government leaders and top scientists as easily as he did with her. How he kept all his contacts straight was a mystery to her.

More than once she had thought Merlin might be an intelligent computer program rather than a human being. But the insight offered and compassion dispensed made that seem unlikely.

What's the buzz, Keypunch?

The familiar greeting appearing on her screen warmed her. Merlin could always be counted on to simply be there when she needed him.

Merlin, so much has happened I hardly know where to start.

Tell me everything. I need my soap opera fix. Lay bare your soul and we'll go from there. Lay bare whatever else you wish, too.

You dirty old man. You ought to be evicted from cyberspace.

She told him about Rick's death, her time with Schultz and his enigmatic phone call, and the girl's death. After some hesitation and gentle prodding by Merlin, she told him about her visit to Schultz's house and the discovery of the empty bottles.

Was it good quality? The booze, that is.

Dewar's. What has that got to do with anything?

Just checking to see if he has good taste. Wouldn't want you hanging out with a cheap drunk.

Merlin!

Yes. Sorry. That was uncalled for. So do you believe Schultz or not?

PJ closed her eyes. At least he hadn't asked if she loved Schultz or not. Or perhaps it was the same thing.

I want to believe him, she typed, *but everything's stacked against him.*

My kind of poker game. What are you doing to find Rick's murderer?

She described everything her team had gone through.

Very pedestrian.

What's your idea, oh great crime-solver?

It's about time you recognized my abilities. Raise up thine eyes from thine own concerns and look about thee.

Merlin, the biblical prophet. I can do better getting an old movie at Blockbuster.

Very funny. Good to know you still have that lightning wit.

Cut the crap and tell me what you're thinking.

Oh, how unladylike. I'll have to tell your mommy.

PJ nearly broke her connection. Sometimes Merlin fell into a loop of mock insults, and she wasn't able to get anything useful out of him. She waited him out.

Oh, all right. You're not thinking in a synergistic way. Look for connections, even ones that don't seem to make sense on the surface.

I'm all ears.

Do you think somebody is out to get Schultz?

I'm not sure, PJ typed. *He thinks so. He said something on the phone about being framed.*

Consider this: a detective who arrests killers suddenly has his life turned upside down. A prominent prosecuting attorney who brought killers to justice is wiped out. Key word in both sentences: killers.

Victor Rheinhardt.

I read the news, cutie.

Do you think they're related? PJ's eyes were wide.

No, but their deaths might be.

I hadn't thought of that, PJ typed, letting his remark slip by.

That's what I'm good for, the Big Picture. Separately, they each have a lot of bad guys in their pasts. Go for the intersection points in their careers.

I need to get on this.

Not before you get your list. The word for the day is "connection" and the list is mercifully short.

1. Connections can be physical, emotional, or spiritual. Physical ones are the most fun.

2. Revenge is a form of connection that isn't on the plus side of the personality ledger.

3. Soap operas = tangled connections.

4. My stomach's grumbling and I'd like to connect with a few enchiladas right about now.

5. The ultimate connection is that we are all made of star stuff.

Take care, Keypunch.

PJ didn't know much about the Rheinhardt case, certainly not any insider details. Ordinarily, Schultz would be her conduit for information about cases that didn't belong to CHIP. She couldn't rely on that. In fact, she couldn't even reach Schultz. She had no idea if he'd contact her again or not.

She was on her own, and she told herself she'd better start dealing with it.

Then she realized that it wasn't really Rheinhardt's death she needed to learn more about, but his life—specifically, where it crossed Schultz's. PJ had one contact she had developed all on her own. She checked the clock on her desk. Would he be there on a weeknight at 9:00 P.M.?

Probably. It's not like he has a wild social life.

Gathering up a few things from her desk, she set out toward the Audiovisual Department in search of Louie Bertram.

The AV lab door was closed, and PJ heard loud music coming from inside. She recognized it as *Mars, Bringer of War,* from the suite *The Planets,* by Gustav Holst. Most people knew it as the music from the movie *2001: A Space Odyssey,* but PJ was familiar with it because her father used to play it at full volume when he finished his editing work for the day. When the arthritis in her father's fingers got worse, he took to working from home so that others wouldn't see him painfully pecking out articles or working with the layout boards. Sometimes PJ typed for him. Other days she'd be doing her homework or reading, and suddenly the music would come booming through the walls of the house, indicating another edition put to bed. It had startled more than one of her young friends who happened to be visiting at the time. She smiled as she heard the familiar music from the lab.

PJ knocked on the door, but had little hope of being heard.

After a minute of ineffectual knocking, she tried the knob. It turned, so she opened the door slightly. Peering in, she saw Louie, one hand moving his wheelchair back and forth in time to the thunderous beat, the other raised and holding an imaginary conductor's baton. His eyes were open but unfocused and his face practically glowed. It was a private moment, and she didn't want to intrude, but she couldn't wait to get started on researching any possible connection between Rick's death and Rheinhardt's. Quietly she closed the door and went to an office a few doors down, far enough so she couldn't hear the music, in search of a phone. She dialed his number, chastising herself for not doing that in the first place.

She hoped he'd see the flashing light on the phone.

The phone was picked up on the tenth ring. The background was silent. He'd turned the music off.

"Bertram."

"Louie, it's PJ. I'm surprised to find you in. I was going to leave you a message." She kept her voice low and the phone close to her face. For all she knew, Louie could hear her through several dividing walls. The man had an uncanny knack for all things audio.

"Always glad to talk with you, PJ. What can I do for you?" he said. She knew his lashes would be brushing his cheeks shyly as he talked. He gave no indication that he knew she was on the same floor of the building as he was.

"Actually I'm still in the building, Louie. Could I come over and talk with you?"

"Sure."

"See you in a few minutes," PJ said. She hung up, waited in the dark office for several minutes, then went to his door and knocked.

"Come in," Louie said cheerfully.

She pulled up a chair so she wouldn't tower over Louie. As a short person herself, she didn't care much for speaking to people's chests, and she imagined Louie didn't like talking to their belly buttons.

To others Louie Bertram was an extension of his audio-visual equipment. Because he didn't relate easily to most people, he became invisible to them, just another one of the levers and knobs to twist or pull when A/V expertise was needed. From the first time she'd met him, PJ had tried to penetrate his shell of isolation. She had been rewarded with friendship, tentative at first, then cemented when she called upon him for help. He'd gotten in trouble once by following her requests, but it didn't matter to him. Friends helped out, didn't they?

He was neatly dressed in a long-sleeved blue dress shirt, open at the neck. Probably he'd worn a tie during the day and loosened up after hours. He wore black trousers and freshly shined black leather dress shoes. From the knee down his legs were spindly and twisted. As his trousers draped against them, she could make out their shape. He was about forty years old, with an unfortunate problem of overly hairy ears but a dazzling smile that she couldn't help returning. After a few minutes in Louie's presence, the ears didn't seem so bad.

"What can I do for you, PJ? A tape enhanced? Voices compared?"

Louie had started out calling her Dr. Gray when they first met, but she had gently insisted on PJ. It was that simple show of warmth that had started a fledgling relationship.

"Louie, I need something outside your area. But I thought you could point me in the right direction."

His smile faltered for a moment. "I'll do what I can."

"I need to know how to search old case files, pulling out ones that match compound criteria. It's important." PJ hadn't had the need to examine archival computer records, and therefore didn't have the access code or experience with the database search. She could poke around and probably hack in, but she knew that any security program worth its salt would record her initial attempts as unauthorized accesses. She'd leave a record, and Wall or someone else would be down on her head in the morning about it. Unless the idea panned out, she didn't want to go public with it. She had resolved to give Schultz his three days, and she felt that she was sneaking around behind his back—which of course she was. She could obtain and use someone else's ID, but she didn't want to risk having anyone else blamed for unauthorized accesses they had nothing to do with.

She could also wait and make a request through appropriate channels in the morning. She was assigned to the Rick Schultz case, and it would be a legitimate request that wouldn't garner any special notice. But her sense of urgency wouldn't hold still for that.

Louie's face lit up. "Oh, no problem. That would be Georgina."

PJ sat back, relieved. He hadn't questioned her reason for wanting the information, and Louie seemed to know everyone. "Great. Let's go see her."

"One small problem. She works days and always goes home right on time. She's got two boys under five years old."

"Oh," PJ said, disappointed.

"I could probably get her to come in if I went over and stayed with the boys," he said. "They're asleep by now, and wouldn't even know their mom was gone. And if they did wake up, they know me from the time I rewired her furnace and helped her put in smoke alarms."

PJ wondered how Louie could possibly help install smoke alarms on the ceiling, then moved on to another thought: *Was there anyone around here that Louie hadn't helped out at one time or another?*

When she thought about it further, she realized that all of his contacts were among the support personnel, technicians, or administrative staff, not the officers. There was an entire network of people who worked within, around, and underneath the visible structure of law enforcement that the public saw as "the police." They were civilians, like herself, highly dedicated to their work.

And Louie was the entry gate.

"I couldn't ask you to do that," PJ said. "I'll just wait until morning."

"Let me give her a call and see if she goes for it."

PJ shrugged. She felt she was imposing too much, but she was eager to see if the connections idea had any merit.

Louie rolled over to a phone. He had a short conversation with his back to her, so she couldn't make out much. Then he spun around.

"It's a done deal. I'll leave now for her house. It's only a twenty-minute drive, so she'll be here in less than an hour."

PJ found herself wishing she could hear Schultz's voice again, even if it was another enigmatic phone call.

By the time PJ got to her bedroom, Megabite had worked the feline magic of being in more than one place at a time—the cat was on the bed, delicately cleaning her whiskers. PJ pulled up the covers and got comfortable with the cat curled under her arm. Doubts mercifully faded, the world narrowed to the darkness behind her closed eyelids, and in moments she was asleep.

Seventeen

Early Thursday morning, Schultz awakened in his motel room. He went to the lobby for a cup of coffee. Heavy dark clouds hung down so low that he could feel them on his shoulders as he walked. The air held a lot of moisture, enough so that he couldn't cool off by sweating, and a thin film of sweat and condensation formed on his skin almost as soon as he stepped outside his room. The hairs on his arms rose with every distant lightning strike. On the way back to the room, a few raindrops dampened his shirt and thunder rolled over the roofs of the buildings like the echoes of a giant's footsteps. The air was oppressive and gloomy, setting the stage for the kind of storm that made people want to stay indoors and pull down their window shades.

He called Anita Collings at her home, looking for information. She came through for him without asking questions, and he'd remember that if he was ever in a position to do her a favor. He also appreciated her being his eyes and ears back in St. Louis.

"Nothing big on Rick's murder," Anita said. She told him about the chemical supplies purchased by Ginger Miller. Bursts of static from the approaching storm punctuated her account. "On the hit-and-run, Wall and company have been inside your house. The liquor bottles didn't help your case." There was no suspicion in her voice, just flat sarcasm.

"Well, shit, I could have figured that out myself." He cursed the impulse that had led to the bottles' presence in the first place, and his stupidity for leaving them there.

"What about Mandoleras?" he said.

"Found him. Personnel had a forwarding address. After his early retirement, he moved to Tucson." She gave him the address.

"And that other thing?"

"No luck yet. I'm going back, and I'll be a little more persuasive this time."

"Good. I owe you, Anita."

"Um, I never did get a chance to tell you directly. I'm really sorry about your son. And the way it happened. What a shitty way to go."

It wasn't the most eloquent expression of sympathy, but Schultz was deeply affected. He choked up for a moment, and tears stood at the corners of his eyes. While he had been on the run, he'd had to put his grief on the shelf.

Static crackled through the phone line.

"Yeah," he said finally.

"Bye, Boss. Call again when you get the chance."

It didn't take Schultz long to pack after he got off the phone. He had acquired a small suitcase that held his supply of cash, a change of clothes, and a shaving kit—plus a .40 caliber pistol, a Glock 22.

The handgun made him feel a little safer, even though he knew he could be taken out by a sniper's rifle before he had the time to use it.

Schultz turned in his rental car, paid the one-way fee for not returning it to the city of origin, and bought a bus ticket to Tucson. He was on his way to find Glen Mandoleras. He wasn't sure if the guy would be at home, in St. Louis, or out on the road searching for his last target. But he hoped that sooner or later Mandoleras would check in at his home base.

Schultz was going to be waiting for him.

One of the advantages Schultz had in his detective work was an uncanny ability to connect with a killer. It came to him as an image of a thread that connected him to the person he was seeking. When he started out, the thread was insubstantial and not anchored on the far end, the end away from him. The far end waved in the darkness. The deeper he got into a case, the more solid the connection became, until it was a gleaming cord that terminated in the heart of the killer. It enabled him to make the last leap toward solving a crime, sometimes crossing a gap of information in a sudden blaze of understanding. It was almost as if he could swing hand over hand along the cord to the person he sought. He knew it sounded crazy, so he kept quiet about it, preferring to say that he had good instincts. He had told one person about it, and that was PJ. She hadn't laughed, but he didn't think she grasped the significance of it either. In any case, they'd talked about it once and then never mentioned it again. Schultz wasn't about to push his explanation.

He didn't fully trust the mysterious ability. It wasn't reliable. It couldn't be commanded to perform. And he was convinced it had misled him before, possibly even more than he realized. If he was pinned to the wall about it, he'd say it was probably just an intense visualization of wishful thinking, like the process cancer patients used to mobilize the body's internal defenses by imagining an army of defender cells.

As the Greyhound moved out into waves of rain, Schultz leaned back, closed his eyes, and cast the thread out to see if the connection was there between himself and Mandoleras.

The thread was cold and dull, and couldn't penetrate the gloom.

Idly, Schultz wondered how many other passengers on the bus were carrying handguns in their luggage.

Eighteen

Thursday morning PJ got an early start, expecting to have to ride herd on her archive records requests. To her surprise she found twelve thick folders in two side-by-side stacks on her desk at 7:00 A.M. She shook her head in wonder. It was probably more of Louie's doing.

The folders represented only a small amount of the actual case material. Homicide cases generated a huge amount of written reports, photographs, interview transcriptions, notes, and evidence logs. If every scrap of paper that existed for the cases had been sent, there would have been boxes filling her office and probably spilling over into the hallway.

Even though the folders were greatly streamlined, it looked like a big job. It was time to call in reinforcements. PJ dialed Dave Whitmore's number. He was already in the office too, and picked up on the first ring.

"What are your plans this morning, Dave?"

"I thought I'd go on over to Schultz's neighborhood later on and do more interviews. If his car was stolen from right out in front of his house, somebody should have seen it."

PJ thought about the flash of reflected light across the street from Schultz's house when she had been there. "No one's said anything?"

"They were all at work or asleep or walking around with their eyes closed, something like that. Neighbors see more than we'd like to think they do, but getting them to open up about it can be tough."

"You don't think he did it, the hit-and-run."

"Who, Schultz? Nah."

He sounded so certain. She wished she could get a transplant of his confidence.

"How do you know for sure?" PJ asked.

There was a pause. She could picture him holding the phone, frowning, his brows creased in deep thought.

"I just know, that's all. He wouldn't have run if he'd done it. Schultz would face up to it, no matter how bad it was."

Then why is he gone? She didn't voice her concerns to Dave. And she didn't mention the potential Mrs. Dollins to him, either.

PJ wanted help, and she had turned to Dave. He was more approachable than Anita, who always seemed aware of the gulf between cops and civilians, and which side of that gulf each of them was on. PJ thought Dave would go along with what she was about to ask. She cleared her throat.

"I've got an idea I'd like you to help me check out," she said. "Is Anita there?"

"I haven't seen her yet this morning. I can leave her a message and come on over to your office."

"No, that's all right," she said quickly. "It's you I want to talk to. Are you willing to help out on something that I'd prefer to keep just between the two of us for now?"

"Sure," he answered immediately. "Just say the word."

She didn't know whether to be pleased that he agreed so easily or worried that he would do and had done the same for others, namely Schultz.

"I've got an idea I'd like to bounce off you, then," PJ said. "See you in a few minutes."

Dave appeared soon afterward, bringing a small sack of homemade cinnamon rolls. He tore open the bag and offered PJ a choice.

"These all look so good. Did your friend make them?"

"She's into that kind of stuff. I think she started these last night. Put them in the refrigerator to rise overnight. Does that sound right?"

PJ shrugged. She had made yeast rolls once in her life, and the results hadn't encouraged repeat attempts.

"Um, could be," she said.

"All I know is when I woke up this morning the place smelled great."

"Marry her."

Dave laughed. "Maybe I will, at that. If she'll have me."

He glanced at the stacks of folders on her desk, then looked at PJ expectantly. She explained her connection theory, including Schultz's phone call during which he said he was being framed. Excitement grew in Dave's face.

"Sounds like there might be something to it," he said when she finished. "What do you want me to do?"

"I don't want Wall to know about this yet," PJ said. "Not until there's something to show for it. And I did promise Schultz three days. He's got until tomorrow."

"My lips are sealed. Except when it comes to cinnamon rolls," he said, taking the last roll.

It wasn't until several hours later, when the smell of the cinnamon rolls had long since dissipated and PJ was beginning to think about taking a lunch break, that she found something that clicked.

"I think I've got something," she said. Dave looked up. His elbow had been resting on her desk, and his cheek on his hand. He might have been asleep. She knew no one on the team had gotten much sleep since Rick's body had been discovered.

"Yeah?"

"Jeremiah Ramsey, executed for murdering his sister Eleanor. Get this, Dave—he was put to death one year ago July twenty-ninth," she said.

"That falls in the range for Rick's time of death."

"One year later."

"Revenge on the anniversary of the death. Like placing flowers on the grave, only a lot worse."

"There's a list of family members in here somewhere . . ." PJ flipped the pages in the folder. "Here. Father, Elijah Ramsey. Mother, Libby. One surviving sister, Darla."

"No girlfriend?"

"Nope. Not in this folder, anyway. Might have been a more recent development, after the trial. Are you thinking Ginger Miller is Jeremiah's girlfriend?"

Dave nodded. His eyes held a light she hadn't seen before, the hard glint of a hungry fox in the dead of winter that's just scented a rabbit. She hadn't thought of Dave as a predator, but prolonged exposure to him in Schultz's absence was changing her mind.

"Let's not get carried away," she said. "This looks like a connection, but it could also be coincidence."

"Party pooper."

PJ smiled as she checked farther into the family information. Dave was coming through loud and clear. Schultz obviously had a dampening effect on Dave.

"At the time of the trial, Jeremiah's dad was a janitor at an elementary school," PJ said. "Mom ran a day care center. Darla worked in a children's clothing store." PJ twirled a pencil between her fingers. "Seems like everybody wants to be around kids, doesn't it?"

"Why does that sound bad when you say it?"

"Because I'm a shrink," PJ said. Her mood had shifted. She felt she was onto something.

"So what's the plan, boss? Jump on this?"

"I think we should finish the last couple of folders," she said. "If nothing more promising comes up, we go on this one. I'll track down the family and find out what they're up to now—there's a last known address in here. It's been about twelve years since the trial, so there's no telling if this information is still accurate. You can check out whether Jeremiah got a girlfriend while he was in prison."

"What kind of girl falls for a guy on death row, anyway?"

"I know of a case where a woman fell in love with a convicted serial killer awaiting execution. They got married over the telephone."

"Different strokes, I guess. But I wouldn't want to live next door to her."

They raced through the last two folders, finding nothing compelling.

"Okay, the Anniversary Killer it is," Dave said.

"I've just had another thought," PJ said. "If revenge by the family is the story here, why stop with the prosecutor and the detective? Aren't there other obvious targets?"

Dave's eyes widened. "The judge," he said.

"And the jury," PJ finished.

PJ sat across from Lieutenant Howard Wall. His face, which could be described as craggy at best, seemed as lined as the surface of Mars, which had deceived early astronomers into believing an advanced civilization had built canals. New worry lines seemed to pop into being as she talked.

After some soul-searching, she had gone back on her decision to give Schultz until Friday morning to resolve things on his own. Dave had pressured her not to keep their speculations secret. Truthfully, it hadn't taken much pressure at all. She felt that lives could be at stake. Her promise to Schultz was important, but it wasn't going to get in the way of saving lives.

"So Schultz called you Tuesday?" Wall said.

"While you and I were having lunch at Subway," she said. Having decided to figuratively bare her chest, she wasn't going to keep Schultz's contact a secret. "The call came on my cell phone while I was in the bathroom."

"I thought you looked a little upset when you came out."

"Upset doesn't quite cover it."

"There's something lacking in our communication," Wall said. "I want you to think of me as someone you can come to with problems."

PJ tried to keep the skeptical look off her face, but apparently didn't succeed.

"I know I've been hard on you before," Wall said. She expected him to smile at the understatement, but he didn't. "Regardless of what you think, I don't care about procedures or chain of command or that civilian versus cop thing you're so hung up on."

PJ kept her silence. It wasn't quite the reaction she expected from Wall. He was hitting too close to home.

"I couldn't give a crap about department politics, either," Wall said. "That's for Wharton and his hangers-on. Now I don't like getting chewed out by my superiors and I've been known to pass it on. But you have to expect that on this job. On any job."

"I understand."

"No, I don't think you do, PJ. I think you're too wrapped up in your own concerns. I don't care about proving you can work with the big guys. I care about saving lives."

PJ began to get defensive. "That's not fair. I came to you with this because I care about saving lives too," she said. She felt heat rising in her cheeks.

"You could have opened up about it on Tuesday. If there's anything to this, there could have been more resources working on it. I think you kept quiet because you didn't want to look bad if you were wrong."

There it was. Did PJ really care more about her own image in the department than helping Schultz? Or, heaven forbid, than protecting innocent people? No, she decided. She had kept quiet at first because Schultz asked her to do so. And she wasn't about to explain the complexity of thought and emotion that went into *that* decision to Wall. She wasn't ready to closely examine it herself. But when it became clear to her that other people might be in deadly danger, she hadn't hesitated to come forward. She forced herself to answer calmly and contritely.

"That wasn't quite it, sir, but I'll work on my communication," she said.

He held her eyes for a minute, then seemed to decide that was all he was going to get from her. "Good. Now what exactly did Schultz tell you?"

PJ went through the conversation in the toilet stall, then told him about her visit to Schultz's house.

"You've got a key?" He sounded displeased.

"Yes." She practically dared him to make an issue of it.

"You didn't by any chance go there right after Schultz disappeared and remove an answering machine tape, did you?"

"No."

So he knew about the missing tape, which meant he also knew about the bottles under the sink, just as Dave did. Wall ignored the fact that he hadn't bothered to tell her of those findings earlier. She bit off a smart remark about communication evidently being a one-way street. Stubbornly, she decided to keep her observation about the busybody across the street from Schultz's house, the person who might be able to clear or further incriminate Schultz, to herself.

Wall listened intently when she got to the connection she was tentatively fashioning among Rick Schultz's amateur execution, framing Schultz for the hit-and-run, and Victor Rheinhardt's brutal knifing. She rushed on before Wall could question the details of how she obtained knowledge of the Ramsey case. PJ didn't want to get Louie in trouble again if she could avoid it.

Wall indicated that he was familiar with the Ramsey case, although he had no direct involvement in it.

"It's possible the killer won't rest until everyone responsible for Jeremiah Ramsey's death has been eliminated," PJ said. "There's no telling how far it will go. There could be a chain of deaths. The judge in the case, the jury, the defense attorney for not getting Jeremiah off, even the warden who officially carried out the sentence."

"The governor who declined clemency."

"That's one I hadn't thought of," PJ said.

"Who do you think the killer is?"

"I don't have any idea at this point. Likely suspects are members of Jeremiah's family, a lover if he had one, or even someone who got to know him in prison who feels the execution was unjustified."

"Like a guard who worked on death row," Wall said.

"Or a counselor of some kind. Here's a thought: instead of the defense attorney being a target, the attorney or someone in his office could be the killer, trying to wipe out a blot on his record, or a perceived injustice," PJ said.

"Then that could apply to any of the possible targets. Maybe a member of the jury feels he was talked into a guilty verdict and is trying to atone."

PJ shook her head in dismay. The list of possible suspects was growing faster than the estimate on her last car repair job.

Wall locked her in his gaze. His eyes gave away nothing, but she knew he was considering where to go next and what her role was to be.

"I want you to stay with the family," he said. "Go do your shrink stuff on the Ramseys. I'll get a task force looking into others who had to do with the case. We're not dropping our other lines of investigation, though."

By that he meant he wasn't going to entirely stop consid-

ering Schultz as the perpetrator in Caroline Bussman's death.
PJ nodded.

"I'll get right on it," she said.

Nineteen

Back in her office, PJ closed the door to shut out the hall-way noise. It sounded as if there was a party going on in the men's room directly across from her office, complete with whoops and hollers. The closed door blunted the noise, but didn't shut it off entirely.

Her desk lamp illuminated the center of her small window-less space, but left shadows at the edge. That made the work area seem even smaller than the converted utility room that it was. It was a good thing she wasn't claustrophobic.

Dave, Anita, and others were going to start contacting peo-ple who had been involved with the Ramsey trial, people who might be in danger. No doubt they'd be setting up protective watches for those people, at least the more prominently in-volved ones. Being on a jury had a sort of anonymity about it, whereas others such as the judge stuck out as individuals. There was another benefit from watching the movements of those involved—the killer might be among them.

She balled her hands into fists and rubbed her eyes. When the surveillance started, would the killings stop? That would be beneficial—no more deaths—but it would also mean that the killer had been alerted to the fact that the police were closing in.

It was her job to talk with the family members, who were unlikely to be targets themselves. So, although her work was vital and could lead to the identification of the killer, it didn't have the same ring of urgency as protecting those in danger. To prepare, she had to do two things: locate as many family members as possible, and learn more about the case itself so that she could talk knowledgeably about it. She had learned from past experience that if she wasn't thoroughly prepared, she might as well have a sign on her forehead reading "loves to be manipulated."

After looking in the case file for the last known addresses of Libby and Elijah Ramsey and their older daughter Darla, she dialed the phone numbers listed. One of them resulted in an automated message that said the number didn't exist and urged PJ to check her directory for the valid number. The other phone number got her a recorded message from a health clinic that offered confidential testing for sexually transmitted diseases. PJ was told that her call was important, and to please call back during office hours Monday through Wednesday.

Opening the phone book, she found over a hundred and fifty listings for Ramseys. None were for the exact names she was looking for, but she called a few promising ones that were listed under the right initials. No luck. It was frustrating, but not unexpected, that after more than a dozen years the Ramseys might be hard to find. It was quite possible none of them even lived in the St. Louis area anymore. Bad memories.

She dialed the number from the case file for one of the Wee Belong Together day care centers that Libby Ramsey had operated. To her surprise, someone answered.

"Mrs. Ramsey, please," PJ said, slipping into her concerned mother's voice.

"There's a name I haven't heard in a long while. She hasn't been around for years," said a woman's warm voice. "Years. Did you know Libby?"

"I'm trying to locate her. We've lost touch."

"Oh, I'm not surprised. After that dreadful business with her daughter . . . Who did you say you were?"

"I'm a friend of hers. Actually an old client. My son used to attend Wee Belong."

"Well, it's run by Mrs. Wellsing now. If you're calling about the center, I'll let you talk to her."

"No, wait. All I need to know is where I can reach Mrs. Ramsey. It's important. I'm a friend of hers, and I have some news for her. Good news, for a change."

PJ discovered that casual lying for a good cause came easily to her. Perhaps she was cut out for investigative work, after all, in spite of the way Schultz sometimes taunted her about only being suited for consumer studies.

Abruptly she felt the phantom pressure of his lips on hers.

"Oh, well . . . I guess it wouldn't do any harm," the woman said. "It's not like she went into hiding, the poor thing. She moved to Jefferson City. I don't know her phone number."

"That's okay. Thanks." PJ hung up hurriedly.

Having gotten one nibble, PJ dropped the search for the other family members and concentrated on Libby. She figured that if she could locate Mom, chances were good that Mom could tell her where the rest of the family was. In her family, that would certainly be the case.

The phone company information line yielded no listings for Elizabeth Karen Ramsey in Jefferson City. A half hour later, after a lesson from a bored rookie on desk duty, PJ got an address from the Department of Revenue's license bureau. Libby had a driver's license.

It was nearly three in the afternoon. Tomorrow PJ would get an early start and drive to Jefferson City to look for the elusive Libby in person. She wanted to talk with her face-to-face anyway, and not over the phone.

She phoned her son Thomas at Bill Lakeland's house. Winston picked up on the second ring.

"Hi, Winston. Could you put Thomas on, please?" There was a pause and a few clunks as the phone was put down hard and then picked up.

"Hey, Mom!"

"Hey, Cuddle Bunny, how ya doin'?"

"Sheesh. Don't call me that."

"Don't complain. Could be worse. I could call you that in front of girls. Specifically, Amanda Franklin."

"You wouldn't!"

"Let's just say I probably wouldn't, but I reserve the right."

"You coming home? We could have dinner together."

That sounded great to PJ, but she needed to get some work done before her trip to Jefferson City tomorrow. She missed her son, and hearing his voice on the phone made her want to see him even more.

"Here's the deal. I'd like to invite myself over to have breakfast with you guys tomorrow morning. Could you ask Winston and his dad if it would be all right?"

"His dad won't be home until five-thirty. Just come over, anyway. I'm sure it'll be okay."

PJ laughed. "You're certainly making yourself at home over there. We'll assume breakfast is on unless I hear otherwise from you. Call me at work if Bill says no."

"He won't. He likes you, Mom." Thomas's voice had gotten low, practically a whisper. She guessed that Winston was nearby, and he didn't want his friend to hear that last part.

"Yes, I know, T-man. I like him, too."

"I mean he really likes you."

"Oh," PJ said. After an initial resentment at the fact that his mom might actually be interested in other men after the divorce, Thomas seemed determined to fix her up with men he liked. He had tried it with Schultz, too. She was sure Thomas didn't realize how obvious and endearing his actions were.

"It's complicated," PJ said. "He's still married, you know."

Bill Lakeland's wife lived in a supervised halfway house, recovering from drug addiction. She wasn't making a lot of progress, and had gone through several setbacks by walking away from the house and vanishing for three or four days at a time, indulging in drugs. Then she'd show up, contrite and ready to start over. Each time, it twisted Bill's heart. He felt responsible for her, but PJ didn't think he actually loved the woman anymore. He was torn—he wanted to stand by her, but he also wanted to make a life for himself and for his son Winston. From the first time they'd met, she sensed that Bill was attracted to her. From time to time, she thought about pursuing that attraction and seeing where it led, but for now it was on the back burner. She thought Bill should get his mind clear about his wife's situation—not to mention get a divorce—before leaping into a romantic relationship.

"Yeah, I know," Thomas said. "But Winston says his dad is thinking about getting divorced."

"We'll just have to see what happens," PJ said, amazed at the serious turn the conversation had taken. "Bill needs time to sort things out for himself."

"You're a psychologist, Mom. Can't you help him?"

"The best thing for both of us to do now is just be friends with him. Be supportive."

"Somehow I knew you'd say that." She could hear the mischief coming back into his voice.

"Tell me what's for breakfast tomorrow."

"I'm voting for chocolate chip pancakes," he said. Her little boy was back. It was remarkable how he could leap from serious grown-up to playful kid. At age thirteen, he had one foot in adulthood already, but the other foot was dragging behind. She hoped it would drag for a while longer.

"Yum. I can hardly wait. Tell Bill I'll bring the chocolate chips. I'm going to be there early, so you guys better be up and about by seven."

"Seven?" He sounded indignant. "This is summer vacation. We're supposed to get to sleep late."

"Not tomorrow, oh lazy one. Seven it is."

"Well, okay. Just this once."

"See you tomorrow. Love you. Bye."

"Bye, Mom. I love you."

When she hung up the phone, she felt energized. It was as though talking to her son had replenished some part of her that had been running low.

She threw herself into the task that was costing her an evening with her son: digging through the Ramsey case file in more depth.

Fifteen-year-old Eleanor Ramsey, daughter of Elijah and Libby, was beaten to death in her bedroom on an unseasonably hot May afternoon thirteen years ago. Her skull was crushed, she had multiple lacerations, and there was internal bleeding due to abdominal trauma. Blood spatter analysis led to the conclusion that the bedroom was the site of the beating. Eleanor didn't die rapidly or painlessly. The killing blow hadn't been the first one delivered. Nor the last. Rage definitely fueled the murder.

The body was discovered on the floor of the girl's bedroom at 3:00 P.M., when Libby returned from a shopping trip. Eleanor had been seen alive by neighbors before lunch, when she went out to get the mail at the curb, so the time of death was between 11:00 A.M. and 3:00 P.M. Libby reported that the front door was unlocked but not ajar when she got home. She was suspicious because she was certain she had locked the door when she left. She entered the house calling her daughter's name with increasing anxiety until she discovered the body. Libby called for an ambulance rather than the police because she wasn't sure, or more likely couldn't believe, that her daughter was dead.

The only fingerprints found in the bedroom were from a couple of Eleanor's girlfriends plus the immediate family: parents Libby and Elijah, her sister Darla, age thirty-three, and her brother Jeremiah, age thirty-one at the time. Darla and Jeremiah each had their own apartments, but visited the parents' home frequently. Eleanor had been the baby of the family, born long after her older brother and sister. The girlfriends were away on a camping trip, and were eliminated as suspects as soon as they returned that night.

The postmortem exam revealed defensive wounds on Eleanor's hands and forearms, and traces of blood on her fingers. She had been beaten with a blunt object the size and shape of a baseball bat.

Eleanor was eight weeks pregnant at the time of her death.

When PJ got to that revelation, she put down the papers and photos she'd been going through. She squeezed her eyes, trying to keep back the tears that had suddenly sprung from them. Homicides involving young people were especially hard for PJ to deal with in the first place, and the added loss of life because of the pregnancy seemed especially poignant.

Her mind took a detour down a path she had been determined not to travel again. She had wanted more children from her marriage. She loved Thomas with all her heart, but always felt that there was a missing face at the table, another little hand that should be clutching hers. She had wanted a second child, but her husband, Stephen, resisted. After the divorce, he married Carla the Home-Breaker, who was half his age and wanted a family. It was like salt in the wound of divorce that they had a child within a year. The baby Stephen refused to have with her was cuddled in Carla's arms.

She gave up on holding back the tears and, glad that the office door was closed, let them course down her cheeks. She was reaching for a tissue to tidy up when there was a quick knock at her door. It swung open without waiting for her to say anything.

Lieutenant Wall took in the scene, including the photos on PJ's desk, and reached an assumption that was only partially true.

"Be back in a couple of minutes," he said. "Left something in my office."

It was clear he was giving her time to shape up. The man

was an enigma to her: harsh, then sensitive, manipulative, then concerned. She never seemed to know which way the wind was blowing with him. The one thing she could count on was fairness, even if it came in tough wrappings.

When the knock came again, she had straightened her desk and started a pot of coffee.

"Coffee?" she offered, as though nothing had happened a few minutes ago.

"Sure. Black. You're not one of those women who thinks it's degrading to serve coffee, are you?"

"Not if you're in my office."

"Well, good. Never did see the point of those women who complain about that," he went on cheerfully, having missed or ignored the qualification. "Any luck with the Ramseys so far?"

She gave him his coffee in a flimsy paper cup. To her disappointment, it didn't spill in his lap right away. But at least it gave her something to anticipate as she talked with him.

She summarized her efforts to reach the Ramsey family, or what was left of it after the murder and execution.

"Good work," he said. "I'll call the Jeff City police as a courtesy. But I think your plan to go in person is a good one. Ow! This coffee's burning my fingers right through the cup. Don't you have any mugs?"

"I did," she said pleasantly, sipping from her own favorite mug, "but they seem to sprout feet and walk away."

"Yeah, Schultz is always stealing coffee mugs."

That reminded her that the man in front of her had a considerably longer personal history with Schultz than she did.

"Tell me," she said, "What do you think of the Ramsey case? I haven't gotten far into it yet. Was it an open-and-shut thing? Did Schultz work on it alone?"

"Nobody's really alone on these things. There's the patrol officer who's first on the scene, the medical examiner's office,

evidence technicians, the prosecuting attorney's office. . . .
It's a team effort all the way."

She gave him a look that said *save the propaganda for the
reporters.*

He sighed. "It was his case. Normally he'd have a partner
and an assistant or two, the way you guys work together. Even
back then we had a team approach. But it so happens Schultz
was on probation at the time and working pretty much alone."

"Probation? He never told me anything about that."

"You wouldn't expect him to, would you? It wasn't one of
his prouder moments."

"Have there been many?"

"What? Oh, proud moments. Yeah, quite a few. He's solid
in the thinking department. Good hunches, too."

She let the silence grow. Wall squirmed a little in one of
her folding metal chairs.

*Serves him right if it collapses under him. Maybe then I'll
get my requisition approved for some real chairs.*

"He's considered a little quick to use his weapon," Wall
finally said.

She wondered how many shooting incidents Schultz had
been involved in. The way Wall was talking, it sounded as if
Schultz were a one-man execution squad. She knew of two
incidents herself when he'd used his weapon with fatal results.

"Is two a lot for a man with his years of experience?" she
said.

"Zero is always best," Wall said. "Two isn't enough to raise
most eyebrows around here, given that Schultz has been here
longer than most of the furniture, and that's saying quite a
bit. But five is. He's no stranger to those investigations for
use of deadly force."

PJ's eyes widened. "I guess I don't know as much about
him as I thought."

"At the time of the Ramsey case he was on probation, but

it had nothing to do with using his weapon. Not his gun, anyway."

PJ kept her face neutral. She wondered if she was about to hear something about Schultz's sex life she didn't want to hear.

"It's not what you're thinking," Wall said, picking up on her sudden stone-faced appearance. "I meant his fist. He arrested a rock musician who was in town giving a concert. The guy was selling drugs out of his hotel room to groupies and others. The bellhop reported it. Schultz had a brief—thank God—stint in narcotics. The musician took a swing at him and Schultz decked the guy. Broke his nose and jaw, and knocked out four teeth."

"And that was police brutality or something?"

Wall waved his hand dismissively. "Nah, wouldn't have stirred up anything ordinarily. Self-defense, and several people saw it. But this guy was semi-famous, and the jerk's father— get this—was a US Senator. Together they cooked up a line where the whole thing was politically motivated, and said Schultz planted the drugs."

"He didn't, did he?"

"What, you don't trust your own team member?"

PJ was a little flustered. She hadn't meant to ask that question aloud. "It's just that I didn't know he killed five people, either."

Wall narrowed his eyes. "Don't worry about that. The killing thing. I'll tell you once, and then we won't talk about it anymore. He did what he had to do. There are tough choices to be made, and Schultz, whatever else I think of him, doesn't shy away from the difficult path."

"So what happened? With the jerk?"

"Schultz got reamed by Internal Affairs for suspected evidence tampering. They flipped him up, down, and sideways. He must have a file about this thick"—Wall held his palms about a foot apart—"by now. Couldn't get anything to stick on him, so they gave him a few months' probation anyway because of the mean look on his face, and the mayor apologized to the senator."

"And the drug charges?"

"Dropped."

"That's unfair!"

Wall grunted. "Welcome to the real world, Pollyanna," he said. "Getting back to the Ramsey case, Schultz was on probation but still on active duty. That meant he could work cases but had IA sniffing his ass all day, waiting for him to make a mistake they could terminate him for. Needless to say, nobody was anxious to work with him, so yeah, in a way he was on the case alone in spite of what I said about that teamwork stuff. Schultz needed something to make himself look good, something redeeming. He wanted a fast arrest and a conviction, and he got it."

"Why do you remember this so well? It was thirteen years ago."

"I was his sergeant. When he got chewed out, so did I."

"Then you were involved in the Ramsey case. I thought you said earlier that you weren't close to it."

"I wasn't front line. I didn't testify at the trial. As far as the killer is concerned, I'm just another guy in a police uniform. He can't wipe us all out, can he?"

PJ left his question unanswered. "I need to know all the background I can find on this case. What do you think of the Ramseys themselves as suspects?"

"The older girl, Darla—I remember her as being very remote. Tried to cut herself off from the whole thing, close off her emotions."

"That's understandable," PJ said. "She had a life of her own stretched out in front of her—she probably just wanted out as fast as possible."

"Libby's a tough one to call. She refused to believe her

son was guilty. Then she seemed to cave in and accept things when it became clear he was going to be convicted."

"Or maybe she just made it look like she accepted it. How did she feel about her daughter's death?"

"She's not a demonstrative woman. You'll see that when you talk to her, no doubt. She probably mourned her daughter's death deeply, but it was all on the inside."

PJ nodded. "Women of her generation didn't feel as comfortable reaching out for help as we do today."

"Stoic."

"Exactly. What about the father?"

Wall shook his head. "One weird guy. Served in Vietnam, never got the military bug out of his system. Went around the world looking for action."

"You mean he was a mercenary?"

"As far as we could tell," Wall said. "He's very secretive. Couldn't get much from the military but the basic facts of his service. You know, years, rank, that kind of stuff."

"Holy cow. I'd better watch my back. He sounds like Rambo."

"Rambo wasn't a mercenary, I don't think. Anyway, you should be fine over in Jeff City."

That made PJ think that Wall was only agreeable to sending her out of town so that the real police officers could catch the killer while she was out of the way. It stung for a moment that she was going off to interview a woman, while the action might be going on behind her back. Anita didn't get sent out of town. She was out on the streets. Then PJ dismissed that thought as inappropriate. If Wall was unhappy with her work, she had no doubt he'd tell her. Tact hadn't gotten in his way before.

When he was gone, she returned to the case file. Libby Ramsey told the police that Eleanor had been dating an older man, twenty-two-year-old Clarence Richman, and that her daughter had confessed to her that Clarence was the father of her unborn child. Eleanor also, according to Libby, told her mother that Clarence was upset about the pregnancy and had strongly urged her to have an abortion. At the time, Clarence had recently enlisted in the army, and was stationed at Fort Leonard Wood in Missouri. The pregnancy dated from when he completed boot camp and had a three-day leave before his assignment.

Libby accused Clarence of murdering her daughter because the girl was pressuring him to get married and make the child legitimate. But he wasn't ready to be locked into such a marriage. Because Eleanor was underage and Clarence was over twenty-one, he feared that if he made any fuss he would be prosecuted for statutory rape. Libby argued that fear was his motive. The fact that the front door was unlocked meant that Eleanor had known her attacker and let him in the house.

Adamant as Libby was, Clarence was found to have an iron-clad alibi for the time of the murder. He was participating in a special training assignment given at the Pentagon, and his presence was vouched for by his instructor and eighteen fellow attendees. PJ tapped her pencil on the table rapidly, her thoughts moving along as fast. What if he hired it done? He could purposely have set it up for a time when he'd be out of town, so that suspicion wouldn't stick to him.

She flipped the pages, found her question dealt with and dismissed. There just wasn't any evidence of a conspiracy. Interviews with Clarence and those who knew him portrayed him as genuinely grief-stricken. He had loved Eleanor, despite their age difference, and had intended to marry her, as he told several friends. In fact, he had already purchased an engagement ring and requested a day's leave after the completion of the training course to deliver it to Eleanor. That didn't sound like the actions of a man who was planning a murder.

The investigation then turned to family members. The older daughter, Darla, worked in a children's clothing store and had been verifiably waiting on customers between 11:00 A.M. and

3:00 P.M., while her kid sister was being bludgeoned to death. Elijah, secretive and known to have a mercurial temper, had no alibi. He had recently returned from overseas and was out looking for work, he said. He was distant from his younger daughter, having been out of the country most of the time she was growing up. Although he was looked at long and hard, there was nothing to pin him to the crime.

Libby, who owned three day care centers, had been shopping for supplies for the centers with her son Jeremiah. She claimed she had dropped him at his apartment immediately before heading home and discovering the body. Mother and son were each other's alibis for the time period of Eleanor's death.

Eleanor's friends said that mother and daughter fought often over control issues, and that Eleanor had said that when her mother found out she was pregnant, she would kill her. From Libby's own statements, it was clear she had found out about the pregnancy. None of the friends took the threats seriously at the time, but after the fact, it began to make Libby seem increasingly guilty. On the surface, it was a direct threat, although couched in a teenager's sometimes exaggerated way of talking. Libby was brought in for questioning.

A surprise confession by Jeremiah turned attention away from Libby. A baseball bat that he was known to possess was missing, and he claimed that it was the murder weapon. He had disposed of it by burning it. He displayed recent scratches on his shoulders, which he said he'd gotten when Eleanor was trying to defend herself. The scratches were so severe that he'd had to bandage them to keep from having blood leak through his clothing.

The blood on the dead girl's hands matched Jeremiah's blood type. Not just a match on the typical ABO grouping, but using HLA typing, which tests for an entire range of proteins that ride along on white blood cells. First developed in the 1950s, it was accurate enough to be the early legal standard in paternity cases. It seemed pretty solid to PJ that Jeremiah was the killer. Except for that one physical piece of evidence, though, the rest of the case against him was circumstantial.

While awaiting trial, Jeremiah suddenly recanted his confession and changed his plea to not guilty. At the trial, his mother pleaded for him, saying that he could not have committed the murder because he was with her. The jury evidently discounted her testimony as that of a distraught mother trying to salvage what was left of her family. They convicted Jeremiah of first-degree murder, premeditated because he brought the baseball bat from his apartment with the intent to use it on his sister.

PJ wondered if DNA fingerprinting was accepted in the courtrooms of 1986, when Jeremiah's trail was held. A few minutes of research told her that DNA fingerprinting was developed in 1985 and was used in trials in the US in 1987. During the late eighties, though, there was doubt about the quality of the testing performed, and some evidence was thrown out of court as a result. It was a period of settling in for the technique.

The Ramsey trial was held right on the cusp of acceptance of DNA evidence in courts, yet there was nothing in the files to indicate it was even attempted. Evidently the HLA blood testing was considered sufficient. If Schultz was there, she would have demanded an answer: was he backward on the subject, or just overconfident?

Even stranger was that none of the numerous appeals leading up to the actual execution involved DNA profiling. It seemed to her that the only reason Jeremiah hadn't insisted on it was that he already knew what the results would show—that it was his blood on Eleanor's hands.

What if Jeremiah had been present at the time of the murder, and had tried to fend off the killer? He might have gotten the scratches not from Eleanor, but from the person who was attacking her. His blood might have gotten on Eleanor's hands as he went to her assistance.

Why was there no mention of that possibility being investigated in the case file? If PJ could come up with it in a few hours, then surely a trained detective could think of it over the course of weeks of investigation. Had Schultz just wanted a quick conviction to make himself look good? Hadn't it mattered to him what the truth of the situation was? The thought shook her deeply. First she had learned that Schultz had killed an entire handful of people, something she hadn't known about him. Could he have twisted the facts of the case to suit his purpose?

PJ took a break and went out for dinner. It was early evening, but the heat and humidity hadn't let up. She felt as though she were swimming through warm water. Shimmery waves of heat radiated from the sidewalk and streets. Inside her shoes, the soles of her feet warmed up and her toes felt clammy. Sunshine was pouring down through the buildings, adding heat to the witches' brew of weather. She could see black, heavy clouds over the tops of the buildings to the west. A summer storm was moving in, but ahead of the storm the air was thick and still.

Her head was spinning from all the facts and images of the case. One thing kept sprouting up in her mind like a dandelion: motive. What reason did Jeremiah have to brutally beat his kid sister to death?

The reason put forth by the prosecution was that Eleanor had taken his car without permission the previous week and smashed it into a light standard in a parking lot, causing thousands of dollars of uninsured damage. Unable to afford to repair or replace it, Jeremiah had been getting around on a borrowed moped. The beating took place on the day the car payment fell due. Jeremiah either had to default on the loan or make payments for two more years on a car he couldn't drive.

That it would make him angry was easy to see. But would it break loose a homicidal rage? PJ knew that some people bottled up their anger for years and then exploded over a triggering event. Wall had said that both Darla and Libby were the type to keep things inside. Maybe it ran in the family. In women, unexpressed anger sometimes turned inward, toward self-destructive activities. Men didn't usually turn their anger on themselves. They found targets. But there were usually signs. Did everyone in the family miss Jeremiah's warning signals before the big blast?

It was possible, she decided. He wasn't living at home. He certainly wasn't under daily observation by trained professionals. Families tended to brush things under the rug anyway, even if they did detect something.

It was only three blocks to the pizza place PJ was heading for, but she was sweaty by the time she was halfway there. The sidewalks were emptying as workers headed out of downtown. There was still a lot of car and bus traffic, but that would die down soon. She wondered if Artie's Pizza stayed open after commuting hours, and quickened her step.

The restaurant was open only until six-thirty. It was almost that time. She tried the door. It swung open and she entered, figuring Artie would have to kick her out personally if he wanted to close up. It was cool inside, and the seating area was dimly lit beyond the reaches of the sun coming through the window.

A kid who didn't look much older than Thomas stood behind the counter. She ordered two slices of mushroom pizza.

"Don't have mushroom," he said. "Got three slices of Super Veggie left. You can have 'em all for half price. We're getting ready to close."

"Do they have black olives?"

"Nope. Not any more."

She wondered if that meant they had stopped putting black olives on the Super Veggie sometime in the past, or someone in the back was listening in to the conversation at the counter and quickly picking the black olives off.

"It's a deal," she said, trying to be optimistic.

PJ paid for her slices and a Diet Coke and carried her tray to one of the tables out of the sun. She put her thoughts on hold and dug in, realizing how hungry she was. Even though they were the last of the lot, PJ found her pizza slices hot and delicious.

After a few minutes the edge was off her hunger. The guy who made the pizzas, who looked only a little older than the first one—*the place is run by children*—had come out from the back and was mopping the floor. She turned her thoughts loose on what Wall had told her earlier about Schultz.

Leo has killed five people. Five. His life has been one long war.

Munching her second slice of Super Veggie, PJ thought about Schultz's circumstances during the Ramsey case. Could he have been guilty of planting drugs in the rock musician's room, as the senator claimed? She shook her head. He wouldn't have done it for political reasons, to embarrass the father. She just couldn't see that. But suppose the musician was selling drugs—the bellhop, who could see the comings and goings to the room, suspected it—but he was smart enough not to get caught at it. Suppose Schultz knew about the situation and felt helpless and frustrated to do anything about it. Would Schultz plant evidence to bring an otherwise untouchable criminal to justice?

That one was tougher.

She thought she knew the man, but the past few days had raised a lot of doubts in her mind. If only he would call again. PJ wanted to ask him some hard questions, pin him down and not let him wiggle out of answering them.

She also wanted to hear his voice and know he was all right.

PJ finished her meal and felt loneliness settle on her. She

missed her son, and she wasn't looking forward to a night in her office, working by herself. She would have lingered and ordered another cool drink, but it was after closing and the kid was eyeing her, waiting for her to go. She tossed her napkin on the tray and left.

On the walk to headquarters, she noticed that the dark clouds had wiped out the sunshine. Her mood was as low as the clouds. Cars were driving with their headlights on, and some of them had windshield wipers clacking back and forth, having come from an area where it was already raining. The temperature had dropped at least ten degrees, and there was a tension in the air, almost an electric charge, as the storm gathered itself. The first few heavy drops hit her on the back as she ducked into the building.

Twenty

When the Greyhound pulled into Tucson on Friday morning, the weather was totally dry. The storm raging in Billings, Montana, had long been left behind. When Schultz stepped out of the station, he felt as though he had been dropped into a toaster. And it was only 11:00 A.M. No one on the street outside seemed to be sweating profusely except him. Of course, everyone else was wearing shorts and casual tops. Abbreviated tops and shorts, he noticed right away, were standard for young women. He thought that he might get to like Tucson on that score, but he'd never convert to wearing shorts. There was nothing about his legs he cared to show off.

The bus driver, who had started congenially chatting with passengers when his destination got within a hundred miles, had suggested that those new to Tucson should buy sunblock before they left the station. Schultz had figured Tucson sun wasn't any worse than St. Louis sun, so he skipped the sunblock. He shaded his eyes with his hand and watched the nicely rounded scenery bounce by, consciously resisting the effort to suck in his gut. To do so would be to admit he had one. If he stood there long enough, maybe someone would ask him to rub sunblock on her back. Or her front. Whichever.

He took a cab to a motel near a shopping mall. After registering, he showered and put on a fresh change of clothes. Then he went looking for a meal. His work wouldn't begin until after dark. He walked a leisurely mile to the mall, watching to see if he had a tail. As far as he could tell, he didn't.

Glen Mandoleras didn't know that his home territory had been invaded. Schultz thought it was clever of the man to establish a base of operations so far from the killing fields. A little inconvenient, but what does inconvenience count for when revenge is at hand?

Inside the mall it was bright and tolerably cool. He circled the food court a couple of times—the hunter stalking his prey, looking for the weak or wounded—and ended up with loaded pizza slices and a Coke. After eating, he would have liked to take a nap, but didn't want to drop his vigilance.

Schultz took in a movie and waited for the persistent sun to go down.

When he came out of the movie theater, he noticed that the heat that seemed to surround him wasn't just the outdoors. He was carrying it around with him. His arms, face, the back of his neck, and the bald spot on top of his head were warm. In the men's room mirror he saw that he was red—sunburned. He must have gotten it during the slow, meandering walk to the mall, when he was checking for someone following him. The top of his head was the worst. He dampened a paper towel and dabbed at the red spot. The towel felt wonderfully cool and soothing.

Shit. I hope I don't get blisters.

Schultz debated going to a drugstore and buying some cream to ease the discomfort. Then he decided to tough it out. It was the image of him confronting his adversary with some greasy white stuff coating every inch of his exposed skin that deterred him. In the morning, if he was still in Tucson, he'd pick up something.

He took a cab back to his motel, which annoyed the driver, who'd been hoping for a longer fare. Schultz slipped on the holster with the Glock. He slid his arms carefully into a sports jacket, hoping he wouldn't look too out of place wearing long sleeves. The pressure of the fabric on his reddened arms was irritating. He tried to put it out of mind. A set of lock picks went into his front pants pocket, which was covered by the jacket. When he stepped out of doors, he found that the evening promised to be quite a bit cooler than the afternoon. His jacket wouldn't be obvious. There would be other men on the street wearing jackets, going out to dinner and to the theater.

Summoning another cab, he was gratified that he didn't get the same driver from his earlier trip. He got out of the cab a few blocks away from the address Anita had given him, surprised to find that he wasn't in a residential area. With the sun well below the horizon, he didn't mind walking. The arthritis in his legs seemed to have benefited from the earlier baking, and he was walking easier on a minimal dose of Voltaren than he had in months. Suddenly he understood why so many cops moved to warm places when they retired. Not only were the T&A prospects good, but maybe the heat eased the aches and pains of decades of legwork.

Eased the pains of the body, maybe, but not of the heart.

The address he had for Mandoleras was in sight. It turned out to be a small hotel in a business district that had seen better days—both the hotel and the district. Anita hadn't mentioned that Mandoleras lived in a hotel. Schultz double-checked the address. He had assumed Mandoleras lived in a house or apartment.

The Oasis Hotel was a three-story building, and he was sure that if the lighting was better he'd see that a couple of the windows were cracked and there was tuck pointing needed. The building was functional, with no effort put into architectural details that might please the eye. It squatted on the street corner like an ugly toad.

He hesitated on the street. It definitely threw a kink in his plans. He had been planning to break into Mandoleras's home unseen, and wait for him to arrive. He didn't know what outcome to expect from the meeting. One possible outcome was that he would kill Mandoleras. In that case, he didn't want anyone to see him going in and out.

Schultz glanced down the street to his right and then left. There was no pay phone available. If there was, he could call the hotel, wangle the room number out of the clerk, and then walk casually through the lobby as if he belonged there. Once at Mandoleras's room, he could pick the lock.

He sighed. It didn't look like the kind of place to have a crowded lobby where a man like him could go unnoticed anyway. He was big and solid and not likely to be missed by any clerk one step above dead. It was also possible all the keys were kept at the desk, and the clerk would remember a person who came in and went upstairs but didn't ask for his key.

He'd have to scrap his whole approach for the night, or go in boldly. If he went in, he'd better not do any killing unless he had a damn good self-defense scenario worked out. And with his record, a self-defense claim probably wouldn't pan out unless he had God himself testifying on his behalf.

He pushed through the revolving door. Against his expectations, the lobby was clean and neat, and cool. Along one wall was a small shop that sold newspapers, Tums, and snacks. There was a grouping of chairs and couches in the center, worn but comfortable-looking. There were no windows, but several lamps provided enough light for conversation. A man whom Schultz judged to be about eighty years old sat in one of the chairs reading a newspaper. He had tilted the nearest lampshade to cast more light on his paper, and didn't look up as Schultz entered.

There was no one behind the front desk.

He decided to go for it, and walked in the direction of the hallway which almost certainly held the elevator or stairs.

By the time he had crossed the lobby halfway, a man had appeared from a back office and taken his place behind the desk. He was in his mid-fifties, and his face held a reserved smile. Schultz had clearly been spotted. He casually veered toward the registration desk, knowing it was time for the direct approach.

"Evening," the man said, agreeably enough. "Looks like you got yourself a little sun."

Schultz's hand automatically went to the tender spot on top of his head. Annoyed, he yanked it back down and scowled at the man.

"I'm new in town," Schultz said.

"I never would've guessed," the man replied. "What can I do for you? Room for the night?"

"No, I'm looking for a friend of mine," Schultz said. "His name is Glen Mandoleras. Is he in?"

"Might be. If he was, would he want to see you?"

Schultz cracked a smile. The guy was not unfamiliar with the routine. That made things easier.

"We're friends from St. Louis," Schultz said. "I've been thinking about retiring here. Glen said he'd show me around."

The man blinked, evaluating the story. Hopefully Mandoleras had mentioned where he was from, so there would be at least a feeble confirmation of his story. The silence stretched out, but Schultz didn't elaborate. He worked on the KISS principle—Keep It Simple, Stupid.

Schultz saw the decision form in the man's eyes.

"He's out," he said. "Went out for dinner. Should be back in an hour or two. You can wait in the lobby if you want. Get yourself a snack." He pointed his chin at the hole-in-the-wall shop across from the counter.

Schultz reached into his pocket and put a twenty-dollar bill on the counter, but kept his eyes on the man's face.

"He's expecting me tomorrow," Schultz said. "I got here a day early, and I'd really like to surprise him. I want to wait in his room."

Another slow blink, but no reach for a key. Schultz sighed and added another twenty. Maybe the cost of living in Tucson was high.

The man reached under the counter, and for a split second Schultz thought he was reaching for a gun. In the space of a heartbeat, though, the man had palmed the money with one hand and produced a key with the other.

"Room three-oh-two. The elevator's down the hall."

"One more thing. Has Glen been out of town a lot lately? I've had a hard time getting in touch with him."

"I wouldn't know. I'm new here."

Yeah, and I'm Mr. America.

The elevator was small and tired. Lifting Schultz's bulk to the third floor almost seemed more than it could manage at day's end. It wheezed to a stop and he stepped off into the hallway. He'd opened the button on his jacket on the way up, and his hand rested lightly inside. The guy at the desk might be in cahoots with Mandoleras, and could have notified him that he had a visitor. After all, if the guy could be bought by Schultz, he could be bought by others.

Three-oh-two was the first room on the right of a narrow but well-lighted hallway. The carpet was worn but freshly vacuumed and free of cigarette burns. Outside Mandoleras's room was a flowery doormat that said "Leave Your Worries Behind." It seemed so out of character for an ex-cop that Schultz pulled up abruptly.

What the fuck? Mandoleras go batty?

Schultz knew that Mandoleras's wife had died twenty years ago and he'd never remarried. Or maybe he had, out here in Tucson.

Schultz nudged the doormat gently with his toe. He wasn't putting anything past Mandoleras. It could have been a trap of some kind. Nothing happened, so he pushed the doormat further until it wasn't in front of the door anymore. There was nothing underneath, so he picked it up and replaced it.

The key turned the bolt with a quiet *snick,* and Schultz pushed the door open a few inches and waited in the hall. No response. Feeling kind of silly standing on the flowered doormat, he ducked low and moved quickly into the room. The room was dark except for the glow of a night-light plugged in near the door. Not willing to stay in one place near the door as an obvious target, with his own eyes not adapted to the dark but maybe someone else making him out clearly, Schultz dove behind a large couch. He came up with the Glock in his hand and peered around the side of the couch.

He found himself staring into eyes that glowed like tiny full moons, reflecting the night-light.

"Ah!"

The cat scurried away at the sound of his voice.

Schultz pulled himself back behind the couch and waited for his heartbeat to slow. He was embarrassed that he had been startled by the cat, and worried that the noise he'd made had pinpointed him for a shooter.

When nothing happened after a few minutes, he stood up slowly, his knees reminding him that even August in Arizona wasn't enough to completely remove years of overburdening his joints. He listened closely. The only sound he heard was the air-conditioner, which was churning out gusts of cool air.

Schultz searched the space thoroughly, making sure Mandoleras wasn't hiding in the bathroom or closet or under the bed. He switched on a couple of lamps when he was certain he was alone, except for the cat. There were three rooms; a bedroom, a small living room and a bathroom. There were no cooking facilities, but there was a coffeepot in the bathroom and a small table with a couple of chairs tucked into a corner of the living room for those homey carry-out meals. The place must have been two adjoining hotel rooms at one time, converted into a tiny apartment for long-term living.

Schultz spent the next forty-five minutes examining the contents of the rooms, looking for something to connect the occupant with the killings in St. Louis. He was accompanied by the cat everywhere he went. The cat was solid gray, young, and sleek, with an incongruously fluffy tail. It had huge white whiskers and soft green eyes, and batted at Schultz's shoe-laces. A couple of times Schultz bent over to stroke it and was rewarded with a jumbo-size purr. Glen Mandoleras might be a murderer, but at least he didn't mistreat his cat.

Mandoleras lived simply. The furnishings, which undoubt-edly came with the room, were sparse and well-used. Schultz searched every drawer and cabinet, every hiding place he could think of, including the toilet tank and inside the refrig-erator. In the bedroom, he found a lot of prescription medicine bottles lined up on top of the nightstand, but no gun inside it, or anywhere else in the two rooms. That could mean Man-doleras had a gun with him. There were two framed photos prominently displayed on the dresser, one of Mandoleras and his wife on vacation, possibly in Florida, and the other of Vince Mandoleras in his police uniform. The fact that Vince's photo was there could mean Dad stoked up his hatred and anger every day by looking at it. Or it could mean that Dad simply missed his son, as he did his wife.

Schultz's own dresser held pictures of Julia, Rick, and PJ. What would someone searching his home make of that?

There was nothing in the compact space that spoke to Schultz of brutal murder. He'd have to get that information directly from the inhabitant, who was expected to return any minute. He slipped off his jacket, which had been irritating his sunburned arms, and draped it across the back of the couch. Then he switched off the lamps and sat in the glow of the night-light, the Glock in one hand, petting the purring cat on his lap with the other.

Twenty-one

PJ stopped at three convenience stores on Friday morning before she found one that sold chocolate chips. She didn't want to arrive at Bill Lakeland's house empty-handed.

PJ felt the weight of her job lift from her shoulders the moment she arrived. Thomas answered the door and then threw his arms around her. She buried her face in his shoulder, marveling at the fact that it seemed only recently that she could rest her chin on top of his head. He had shot up in height in the last year, and his dancing dark eyes were level with hers.

Bill greeted her with a more restrained hug. She closed her eyes and took in his clean scent. The man always seemed to smell good, which was more than she could say for Schultz.

Breakfast was loud, messy, and great fun. She couldn't remember the last time she'd tossed chocolate chips up in the air and caught them in her mouth. None of the others seemed to have the knack, but it wasn't for lack of trying. The floor was littered with the failed attempts.

"Aren't you going to be late for work?" she asked Bill. It was eight-fifteen. He was a lab technician, and staffing was generally tight in his line of work, calculated right down to the projected number of tests for each hour of the day. She knew that coming in late was frowned upon.

"I got somebody else to cover the first hour of my shift,"

he said, glancing at the clock. "It's about time to head out, though."

PJ gave the kitchen a hard look. There were pans and dishes in the sink, drips on the stove, and chocolate chips and pancake flour on the floor. There were hardly any surfaces that didn't have sticky syrup on them. She shook her head. Too bad the Lakelands didn't have a dog. At least the floor would be taken care of.

"You guys go ahead," Winston said. "We'll clean up."

Thomas nodded in agreement.

PJ laughed. "That's one thing I never thought I'd hear. I think I've died—"

"And gone to heaven," Bill finished for her.

"Seriously?" PJ said, looking at the boys.

"Seriously, Mom. It's a done deal," her son answered.

Bill went off to change for work. PJ hugged her son again, and affectionately licked a drop of syrup from his chin.

"Yuck!" he said, pulling back.

"Isn't that my line? I thought you were the one who did gross things."

"Hey, I'm thirteen. I'm grown-up. Gross is kid stuff."

"Well, Mr. Gray, I'll leave you to your work," she said, gesturing to the kitchen.

"I like the sound of that. Mr. Gray. You should call me that all the time."

"Does Mr. Gray think he can fit a movie into his social calendar tonight?"

"That'd be great, Mom. Winston and I get to choose."

"I had in mind a little mother/son kind of thing," she said. "I think we could use some time alone, if you're not ashamed to be seen with your decrepit old mom."

"Yeah, okay. It's a date."

"I'll call this afternoon. Maybe we can fit dinner in, too."

When she drove away, she waved until he was out of sight. Their push-pull relationship seemed to be improving at a time when most parents were losing touch with their children, during the early teens. Part of it was due to the scare he'd had months ago, when his exposure to evil had briefly driven a wedge between them. Since then he'd moved closer, putting himself into her protective circle, as a wolf cub might move close to its mother when it first senses danger. But there was no stopping nature—he was getting older, and more independent. The struggle in him was a hard one for her to watch, as it was for every parent of a teenager. It was amazing how lost she could feel as a parent at times, and she was a psychologist, who ought to have the inside track. She only hoped they made it through with their good humor and communication intact.

Having a father would help, she thought. Images of Schultz with his arm around Thomas and roughhousing the way she'd seen the two of them popped into her mind. Instead of immediately squashing the images, she considered them. With the things she was learning about Schultz, would he make a good father?

Then she dared to think it: *Look at the way his own son ended up.*

PJ headed west on Interstate 70, after putting gas in the Escort at Warrenton. The storm the night before had left the countryside sparkling clean, and the sky was deep blue with spotty clouds of purest fluff. Rolling forested hills were interspersed with lush cornfields and pastures. She would have relished the trip as a break from her routine if it hadn't been for the circumstances.

She pulled off the highway to take a break and buy herself a pack of M&M's. Using her cell phone, she contacted Dave. He had discovered that Jeremiah Ramsey hadn't had a girlfriend—or boyfriend—during his stay on death row. She knew from the case file that there hadn't been a significant other on the scene before the murder, either, so that path was ruled out.

She went over the Ramsey case in her mind, trying to fit the pieces together and tie them to the recent killings: Rick Schultz, four-year-old Caroline Bussman, prosecutor Victor Rheinhardt. Elijah Ramsey was a man trained to kill in the military, one who had probably continued to practice that art as a mercenary. He had the ability to carry out the murders, including the expert knife attack on Rheinhardt. The photo of him in the case file showed a lean, hard-looking man. It didn't take much imagination to cast him as a killer. But she had been led down the easy path before, where assumptions outpaced facts.

It all came down to motive. Was Elijah a bitter man, as well as a violent one?

She wondered if it was correct to lump Caroline Bussman in with the other victims. What evidence did she actually have that the hit-and-run was an attempt to frame Schultz? What she had was Schultz's word, his ex-wife's alibi for him, and an unexplained missing answering machine tape that might or might not support it.

And the principle of innocent until proven guilty.

She had raised the alarm and sent people scurrying off in all directions, based on the seed of an idea Merlin planted in her mind. Based on—*admit it*—a hunch. Maybe based on wishful thinking about Schultz.

If nothing came of it, she was going to look foolish. She smiled grimly to herself. It wouldn't be the first time, or the last.

Thinking about looking foolish, PJ remembered the day she had discovered her husband, Stephen, wanted a divorce so he could marry Carla. The affair had been going on right under her nose for months, and she hadn't noticed. Her relationship with Stephen had been so distant by then she probably wouldn't have noticed if he'd moved Carla into the guest bedroom. Her cheeks burned at the memory, made especially painful by her more recent realization that the divorce hadn't been entirely Stephen's fault. It had taken PJ some time to come to the conclusion that she hadn't worked as hard on the marriage as she could have. And the only reason she could muster to hold up to the cold light of analysis was that she had loved her job more than she loved Stephen. She'd had an affair too—with her career.

Since that time she'd examined her priorities, and taken a giant step away from her all-consuming, high-powered position in state-of-the-art market research. Her work with the St. Louis Police Department was demanding, and she was deeply committed to it, but there were short lulls when she could recharge her batteries and spend time with her son.

The turnoff to Jefferson City on Highway 54 came up, and PJ almost missed it. Putting aside her doubts about wild-goose chases, she focused on what information she wanted to learn from Libby. The Missouri River bridge came into view a half hour later. The dome of the Missouri State Capitol Building, an impressive sight from the bridge, glinted in the sun. It was a little before 11:00 A.M., too early for lunch, so she decided to check out Libby's address. PJ got off Highway 54 and asked for directions at a gas station.

It took one more stop for directions before she located Libby's street. It was an area of small homes, little brick boxes with awnings. About one out of four had a detached garage in the back of the lot. Most of the houses were festooned with several window air-conditioners, keeping individual rooms cool for owners who were at work. What was the sense in that? PJ rolled down her window and discovered that the air-conditioning units actually gave the neighborhood an audible hum. She drove a few blocks and circled back. She had seen only a couple of children outdoors, and they were taking turns with a hose, squirting each other and giggling. There were few cars in the driveways.

Libby's house was tan brick with a concrete front porch edged with wrought-iron railings. The lawn was small and well-kept, but there were no flowers or bushes, just a single oak tree in the center of the yard that looked as if it might predate the housing development. There was no obvious sign that anyone was home.

PJ parked a couple of houses down and across the street. After just a few minutes without air-conditioning, the car got hot and stuffy, so she rolled down the front windows on both the driver's and passenger's side in the hopes of getting a breeze going. Yesterday's rain hadn't had any effect on the temperature, which she was sure was in the nineties. She sat and sweated, and thought about her options.

They were pitifully few. She didn't know where Libby worked, if she did work outside the home. It was important to learn as much as she could about the family dynamics, particularly the attitudes of Elijah Ramsey, and she wasn't getting that done while roasting in her car. Frustrated and hot, PJ decided to try the direct approach. She rummaged around in the backseat for the notebook she always kept there, slung her purse over her shoulder, then got out of her car and strode up the concrete steps as if she had every right to do so. She rang the doorbell. Just in case she actually found her target, PJ reached inside her purse and pressed the RECORD button on the small tape recorder she had hidden there.

A long minute later the door opened slightly. There was a security chain, and the person who opened the door stayed out of sight.

"Yes?" It was a woman's voice. She was cautious but not totally unfriendly.

"I'm looking for Elizabeth Ramsey," PJ said. "I understand she lives here."

"Who wants to know?"

"I'm Roberta Lakeland, a reporter for the *St. Louis Post.* I'd like to interview Mrs. Ramsey. The *Post* is doing an article on how the death penalty affects the families of the prisoners." PJ hadn't known she was going to say that until the words were actually out. She thought it sounded pretty good. Mrs. Ramsey had been outspoken at the time of the trial. Perhaps she couldn't resist the opportunity to get her side of the story out years later.

PJ wondered how Bill Lakeland would feel if he knew she had taken on his last name. And she wondered why she didn't have the confidence to simply identify her association with the police department and ask questions directly. She couldn't imagine Schultz taking such a roundabout way to get information.

"Ramsey doesn't live here anymore."

PJ was almost sure her quarry was right behind that door. If she had Schultz with her, she wouldn't have any trouble getting in. Either he'd think of something compelling or he'd bully his way in. She searched for inspiration.

"Sorry to bother you," PJ said. "Mrs. Ramsey was first on my list, and I was really interested in what she had to say. But I guess I'll just have to use my second choice in Springfield. If I leave right away, I still might be able to get an interview this afternoon."

There was no reaction. PJ assumed she'd played it wrong. "Bye now," she said. The disappointment in her voice was real. The door closed.

And opened again, without the security chain.

PJ recognized Libby from her case file photo, although the intervening years hadn't been gentle. Libby was shorter than PJ, which put her at about five-foot-two. She was wiry, not a term often used to describe women, but that's what came into PJ's mind. She had short, curly, white hair that showed no sign of thinning, and clear gray eyes that shone with friendliness on the surface but held shadows in their depths. Her face was wrinkled as if from a lifetime of outdoor living, and reminded PJ of a jack-o'-lantern that was past its prime. She was wearing a sleeveless blouse and shorts, and the arms and legs that were revealed showed good muscle tone. She was probably a loyal mall walker, following the lines on the tile floor and daring any loiterers to get in her way.

"Come in out of the heat," she said. "Would you like some ice tea?"

PJ sidled past her. "Are you Mrs. Ramsey?"

"Can't be too careful these days," Libby said.

"Oh, I agree," PJ said. She hoped she wasn't going to be asked for press identification. "I'd love some tea."

The living room was small but pleasantly furnished. The wood floor gleamed, and there was a faint scent of pine cleaner that called up images of shining tubs and toilets. The air-conditioning was set frigidly low. Sitting on the couch, which took up one whole wall of the room, PJ felt the sweat starting to evaporate on her back. Libby disappeared, presumably into the kitchen to prepare tea. PJ put her purse on the floor at her feet and propped it open enough to see the tape recorder inside. She wondered if the microphone was sensitive enough to pick up their conversation.

PJ spotted some family pictures hanging on the wall opposite the couch. She got up and took a closer look, matching the faces to the pictures in the case file. Eleanor looked a lot better than she did in the crime scene shots. She was a blossoming teenager, with a glow in her cheeks and her mother's intriguing gray, almost colorless, eyes. PJ narrowed her eyes. She thought she recognized that glow. Eleanor might have been pregnant when the picture was taken.

"Pretty, isn't she? It's a terrible tragedy. I don't know why God saw fit to visit this hardship on us." Libby was at her elbow.

"You must have been very proud of her," PJ said.

"Smart, too. Just like my son Jeremiah." Libby reached out her finger and touched Jeremiah's photo lovingly.

PJ resettled herself on the couch, with a glass of ice tea on a coaster on the coffee table. She opened her notebook.

"I thought all you reporters used tape recorders," Libby said. There was the slightest twinge of suspicion in it.

"I found that it makes people nervous sometimes. They start talking to the tape recorder and not to me."

Libby nodded. "I hate 'em. I'm one of those people who would clam right up."

PJ kept her eyes on Libby's face, resisting the impulse to cast a guilty glance at the purse at her feet.

"So you want to know what effect Jeremiah's execution had on us," Libby said. "I don't mind talking about that, and I'll tell you right out. It was devastating, and it still is. My son was innocent."

"I understand you believe another man was guilty"—PJ pretended to consult her notes—"Clarence Richman, Eleanor's boyfriend."

Libby's face hardened. "He was more than just her boyfriend. He was the father of her child. And him twenty-two years old, taking advantage of a teenage girl like that. A minor. He killed her, all right. The police just didn't look hard enough."

PJ jotted notes. "Why do you think they didn't, Mrs. Ramsey? Did they have it in for your son, somehow?"

"The boy confessed. The fool thought he could protect his little sister's reputation, or something. Who knows what was in his mind, but as soon as the police got that confession they didn't let up on him. Even after he took back every word he said."

"Speaking of little sister, I've noticed a big age difference in your children, Mrs. Ramsey. Eleanor was the baby of the family by quite a few years. Why did you and Elijah have a daughter after your other children were grown?"

Unexpectedly, Libby laughed. "You're too damn nosy," she said. "Now I know you're really a reporter."

"You mean you had doubts?" PJ said innocently.

"Honey, a lot of people have wanted to talk to me about

our family's tragedy. Not all of them had good intentions." Libby left unfinished what those bad intentions were, such as putting her son on trial for murder and executing him years after a conviction.

"Elijah and I got married when I was fifteen years old. I had Darla six months later, if you catch my drift. Then Jeremiah right after that. Got pregnant as soon as I took Darla off the breast. Hormones or something. I worked my tail off with those kids. Never had much of a childhood of my own, you know. Never got to enjoy the time when I had a good figure and the boys wanted to put their hands on me every chance they got. And I'd give 'em plenty of chances." Libby smiled, remembering. "You got any kids?"

"One. A boy, thirteen."

"Something special about a son, isn't there? Just looking at my boy positively filled up my heart. You should get yourself some more kids, though. Isn't natural to raise an only child. You're not too old."

PJ felt the tips of her ears burning. She hadn't expected to become the interviewee. She lowered her eyes to her notepad, absorbed in the squiggles she was making there. "I'm divorced."

"So?"

PJ cleared her throat. "Getting back to the question about Eleanor, Mrs. Ramsey. Was she a welcome addition to the family?"

"Holy shit, you got nerve," Libby said, ignoring the fact that she had just questioned PJ's sex life. "You'll go far as a reporter, you'll see. The only reason I'm going to answer that is I like a woman who goes after what she wants. Of course she was welcome. I was only thirty-three. My own mother had kids up until she was forty-four."

"So you'd describe her as your midlife treasure? Just trying to get quotes for the article."

"You could say that. Sure, that sounds good." Libby seemed amused, but the joke was a private one.

Libby was answering questions easily enough, but PJ had the strong sense that the woman was in charge of the conversation even though PJ was asking the questions. PJ wasn't getting the insight she needed, and she couldn't seem to read the woman as she could other people after a brief conversation. Libby's body language gave away nothing. PJ would have to knuckle down and dig for both information and attitudes. There was no telling how much longer she'd be allowed to stay in Libby's small living room. PJ shuffled her feet on the wooden floor and kept up her side of the interview.

"How did the other children react?"

"Darla, I don't think she was thrilled. Always wanted the spotlight, that one. She didn't take to having a baby in the house when she was already high-and-mighty eighteen years old. She moved out right after that, come to think of it. Jeremiah, he was excited. Took to the baby from the start. Diapered her and everything. He said he was practicing for when he got married."

Libby seemed lost in thought for a moment, and in that unguarded moment her face showed something frightening. Jealousy? Hatred? Anger? PJ couldn't say for sure, but whatever it was caused her to recoil from the intensity of emotion that Libby was radiating. Then the mask slipped back onto Libby's face, and PJ had the sinking feeling that everything she had seen and heard up until then had been a performance.

To what end? Normal caution with a reporter? Or something deeper?

The emotions had been revealed when Libby talked about Jeremiah getting married. PJ remembered Dave's report that Jeremiah was a bachelor. Either Libby had resented the fact that he wasn't married yet, or she hadn't wanted him to marry. PJ couldn't make sense of that, but marked it "raw data" and filed it away.

"And what about your husband? How did he feel about Eleanor?" PJ asked without missing a beat.

"Oh, you know. Another mouth to feed."

"Let's move forward," PJ said, consulting her notes. "During the trial, you said you were with Jeremiah at the time of Eleanor's death, so you were his alibi. What effect did it have on you when the jury didn't believe you?"

"Honey, it doesn't make any difference what I think of the jury. They're already damned and going to hell."

PJ blinked. She was getting somewhere now. She hoped the microphone in her purse was recording it all.

"That's the Lord's judgment, not mine," Libby said. "They knew in their hearts that my son was innocent, but they didn't listen to their hearts. They listened to the lies of the police and the lawyers. They know what's waiting for them, and they should be afraid. Damned afraid."

"Do you think they deserve to die?" PJ asked. Her voice trembled. It had occurred to her that things could get dangerous. She was starting to become afraid, herself. "I'm asking for the article, I mean."

Libby gave her an odd look. "Of course not. The Lord will get around to them in His own sweet time. Aren't you a believer in the day of judgment, honey?" She smiled, and her pumpkin face lit up as though a candle had been lighted inside it. There was nothing but sincerity in her face and voice. Or was that part of a superb performance?

"Um, how did Elijah take the guilty verdict? His own son convicted of murdering a family member?"

"Makes a great headline, don't it? I think Elijah kind of died that day. Inside someplace. He's been a broken man since then."

PJ nodded. "Doesn't he feel an injustice was done?"

"Hard to say. He didn't talk much about it. I always had the feeling he thought Jeremiah actually did it. He loved the boy dearly, so it's beyond me how he could have thought such a thing of him. It broke us apart, too. We're divorced now, you know. I haven't seen him in years."

PJ was taken by surprise. "No, I didn't know that." She almost said, *That wasn't in the case file.*

"It's been hard on me. I lost Eleanor, then my business. The day care centers. Parents wouldn't bring their kids. They thought the whole family was tainted and we were a bunch of killers, I guess. Then Elijah couldn't stand it anymore and moved out. Darla turned her back on the whole thing. When Jeremiah was murdered by the state, it was the last straw for me. I got out, moved away from St. Louis. I didn't have anything there." She sank back in her chair as if she didn't have the strength to sit up.

"So what's happened to you since? This is great stuff, if you don't mind my saying so." *Spoken like a true reporter.*

"I had a little money from the sale of the Wee Belong centers. I bought this house with it," Libby said, gesturing vaguely around her. "For my living expenses, I work in a Burger King. Do you want fries with that, Ma'am?" The last part she said in a flat singsong voice that would have been comical if it weren't for the context.

PJ drank some of her tea, and took the opportunity to look quickly down at her purse. She could see the tiny reel on the recorder spinning. So far so good.

She felt sorry for Libby, and was beginning to think of that bit about the jury being damned as nothing but a despairing woman looking to religion for comfort. PJ searched her face carefully, and saw no trace of the deep emotion glimpsed earlier. Libby had suffered so many losses.

If Thomas was brutally killed—PJ didn't allow herself to think of the way Rick Schultz had looked—there was no telling how she would react herself. Perhaps she'd turn to religion too, consoling herself with thoughts of the kind of final justice that wasn't available on earth.

"So you don't know where Elijah is?" PJ asked. "I was hoping to interview him also."

Libby shook her head. "Not that he was home much during the marriage either. Always off in some godforsaken jungle, wherever there was a fight going on. I raised those kids alone."

Libby had been like a single mother even though she was married, PJ thought. Her sympathy went up a notch.

"Too bad," PJ said, speaking of both Libby's experience and her own disappointment in not locating Elijah. "How about Darla?"

Libby's lips narrowed into a tight line. "I don't know where she is. Haven't heard from her in ten years. That's what kind of a grateful daughter I've got left."

PJ imagined what Libby's life was like. Everything that was important to her, everything she loved, had been yanked out of her life or moved out voluntarily. Most likely all of her friends had edged away from her as well. She lived in a tan brick box, worked at a meaningless job, and had only memories of better times to brighten her existence. PJ shuddered. Would she ever end up like that? Old and alone?

"Eleanor's friends said that you had a . . . difficult relationship with her," PJ said. "They even said that you would kill her if you found out she was pregnant. Is there anything to that?"

"You don't have a teenage daughter," Libby said. "You don't know what it's like. They fight you every step of the way. Between mother and daughter is the roughest."

"I know teenagers can be difficult to get along with."

Libby snorted. "That's not the half of it. Eleanor had a temper, bless her soul, just like Elijah does. That man has a cruel streak in him. I always thought he had a cold snake curled around his heart. You got to know how to handle him. But Eleanor, she knew which buttons to push on good old Mom. She did love her brother, though. That's one good thing.

But I knew from raising Darla that all that defiance blows over when a girl gets into her twenties. Then she's ready to listen to Mama again. In the meantime, I came down hard on her. I wanted so much more for her than I had."

Libby looked away, focused on the photographs on the wall. "Don't get me wrong. By some people's standards, I had a good life with Elijah. I mean, he didn't beat me or drink away the family's money. But I didn't want Eleanor pregnant at fifteen, the way I was. I wanted her to make something of herself. Go to college. She was smart, damn it." When Libby turned back to face PJ, tears moistened her eyes and turned the cool grayness into soft colorless pools.

PJ took it all in, tried to fit the grief against the earlier violent emotions that had peeped through the mask. It didn't make a coherent picture.

While Libby was distracted reaching for a tissue, PJ leaned over, dropped her pen into her purse, and snapped the purse shut.

"Thank you for your time, Mrs. Ramsey. I know it was difficult for you."

"I want you to make it clear in your article how much this whole thing has hurt us. We're all victims, including my innocent son. Our lives were shattered on the day I found Eleanor's body."

"I'll tell your story just the way you want it," PJ said. "It's good copy."

The heat was like a visible barrier outside Libby's front door. PJ steeled herself and returned to her car, clutching her purse. She had pulled it off. She had tracked down Libby Ramsey and gotten an update, of sorts, on the rest of the family.

She started the car and moved off to a parking lot a few blocks away, then opened her purse and turned off the tape recorder. The air-conditioner was beginning to cool the car down. She used her cellular phone to call Lieutenant Wall.

She told him she was bringing back an interview tape. He berated her for not having authorization to tape, but seemed pleased, nevertheless. She asked if he could contact Dave or Anita to start the search for Darla Ramsey. PJ had two strong impressions about Darla: that she needed to talk to her to learn more about the Ramsey family, and that it wasn't going to be as easy to find her as it had been to find Libby. From what Libby had said, Darla wanted nothing to do with the rest of her family.

On the drive back to St. Louis, she tried to sort things out. The mysterious Elijah still looked like a good bet for the killer. His whereabouts were unknown. He was a broken man after the trial. He had a bad temper and a cruel streak, and it was likely he blamed the justice system for everything from the loss of his son to the breakup of his marriage. From what Libby had said, Elijah seemed like the type of man to look outside himself when there was blame to be assigned.

A bag of jelly beans from a food mart provided comfort food. She drove along, popping them in her mouth. It was something she did when she was nervous. She didn't know what her next step should be. It was exactly the kind of thing she wanted to talk over with Schultz.

PJ was discovering that he was an equally hard man to be with, and be without.

She went straight to the headquarters building and gave the tape from her purse to Louie. If anyone could make something of it, he could. His eyes gleamed when he turned it over in his hand. She felt sorry for the poor tape. It was at Louie's mercy.

Thomas was pleased when she turned up early at the Lakeland's house to take him to dinner and a movie. She turned the volume down on her jumbled thoughts and enjoyed an evening with her son.

Twenty-two

Schultz didn't have long to wait in Glen Mandoleras's tiny dark apartment. Fifteen minutes after he finished his search he heard the key in the lock. He gently pushed the cat off his lap in case he had to move fast.

Schultz's eyes were fully adjusted to the dimness, so he could make out a hand that moved inside the door and groped around on the wall. He tensed and aimed his gun at the door, holding it with both hands, arms raised to slightly below shoulder level. The moving hand found a light switch and flipped it. A small ceiling light came on in the entryway. The light barely reached to Schultz's feet and outstretched arms.

The door swung open and Mandoleras walked in, carrying a grocery bag with one arm.

"I'm home, O'Brien," he said. "Gotcha some treats." Then he stopped abruptly. He had spotted a shadowy figure on his couch and a gun pointed in his direction.

"I'm unarmed," he said, holding perfectly still.

"Put the bag down on the floor and close the door," Schultz said.

Mandoleras complied. His back made a nice big target. Schultz could end the chase right then, with no risk to himself. But his search of the apartment had turned up nothing, and he had to be sure.

"Sit down on the floor," Schultz said.

"My knees hurt. That'd be very hard for me."

"Do it."

Mandoleras slowly lowered himself to the floor. It was clear that he was in pain doing so. He kept his legs spread out in front of him, not folded in a pretzel shape. The moment he was settled, the cat was between his knees, kneading on his thigh and purring noisily. Mandoleras began to stroke the cat, and it was clear that O'Brien had him well-trained.

Schultz reached over and turned on the lamp on the end table. There was a brief silence as Mandoleras stared first at the gun and then at Schultz's face. Schultz saw the moment recognition came into his eyes.

"Schultz? What's going on?"

"That's what I'm here to find out."

Mandoleras squinted at him. "Damn, man, you got yourself some sun. You should get something to put on that."

"I'm looking for the man who killed my son," Schultz said, his voice barely above a whisper and sharp as a razor. "Would that be you?"

"What?"

"You heard me, Ginger."

"What the fuck are you talking about? That sun must have fried your brain right through that bald spot of yours."

"You saying you had nothing to do with that?"

"Shit, yes, that's what I'm saying. I heard about it. It was in the papers here."

There was a pause while Schultz examined his quarry. The Glen Mandoleras that Schultz had known was a vigorous, hard man, secretive about his private life but a damn good cop. On the floor in front of him was a man who had aged badly: thin white hair askew, the beginnings of a pot belly, legs splayed out, his shorts displaying knobby knees. There was an unhealthy pallor in his face. The only thing that reminded Schultz of the old Mandoleras was the stubborn gleam in his eyes.

"Can I get up now? The floor is uncomfortable."

"Yeah. Go sit in that chair." Schultz gestured with the gun. He had already searched the chair cushions and knew there was no weapon there.

Gathering his legs under him and wincing from the pain, Mandoleras awkwardly got to his feet. He limped over to the chair and sat down with a sigh. "Put that gun away, asshole," he said, "before you blow a hole in my wall."

"I haven't heard any proof yet. And I want to know about the little girl, too. You shithead. A four-year-old girl."

Mandoleras's face was getting increasingly red. "Are we just going to sit here and call each other names? What do you want to hear? I didn't have anything to do with your son's death. Or this girl you're talking about. Why should I?"

"Because you blame me for Vince."

"Oh," Mandoleras said, sitting back in his chair. "That." The cat jumped up on his lap and made a bid for attention, but was ignored. "After all this time, you think I got a grudge? Maybe you think I got something against Rheinhardt, too?"

"What?"

"Is there an echo in here?" Sitting in the chair had taken away some of his vulnerability, the same way that wrapping a robe around his body would have if he'd been naked. Mandoleras had regained most of his composure, and he faced the Glock steadily. He clamped his lips together. For a moment the two men glared at each other.

Schultz's curiosity and doubts won the moment. He lowered the gun. "Tell me about Rheinhardt."

"Our old buddy Victor Rheinhardt got himself knifed a little while ago. Very professional hit, no wasted effort. Tuesday. Might have been Wednesday."

Schultz hadn't heard about Rheinhardt's death. He had been moving fast, and couldn't recall immediately where he was on Tuesday. He was almost sure he'd talked to Anita since then, and she hadn't said anything about it. Probably she assumed he had seen it on the news. Suddenly he remembered that night in Billings, when he'd glimpsed Chief Wharton on TV and thought a politician got arrested for drunk driving or something. That must have been the news coverage of the murder.

"It was Tuesday," Schultz said.

"So who's this little girl you're talking about?"

Schultz told him how he was framed for Caroline Bussman's death.

"Jesus, that's a hard thing," he said. "Four years old. Her parents must feel like their hearts have been ripped out."

"Yeah, like you feel about Vince. I saw the photo of him you keep in your bedroom. I still haven't heard anything convincing from you."

Mandoleras shook his head. "Schultz, you are the world's biggest dumb shit. It's a wonder you found me. You probably can't find your own ass in the dark."

Schultz sat and tried to pull his whirling thoughts together. The timing of Rheinhardt's death could be a coincidence, or it could be the result of some case, past or present, that Schultz had nothing to do with. How did the message on his answering machine fit in?

You think about that, Detective Schultz, you think about him tied up helpless like that and gasping for air. Then think about what I'm going to do next.

Schultz rubbed his chin with one hand, still keeping the gun trained on Mandoleras with the other. Was Rheinhardt part of a wider pattern of revenge?

"What makes you think there's a connection?" Schultz said.

"I'm psychic," Mandoleras said sarcastically.

"What do you know about Ginger Miller?"

"Not a thing."

Schultz studied his face. Either he was telling the truth or he was the most accomplished liar Schultz had run across in thirty years of dealing with people who would have denied they'd ever seen their own shadows if they'd thought it would shave even a few days off their sentences.

Rheinhardt's death might change everything. If the connection was there, then the idea of Mandoleras taking revenge for his son's death didn't fit the picture. The picture had suddenly gotten much bigger.

"You been back in St. Louis lately?" Schultz asked. He wasn't willing to give up on his theory yet.

Mandoleras shook his head. "In case you haven't noticed, this old body ain't what it used to be. I can barely walk." He patted his knees. "I'd be a candidate for knee replacement surgery, except for another little health problem I've got. Cancer. I've got less than a year to live. The most traveling I do is back and forth to the hospital."

"Tell me how you feel about Vince," Schultz said. They had never really talked about it. Neither of them were good at talking about their emotions.

Mandoleras closed his eyes. "I never wanted him to be a cop. It was okay for me. I'd been in worse situations, and I knew I could handle whatever came at me on the streets. I was Mr. Tough Guy with more kills to my credit than I could keep track of." He seemed to grow smaller in the chair, to sink into himself. "As if that's a good thing. You know a little about that, don't you?"

Schultz nodded. He'd killed in the line of duty, and he felt that taking someone else's life diminished a person in some way, took away a little piece of the soul. Or maybe put it in layaway to be redeemed later.

"Vince was different. He was sensitive. I always thought he'd be a teacher, something like that. But he wanted to follow in his old man's shoes. I almost changed my mind about being a cop then, but what else was I fit for? A security guard? Shit."

Schultz grunted. "You could have been a private investigator."

"And take photos of people screwing or tail some jerk of a husband all day, waiting for that one minute of action out of a whole year? That wasn't for me."

"So Vince was sensitive. That wasn't why he got killed." Schultz tapped his chest. "I pulled that little trick off myself."

"No. You fucked up by not doing more background work on Lemont Clark. Vince got the hots to make a bust, and you let yourself get carried away with the thing. Vince could wear a guy down, I know that."

Mandoleras paused for a moment, marshaling his emotions. "It was Vince that got himself shot," he said. "What the hell was that kid thinking, standing right in front of that door like that? He should have been off to the side, against the wall. When Clark yanked that door open, Vince shouldn't have been looking down the barrel of that shotgun. Vince could've got the drop on that guy. He just screwed up, is all. And he paid for it."

"It was my job to see that he didn't screw up," Schultz said. His voice was small and came from a long way back in time.

"Gimme a break, Schultz. You know you can't do that. You're not God Almighty, last time I checked."

"So you didn't blame me?"

"Oh, hell, of course I did at first, because it was easier than blaming Vince. I've come around since then. You want something to drink?"

"No," Schultz said, putting his gun back in his holster. "But you go ahead. Better put those groceries away too."

"Lucky I didn't buy any ice cream this trip. Would've had a mess to clean up by now."

Mandoleras went into the kitchen with the bag. The cat followed hopefully. Schultz had his own opinion of who was responsible for Vince's death, and it hadn't changed any in the last few minutes. But what mattered was how Mandoleras felt.

There was another factor. The psychic thread that should ave been connecting him to Mandoleras, had Mandoleras een the killer, simply wasn't there. He had felt the stirrings f the familiar feeling when Rheinhardt was mentioned, which e took to mean that his search lay in that direction. But there vas no brilliant streak of gold luminescence, a twisting living ord linking him to Mandoleras. Could he trust that absence? lot completely. The cord didn't perform on cue; it hadn't in he Ramsey case, and others. He'd have to make up his own nind. Schultz held up a mental finger to see which way the nternal winds were blowing.

Mandoleras was no longer a candidate for being Ginger Miller.

Schultz tried to enlarge his thinking to deal with Rheinardt's death. Assuming the same killer was involved, Rick's leath and the frame job were pieces of a much bigger puzzle. t had to be something that connected Schultz and Rheinhardt. Since it wasn't in their personal lives, it had to be in their areers, and that meant cases they'd worked on together.

He needed access to police records. He had to go back in, o matter how dangerous it was for him. With any luck, Anita vould hand him what he needed to do that. He'd call her oon. In the meantime, he needed to get to the airport.

Mandoleras came back in from the kitchen. He tossed a ube of aloe cream at Schultz.

"Here, you old bastard," Mandoleras said. "This'll take the ting out."

Twenty-three

Cut knew it wasn't good to approach a home on foot at 1:00 A.M. A lone man out walking, without even a dog on a leash as an excuse, would attract attention. A patrol car or even a neighbor glancing out the window when he got up to take a piss could mess up his plans. He didn't want to park in the street either, because all of the upscale townhouses had their own garages and there were few cars on the street. He couldn't count on blending in, even for a short while.

Fortunately the apartment complex had common ground. There was an open field and a large lake backed by woods. The woods adjoined a county park, and the park was within walking distance of an all-night supermarket.

Cut didn't mind a little exercise. It would do him good to work off some of those steakburgers.

He parked in the supermarket lot and waited until there was no one nearby. He stepped out of his car, took a deep breath of humid night air, and started walking. The woods slowed him down somewhat, but he wasn't in a hurry. His dark clothing blended with the night, and he passed through the trees as silently as a shadow cast by the moon. At one point he was downwind, and so near to a couple of deer that he could have reached out and tweaked their tails.

It was the third night in a row he'd used the supermarket lot. If his target didn't show that night, Cut would have to get a different car. He didn't want his car to become a regular in the lot.

The lake was beautiful in the moonlight, with the lights on the apartment complex gleaming from the far shore. He skirted the lake carefully, staying far enough away from the shore so that he wouldn't leave any footprints in the mud. Crossing the open field bothered him, and the first two nights he'd crawled through the tall grass, getting spiderwebs plastered across his face and coming nose-to-nose with startled rabbits. He'd gotten bolder—or stupider, he told himself—and on his third trip he stayed on his feet, flitting from one widely spaced tree to another.

The town house that was his destination was quiet, and there was no car in the driveway. He leaned against a tree at a good vantage point he'd found and waited.

The street was deserted. Streetlights that were more decorative than functional spread small cones of yellowish light that didn't reach far into the driveways. Cut watched moths dance with abandon in the grip of the lights, and appreciated the swooping flight of the bats who came to the midnight buffet. Time passed, an hour or a little more. Cut was good at waiting.

Headlights. The car turned into the right driveway. Cut was close enough to see that it was a Lexus, just the type he was looking for. A man got out and went to the door. Before he could knock, the door opened, a rectangle of warm light. From where Cut was, he could see the front of the man's face illuminated in the open door, confirming his identity.

As soon as the door closed, Cut started to move toward the car. A sudden cautious feeling made him wait, in case the target had left something in the car and came back outside. The Lexus sat silently, obediently, the hot engine clicking. Cut patted the bomb that was taped under his dark shirt, snuggled on his left side. It had ridden there securely for three nights, and would finally get the chance to do its work.

Cut was about to step out when another set of headlights turned the corner. Almost as soon as they did so, the headlights were turned off. That wasn't standard behavior for a car just driving through, so Cut pulled back and pressed himself against the side wall of the town house. The car continued on past and turned around in a driveway three doors down.

The driver pulled up to the curb on Cut's side of the street at a spot midway between streetlights to remain as hidden as possible.

Not good, Cut thought. The target was being followed by someone else. Cut thought he knew exactly why, too. The target was in the home of his mistress. The suspicious wife must have hired a private investigator to document the visits. In that case, the person in the car probably had a low-light camera, and that was dangerous to Cut. He pulled even farther into the shadows, feeling sweat trickling down his back. He reached in his pocket for a peppermint candy and found it empty.

There was another possibility—that the police had put the earlier killings together and found the pattern too soon. They'd anticipated his next move and assigned police surveillance to the target. If that was the case, Cut could still accomplish his task, but then he'd have very little useful working time left. He frowned in concentration. The bomb blast would give him a window of time in which no one would expect another hit.

He'd have to go after Schultz right away. Tonight. There wouldn't be a chance for anything dramatic, so it would have to be a straight hit.

He watched the car carefully. In a couple of minutes, the windows were rolled down on both the driver's side and passenger's. It was too warm and stuffy to sit for an extended period of time in a closed-up car, even in the middle of the night.

Cut circled around the rear of four townhouses and came out behind the car. The open front windows were handy. He planned to move closer, aim through the window, and take out the driver. He probably couldn't get close enough for the skin-touch range he preferred, which would muffle the shots efficiently, but field conditions rarely turned out perfect.

Cut eased the Ruger Mark II with its suppressor into his hand and started moving in. He was glad he'd brought it along. He hadn't thought he would need a gun, but being prepared paid off.

Twenty-four

After the movie, PJ brought Thomas back home with her, as she had worked out with Bill Lakeland. She and Thomas had gone to Union Station, an authentic train station that had been remodeled into a unique shopping area. They'd walked the length of the station, window-shopping, then had a relaxing dinner and taken in a late movie. Rather than wake Winston and Bill up at midnight, she simply drove home. She was thinking that with Schultz out of town, Thomas might as well end his stay with the Lakelands, anyway. She had originally made that arrangement so she could stay out long hours at night or even the entire night consoling Schultz without worrying about someone to stay with Thomas. Since Schultz took off, there hadn't been much call for consoling.

Their evening together had gone well, but by the time they got back to the house her son was drooping and ready to fall asleep. He took a warm bath and then she tucked him in. Megabite had taken her customary place on his pillow, so he scrunched his head to the side to leave the cat undisturbed. PJ went to bed shortly after him, and fell asleep quickly.

She was jolted by the phone ringing in the middle of the night. She looked at her clock as she grabbed for the phone. It was 3:00 A.M. She'd only been asleep for a couple of hours.

"I'm sorry to wake you, PJ. It's Bill."

"Is there anything wrong?" PJ had gone rigid with worry

when she heard him, thinking something bad must have happened to Thomas, until she remembered that he was asleep in his own room down the hall.

"No, everything's fine here. I was just watching a movie and I fell asleep on the couch. When I woke up, there was a news bulletin on the TV. I wanted to make sure you caught it."

She felt goosebumps rising on her arms. Since Thomas was okay, her concern had shifted to Schultz. Had he been brought in by the police? She waited breathlessly.

"Flip on the TV and check out local news," Bill continued. "It's on all the channels. Any that are still broadcasting at this hour, anyway."

Bill seemed to be rambling. She would do better going right to the source. "Yes, all right, I'll go find a TV."

She got off the phone and hurried downstairs. She had a TV in her room, but she didn't want to risk waking Thomas with the noise. She caught the broadcast right away.

The Honorable Edward D. Canton, of the 22nd Circuit Court of St. Louis City, had just been blown up, along with his car, outside his mistress's home.

There was a brief statement from Chief Wharton. Yes, there was an explosion. Yes, it was a car registered to the judge. Yes, there was a person inside, but that person had not been identified definitely as the judge. End of statement.

The chief tried to look concerned and grave, but he came across as rumpled and irritated about being pulled from sleep.

The rest of the information was liberally filled in by the reporter on site. As PJ continued to watch, a parade of neighbors and associates of the judge appeared, obviously rousted from their beds by the media, to say what a nice guy the judge was, and how he had carried on a ten-year affair that his wife didn't seem to mind. Evidently everyone who was anyone in St. Louis society had known about his extramarital relationship with Natalie Dorale. That left out PJ, who was mildly shocked to see footage taken a half hour earlier showing the wife and mistress sobbing together and comforting each other.

TV reporters were indulging in gleeful speculation while trying to keep funereal looks on their faces. The city prosecutor flamboyantly knifed to death and a leading circuit court judge blown to bits within a few days of each other—it was the stuff that crime reporters' wet dreams are made of.

"Revenge killings," she heard. Someone was presumed to have a reason to hate, a reason that tied those two men together.

No one mentioned a lone ex-con put to death in a hellish apartment. But the link was clear to PJ.

Canton had been the judge in the Ramsey case.

The phone rang and she picked up on the first ring. It was Wall.

"Thought I'd be waking you," he said.

She ignored his comment and rushed on. "I already know about Judge Canton," she said. "It looks like the Ramsey case is the key factor."

"Can't dispute that. We're looking hard and fast for Darla and Elijah. I'm thinking Darla might be Ginger Miller. What do you think of the mother?"

"As the killer, you mean?" PJ was taken by surprise. She searched her feelings quickly. "I don't think so. She still thinks Jeremiah was innocent, and she'll probably go to her grave thinking that. But I can't see her being a knife-throwing or bomb-building expert."

"There's something else, PJ, that wasn't on the TV news." His voice had taken on a somber tone. She sensed that there was something he hadn't wanted to tell her right away, and immediately the sense of dread came back, the one she'd felt when first awakened by Bill's phone call. She stilled herself and waited to hear the worst about Schultz.

"Because of your warning about people associated with the

case being in danger, we had surveillance on Judge Canton and a few others. The tail followed him to the mistress's house and kept watch outside. Canton wouldn't let anyone into his house, and he refused to have anyone ride with him. Obviously the mistress was the reason for that; it's plain now. He didn't want to give up his middle-of-the-night visits."

PJ shook her head. However the judge had managed to get out of the house, he wouldn't be doing it anymore.

"Someone else was hurt in the explosion?" PJ asked, puzzled. She was breathing easier. At least it didn't seem that he was going to drop some news on her about Schultz.

"Not exactly. The tail was spotted. He was shot twice while sitting in his car. It was Dave Whitmore."

Twenty-five

PJ dropped the phone.

Not Dave! Oh, no . . .

She scrambled for the handset and snatched it up from the kitchen floor. "Tell me he's not dead," she said, her voice cracking with emotion.

"I can only tell you he's not dead yet," Wall said. "He's critically injured, and he's in surgery now. His chances are not good."

"Oh God, Howard . . . I feel so terrible. Has anyone contacted his girlfriend?"

"She's at the hospital. I thought she could use some company there."

"I'll go immediately. What hospital?"

She got the information and hung up. For a few moments she sat in the kitchen, immobilized. All she could think was that someone she cared about had been killed because of her suggestion. If she'd kept her theories to herself, Dave would still be alive. Who cared about protecting some judge who was fooling around, anyway?

She shook herself. Her thoughts had been spinning down strange paths. Of course it was important to protect others if she could—she had been right to pass on the information she had.

And Dave wasn't dead yet.

She forced back tears and went upstairs to wake Thomas. It looked as though he was going to have to stay with the Lakelands a little while longer.

She went into his room, turned on the lamp, and touched his shoulder gently.

"Thomas, wake up," she said. "I have to go out." She was worried that taking him back to Bill's house would send Bill into a tizzy. Rapid changes in plans had that effect on him. He would just have to cope.

Thomas was groggy and slow to wake. Agitated and anxious to get to the hospital, she shook him roughly.

"What is it?" he said crossly.

PJ didn't have time for elaborate explanations. "Dave Whitmore's been shot. I have to get to the hospital right away. You're going back to Winston's house."

"Mom, it's the middle of the night," he said. "I just got to sleep."

"Didn't you hear me?" Her voice edged up toward shrillness. "It's important. Get up!"

She pulled on his arm.

"Just leave me here, okay? I'll be fine. You go on."

"No," she said stubbornly. "Get dressed and meet me downstairs in three minutes."

He made it in time, but there were thunderclouds on his face and lightning in his eyes. He kept silent as they got into the car.

Finally, when PJ turned onto the block where the Lakeland home was located, she couldn't stand it any more.

"What's the matter with you?" she said irritably. "I thought you enjoyed staying at Winston's."

"I do, Mom, but his dad isn't your baby-sitter. There's such a thing as imposing."

She glanced at him as she drove and saw that his eyes were brimming with tears. There had to be more to it than what he'd already said.

"If you loved me like you say you do, you'd get a job where you don't have to shuffle me around like a loaf of bread in a shopping cart," he spat out.

His words sliced deeply. She thought he understood about the demands of her job, and that they had enough communication to prevent the buildup of resentment that she heard in his voice. Obviously he'd been hiding his disappointment. She chided herself for thinking that their relationship had been getting better and better. She should have known that his behavior was too good to be true, but she'd blinded herself to that.

"Sweetie, the past few days have been really tough on both of us," she said. "I apologize for thinking I'm the only one who's worried about Schultz. And I also apologize for thinking that spending a few fun hours with you makes up for everything else." She looked over at him. Tears had spilled down his cheeks.

"I'm not a little kid anymore, Mom. You don't give me credit for understanding anything."

"You've been very brave," PJ said. She slipped the car to the curb in front of the Lakeland house and turned off the engine. All the windows were dark. Bill had spoken to her not long ago, but he must have gone directly to bed afterward.

"Take me with you," he said softly.

"What?"

"Take me with you to the hospital. I like Dave Whitmore too. I might be able to do something to help."

In his dark eyes there was an unspoken challenge: *Go ahead. Treat me like a little kid and ignore me.*

She felt as though the ground were shifting under her, or all the stars were realigning themselves in the sky. It was too soon, too soon. Wasn't this supposed to happen later, when he was sixteen or seventeen? She knew he had matured tremendously in the past couple of years, but he was still her baby. He was asking her to change the rules—to change the entire way she perceived him.

"Can't we discuss this later?" she asked feebly. Too many things were crowding in at once. The past week would go down in her personal history as a record-breaker in terms of loss, doubts, and forced readjustments.

He turned his head away and stared out the front window in answer. His profile looked so much like his father's.

Was that it? Was she afraid that when he became a man, he'd be like his father?

PJ started the car and drove toward the hospital.

Twenty-six

There was an alley behind Schultz's house on Lafayette Avenue. Cut made his way down it, sticking to the shadows, slipping around the edges of the bright circles cast by the occasional dusk-to-dawn light. It was three o'clock on Saturday morning, and Cut didn't think anybody would be watching the alley, but he was careful anyway. He lived by three things: have a plan going in, always follow orders, and don't waste anything. He had come straight from the bombing, and that bothered him a little because that hadn't been in the day's plan. But he knew that the bombing was going to be occupying the police in general, and maybe Schultz in particular. No sense wasting opportunities.

Schultz's house had respectable locks on the doors but no alarm system. He smashed a basement window with a cloth-wrapped hand, removed the shards of glass, and slithered in on his belly.

The basement was lighted only by moonlight slipping in the same window he'd used. The moon was half-full, but hazy clouds drifted over its face, blocking most of the light. After his eyes adjusted to the darkness, he still couldn't see well enough to move around. He turned on a small flashlight and played a thin beam over his surroundings. After thirty seconds, he turned it off and moved with confidence, having memorized the placement of obstacles and the direction of the stairs. It was a skill that had come in handy a number of times.

He was hoping the basement door wouldn't be locked on the other side, and it wasn't. He opened it cautiously and found himself in a short hallway. He stopped and listened. The refrigerator hummed from down the hall. It was cool in the house, but the air-conditioner wasn't running at the moment.

The house was so quiet that Cut knew Schultz was either asleep upstairs or had been called out to the scene of the bombing.

A third possibility occurred to him, one that went along with the surveillance man he'd taken out at the judge's house. If the man hadn't been a private investigator, then he was a cop. He should have taken the time to ask the guy before pinning him with a couple of shots. If the police already had the full pattern, then Schultz might have made a cowardly exit. He could be in hiding somewhere, and Cut could wait in the house, and wait, and Schultz wouldn't show his face to have it blown off.

If the cops had the pattern, they'd probably expect him to go after Vince's lawyer next—Arnold something. Arnold Cartwright. That had been considered early on, but the more thought that went into it, the more it became clear that Cartwright was the only one who had spoken out on Vince's behalf. Even if the guy was inexperienced, he had done his best. That still counted for something, at least in Cut's world.

Cut made his way up the stairs, looking for Schultz's bedroom. Floating in like a malevolent fog, Cut entered the bedroom and found no one sleeping. He used his flashlight, shielding the beam with his slitted fingers. The bed was rumpled, but that didn't mean anything. Most men living alone didn't make up their beds every day, unless the odds were good they'd be bringing home a woman. Cut checked the closets with his flashlight and found that only two of the numerous hangers were empty, so Schultz hadn't packed up and left entirely.

On the dresser he found framed photographs. One was of Julia, one of Rick, the last of a woman and a young boy. He studied the third picture, and recognized the woman he'd seen inside Schultz's house when he'd been across the street playing gardener while spying. He hadn't been directly across the street, so he'd seen everything from farther away and at an angle, but he was fairly sure it was the same woman.

So there was already a new woman in Schultz's life, after Julia left.

Cut would have to find out who the new woman was. Julia wasn't where she was supposed to be, which had been a disappointment. Her answering machine message said she had gone to visit a sick friend and didn't know when she'd be back. It was either true or a clever diversion, and Cut didn't have the time to dig into the situation to locate her.

The new woman would make a good substitute. Cut filed the information, and the image of the woman's face, in his mind. When he had a chance, he'd look her up.

The bathroom had the basic toiletries in it, plus a book laying open next to the sink. Schultz read in the bathroom. Cut smiled. He and Schultz had something in common besides the executions of their sons.

Deciding that Schultz was out on police business, Cut went back downstairs to choose a spot for the shooting. If he was lucky, Schultz would be back while it was still dark. If not, he could still manage. He wasn't planning to fool around. A couple of quick shots, and out.

In the kitchen, he found a good spot where he could sit down while waiting and still cover both the rear and front doors well enough. He figured he'd hear the key in the lock, and that would tell him which door to head for. There was a night-light plugged into one of the outlets above the kitchen counter. He went over to unplug it so that its light wouldn't give him away.

On the counter underneath the night-light was a stack of mail. It caught his attention as something out of place. Didn't Schultz open his mail regularly? Cut could see that some of the pieces were junk mail. He narrowed his eyes. Most people pitched junk mail immediately. They didn't stack it on the counter.

Suspicious of anything out of the norm, he flicked on his flashlight and took a closer look. The most recent postmark in the stack was several days ago. Schultz, or someone else, had stopped his mail.

Schultz was gone. It was time for Plan B.

There was always a Plan B, and this one was sweet.

Twenty-seven

PJ found Melissa Hawkins, Dave's girlfriend, in the surgery waiting room. Melissa was a graduate student in Mechanical Engineering at Washington University. PJ knew their relationship had progressed to the point where they were living together. She greeted Melissa and then turned to introduce Thomas.

She noticed how composed her son was. There was no sign that a few minutes ago he'd been sitting in her car crying in frustration. Even his voice seemed different to her.

Where did this handsome young man come from, anyway?

"May I get you two some coffee?" he asked. She realized that he sensed the two women wanted to talk alone.

Sensitive as well as handsome.

She sent him away with a few dollars in search of coffee. He came back carrying a cup in each hand and a can of soda for himself stuffed into his pants pocket. By that time, she and Melissa had hugged and cried and wiped their faces with tissues. He had stayed away just long enough.

Sensitive, handsome, and with good timing.

An hour or so later, Anita arrived. Her face was grim, but PJ suspected that tears weren't her way of expressing herself. Anita explained that the bomb had gone off not long after Dave was shot. The fiery blast attracted the police immediately, and Dave's wounded body was discovered before too much time had gone by. If Judge Canton had stayed with his lover a long time, the discovery of the wounded officer would have been delayed, and Dave would have died in his own bloodstained vehicle.

"Thank goodness," Anita said, "that it was a quickie." She lapsed into silence after delivering her news, and they all drew strength from her quiet presence.

Hours later, the three women plus Thomas stood together as they got the news from the surgeon. One bullet had ripped through Dave's right lung at an oblique angle, nicked the pericardium, the membrane that surrounds the heart, and come to rest perilously close to his spine. The other, delivered from a different angle as though the attacker had been running and fired from two different positions, had traveled completely through the base of his neck, a fraction of an inch from his jugular, just missing his cervical spine.

Either of the bullets could have ended his life if they had taken just slightly different paths. He was still not out of danger, even though the surgery was as successful as could be expected. The bullet in his neck had damaged his trachea, but that was not life-threatening after the surgery. It was unclear whether his voice or breathing would suffer. There would be swelling for a few days, and Dave would be breathing through a temporary tracheotomy. The bullet near his spine was still in place. Dave's condition needed to stabilize before a second operation was attempted to remove it. There was the possibility of leaving the bullet in his body because of its precarious location. It had chipped one of the thoracic vertebrae, but not damaged or severed the spinal cord cradled inside. Half of his right lung had been removed. It had been irreparably mangled, and had been leaking blood into his abdomen. If he hadn't been discovered so soon, he would have died of internal bleeding, shock, and hypoxia, any one of which could have killed him.

Dave was incredibly lucky to be alive.

PJ sank into her chair, relieved that Dave had made it through the initial surgery and that there was hope of recovery.

Melissa and Anita seemed to have grown roots in the waiting room, and PJ knew they'd be there when Dave woke up. She would have liked to stay also, but an idea had been growing in her mind as she sat anxiously waiting for the outcome of the surgery. She felt the need to act on it, so she took Thomas aside.

"I'm going to work for a while," she said. "There's something I need to do. You can stay here if you want, or come with me."

"I'll come," Thomas said.

It was seven-thirty Saturday morning. She and Thomas ate breakfast at Millie's Diner. Fortunately, Millie wasn't there. PJ didn't want to explain, and Millie would have immediately picked up that something was wrong.

It was an odd experience sitting at the counter with her son, not with Schultz. The wobbly stool stood between them, and they shared breakfast and talked like adults. It was going to take a lot of getting used to, but PJ had decided to take Thomas up on his challenge. Teenagers definitely needed limits and guidance, but the past few hours had been an eye-opener about Thomas's level of maturity. She had a lot of catching up to do—he'd outpaced her expectations.

She offered to drop him off at home for a few hours' sleep, but he wanted to stay with her. So she took him to the headquarters building and got him a visitor's pass. It was only the second time she'd taken him to her office. The first time was when he helped paint the walls, turning a sickly green utility room into a fresh white office.

He eyed her Silicon Graphics workstation, a benefit of the grant that had set CHIP in motion in the first place. She was sure he'd love to get his proficient hands on it. She tucked him into a corner of her tiny office with the morning *St. Louis*

Post-Dispatch and angled the monitor away from his line of sight.

She called Lieutenant Wall and asked about locating Darla.

"No progress," he said. "There was distraction with the situation last night. But I've had someone on it since I listened to that tape you made at Libby's house. Asked the FBI for help after Judge Canton was killed. Nothing there yet, but they've only had the basic info for a few hours."

"That's what I thought," PJ said. "Darla really wanted to take herself out of things. She might have hired a professional to help her disappear. What's she running from, anyway? Embarrassment about her family? The media?"

"Seems to me like she's afraid of something," Wall said. "Or someone."

When she got off the phone, PJ hesitated for some time before making a dial-up connection with her computer. She wasn't at all sure what she was about to do was right. But it was necessary.

What's the buzz, Keypunch?

Merlin, I need to get in touch with someone, she typed without preamble.

Have you tried the social chats? Maybe you'll meet someone with common interests. Although in your case, I doubt it.

Knock it off, funny man. This is important.

I see. Go ahead.

I want to talk to Cracker.

There was a long pause, as she'd expected. Cracker was the screen name of a computer genius she'd encountered in one of her earlier cases. He was extremely resourceful, and highly skilled at breaking into supposedly secure systems. He sifted information through his fingers and came up with answers, and he did it for money.

Cracker was also a killer.

He never did the dirty work himself. He worked through

machines whenever possible, through people when he couldn't find a computerized way to kill.

He had taken a liking to PJ, seeing her as a skilled adversary—one who wasn't up to his level, but few were.

Merlin finally responded. *I don't know who Cracker is.*

She wondered if that was completely true. Cracker had told her that Merlin was their link, that Merlin knew him, but in an unexpected way. Merlin could well have figured out the connection by now.

This is no time for games, PJ typed. *This could be life or death, Merlin. Schultz's life, and maybe others.*

I don't know who Cracker is.

He broke his connection. It was the first time in their lengthy relationship that Merlin had gotten genuinely angry with her, with something she implied. She waited tensely in the private chat room, worrying about the morality of what she was trying to do: bargain with one killer to catch another. Finally she shook her head. She'd have to sort it all out later. There wasn't time to deal with it now.

Merlin rejoined her after ten minutes.

All I can do is broadcast a message to everyone I know and hope he sees it or that it's passed along to him.

Then that's what I want you to do. Tell him Lucky Penny needs to talk to him.

Your wish is my command.

He disconnected again. PJ couldn't tell if his last remark was sarcastic or his usual brand of weird humor. She hoped their relationship wasn't damaged beyond hope. She knew she was intruding on his very private existence by making that request. The fact that he hadn't given her the customary list before signoff was an indication of his emotional state.

Add another loss to the week's total, she thought.

PJ looked over at Thomas. He was sitting at the small table that held her coffee machine, and he'd fallen asleep with his head down on the newspaper. He wanted to stand by her, and he couldn't even stay awake. Poor kid.

Poor young man, she amended.

She wanted to fix herself some coffee, but that would wake him. She left him there, gently snoring, and went to work on a virtual reality simulation of the Eleanor Ramsey murder. She spread the file photos out on her desk and selected some for the scanner. Then she set about designing the Ramsey home in the computer, quickly sketching in Libby Ramsey's path from the front door to the bedroom where she found the girl's body. Rooms that weren't entered by Libby were stubbed for later development. The final step was to add details from the police report and the postmortem exam concerning the condition of the scene and the victim, so that the computer could make the simulation consistent with reality.

The phone remained quiet while she worked. Everyone else was busy with their own tasks aimed at finding and stopping the killer. At about eleven o'clock, she called the hospital and spoke to Anita. She got the depressing news that Dave hadn't awakened yet from the anesthetic. His doctor was probably thinking coma, although no one wanted to say the word and make it that much more real. Melissa was a real trooper, and had faith that he would wake up soon. She said he always did sleep late whenever he got the chance.

PJ was ready for a run-through on her simulation. She decided to skip the preliminaries and go directly to immersion, although she knew the experience wouldn't be fully realized at such an early point in her work.

She closed her office door. She always did when she used immersion, because she had a tendency to wander around the room, to move in reality as well as in virtual reality. She pulled on the data gloves. They felt like a light metal mesh, and picked up the movements of her hands. She could perform actions in the virtual world by tapping one finger against the palm of the other hand to move in the direction she was looking, or clenching her fingers to pick something up. The gloves felt cool against her skin, but after a time she wouldn't notice their presence.

Next she put on the Head-Mounted Display, or HMD. It wasn't a sleek commercial style. She had obtained both the gloves and the HMD on loan from Mike Wolf, her friend and a researcher in virtual reality at Washington University. She had put in for a requisition for a purchase of her own peripheral devices, but the items were expensive and hadn't yet found a place in the department budget. She was new enough to the department to still have a shred of hope for eventual approval. The pieces of equipment she got from Mike were considered spares, replacements to be used in case of malfunction of the primary items used in his research. One of these days he was going to ask for the items back. When that happened, PJ would have to find another "donation" or CHIP would go without. A VR team without immersion capability wasn't exactly working on the cutting edge.

The HMD looked like a mad scientist's helmet from an old B movie, but it worked. She lowered it onto her head and gave her eyes a few minutes to adjust to the blue screens. In a couple of minutes, her whole world would narrow to what those two screens presented to her. The HMD blocked out input from the outside world. Vision was totally restricted to the screens, and hearing somewhat restricted to the foam speakers that cradled her ears inside the helmet. If someone were to come up and shout near her head, she might react to it, but ordinary room noises were blocked out.

The blue screens were actually small computer monitors a few inches from her eyes. Each monitor would present a scene to one eye, angled from the view in the other monitor, the same angle at which light naturally fell on a pair of human retinas, which were about four inches apart. The result was similar to a moving, life-size ViewMaster scene. After a short period of adaptation, she found it easy to accept the world as real because everywhere she turned her head—slowly, unless she wanted to blur everything—another part of the world was revealed, just as in real life. In virtual reality, though, the only portions of the world that existed were the ones she was looking at. When she turned her head, the old images were swapped out of memory. The computer was fast enough, and had enough memory, to make the swapping out almost seamless, so that there was minimal jerkiness to the motion.

PJ closed her eyes, pressed a function key on her keyboard, and waited a few seconds. She preferred to have the setup done while she wasn't looking.

Opening her eyes, she found herself standing in daylight outside the Ramsey home. She noticed that her shadow didn't have its familiar contours, and then she remembered that she'd chosen to play the role of Jeremiah Ramsey. She had a male-shaped shadow, and it was foreshortened close to her body, because the time was a little past noon and the "sun" was high overhead. There was a projection on one side of the shadow that puzzled her, but she put it down to a simulation inaccuracy. At such an early point in the development, she expected to see a lot of those blips.

In front of her was the brown door from the case file photos. She turned her head, scanning the houses on either side. They were generic-looking, and repeated in patterns of three, because she had not scanned in images of them or developed them individually. The computer had inserted the three basic house images that were available in its database. Actually, the effect wasn't dissimilar from new subdivisions that had a limited choice of home styles.

PJ moved forward in the scene by tapping her palm, each tap equivalent to a step. She pushed on the door by extending her hand out into the air in front of her. The data glove picked up the motion and translated it appropriately in the scene. She also tried turning the doorknob, but the door was locked. She reached into her pocket for the key, and that's when she noticed one of her hands was encumbered. She looked down at her hands and saw that she was carrying a baseball bat in her left hand.

Of course. The bat.

Jeremiah had claimed in his early confession that the murder weapon was a bat, and that he'd brought it from home. He couldn't exactly have put it in his pocket, so he had to carry it openly. And hadn't his statement said he was riding around on a moped since his car was wrecked? How had he transported the bat? He couldn't just toss it into the trunk. He would have had to tie the thing on the moped somehow. She couldn't recall anything on the subject from the case file. Had Schultz deliberately overlooked an incongruent piece of evidence to get a conviction in the case? She tossed that question on the mounting stack of doubts she had about Schultz's past and his integrity. Would he allow an innocent man to be sentenced to death to restore his own image in the department? She reminded herself that the conviction was reinforced by physical evidence—the blood on Eleanor's hands that matched Jeremiah's.

Instead of opening the door with a key, PJ knocked on the door with the bat. Jeremiah was supposed to be angry about the wreck of his car, so it seemed like a natural thing to do. She had to get into character.

Eleanor opened the door almost immediately. The girl was done with scanimation—the process of animating a scanned-in image. Her features and body language were brought to life by the computer, so that her face moved when she talked and her body had motor functions. At the moment she was standing with her hands balled on her hips, an arrogant posture. Eleanor was several inches shorter than PJ, which startled PJ until she realized she was looking down on the girl from Jeremiah's simulated height.

Jeremiah reached out with his right hand and shoved Eleanor back into the foyer. She glared at him, her computer-generated eyes narrowing to slits, and slipped around him to close the door. She stood with her back to the door.

"What do you want?" Eleanor said. It came out flatly, as what-do-you-want. PJ would have to work on her voice intonation.

"You wrecked my car," Jeremiah responded. PJ kept her "Jeremiah" voice low. She didn't want to wake Thomas. There was no record of the exact conversation between Eleanor and Jeremiah in the court transcript, so she and the computer were improvising an angry confrontation.

"It was a rotten piece of shit, anyway," came the retort. PJ briefly wondered where her computer had learned bad language.

Must have picked it up from Schultz.

Eleanor turned her back and strode into the kitchen. Jeremiah followed. PJ noticed that rooms leading off the hallway, rooms that she hadn't defined yet in the simulation, appeared as black gaps in the wall. It was a little disorienting, but she had been expecting it.

"I expect you to pay for it," Jeremiah said when he reached the kitchen.

"Yeah, sure. I figure it was worth about five bucks." She reached into a purse on the counter and produced a five-dollar bill.

Jeremiah shoved her hard against the kitchen counter. The case photos indicated that there may have been a struggle in the kitchen. He advanced on her and raised the baseball bat threateningly. She side-stepped, but swiped her hand along the counter, spilling papers, plastic cups, pill bottles, and the telephone to the floor.

"I want my money and I want it now. If you don't have it, I'll take it out of your hide!" Jeremiah brandished the bat again.

Eleanor ran past him, heading for the front door. Jeremiah put his foot out and tripped her. She went sprawling on the kitchen floor, knocking her chin hard and turning over a chair with her legs. The kitchen then matched the crime scene photos: overturned chair, items scattered on the floor. Jeremiah went out of the kitchen and locked the front door with a security chain so she couldn't make a quick exit. By the time he returned to the kitchen, she was gone. He heard her slam the door to her bedroom upstairs.

Jeremiah went up the stairs. PJ was breathing fast by the time her character got to the upstairs hall. She was caught up in the chase.

Jeremiah knocked roughly on the door. "Come out of there. You can't get away with wrecking my car this easily."

Eleanor kept him waiting in the hall, getting angrier at being shut out. When she did open the door partway, she had a portable phone in her hand, the one that had been found smashed on the floor at the crime scene.

"I'm calling the cops. You better get out of here, if you know what's good for you."

Jeremiah slammed his body against the door, sending Eleanor flying backward. The phone was knocked out of her hand and went spinning across the floor. He went over to it and stomped it. There was a satisfying crunch, although it sounded a little like popcorn popping. The simulation had a long way to go.

"Hey!" Eleanor said. "I bought that phone out of my allowance! You're going to pay for that." She rushed toward him.

Caught unprepared, Jeremiah took quite a beating. Eleanor came at him with her fists clenched, meaning to do harm. She pounded his left shoulder repeatedly, trying to get him to drop the baseball bat. Angrily, Jeremiah pushed her away and swung the bat with both hands, just as he'd swing at a pitch. It caught her in the ribs, and there was a sickening crack.

PJ, breathing hard and with her heart racing, reached out to stop the simulation at that point. She knew what happened next. Jeremiah struck Eleanor repeatedly with the bat, sending her blood flying in patterns that were telling to those who studied that sort of thing. Then he fled from the house, leaving the front door unlocked behind him.

Playing the role of killer through to the bitter end was repulsive to her, although she'd do it if she thought there was something fresh and important to be learned. Whenever possible, she left that to Schultz and others who weren't fazed by it. Not that it didn't affect them—she'd seen Schultz's face after simulations—but they absorbed it better than she did.

When PJ lifted the HMD off her head, she found herself across the room from the computer, nearly at the limit of the cables that connected the device. Her feet had responded to the VR motion by moving her around.

Something nagged her about what she had just seen, some inconsistency, but she couldn't pin it down.

Thomas was watching her, eyes bright. She knew her face reflected the emotions she'd just experienced in the simulation, and she wondered how much of Jeremiah's part of the argument Thomas had heard.

"Can I try that?"

"No," she said. Her tone allowed no room for discussion.

"You got a fax while you were dancing around."

"I did?" PJ had gotten exactly three faxes since her machine was installed. Not many people had reason to send directly to her. She had been hoping that no one would notice that fact and reassign the machine. She went over, lifted out the single sheet, and read it.

> *Lucky Penny,*
>   *Merlin says you need something. Be at the White Castle off Interstate 44 at Bowles Avenue at 2:00 P.M. And bring something to trade. Information doesn't come free.*
>   *Cracker*

She sucked in her breath and held it. Her hands shook slightly. It sank in on her what she'd done, and who was on the other end of the fax. She looked for a return phone number or other identification, and found none.

"What is it, Mom?"

She started to say it was nothing, then remembered her decision to treat Thomas like a grown-up, at least most of the time.

"I've gotten in touch with a person who might be able to track down more information about the killer," she said. "About who shot Dave, too. The problem is, he's a scary guy himself."

"You've got to talk to him," he said. "You don't want Schultz hurt too, do you?"

She folded the fax in half and stuck it in her purse. It seemed less threatening when it was out of sight. "No, of course not. I have to be somewhere at two, and this time I don't want you to go with me." She had no idea what the meeting would be like. In the unlikely event that Cracker was there in person, she certainly didn't want to introduce him to her son.

Talk about a bad influence.

"Okay. No problem. Do you have time to drop me off at home?"

The argument she'd expected didn't materialize. She checked her watch. It was ten after one.

"Just barely," she said. "Let's go."

Later, traveling west on Interstate 44 toward Fenton, she remembered a portion of Cracker's message. *Bring something to trade.* What on earth did she have that he could possibly want?

Twenty-eight

"It's Schultz."

"About time you called," Anita said. "A lot's been going on here."

Schultz didn't bother to say that a lot had been going on with him, too. He was back in St. Louis, although not at his home. He was staying in a flophouse downtown where questions evaporated at the sight of cash. It wasn't one of the nicer places he'd stayed in, but at least the sheets and towels he paid extra for had actually been laundered since their last use. That alone elevated the place to the top rank in its category.

"First let me tell you that Julia is okay," Anita said. "She's in Florida with her friend, and nothing threatening has happened there. It took a few phone calls, but I even talked with her on the phone. By the way, Cassie says hello to Burpy."

"That's a load off my mind. Thanks."

"You know about Rheinhardt, don't you?"

"I do now." He didn't mention that he'd learned about it while holding someone at gunpoint.

"Have you heard about the bombing last night?"

"Bombing? Shit. Who got hit?"

"Judge Canton."

"Jesus Christ, I hate to hear that. Didn't like the guy personally, but he was fair in court."

Wheels were spinning in Schultz's head. He'd been traveling

again, hadn't caught the story, although he was sure it would have made the news broadcasts in Arizona. The latest death lent credibility to his theory, and sent shivers up his spine.

"You had quite a few cases in his court, didn't you?"

"Sure. Wharton must be crawling up Wall's butt on this. A prosecutor and a judge. You sound tired." The fatigue in Anita's voice had finally registered on Schultz.

"I've been busy. Another thing. Something you're not going to want to hear."

"I'm listening." He figured she must have told someone about their behind-the-scenes collaboration.

"Dave's in the hospital. He was outside the judge's house, doing surveillance. He got shot in the chest and neck."

Schultz took the phone away from his ear and held it against his chest. He was standing at a pay phone a couple of blocks from his hotel, and for a few moments he let the street noise wash over him. Then he put the phone back to his ear.

"Dead?"

"No. The surgery went well, but he didn't wake up afterward for a long time. We all thought he was in a coma. He's alert now, and responding. Whatever strange place he was in, he's back from it, as of a couple of hours ago. Looks like he's going to be fine, except maybe for his voice. Too early to tell on that."

"Thank God. What a relief." Schultz sighed deeply. Dave's loss would have affected him almost as strongly as his own son's. He was fiercely protective of the young detective, but he just didn't express it. It wasn't something he could tell a male coworker: *Hey, guy, I really care about you, you big teddy bear.*

"One last thing," Anita said. "You were right about the woman across the street. Good pickup on that."

"I knew she was a snoop. I kept my drapes closed, but I always thought she had X-ray vision. She saw my car stolen?"

"Yeah. Loretta Trent saw you come home, park the car, and

leave on foot. Your car was stolen by a man wearing a hat and then returned about an hour later, complete with broken headlight. The time frame fits for the hit-and-run. She didn't get a good look at the guy's face, but it wasn't for lack of trying. The hat he was wearing blocked her view, since she was looking down on him from the second floor. Lean, moves like a cat. That's all she got."

"Is old Loretta reliable, or has she got too many screws loose?" Schultz had seen the woman several times, in the second-floor window of the house across the street. She liked to spy on others in the neighborhood. Schultz didn't like it, so his habit of keeping the drapes closed on the front windows of his house all the time probably frustrated the woman.

"Oh, she's reliable, all right. She's got excellent eyesight and get this—she uses a spotting scope. And she keeps a journal of the comings and goings of her neighbors. I've already verified some of her other journal entries with people who live on the block. They're dead on."

"How'd you get her to 'fess up?" Schultz had encountered the type before. Loretta Trent had a "little vice" of spying, around which her whole life revolved. Telling the police about it would be the last thing on her mind.

"You don't want to know."

Schultz laughed, a short ironic bark. "You're probably right. I hope you didn't hurt her."

"Not physically."

He could see he wasn't going to get anything else out of Anita on that subject. He knew she had a hard edge to her, and basically he liked her that way. He saw himself in her more than in Dave, who talked tough but had a marshmallow center.

"Have you told Wall about Miss Loretta yet?"

"Just a little while ago. You're pretty much clear on the hit-and-run. Wall was relieved, to say the least. He didn't like the idea of somebody under his command freaking out like that."

During the conversation, Schultz decided that he had to trust Anita with what he knew about the recent deaths. He took a deep breath and launched into it.

"I think the recent deaths are connected, Anita. Starting with Rick's and Caroline Bussman's, and including Rheinhardt and Canton."

"No shit, Sherlock," she said.

"What?"

"Tell me something I don't know already."

"You mean you're already working on digging up past cases all the parties were involved with, looking for a revenge killer, that kind of thing?"

"Doc was way ahead of you," she said smugly. "We've even got the killer identified, we think. Doc's been out pounding the streets and making secret tape recordings."

"Holy shit!"

"Yeah, we're all kind of proud of her. Don't tell her I said that."

"Who do you think it is?"

"Elijah Ramsey. His son was executed last year. Remember the case?"

"Of course I remember the case. Man beat his kid sister to death over a wrecked car."

"Good old Dad Ramsey has vanished from the face of the earth."

"Why doesn't anybody tell me this stuff? Hell, it's not like I'm involved or anything."

"Need I remind you that you're the one who's been slightly out of touch?"

Schultz pictured himself sitting in Mandoleras's darkened living room, thinking seriously about blowing the guy away the minute he opened the door.

It wasn't a pretty picture.

"Okay, so I'm back. I want in on this."

"Don't talk to me, Boss man. I figure you got some talking to do to Doc and Wall."

"You're right," he said. He reached to hang up the phone, then pulled it back toward him. Anita was still on the line.

"Thanks, Anita, for all you've done. I won't forget it."

"You got a memory like an elephant and a prick like a mouse, ain't that what they say?"

He hung up on her, smirking. That woman had potential.

Schultz tried PJ's number first. She was out of the office, and he didn't want to try her home phone. He didn't want Thomas to pick up and have to talk to the boy right then. He dialed her cell phone number, but got the message that it was unavailable, so she'd turned it off. So he did the only thing left: he called Wall.

Fifteen minutes later, after a blistering tongue-lashing and acknowledging numerous times that he ought to be tossed out of the department on his sorry ass, he was back on the case.

Twenty-nine

PJ got to the fast-food restaurant with five minutes to spare. She'd missed lunch, so she bought a number two combo—two double cheeseburgers, no pickles, fries, and a soda. Her small square burgers came on a white paper plate, and her fries came in a cardboard box with a tiny package of salt inside. She sat at a booth next to the window. The only other customers inside were two couples, motorcyclists judging by the Harleys parked outside, sitting several booths away. There was a steady parade of vehicles through the drive-through right outside her window.

The cheeseburgers were hot, covered with diced grilled onions, and had the distinctive White Castle taste, something which has to be experienced rather than described.

As she ate, she watched the drive-up activity, wondering idly if one of the people was Cracker checking out the situation, or if he was somewhere remote like the Fiji Islands.

Thick gray smoke started to pour out from underneath the hood of a Chevy pickup in the drive-up lane. It was old, dented, and had rust along the rocker panels that reminded PJ of reddish lace edging. The driver flung the door open and raised the hood, then angrily kicked the tire. An employee glanced out the window, then sauntered outside with a fire extinguisher and sprayed the engine. He helped the irate driver push the vehicle out of line.

The lack of excitement and the relaxed pace of the employee led PJ to think vehicle fires might not be an unusual occurrence.

She ate her meal with no sign of any contact by Cracker. At two-twenty, she was about to give up and leave. The motorcyclists cleaned up their table and walked toward the door. One of the women dropped a piece of paper on PJ's table as she walked by.

Pay phone at west corner of lot, five minutes.

PJ hurried to her car and looked for the pay phone outside. It was one of the type intended to be used from a car, and fortunately it wasn't in use. She backed her car into the parking spot next to it and rolled down the window. She didn't have long to wait before the phone rang.

"Hello," she said nervously.

"It's Cracker. What can I do for you?" His voice was flat and distorted, in the same way that Eleanor's voice had been during the computer simulation. Startled, she wondered if Cracker was someone she knew personally. Would she recognize his unaltered voice?

"I need to locate a person," she said. "It's important."

Of course it is, or I wouldn't be talking to him. Get a grip.

She felt that every word she spoke to this genius would be analyzed, considered, undoubtedly recorded. She had to think before she spoke.

"I have some skill at that. Is this person a fugitive from the law?"

"No."

Technically.

"Good. If so, I wouldn't take the job."

PJ's silence asked the question for her.

"Because I'm only willing to help the police so far. I have a certain compassion for fugitives."

There was no arguing with that, given his situation. Cracker was a wanted man himself.

"I need to talk to Darla Beth Ramsey, born April fifth, nineteen fifty-three, in Springfield, Illinois." PJ gave him Darla's last known address and place of employment. He asked for her social security number, but PJ didn't know it.

"How do you plan to pay for this information?"

"I don't suppose you take credit cards?"

There was a brief pause, then eerie mechanical laughter.

"It so happens I do," he said. "Although it's usually without the owner's consent. I happen to know that your credit limit isn't high enough on either of your two cards, and that your bank balance was exactly fourteen thousand, four hundred thirty-nine dollars and twenty-nine cents as of this morning. That's checking plus money market account. You have some old Series EE savings bonds, which by the way you should cash in, since they've matured. You could get a better rate elsewhere."

It was disconcerting to hear her finances discussed and know that he had been prying into her life. But she should have expected that when she asked Merlin to broadcast the message. Having attracted Cracker's interest, she'd opened the door herself.

"What exactly is your charge? Maybe I can make installment payments."

"I'm not a used car dealer, Lucky Penny. It's cash up front. My usual fee is thirty-five thousand dollars."

It was PJ's turn to be silent. There was no way she could raise that kind of money. With the divorce, she had walked out on her old high-paying job, their house, and their savings just to retain custody of Thomas. PJ might be able to borrow it from her ex-husband, Stephen, but the thought turned her stomach.

She remembered the informal help network run by Louie, the A/V technician. There was no cash exchange there, only favors.

"You mentioned that I should bring something to trade," she said.

"So I did. You have something interesting?"

"How about the promise of a favor in the future? Anything I can do that isn't illegal."

"Hmm. Let me think about that."

PJ waited in the heat of an August afternoon. The sun was hot where it poured in the open window onto her left shoulder, and beads of sweat ran down her forehead and the back of her neck. She blinked as the salty drops rolled into her eyes. The double cheeseburgers made their presence known in her stomach. The heat and her nervous state would make her nauseated if things went on too long.

"It's a deal. One future favor for the delivery of one Darla Beth Ramsey. Don't worry, I won't ask for your firstborn son or anything like that."

"That's—"

The connection was broken, and she was left sitting there wondering what she'd gotten herself into. It was going to have to be some favor to be worth thirty-five thousand dollars.

The things I do for that man, she thought as she rolled up the window, started the car, and switched on the air-conditioning. She tried to tell herself it wasn't strictly for Schultz. There could be other lives still at stake. And anyway, it was part of her job to bring the killer to justice.

Thirty

PJ was back in the headquarters building, trying to shake off the disturbing feeling of having sold her soul. She was walking toward her office when she heard a familiar voice coming from around the corner. She quickened her step.

She came around the corner and there was Schultz, standing outside her office talking to Anita. The two of them were intent on each other, and hadn't noticed her yet. PJ's face cycled through several different emotions in succession, like an actress practicing before a mirror. By the time they turned toward her, she had regained her composure.

"Long time no see," she said evenly. "Looks like you've been lying on the beach while the rest of us were working."

She was pleased to see his hand start to rise to his sunburned head, then stop midway by a clear effort of will.

Score one for me.

"Good to be back, Doc," he said, ignoring her comment after the damage was done. "I was just telling Anita that I'm glad Dave is doing so much better. Looks like it takes more than a couple of bullets to do that guy in."

"Like one of those dinosaurs in old movies," Anita chimed in. "Had to shoot 'em right in their little pea brains to kill 'em."

"He should patent that luck of his. Could've sold some of it to Judge Canton."

PJ frowned. Leave it to the two of them to make a joke out of a serious situation. She knew it was an example of the defensive kind of humor she frequently encountered on the job, but she never seemed to get into the spirit of it herself.

She had been elated to hear of Dave's improvement, and she said so. Heads nodded in agreement.

She took a closer look at Schultz's face. "Is that a—"

"Yes," he said curtly.

Apparently he didn't want anyone to notice the blister on his nose.

"Has Anita filled you in on the hit-and-run yet?" he asked.

"No, I've been . . . out of the office," PJ said.

Just having a phone conversation with a killer. And what did you do over lunch?

Traffic flowed around them in the hallway. Frequently someone nodded to Schultz or stopped and clapped him on the back and said how glad they were he was back in the fold. PJ thought that he must know every single person in the department.

"There's something I have to ask," PJ said. Both pairs of eyes turned to her expectantly. "When you were working on the Ramsey case originally, did you consider the possibility that the victim got Jeremiah's blood on her hands when Jeremiah defended her from an attacker? That there was another person present, someone Jeremiah later tried to cover up for?"

Schultz blinked. She could see him sorting back through his memories.

"Yeah," he said. "No defense wounds on Jeremiah's arms or hands. Check the photos taken during his physical exam. All that shows up is the scratch on his shoulder. If he'd been fending off somebody who had a baseball bat, he would have shown more damage."

"Oh," PJ said. She was mollified that Schultz had an answer.

The conversation veered off into details of the bombing,

and PJ had to force herself to focus on what they were saying. Something inside her was in turmoil, and it had to do with how close Schultz was standing to her.

Anita went through the explanation about Loretta Trent, the witness who saw Schultz's car stolen.

"Ah, the busybody." PJ nodded. At least she could firmly set aside her doubts about Schultz on that score. She tried to recapture the feelings she'd had about him getting a man sentenced to death in order to further his own career. In the hallway, with his image filling her eyes and his presence raising goosebumps on her arms, those conjectures seemed far away and trivial.

"You knew about her?" Anita said.

"I caught a glimpse of her when I was at your house. I wondered if she might have seen anything."

"Nice of you to come forward about it," Schultz said sarcastically.

PJ's eyes flashed as the stress of the past few days surfaced.

"I didn't want to," PJ snapped back. "I was convinced she would confirm that you were the driver. That you did it."

The three were frozen for a moment. No one seemed to know what to say. The toilet flushed in the men's room across from PJ's office, and that broke the uncomfortable silence.

Anita punched Schultz lightly in the arm. "Well, I'll leave you two to get reacquainted."

Schultz rolled his eyes at her, and Anita walked away smiling.

"I guess we need to talk," Schultz said to PJ.

PJ folded her arms across her chest. "You might say that."

He opened her office door and gestured inside. She preceded him, and he closed the door when they were both in the small room. She turned to face him, not knowing what she was going to say. There seemed to be a white noise in her mind.

"C'mere, you," he said. He grabbed her around the waist

and pulled her toward him, wrapping his arms around her as though he thought she'd try to escape. His mouth found hers.

PJ resisted, but only briefly. His arms felt so good. She gave herself up to the kiss, melted into it, let all the emotion she'd been bottling up pour through her lips into his. She pressed the length of her body against him and thrilled to the warm delicious feeling that came over every inch of her body that was in contact with his.

Doubts? What doubts?

The first kiss was followed by many others.

Breathlessly, they pulled apart. He held her at arm's length.

"Are we done talking?" he said.

"For now," she answered. "But I want you to know I don't usually hold meetings like this."

There was a rapping on the door. They moved apart. PJ straightened her blouse, and Schultz ineffectually ran his fingers through the long strands of hair he combed over his bald spot.

"Yes," PJ said. "Come in."

Anita practically burst through the door.

"They found him," she said. "They found Elijah Ramsey. We got the son of a bitch."

Thirty-one

"Is he in custody?" PJ asked. Relief was already coursing through her body. It was over.

"I hope not," Schultz said. "We have nothing on him but a lot of suspicion."

"He's still out there. It was pure dumb luck," Anita said. "Gregor and Ullman, over in Vice, went to a hotel to talk to a contact. They're standing there, passing the time of day with the jerk, trying to get something out of him about a big transaction that was supposed to be going down soon. Who walks out of the room a couple doors down but our guy."

PJ remembered that Lieutenant Wall said he was going to work hard and fast to find Elijah and Darla, and that must have included broadcasting their pictures to every member of the department, especially those out on the street. It had paid off, at least in one case. PJ didn't think Darla was going to be found walking the streets of St. Louis.

An uneasy thought slid across the surface of PJ's elation. Darla might be dead.

"He make 'em as cops?" Schultz asked. PJ noticed that his eyes held cold sparks.

"Nope. They were cool. Ullman started a shoving match with the contact, even threw a punch at him. Must have surprised the hell out of their contact, but to Elijah it looked like a little disagreement over a payment or something. He walked right on by, and they didn't trail him."

"How sure are they that it's him?" PJ said. "The case file picture is over ten years old." Her good feeling had started to evaporate since she'd found out that Ramsey wasn't in custody, but Schultz and Anita still seemed buoyed by the news.

"Detectives have to be good with faces," Schultz said. "Really good. Their lives depend upon it sometimes."

"Oh. So you trust the quick look these two men got as they were busy scuffling with their contact."

Schultz and Anita gave each other a knowing look, a look that told PJ exactly what they were thinking: *Civilians don't know shit.*

She put her fingers up to her lips and caught the retort that sprang to mind while it was still in her mouth. It wasn't the time or place to be petty.

"Yeah, I trust their ID," Anita finally said. "No reason not to. Got a make on the vehicle, too. A rental car, nineteen ninety-four blue Hyundai, rented in the name of William Penn."

"Got a sense of humor, does he?" Schultz asked with a grim smile.

Anita nodded. "Wall's called a meeting. His office, fifteen minutes."

Schultz watched as PJ entered Wall's office. She was on time to the minute, and carried her coffee cup in one hand and a notepad in the other. She treated the whole thing like a business meeting from her old corporate job. Most likely there was a fresh pen tucked inside the notepad, and the date and time of the meeting were already written at the top of the first page.

He saw the surprise register on her face as she discovered it was standing room only in Wall's office, followed by brief indignation that no one, including himself, offered her a chair. First come, first served, was the rule of the day, regardless of gender or rank. She dropped the notepad to the floor near her feet and gripped her coffee cup with both hands, studying the people around her. Her hold on the cup wasn't quite strong enough to produce white knuckles, but it was clear that the cup wasn't going anywhere.

A good number of the faces must have been unfamiliar to her, because her gaze bounced off them quickly and continued the journey around the room. Her eyebrows slid up when she got to Ullman's bruised jaw. Ullman was scruffy looking even when he was trying to look respectable, and the discoloration on his jaw didn't help. PJ bit her lower lip in that manner she had when she was nervous.

He smiled inwardly but had no intention of easing the way for her. He might as well have stood up and shouted through a bullhorn that he was sweet on the boss.

Schultz, of course, had headed for Wall's office immediately after the announcement and claimed a chair front and center, even before Wall came to his own meeting. He was heartily greeted by everyone who arrived afterward, since word had spread that he was somewhat back in good graces. There was a good-size crowd in the office, even though it was late Saturday afternoon. Most cops put their work ahead of their personal lives, and sometimes their marriages paid the price. Like his.

Wall arrived right after PJ, his arms occupied with a large box containing a couple dozen doughnuts. He plopped the box in the middle of his desk and lifted the lid. Ullman stepped up and claimed his choice like the leader of the pack. Gregor took the next pick. Schultz selected a fat jelly-filled one, and then the rest of the people in Wall's office crowded around. PJ held her spot against the wall. He could see in her eyes that she didn't know if she was invited to the feeding frenzy.

For a shrink, she's damned unsure of herself sometimes.

Then he chastised himself. There were a lot of unwritten rules in the department, and he couldn't expect PJ to absorb them all in a little over a year.

His thoughts strayed outside Wall's office. He knew that sometime soon PJ would want to talk about Helen Boxwood. Helen was a nurse Schultz had met the previous year. He'd been freshly separated from his wife, and Helen had hit him like the proverbial ton of bricks. He'd thought he was in love with her, and had confided that to PJ in an effort to enlist her in breaking through Helen's reluctance to accept his advances. He should have kept the whole thing to himself. He had made a fool of himself over Helen, and surely PJ must wonder about his sudden change of affection. PJ probably thought she was just another rebound romance.

It was a good thing Schultz had picked up a few women's magazines to read up on that stuff. He had the terminology down.

He didn't have the slightest idea how he was going to explain his feelings for Helen, which had abruptly plummeted to the level of respect and cautious friendship from flat-out romantic pursuit. He shook his head, thinking that at his age he ought to be better at dealing with women.

He looked over at Anita and raised his doughnut to her in a salute, like honoring her with a toast. She smiled back, a little wisp of a woman with an iron rod for a backbone. Now there was someone he could deal with, because he could relate to her as he would another man.

He had no idea how he and PJ were going to handle it, the details of having a personal relationship outside work. It was uncharted territory. Would it affect them when word got around? And he didn't kid himself. He knew word would get around. For the time being, he had to put all that aside and bring the man who'd killed his son to justice.

Wall let the chatter and the munching go on for a few minutes before getting everyone's attention.

"Listen up, ladies and gents," he said. "I don't think I need to remind you how hot Wharton is on this one. You can't get much more high-profile in this town than what this killer's done. Not to mention he's hit the son of a fellow officer, and nearly killed one of our own."

The room became somber. Schultz kept his expression blank at the mention of Rick. He was aware that several people in the room were looking at him, practically crawling over his face.

"How's Witless?" Ullman asked.

"Dave's doing better than expected," Wall said. "There's a chance the tracheotomy will be permanent. That means he'll have a breathing hole at the base of his throat. There will also be physical therapy needed to regain stamina because he has diminished lung capacity." He sounded like he was repeating, word-for-word, what he'd been told by a doctor.

Wall's gaze swept the room. "I fully anticipate having him back on active duty. The department stands by officers wounded on the job. He's getting the best care there is to offer. I expect each one of you to be supportive."

"Yes, Mom," said a voice from the corner. There was laughter all around, but the point was made and taken.

Schultz produced the answering machine tape he'd taken from his house, and everyone listened to the threatening message.

He didn't die fast, you know. You think about that, Detective Schultz. You think about him tied up helpless like that, and gasping for air. Then think about what I'm going to do next. Oh, and have a nice day.

Schultz watched the horror spread over PJ's face. She didn't bother to hide it. There was something else there that he doubted if anyone could pick up but him. She was angry that he'd held the tape back from her, that he'd left St. Louis without a word to her. He had wanted to protect her, to make sure whatever evil shadow he was casting didn't fall on her. And even though he knew it had probably hurt her feelings, he'd do it all again.

Around the room, expressions were grim.

Ullman gave a firsthand account of the incident at the hotel; then Wall moved on to the follow-up situation. Photos of the rental car were handed around, and then current, although slightly blurry, photos of Ramsey. It was a profile shot.

Schultz would have liked to look directly into the eyes of his son's killer, but he figured that time would come soon.

When the recent photo of Ramsey was placed in his hands, Schultz had felt a sudden strong tug from the psychic thread that helped him seek out killers. He closed his eyes and focused inward, momentarily shutting out the discussion around him and giving himself over to the visualization. The thread leapt to life, golden and coiling, dancing in the air in front of him, stretching out from his own heart. It crossed the short distance to the photo he held in his hands and flared so brightly the light burned the inner surface of his eyelids. It was a thick fiery rope, and when it impaled the photo it burned away Ramsey's face, leaving a hole with charred, smoking edges. But it didn't stop there. It kept going, speeding away into the darkness, pulling Schultz further out into the world, until the glowing end faltered. Schultz snapped his eyes open. The photo was whole in his hands.

Jesus Christ, Ramsey is the one. He killed my son.

The certainty of it struck Schultz hard, and he struggled to keep his face impassive. He felt as though his heart had stopped beating for a moment, and a silent shout of grief reverberated in his body. When the surge of emotion passed, he puzzled over the fact that the golden cord had kept going past the photo, as though it had overshot. He put it down to the fact that he was reaching outside the room to try to locate the man physically.

"Suggestions?" Wall asked.

Schultz wondered what he'd missed. PJ could fill him in later, assuming she was still speaking to him.

"Yeah," said one of the detectives, "let's find this scum bag and cut his balls off real slow."

There was laughter, but the kind of laughter that said everybody else had been thinking the same thing.

PJ cleared her throat. "Has anyone considered the possible next targets?"

"Enlighten us," Wall said when no one responded.

PJ glanced down at her notepad on the floor. Schultz realized she had prepared some notes to speak from during those fifteen minutes since the meeting was announced, during which he'd parked his butt on a chair and cleared his mind of any useful thoughts. She decided to go on without bending over and picking up her notes, which was probably a good thing. A woman bending over in front of the crowd in Wall's office was guaranteed to elicit at least a couple of obnoxious comments even if she was forty-one and a little bottom-heavy. It wouldn't matter in the least that she had a doctorate in psychology and a glare that could cause a hard freeze in the tropics.

"The suspect has attacked Schultz, indirectly, through his son and an attempt to frame him. That was followed by the deaths of Rheinhardt and Canton. The arresting detective, the prosecutor, and the judge. He's probably working on what he perceives as a decreasing order of responsibility for the death of his son, like a score he's assigned to each person."

"You mean, Schultz gets ten points for arresting him and collecting evidence, the prosecutor gets eight points for building a case against him, the judge gets six points for presiding over that case, and so on," Wall said.

PJ nodded.

"So why am I still alive?" Schultz asked. "I'm a perfect ten."

"He's not done with you," PJ said. "You're the prime target.

He wants you to realize what's going on, that you're responsible not only for the death of his son, but for all the other deaths happening now because of your investigation years ago. He's pushing the blame off on you for all his actions." PJ looked thoughtful. "There might be some religious element here. Come judgment day, he wants to make sure all the bad stuff is on your side of the ledger, not his."

"When you say he's not done with Schultz," Wall said, "you mean there are other targets before he comes back to Schultz at the end of everything?"

"Exactly. I think the next target might be Jeremiah Ramsey's attorney, Arnold Cartwright. He was the public defender assigned to the case when Jeremiah couldn't afford a private attorney and none of his family members jumped in waving cash. After that, it's possible he might start in on members of the jury. I'm not sure how long he intends to drag this out. He's very organized, so he probably realizes he can't carry this on long enough to get all the jury members. So my guess is that he won't bother with the jury because he knows there's an excellent chance he'd be caught before he could finish. He wants closure, and that means he starts and ends with Schultz. One more killing, then Schultz."

PJ had put on her shrink hat, and everyone was listening carefully to her chilling words. She'd been right more times than wrong, and they were willing to pay attention to her expertise in her own field. It didn't hurt that her voice had gained in confidence.

"How likely is it that we've even got the right guy?" Ullman said.

"This particular combination of victims, the timing that is related to Vince Ramsey's death, Ramsey's presence here in St. Louis, his military and post-military experience with killing, the violent cruel personality that his ex-wife admits he has—those things are hard to ignore. It's as close to certainty as we're likely to get without finding Ramsey in the act."

Damn straight.

There was a buzz of conversation when she finished. Wall picked up the phone and the buzz tapered off into a low hum.

"Find out where Arnold Cartwright is," Wall said into the phone. "He needs to disappear for a while."

There were several nods in the room, including Schultz's.

"You're going to mess up Ramsey's schedule," PJ said.

"Put him off balance," Schultz said. "Off balance people make mistakes."

"That means he'll go after you in earnest," PJ said. "If he can't get at his next planned target."

"You mean killing my son and framing me for murder wasn't going after me in earnest?"

PJ's cheeks colored. "You know what I mean. Don't twist my words."

Schultz didn't react. His thoughts had already moved on. "That means I'll have to get out there and wag my tail for attention," he said.

"Like a puppy that wants to be petted," Wall said.

"Or a stripper who needs extra cash," came another response from the group.

"A prostitute on a busy corner."

"A new convict . . ."

"Enough," Wall said, cutting off the comments.

"You mean you're deliberately going to dangle Schultz in front of Ramsey?" PJ asked.

"Yes," Wall said. "We have a killer to catch. You have a problem with that?"

All eyes turned toward PJ. Schultz held her gaze. Was what they had together going to get in the way of their jobs? So soon?

"No," she said firmly. "How do we get started?"

That's my gal.

Thirty-two

Sunday morning PJ and Thomas got up early and ate a breakfast of fruit, cheese, and crackers. Megabite graciously accepted bites of cheese. The cat hopped up on one of the empty kitchen chairs and put her paws on the edge, poised there like a polite diner keeping her elbows off the table. PJ and Thomas had given up all pretense of not feeding Megabite during their own meals.

Megabite was gray tiger-striped on top, white on her belly and paws, with a band of orange fur making a circle around each leg. PJ thought about how much enjoyment the cat added to her life. Her ex-husband, Stephen, had been allergic to cats, or so he said. She had gone years without one, and vowed never to do it again.

She watched the white tip of Megabite's tail flick in metronomic appreciation as the cat pinned down a piece of cheese that Thomas had sent rolling toward her.

After breakfast she and Thomas took off for the Missouri Botanical Gardens, called Shaw's Garden by longtime residents of the city, after its original owner. She had used some of her limited funds to buy a family membership so that they could indulge themselves in a stroll around the gardens whenever they wished.

They each had their favorite spots. Thomas, much to her surprise, loved the ordered serenity of the extensive Japanese

Garden. PJ liked the profusion of blooms in the perennial beds that flanked the Linnean House. The Linnean House used to be the greenhouse of the old Shaw estate. It had huge windows that gathered light, and it was filled with fragrant camellias. It was too early in the year for the camellias to be at their best, but the perennial gardens right outside were lovely. Reflecting pools mirrored lily and lotus blossoms held grandly above the surface of the water. Morning dew was bright with trapped sunshine, like handfuls of diamonds cast over the plants. The air was smooth against her skin, and the mixed scent of the flowers was intoxicating.

PJ gave herself over to the moment. She found a bench in the sun. Later the heat would be oppressive, but in the early morning it was comforting. Her muscles relaxed and her thoughts flowed easily, like melted chocolate.

An hour later she noticed a chill. Clouds were moving in. It looked as though the sun would be hidden the rest of the day. There was a breeze stirring, possibly bringing rain. Her delightful interlude was over. Thomas appeared on cue, having used up the coins he brought with him to buy food pellets for the koi in the Japanese Garden.

PJ congratulated herself on having gotten through the first morning of Schultz serving as bait, and in such a peaceful way. She dropped Thomas off at home with the promise of an early dinner together, if she could make it.

Schultz had gone back to his house the evening before, conspicuously arriving with bags of groceries to indicate he'd be in residence for a while. He was wearing a small tracking device fastened to his chest with first-aid tape. She knew he had a gun in the house and was probably eager for a chance to use it. To her consternation, Anita had reported that he had spent most of the evening parading himself outside, barbecuing hamburgers, slapping at mosquitoes, and sipping beer in his front yard.

Ramsey had checked out of the hotel where he had been

spotted and moved to another in South County. His movements were being closely monitored by the St. Louis County Police.

She was still worried.

Ramsey was trained to kill. He was an expert in approaching by stealth. He had apparently taken Dave by surprise, and he had demonstrated that he was capable of putting together an elaborate plan.

She had given Schultz her cell phone, since his house phone was tapped and she wanted to be able to talk with him privately. So far, she'd resisted calling, but the tug was always there.

PJ decided the best way to spend the rest of the day was to refine her simulation of Eleanor's murder. During her first immersion, there had been something that bothered her, but she was unable to pin it down. A few quiet hours in the office gave her the perfect time to work on it.

She closed her office door and went through the simulation again. She came out of it convinced that she was overlooking something.

The light on her fax machine was flashing. Thinking that it was becoming a tradition that she would receive a fax every time she put on the HMD and stepped into the VR world, she went over to pick up the single sheet of paper lying in the tray.

Cracker had found Darla Ramsey. The paper contained the woman's assumed name, her address and phone number, place of employment, new social security number, and a description of the type of car she drove.

There was a cryptic typed note at the bottom.

She covered her tracks well, but she should have hired me to make her disappear. She had one weak link—a man of the cloth, no less. By the way, she has a high-quality alarm system on her house, so don't try to break

*in. You'd blow it. I'll be in touch about the favor. It could
be a while before your number comes up.*
C.

PJ tried not to think too much about the last two sentences
of the note and concentrate on the good part: Darla was within
reach.

She wondered if it still mattered. After all, Elijah Ramsey
had been located. Did it matter what Darla had to say?

She thought about that, and decided that everything she
could learn about the Ramsey family would be important. The
very fact that Darla had gone to so much trouble to hide had
to be significant.

The first thing she did was contact Merlin using a dial-up
connection. Their conversation got off to an uncomfortable
start. He didn't use his usual perky greeting.

I know you're mad at me, she typed. *You think I took advantage of you. I did, and I want you to know I feel bad about
that. But I had to, Merlin. Leo's life was on the line.*

There was a long pause, and she thought he wasn't going
to answer her. Finally words appeared on her screen.

So. You have any idea which of my "friends" is a killer?

So that's bothering you, too?

*You bet it is. I didn't actually think it would work, that
anyone would get in touch with you. I thought all my contacts
could be trusted. My confidence is shaken.*

I don't know what to say.

*<Giggle.> That's the first time I can remember that words
have failed you, Keypunch.*

She was encouraged by his light-hearted response and the
use of her nickname. *Am I back in your good graces, then?*

*No. But you're on probation. Oh, let's just skip the proba-
tion. You know I can't stay mad at you.*

I've got to go now. I just wanted you to know how helpful you've been.

In the interest of saving time and lives, I'll spare you my list this time. But the next time we talk I expect the full low-down on this thing with Leo Schultz. Do you have stars in your eyes, my dear? Are you sleeping with him yet?

Bye, Merlin.

The next thing PJ did was tape a piece of blank paper across the bottom of the fax, covering Cracker's note. She didn't especially want Wall to know her source of information, and she particularly didn't want him to see that line about the favor. She fed the sheet back through her fax and made a copy of it. She hid the original in her desk and dialed Wall's number.

Not surprisingly, he was at his desk even though it was Sunday morning.

"I need to go to Dayton," she said without preamble. "I want to talk to Darla Ramsey."

"What makes you think she's in Dayton? I've had people looking for her and they haven't come up with anything."

"I, uh, I have a source."

There was a long silence. She could visualize him doodling on a piece of scratch paper, drawing tiny animals. She'd seen the discarded sheets in his trash can. She wondered if he'd press her to reveal how she'd located Darla. Nervously she jumped into the silence.

"You don't ask your detectives to disclose their sources, do you?"

"Ordinarily, no."

But you're not a detective. She easily added on the sentence in her mind.

It was her turn to let the silence stretch out. She was sure a lot of things were running through his mind, including whether she'd done anything illegal and whether he cared.

"All right," he said. "I'll get you on the first flight out. I don't know anyone on the Dayton force, but I know somebody who does. I'll set you up. We'll do it right, get you wired. I think we've got cause."

"I don't like the idea of wearing a wire. I want to handle this my own way."

"What, your ten dollar tape recorder in your purse?"

PJ stubbornly kept her silence.

Wall sighed. "All right. But you're not going in there without backup."

"I can't just drive up to her house in a police car. She'll get spooked."

"So they'll be subtle about it."

"Lieutenant, I still don't think that's a good idea."

"Doctor, take it or leave it." He'd reached the end of his willingness to go along.

"In that case, I guess I'll take it. Your concern is touching."

"Concern, hell. I just don't want her to escape out the back door while you lumber up to the front door. She can probably smell a shrink coming."

PJ laughed. "I'll approach from downwind."

She contacted Helen Boxwood, who was wonderfully free that evening and volunteered to stay overnight with Thomas, no questions asked, if PJ didn't make it back in time. She phoned Thomas and canceled their dinner together. He didn't seem upset with the substitution of Helen, blurting out that she would bring over great movies on tape for them to watch together. When asked exactly what movies, he got evasive. She remembered that Helen once said she enjoyed R-rated police thrillers, so it was no wonder Thomas clammed up. It wasn't the type of entertainment PJ would have chosen, but in the spirit of her new attitude toward him, she didn't press it.

She caught a ride to Lambert Airport with a couple of rook-
ies who didn't mind stopping at the hospital so that she could
take some flowers to Dave. He was asleep, so she quietly left
the flowers, patted his arm, and left.

Thirty-three

Cut looked out the window of the hotel, checking the logical vantage points for surveillance. His room was on the third floor, with a view of the parking lot as he'd requested. He had just finished watching local news. There had been a segment on the hit-and-run which indicated that Schultz was cleared of suspicion, although police weren't releasing details of why he was cleared. The item hadn't gotten much coverage in the first place, so he was surprised to see Schultz's mug on the tube.

Then he figured it out. Schultz had left town, or so Cut thought, right after getting the message on his answering machine. Cut assumed he'd fled in blind fear. The fact that he was back meant he'd been ordered to serve as the sacrifice to bring Cut out into the open. They'd be making Schultz as visible as possible, probably have him dancing under the Arch downtown in a tutu any minute.

Most likely the police had not only figured out the pattern but located Cut and had him under observation. Without observation, they'd practically be throwing Schultz's life away. Cut could come out of nowhere and vanish just about as fast, and they must be aware of that by now. If the police weren't trailing him, they wouldn't be able to get to him in time to stop a lightning attack on Schultz. Even with someone on his tail, Cut knew he stood a fair chance of getting the task done and escaping, as long as he only had to do it once.

A few more minutes of thought and a couple of peppermint candies led him to believe that the police probably assumed Arnold Cartwright was next on the hit list. That accounted for the timing. That was why they were waving Schultz around like a flag made out of red underwear, to divert Cut from another civilian target.

It was a wasted effort, because Cartwright wasn't even on the list. Wasted.

Cut wondered how they'd found him, then realized his picture would be out on the street, and the clerk in his previous hotel had most likely turned him in for money.

That blue sedan in the southwest quadrant of the parking lot—the driver had pulled in an hour ago but hadn't gotten out of the car. That had to be one of them. And if there was one in view, there were probably three or four hidden. Just like cockroaches. It didn't make things easy for Cut, but he never expected to set his feet on the easy path anyway.

He felt a little stab of liking for Schultz, who was obviously following orders to return and had conquered his fear to do so. That was an admirable thing to do, but it wasn't going to earn him a pardon.

Cut propped himself up with pillows on the bed to watch TV. He didn't like being stuck in his room, even for a little while, because the one thing he hated most to waste was time.

He consoled himself with the thought that by this time tomorrow Schultz would be dead.

like the fairgrounds that attracted events from nearby counties and the placid, at least in August, Great Miami River that Interstate 75 crossed. There were other rivers in town. She didn't catch the other names, but had the impression that there must be a lot of bridges. He seemed to want to treat her like a tourist, so she obliged and asked the usual questions about what made the town distinctive. It seemed Dayton had a decidedly military flavor, with Wright-Patterson Air Force Base on the edge of town and the Air Force Institute of Technology soaking up young talent.

Darla lived just outside the city of Dayton, in a southeast suburb called Oakwood. Rob drove her past the house. It was a typical suburban ranch—brick front, two-car garage, evergreen bushes planted under the front windows, and a shade tree in the center of the lawn. Nothing distinguished it from the others on the block, and PJ was sure that was exactly what Darla had in mind. There was no car in the driveway.

"Do you know if she's home?"

Rob slurped on the soda he'd bought for himself. "Yeah. She went to church this morning, got back around noon. No visitors. She's alone in the house, as far as we know."

He circled the block and pulled up to the curb a few houses away. It was just as hot and humid in Dayton as it had been in St. Louis. There was a small group of kids down the block writing with sidewalk chalk, and the buzz of a lawnmower running somewhere out of sight, but everyone else was inside staying cool. It was eerily similar to Libby's neighborhood in Jefferson City.

PJ took a deep breath and reached for the door handle to let herself out of the car. Rob put his hand on her arm.

"I did a little reading up on this after my dad called. He works for the SLPD, you know."

Lieutenant Wall had said he knew someone who was with the Dayton Police. Evidently that was Rob's father. She wondered about this father-son, and more rarely, father-daughter, thing she kept running into in law enforcement. Did children so admire their parent's line of work that they wanted to go into it themselves, or was there pressure? With more women in law enforcement, would there be a similar pattern in the future of the children of female officers entering law enforcement? The psychologist in her was stirred, and she filed away the thought. Research and publishing hadn't been on her plate for some time, but if she got the chance, that would make an interesting long-term study.

She realized Rob was staring at her, expecting some answer. "Uh, how was that again? I'm sorry, my thoughts strayed."

He frowned at her, and she saw a young Schultz in the making. "This isn't a time for scattered thoughts, Dr. Gray. You'd better focus real tight on this. I said, are you carrying?"

"I don't suppose you mean a purse?"

The frown deepened, and his brow wrinkled. "A weapon. You do have a weapon?"

"I left in a hurry," she said. "No time to pack."

The sarcasm flew right over his head. He reached underneath his seat and removed a handgun.

"You are qualified, right? I checked out a .38 for you, just in case you came unprepared."

It didn't seem like the time to admit that she had never gotten around to the weapons qualification course Wall had urged her to take.

"Uh, sure."

She took the gun and tucked it into her purse with what she hoped were confident moves. Rob's face reflected no suspicion. He assumed anyone referred by his dad came with built-in credibility. Sweet, but gullible.

No harm done. I'll just return the thing when I'm finished.

"There's another officer watching the rear of the house from the next block over. You can see right through the backyards to her back door. If you get in a bind, make a dash for either door, or fire a shot if you absolutely have to. We'll be in there fast."

He was starting to spook her. It had occurred to her that talking to Darla could be dangerous. She knew little about the woman, except that Darla would almost certainly be upset right off the bat that someone had been able to find her. The news reporter spiel probably wouldn't work.

"Okay. Got it," PJ said, building up her own confidence. She left the car and walked down the block. She had a momentary panic when Rob passed her in the car and didn't even glance her way. She'd thought he was going to remain where he was, but he'd driven off to park somewhere less obvious.

Doubts built, and she slowed her pace, so it seemed that even the dense, humid air was keeping her from reaching the house. What made her think she could do this? Why hadn't Wall sent someone more experienced? Someone who wasn't thrown off balance by the weight of the gun in her purse?

Because I can do it. Because I should be the one to do this, for Leo Schultz.

She squared her shoulders and went to the front door. There was no doorbell in sight, so she knocked with all the confidence she could muster. Not long ago she had been standing on Libby Ramsey's front steps, and that had turned out well enough.

The door opened. A thrill went through PJ when she recognized Darla. The years hadn't treated her well, though. She was as slight as a bird, in contrast to her well-muscled mother. Thin legs stuck out from bright yellow oversize shorts. A T-shirt with an eye-catching stain in the region of Darla's navel covered sagging breasts that swung gently without the support of a bra. She had short hair in a choppy cut that hugged her skull. Watery gray eyes peered at PJ from a face that was sunken on the lower half, the lips formless and wrinkled. She had no teeth.

PJ had to remind herself that Darla was only four years

older than her own age. The woman could have passed for sixty-five or more, except for the startling bottled red color of her hair.

PJ put a welcoming smile on her face. "Mrs. Archer? Nadine Archer?" She figured she'd start out with the name Darla had assumed.

"I wasn't expecting company," the woman answered hesitantly. Her voice was slurred, and her chin flapped almost comically as she spoke. "You're not selling anything, are you? If you are, I'm not interested."

The door began to close. PJ had only moments to read the situation, and she determined that the best approach was a direct one. She stuck her foot in the rapidly narrowing space and was rewarded with a sharp pinch. The woman pushed a little harder, and seemed perplexed that her door wouldn't close.

"My name is Penelope Lakeland. I want to talk about your brother Jeremiah," PJ said. "May I come in?"

There was a soft intake of breath. The woman's eyes darted across PJ's face like the hummingbirds she'd seen that morning at the Botanical Garden. Had that been only a few hours ago? Everything was moving so fast, sliding loose like an avalanche, and Schultz was in its path.

"Did Libby send you?" Her voice was barely audible.

"No."

The gray eyes slid shut. PJ was reminded of a rabbit pinned down by the shadow of a bird of prey.

"Come in," she said. "Give me a few minutes to make myself presentable. You can wait inside out of the heat, though."

"Thank you." PJ tried to make her voice warm and supportive, and her presence in Darla's front room nonthreatening. The gun in her purse swung against her hip as she moved, and PJ nearly yelped at the sudden surprising feel of it.

The house was stuffy, and not much cooler than the outdoors. The air-conditioner was running, because she could feel air moving, but it was just barely cool on her skin. The living room smelled sharply of cigarette smoke, even with the air-conditioning circulating the air. It reminded her of a tobacco shop PJ had once ventured into to buy a pipe for a friend from her old life in Denver. In fact, the tobacco shop had smelled better.

She gingerly seated herself on a green velvet upholstered couch. Everything in the room—the couch, the draperies, the carpet—had absorbed the smell, and there was a dirty brown film on the walls, which might have originally been white. Even the lampshade was tinted brown. There was an oil painting on one wall behind PJ, a tapestry with a Chinese scene on the adjacent wall, and a simple wooden cross hanging over the doorway to the kitchen. The painting and tapestry would have been attractive, but the colors were dulled from the smoke film. An overflowing ashtray sat on an end table next to a recliner chair that faced a small TV. Although the room was dusted, vacuumed, and uncluttered except for the ashtray, the smoky overlay gave the impression it hadn't been cleaned in years. By the time the woman returned almost fifteen minutes later, PJ's eyes were burning, and she was certain her clothing and hair had taken on the smell.

The personal transformation was remarkable. "Mrs. Archer" had put on beige tailored slacks and a short-sleeved blouse in crisp white. A gold cross nestled at the base of her throat. Her lower face was filled out and defined by her dentures, her short hair neatly combed, and lipstick added a little color to her face. She smiled, showing the tips of clean white teeth with no smoker's stain. PJ registered that she was a woman who cared about her appearance even though she didn't have much to work with. That was something PJ could relate to.

She settled into the recliner across the room and shook out a cigarette from a pack for PJ, who politely declined. Shrugging, she took the cigarette herself and lit it. She inhaled deeply and sent the smoke out her nostrils. She slid the lighter back into her pants pocket and placed the pack of cigarettes close at hand on an end table.

"Would you like something to drink? I usually have a beer after lunch."

PJ shook her head no, then regretted it. The woman's face flashed disappointment. PJ had missed an opportunity to connect with her.

"Well, then, what can I do for you?"

"I'm looking for Darla Ramsey," PJ said. The direct approach had gotten her in the door, so there was no reason to change. "I have reason to believe that's you."

A thin stream of smoke traveled up toward the ceiling. Tension grew as PJ held onto eyes that showed no trace of the earlier indecision. PJ had indeed caught her off guard, but now all the sentries were on duty. Probably PJ had been let in the front door so that the woman could determine just how much the brash intruder knew.

"Nope," she said with a face as closed as a turtle inside its shell. "You've got the wrong person."

PJ unzipped her purse, and saw the woman tense out of the corner of her eyes. While reaching for the copy of the fax Cracker had sent, she switched on her tape recorder. She read the fax aloud. The woman smoked impassively during the recitation of bare facts about Darla's life, then stubbed out her cigarette.

"Darla and I used to be friends," she said. "She lived here for a while, but we had a disagreement and she moved out. I haven't seen her in a couple of years."

"I don't believe you," PJ said. "Why did you ask if Libby sent me?"

"She told me that someone named Libby might come after her some day, and if I knew what was good for me, I'd shoot her on sight."

The words were said in a matter-of-fact way that sent shivers racing down PJ's arms to her fingertips. She thought about the gun in her purse, and she wondered if the temperature in the room had suddenly dropped, because goosebumps were forming on her arms.

"I have Darla's picture," PJ said. "It's you. There's no doubt. I just want to talk to you. I mean you no harm."

"You by yourself?"

"No." *And if I was, I certainly wouldn't tell you.*

"Sure I can't get you a beer or something?"

"No." There were knives in the kitchen, at the very least.

Realization burst on PJ during the awkward moment that followed. It was the thing she'd been missing during the simulation. Her mind had been working on it as background processing, and had finally come up with an answer to the question that had bothered her. When PJ had played the role of Jeremiah in the simulation, the victim, Eleanor, used her balled-up fists to strike Jeremiah's arm to get him to drop the baseball bat. The computer developed that physical action based on the postmortem injuries to Eleanor's hands, data that PJ had entered.

Balled fists. Yet there was blood on the victim's hands.

There were scratches on Jeremiah's left shoulder, photographed, measured, and described in the case file. The blood clearly came from the scratches, because he had no other breaks in his skin at the time he confessed and submitted to a physical exam.

But there had been no mention of skin and blood cells under Eleanor's fingernails. Her nails were short and very clean. That was a fact of the postmortem exam. How did the girl draw blood with her closed fists?

She could have caused bruises, certainly. But deep scratches? Impossible.

Involuntarily, PJ looked down at the fingernails of the woman across from her. They were long, well-cared-for, and painted with a clear polish. They took on the look of talons.

"Jeremiah didn't kill Eleanor, did he?" PJ asked, her voice trembling.

"Haven't the slightest idea what you're talking about. I think you'd better leave."

"Did you kill her? Or was it Libby or Elijah?"

The woman reached for another cigarette and then slipped her hand into her pocket.

PJ reacted to the movement as a threat. She reached into her open purse and drew out the gun. Gripping it tightly in both hands, she pointed it at the woman.

"You are Darla, aren't you? You might as well admit it."

"Yes, damn it. How the hell did you find me?" The cold eyes flared with a hateful light.

The presence of the gun seemed to make Darla angry, not fearful. PJ's own fear skyrocketed, and her finger started to squeeze the trigger. It seemed as though her body wanted to fire the gun and call for help. She pictured Rob circling the block outside, and another officer watching the back door. The images of police presence calmed her down and stopped the motion of her finger. She took a couple of deep breaths, and her rationality returned from its brief vacation.

"It wasn't easy," PJ said. "You did a good job of disappearing."

"You a reporter, then? I wish that child had never been born."

"I'm not a reporter. I'm with the police in St. Louis." She saw Darla stiffen. "People are dying, Darla, and there's a connection to your brother's execution. I need to know the truth to stop the killing."

"Can I light my cigarette now?"

"Sure," PJ said. "Slowly."

Darla's hand slowly withdrew the lighter from her pocket. She pressed the cigarette to the flame and sucked in gratefully. PJ tensed, half expecting Darla to toss the cigarette lighter at

her as a distraction. Instead, the woman placed it in easy reach
next to the pack of cigarettes on the end table.

"What the hell do I care about the truth?" Darla said. "It's
over and done with as far as I'm concerned."

"Maybe you should care, because I'm holding this gun on
you, and I'm prepared to use it."

There was a short bark of a laugh. Darla smiled grimly and
locked her eyes onto PJ's.

PJ felt the challenge as a physical force, stabbing out and
pinning her to the couch cushions. If she relented, she'd get
nothing from Darla. She thought about Schultz and the others
that might still die, and then gave as good as she got.

Darla was the first to look away. "So what do you want to
know, anyhow?"

On the offensive, PJ leaned forward, still keeping the gun
aimed at Darla's midsection. "Everything," she said. "I want
to know everything, starting with which one of you killed
Eleanor."

"Wasn't me. I had no reason to."

"Maybe you should go back to the beginning."

Darla puffed and thought. "I suppose the beginning," she
said, "was back when Jeremiah grew some hair on his balls."

It took a lot of self-control not to react to the odd statement.
Darla showed no sign of continuing, so PJ raised the tip of
the muzzle so that it pointed at Darla's head.

"I think it started when he was fifteen. Yeah, right about
then. He'd go to Mama's room at night, and it wasn't to fluff
her pillow or take her a glass of milk, like she said. She must
have thought I was plumb ignorant. Good God, I was thirteen
then myself. I'd had a boy's hands on me."

"You mean Libby and Jeremiah were lovers?" PJ's eyes
were wide.

"Well, I'm not sure Mama had love on the brain, but Jeremiah, he was like a puppy, following her around. The fool
thought he was in love with her, and she encouraged him.

Later on, she just came right out with it. She said Pop was away all the time and she needed a man in her bed. Should have looked around down at the bowling alley. Could have had her pick there, but she wanted something a little closer to home."

"Then Eleanor wasn't Jeremiah's sister," PJ said, following the train of thought that was chugging through her mind. "She was his daughter by Libby."

"Say, you catch on fast," Darla said. Her mouth twisted into a sarcastic grin. "They must be getting a better grade of police officer these days than when Eleanor got killed. Anyway, I guess Mama was just carrying on her family tradition. Pop told me once that she'd spent a lot of time squirming underneath her own old man since she was ten years old."

"Who knew about it? Did Elijah know?" PJ pictured Elijah in a towering rage, cuckolded by his own son, and taking out his anger on the product of that incestuous union.

"Pop didn't know who the father was, but he knew it wasn't him. He was overseas when the seed was planted. Mama told him she'd had an affair and dared him to make anything of it."

"So Eleanor was raised as Elijah's daughter. That's why she was so much younger than the other two children in the family."

Darla's face softened. "You'd think Pop would have hated her, the way she was brought into the world. But he loved that girl like his own. I guess he figured it wasn't her fault who her mama spread her legs for."

"So he wouldn't have killed her."

"She grew up fiery, that girl," Darla said, evading the question. "Certainly didn't get it from Jeremiah. It got even worse when she found out her true beginnings."

PJ lowered the gun and put it in her lap. She didn't want to stop the flow of words. Once Darla got started, it seemed she wanted to tell the story. There had been no one to tell for years. No one safe to tell, at least. Anyway, she was across the room from Darla. Even if Darla made a sudden lunge for the weapon, PJ would have time to raise it and fire.

"Who told her? Did you?"

"I didn't think it would be good for her to know. Some things just ought to be left on the inside. But Mama and Pop got into a fight one night, and they were yelling about it. I think it started over money. They didn't fight about much else, 'cause Pop just gave in on everything else. But he couldn't stand to see a penny spent when it could have been saved. It came out that Mama and Jeremiah were still doing it, even though Pop was home more and more. I don't think Jeremiah was the one asking for it, but he just couldn't say no even though he was torn up about it. Eleanor heard everything. She was thirteen or fourteen then. Hell of a thing to find out."

"Jeremiah never married," PJ said. "At least not that the police know about."

Darla snorted. "Nope, he didn't. I see what you're getting at. If he'd gotten married, maybe he could have broken away. I think he was too ashamed about what he'd done to look at other women. Guess he figured he was ruined that way."

Darla stabbed her cigarette into the ashtray and stood up. Alarmed, PJ grabbed for the gun.

"I'm going in the kitchen to get me a beer," Darla said. "You can follow along waving that gun, or you can sit here. Suit yourself."

PJ nodded toward the kitchen. It was a risk, but also a way to express confidence that she and Darla were working together. Darla was back in less than a minute. She had three cans of beer. She offered one to PJ, and PJ took it. She popped the top and tipped back the can for a big swallow, turning her head to keep an eye on Darla, who was watching critically. The psychologist in her said that she was building a trusting relationship with her client. The rest of her simply wanted a beer. She hadn't had a beer in years, and the taste hit her

strongly, like the first time she'd gulped a beer down as an
eager thirteen year old—the same age as her son was now.

She wondered if Thomas had ever had a beer.

"Thanks," PJ said, and meant it.

Darla plopped back down in the recliner and opened one
of the two beers she'd fetched for herself.

"I don't know why I'm telling you all this," she said. "I
guess it's because it can't do any harm after all this time.
Eleanor's long in her grave, Jeremiah's gone, Mama and Pop
don't live together anymore, and I haven't heard my real name
spoken in years."

There was nothing PJ could say to that, so she nodded and
took another swallow of beer.

"It's my turn to ask a question now," Darla said. "You said
at the beginning that people were dying and there was a connection to Jeremiah's execution. Care to explain that?"

Darla looked at her shrewdly, and PJ knew that there was
a keen intelligence behind those gray eyes, no matter what
outward appearance Darla might make or how casually she
might ask questions.

"You don't watch the news much, do you?"

Darla shrugged.

"Jeremiah's sentence was carried out in July a year ago.
On the very same day this year, at least we think it was the
same day, the son of the detective on that case was killed in
a way that simulated a gas chamber execution. Since then, the
prosecuting attorney and the judge have been killed. A four-
year-old girl who had nothing to do with the original case is
also dead, her life tossed away in an attempt to frame the
detective. A man who works for me was shot twice while
trying to protect the judge. Jeremiah's lawyer might be next.
The detective is certainly on the list."

PJ stopped to take a few calming breaths. "It looks to us
like Elijah is the killer. I'm here to learn anything I can about
the Ramsey family that will help us stop the killing."

"And?"

"And what?"

"And what is your personal involvement, Ms. Lakeland, if that's your real name? There's a fire in you about this, finding me and all."

There was a give-and-take developing between the two women, and PJ knew she couldn't expect to do all the taking.

"The detective," PJ said. Her lips were tightened into a line, challenging the woman to take the questioning a step further. To her relief, Darla simply nodded.

"My turn," PJ said. "I ask you again: Why did you think Libby sent me? The first time you answered that question, you hadn't even admitted to being Darla."

There was a long pause, and PJ didn't think Darla was going to answer her.

"Eleanor liked her big brother," Darla said. "Especially after she found out he was actually her daddy. She wanted to do something for him. She wanted to get Libby to leave him alone. Release him from the incest so he could make a life for himself. When she got pregnant by Clarence, she saw an opportunity."

"What opportunity? Did Clarence really love her, by the way?"

"Oh, yeah. The two of them were good for each other. They would have made it out, away from the family and everything. But Eleanor wanted to help Jeremiah, kind of like a parting gift before she took herself out of the family's affairs. So she thought up a way to blackmail Libby into letting go. She told Libby that unless Libby let Jeremiah alone starting right then and there, she was going to announce to the whole world that Elijah had molested her and that he was the father of the baby inside her. On top of that, she was going to say that Elijah molested children at the Wee Belong centers, where he sometimes worked as a handyman. At the very least, it would have meant the end of the business."

"Holy cow."

"Holy shit is more like it. Another beer?"

PJ shook her head. "So both Elijah and Libby had reason to want Eleanor to shut up."

"Jeremiah, too," Darla said. "Don't forget that he loved Mama. He wouldn't want to see her hurt." She blew smoke up toward the ceiling. "Such is the power of love."

"What about you? How did you stand in all of this?"

"Me? I just wanted out. Way out. If you had a family like that, would you want to hang around?" Darla lit another cigarette with the one she had smoked nearly all the way down. "When Eleanor got herself killed, it wasn't much of a surprise to me. I was already planning to get out, and that was one hell of a motivator. I stayed for the trial 'cause I didn't want the police thinking I was running away out of guilt."

"None of this came out at the trial," PJ said. "Why didn't you open up then?"

Darla gazed at her in silence, and PJ answered her own question. To tell everything would have made Darla as vulnerable as Eleanor. All she could do was keep quiet and hope to take herself out of the circle of danger.

"How do you know all this, anyway?" PJ asked.

"A fair question. I was born with good ears and a lot of common sense," Darla said. "I still got 'em both. Besides, Eleanor liked to confide in her big sister. She and I were close. I knew she was pregnant practically before she figured it out herself."

"Why are these killings happening now, years after Jeremiah's conviction? Why didn't all this erupt after the sentencing?"

"I guess nobody ever thought he'd really die, that he'd get out on appeal or get a life sentence instead. Mama and Pop loved Jeremiah, you know, although they may have picked strange ways of showing it. I suppose I did, too, in a beaten puppy way."

"Did he really do it? Kill his own daughter?"

"I'll be damned if I know," Darla said. "What difference does it make now, anyway? He died for the crime already. All I want is to be left alone." Her expression closed up, and PJ felt she was hiding something.

"It makes a lot of difference to me. Somebody is taking revenge for Jeremiah's death, and a person I care a great deal about is swept up in it." PJ put her hand on the gun in her lap, making it clear that she wasn't going to put up with lies or withheld information. She saw Darla pick up on the threat. "The man I care about is not going to pay the price for the sickness in your family."

"Sickness. Well, I guess you could put it that way. A bit unkind, but what the hell."

PJ let the silence drag out, but didn't yield a bit. Tension crackled between the two women like lightning along power lines.

"Shit," Darla said finally. "There's one more thing."

Darla stood up again, and PJ came alert immediately. She stood up to face Darla. The gun fastened itself on the woman's chest. PJ wondered if she'd really pull the trigger.

"Take it easy, Ms. Lakeland. You want your answers or not?"

PJ thought of Schultz waiting around for a killer to make a move against him, and her eyes flashed with determination. "Yes. Just tell me what you're going to do before you do it."

"I'm going to my bedroom to get something out of my closet."

"Something?"

"A letter. Jeremiah wrote me a letter from death row. I never opened it, but you might want to."

PJ's heart and hopes soared. Jeremiah's own words might make sense of the tangled mess of the Ramsey family relationships. She followed Darla into the bedroom and stood by nervously while the woman rummaged around in some boxes on the shelf in the closet. PJ watched closely, knowing that people sometimes kept guns in that kind of location.

True to her word, Darla came up with a sealed business-size envelope. She gave it to PJ, who inspected it.

"I thought letters that convicts wrote were read by prison officials before they were sent out," PJ said. "How come this one still looks like it has the original seal?"

"Turn it over. You'll see there's no postmark. Jeremiah gave the letter to the prison chaplain and he passed it on to me privately, like a last wish thing. The chaplain probably figured it was a confession, and confession was good for the soul." Darla snorted, sending plumes of cigarette smoke out of her nostrils. "Nobody's read it."

"You weren't curious what your own brother had to say before he was executed?"

She shrugged. "I suppose I already knew what was in it, or maybe I just didn't want to find out."

Back in the living room, PJ slipped the envelope into her purse, along with the gun. She turned off the tape recorder, too. To her chagrin, the off button made an audible click.

"Got it all on tape, I see," Darla said. "Well, what the hell. You really from the police?"

"Yes."

"I'm going to ask you for something." Darla's eyes showed the cold fire PJ had seen earlier. "I'm going to disappear again. Don't come after me. You got everything you need from me."

"I can promise you that if anybody finds you again, it won't be me." PJ started to walk out the door. She felt Darla's hand on her arm, a delicate but remote touch, like cold mouse feet.

"Good luck with your man," she said.

Thirty-five

Schultz was restless. He'd gotten word that Elijah Ramsey was holed up in a motel room. The bastard was probably sitting around eating Doritos, sucking up Cokes from the vending machines, and watching HBO. Schultz wanted to make something happen, and he didn't think he'd do it by being a prisoner in his own house.

There was no telling what Elijah's timetable was. He could have hired somebody to watch Schultz's house and let him know when the rabbit was out of the burrow. Schultz thought about the woman across the street, with the spotting scope. He wondered if she had any debts she needed paid off.

Strolling into his living room, he opened the drapes that faced the street. He stood there for a few minutes looking out, aware that he was a good target for a sharpshooter, and he had no doubt that Elijah fit that bill. When he was sure the lady across the street had gotten a long look, he left the house by the front door, walking in a leisurely fashion down his front walkway to his resurrected Vega. The car was so dusty he couldn't tell where the dust ended and the shit-brown paint color began. He'd moved the car out of the garage that faced the alley behind his house and parked it at the curb. A good thunderstorm or two would remove the dust, and Schultz was content to wait. He'd never been one for wasting labor on car washing when nature could do the job for him.

He'd been forced to use his own old, unreliable—but paid for—car since the one assigned to him by Vehicles still hadn't been returned after the hit-and-run. Most likely he'd never see that faded red-orange Pacer again. He couldn't decide if that was cause for celebration or not. He'd grown accustomed to it.

He was wearing a summer-weight sport coat that covered his shoulder holster but didn't completely conceal the outline. On his belt was a small pouch that held PJ's cellular phone. The tracking transmitter taped to his chest itched.

Every inch the modern cop, he thought.

In a little while, the itching would get worse as sweat worked its way around and under the tape on his chest. He knew from past experience it would hurt when it was ripped off, too. He blocked out the whole idea.

Schultz didn't have a destination, but he figured that moving around might jar Elijah into action, if he was having Schultz watched. If not, then at least Schultz wouldn't spend the day cooped up.

After reintroducing himself to the joy of driving a stick shift with a reluctant second gear, he ended up at the art museum in Forest Park. He supposed he'd been followed by a police tail, but he hadn't been able to pick it up in his rearview mirror. He could barely see anything out of the mirror because the back window was so dirty, so there could have been a tail right behind him in a Mack truck and he might have missed it.

The art museum was a grand old building, at least from the front. There was a modern wing, but Schultz liked the original part best. He climbed the steps and looked out over Art Hill, where kids sledded in the winter, then sat down in the shade, feeling the cold stone of the steps on his rump. A slight breeze stirred the long hairs that worked overtime trying to cover his bald spot. It was more comfortable sitting there than driving around in the Vega, which did not list air-conditioning among its few amenities. A car went by which he thought might have contained a couple of detectives, but it didn't stop. He figured that once they'd gotten a line of sight on him and verified he was okay, they'd rely on the transmitter to keep track of him until he made a major move again.

No one seemed to be paying any special attention to him. Older, slightly disheveled guys like himself—Schultz knew what kind of impression he made at a quick glance—didn't merit a second look from most people.

Of course, they don't know the sexual dynamo on the inside.

He chuckled to himself and started girl-watching. The roster in his fantasy harem could use a little shoring up.

Twenty minutes later, the sun had crept over to his spot, and he pushed himself up to avoid sitting in the direct sunlight. The top of his head was still a little sensitive. Pain shot through his left knee as he rose, reminding him that he'd been negligent about taking his arthritis medicine since he got back from Tucson.

Poking around the grounds of the museum, Schultz found a path that connected to the hiking trail system in the park. Even though he looked out of place on the trail in his sport coat and long pants, he turned onto it anyway. It looked like an ideal place for an assault, and that's what he was doing out there, wasn't it?

Shortly the trail wound its way into the woods. Sunlight filtered through the leaves and dappled the ground under his feet, making a spotted pattern. He imagined he was walking along the spine of a huge leopard.

Twice, joggers passed him. A lone man, sweating, lost in the music that played into his ears. Two young women in halter bras and shorts running together, carrying on a smooth, lilting conversation in spite of their exertion.

He felt the presence behind him moments before he felt the gun in his back.

"Walk with me," a vaguely familiar voice said. "Don't turn

around, and don't try anything funny. I don't want to shoot you out here, but I will if I have to."

He moved forward, walking in step with the person behind him. His right hand edged inside his coat, toward the holster. He hesitated, knowing that if he resisted now, all he could smack on the person was a mugging charge. He was going to have to let things get a little further along, and hope that he could be extricated before he ended up a corpse.

He'd known the moment would come, but now that it was here his stomach was doing flip-flops and his heart was pounding so hard he felt it might break loose from his chest and gallop down Art Hill without him.

The muzzle pressed hard against the small of his back. "Hands at your sides."

The voice clicked—he recognized it. He stopped suddenly, surprised. Despite what he'd been told, he turned slowly to face his assailant.

"Hello, Libby," he said.

She whacked him on the side of the head with the gun, and he went sprawling onto the leopard's back.

Thirty-six

When PJ got to the airport in Dayton, she checked in for her flight and then found a pay phone. She called the cellular phone she'd given Schultz.

The call didn't go through. The phone was turned off.

Apprehensive, but thinking that most likely Schultz was a techno-idiot and had hit the wrong button, she called Wall. He reported that Schultz had left home and was being followed at a distance using the radio tracker. He had gone to the art museum. A drive-by had verified that all was well—the dirty old man was scoping out the young things in the park. Elijah hadn't budged from his digs, so there was no cause for alarm.

"I'm not so sure about that," PJ said nervously. She relayed to him what she had learned about the Ramsey family. She didn't mention her use of the gun to threaten Darla. She had a feeling that was not an approved interrogation technique. "I have the tape recording and the letter in my purse," she said.

"Don't fool with the envelope," Wall said. "We'll want to check it for fingerprints, see if it was really written by Jeremiah. You should have turned it over to the Dayton police. They could have bagged it up properly."

"Too late now," she said, annoyed with his attitude. "My flight leaves in a few minutes."

She was also irked that Wall hadn't said a word about a job well done.

"I think you should have someone make personal contact with Schultz," she said. "What I've uncovered casts doubt on Libby, too. Maybe someone in Jefferson City could check on her whereabouts."

"That's reasonable, given what you've just told me about the family. We'll take care of things here. You go directly home when you get back in St. Louis. I'll send Anita by to pick up the letter."

"How's Dave?"

"Ornery." She heard a smile in his voice.

"See you soon."

The flight was uneventful. She took a cab home from the airport. It was almost six o'clock, and the evening brought no relief from the heat. The two flights in such a short period of time had tired her out, and she was emotionally drained from the interview with Darla. Helen Boxwood arrived shortly after PJ did. Helen hadn't heard from PJ, so she had come over to spend the night in the house with Thomas, as arranged earlier in the day. PJ invited her to stay for dinner and ordered a jumbo pizza delivered, thinking that pizza had become a major food group for the Gray family.

With satisfied hunger and the smell of green pepper and onion lingering in the air, Helen and Thomas retired upstairs to watch the videos Helen had brought. Megabite trailed after them, in hopes of something more appetizing coming her way than a leftover slice of veggie pizza. Left alone on the main floor of the house, PJ started sorting through her thoughts.

Foremost in her mind was the conviction that she wasn't going to surrender that enticing letter from Jeremiah without reading it first.

She got out the letter and, wearing gloves, carefully unsealed the envelope using the time-honored steam method. After thinking back over her conversation with Wall, she was sure she hadn't mentioned that the letter was still sealed. The letter was several pages long, and she didn't have time to read and study it, so she loaded it into her fax machine to make a copy. While the pages were slowing feeding through, she erased the last portion of the interview tape, the part where Darla talked about the sealed envelope. It was almost at the end, anyway, so there wasn't much to erase. While doing that, she realized that there was ample documentation of her use of the gun on the tape. She couldn't possibly erase all references, or the tape would have suspicious gaps. She sighed. She'd have to take whatever Wall doled out about it.

Once she had the letter copied, she put the original back in the envelope and tucked in the flap. Microscopic examination of the envelope would reveal traces of adhesive, showing that it had been sealed. But she expected the situation to be resolved by that time. She had a strong feeling that things were going to move fast.

Slipping off her gloves, she folded the copy as compactly as she could and put it in her pants pocket where she could have access to it later. Her loose T-shirt covered the slight bulge. Anita had called, verifying that PJ had gotten in from the airport, and said she was on her way over to pick up the letter. PJ didn't want to be caught with the copied pages spread over her kitchen table when Anita knocked at the door. With the copy safely settled in her pocket, PJ gave herself over to worry about Schultz.

It wasn't entirely Schultz's safety that was occupying her mind. There was the big issue of having a relationship with a man who worked for her. From what she had seen of other couples who worked together on a daily basis, few of them could make it last. She certainly couldn't ask Schultz to leave his job, and her commitment to CHIP was solid, so it was an issue that wouldn't go away on its own.

Would they have to keep their relationship a secret at work? Sneak around like they were having an affair?

There was only one place in the department where PJ fit in, and that was with the CHIP project. But Schultz was flexible. He could request a transfer. That would solve the direct boss-employee setup, but Wall would want to know why Schultz was transferring. Was that a problem? Were romances within the department accepted or frowned upon? In her old field of marketing research, she could have answered that question. But in law enforcement, she just didn't know, and she had no one she could ask except Schultz himself. His view was bound to be biased.

Another thing: Schultz was walking around out there, deliberately exposing himself to a killer. It was part of his job, she knew, to put himself in the path of danger, but she had Thomas to consider, too. She sensed that her son would come to love Schultz as a father—the seeds of it were already sprouting. Could she ever really accept the risk that went with his job on the front lines of law enforcement?

To be brutally honest, were the risks he was taking so different from the ones she had taken upon herself since she'd joined CHIP? How did anyone involved in law enforcement handle the idea that their children could be left alone? Would it be easier to deal with as a married couple than as a single parent?

There were so many problems, so many considerations, and all of them striking deep.

She imagined what it would be like if the door shut inside her, closing off the relationship before it could go any further. If it was going to end, it would have to be done by her, because she was sure Schultz couldn't do it. The thought of ending it made her terribly sad. Tears of loss and stress painted her face with hot streaks. She put her face in her hands and quietly sobbed.

The phone rang. She sniffled and took a couple of deep breaths to calm down, then picked it up. It was Wall.

She didn't hear anything of what he said after the first sentence: Schultz was missing.

Anita Collings walked in. PJ had left her office door open after a hasty trip to headquarters. Anita didn't say anything, just puttered around fixing coffee. The familiar noises and aroma seemed to settle PJ's chaotic thoughts. Anita passed her a cup.

"Thanks," PJ said. She wrapped her hands around the warm offering, wondering how her fingers had gotten so cold. "Did Wall send you to baby-sit me?"

"I wouldn't call it baby-sitting exactly," Anita said tactfully. "He just said that you might want somebody to talk to."

Of all people, PJ thought, *it has to be Anita.*

PJ found it hard to relate to Anita. She was the only daughter of a career cop, and had been immersed in the camaraderie of the department from the time her father brought her in to show her around when he was off-duty. Even the scars on her face, on the forehead and at the corner of her right eye, seemed to preclude confidences. There was a gulf between them of experience and attitude that being the same gender hadn't put a dent in, much less overcome.

"I'm all right now," PJ said evasively. "I just overreacted to Schultz being out there." She waved her hand vaguely.

Anita held her gaze, maddeningly waiting her out. PJ sipped her coffee and wondered if it would be too rude just to get up and leave.

"I grew up in a rough neighborhood," Anita said. "And I wasn't exactly a little angel. When Dad worked evenings or nights, I sometimes sneaked out and met with my friends, just to talk, you know, hang out. Since it was just Dad and me, I didn't have a lot of supervision."

PJ thought how different that was from her own childhood.

She had grown up in Newton, Iowa, a small town bounded by cornfields, pig farms, Interstate 80, and the midwestern work ethic. Her mother had always been there for her and her sister, Mandy. Her father had been the editor of the *Newton Daily News,* and frequently came home for lunch. Her father died years ago, but her mother still lived in Newton, in the white frame house with the big porch on the edge of town. The house, her parents, the whole town—everything smacked of stability and normalcy.

The naughtiest thing PJ could remember doing as a child was sneaking out at night with her sister and writing "cock" on the side of the school building with red paint. She had just learned that a cock wasn't only a rooster, and was eager to show off her knowledge. Mrs. Reardon, who taught seventh grade and lived next door to the school, saw them. The next day, PJ and Mandy scrubbed their handiwork with stiff brushes and buckets of soapy water, while classmates taunted them from the playground.

"One night we saw a liquor store robbery," Anita continued. "Cal—that was my best friend at the time—and I heard the shots and saw the creep run out. We went inside before the police got there. Stupid shits, that's us, because there could have been more than one robber. Mr. Li was lying on the floor. His chest was covered with blood, and there was blood on the floor. He wasn't dead yet. He was having some kind of convulsion, his whole body rigid and shaking, practically bouncing himself across the floor. Never seen anything like it before or since. It shook me up so bad I couldn't eat or sleep for days."

PJ closed her eyes. She could picture the scene vividly, but she didn't know why Anita had chosen to tell her the story.

"Cal and I had been in the store pestering Mr. Li five minutes earlier, trying to get him to give us a free soda, I think. Then those bullets had a death grip on him, they were shaking the life out of him. He was dead by the time the police came in and shooed us out."

Anita paused and drank some of her coffee.

"I've seen dead people since then," she said. "Traffic accidents. Elderly people who died at home. Suicides. OD's. Murders. I've even seen a woman who died after trying to give herself an abortion when she was seven months pregnant. But it's Mr. Li I see when I wake up in the middle of the night—the way his head kept hitting the floor, and his eyes were rolled back. Jesus, the whites of his eyes were blood-red." Her hands tightened on the coffee cup, and PJ saw tiny bumps rising on Anita's forearms.

"You never know how you're going to react to stuff like that," Anita said. "Or to the threat of it. Or of seeing people you care about walk into danger. What I'm trying to say is any reaction is all right. Just don't hold it in."

PJ felt emotion sweep through her, slam her hard, an emotional mix she couldn't even define. A cacophony of powerful impressions, each demanding acknowledgment, flashed in her mind. Her father's death. Stephen saying he wanted a divorce. Loss, pain. The death of a newfound friend at the hands of a brutal killer. Eleanor's blood spattered on the wall from the blows of a baseball bat. Schultz's son under the terrible hand of death.

Her heart wailed when she thought of Schultz looking the same way.

When she could talk, she looked into Anita's eyes, and wondered how she had ever thought the woman cold and distant.

"It's so many things," PJ said, knowing there were things she couldn't say directly to Anita. She had to keep the depth of her feeling for Schultz a secret, at least for now.

PJ's gaze flicked down at her own arm, where the thin line of the scar inflicted by a psychopath lay. She looked up and saw Anita looking at the scar.

"When *he* was killed," PJ said, tapping the scar, "my God, Anita, when he was killed, his blood splashed on me and mixed with my own in my wounds." PJ lost her voice for a moment. "How do you do this, year after year? Doesn't it make you crazy?"

"Welcome to the job," Anita replied. "I can't say that it gets any easier. You just go on. You have to believe that you're making a difference."

PJ wondered why she couldn't talk to Schultz about those things. Anita seemed to read her thoughts about him.

"Some cops just can't talk about it. Or won't."

"I guess you'll have to be my safety net," PJ said. The two women sat quietly. PJ felt something pull together inside herself, an inner strength that, just three years ago, she wouldn't have believed she possessed. That strength got her through the divorce, through the first challenging months of single parenthood, through the soul-searing cases she had been involved in, and it would serve her now, as well. In her work with the St. Louis Police Department, PJ had discovered a new level of commitment that flowed deep within her psyche, like the cold, relentless currents that ran far beneath the ocean, down where the sunlight never penetrated.

Where was there room for love? Floating on the surface, perhaps, like a life raft. She liked the image. It was one she could hang onto until she had time to think the whole situation through.

PJ rubbed the scar on her arm. The skin there felt colder than the surrounding area, but she figured that was her imagination. "How did you get those scars on your face?"

Anita blinked. That was a question she wasn't expecting. "You probably think it's something sinister. Far from it. This one," Anita said, brushing her hair away from the half-inch long depression that was like a notch in her forehead, "was from running into the corner of a brick building. I was chasing some friends when I was six years old, and took the corner too tight. Really laid myself out. It probably should have had stitches." She took a sip of her coffee, evidently reliving the event.

"This one," she said, her finger tracing the slash at the outside corner of her right eye, "came from an old phonograph player. You know, the kind they had ages ago with long play records."

PJ nodded, feeling old.

"Dad had one, and some old records he and Mom used to play. I was putting a stack of them on that post in the center, and I fell over on it. I was about ten years old. Just toppled over. Clumsy kid, I guess. The doctor said I was lucky. The post glanced off the bone right here at the edge of my eye and slid to the outside. If it had slipped the other way, I would have lost my eye."

Anita smiled and raised her coffee cup to PJ in a salute. "Now you know some of my deep dark secrets."

"If that's all you've got hidden in your past, you're one fortunate woman."

"Well, I didn't say that was all . . ."

The office door opened a crack, then widened, and Wall's head popped in briefly. Evidently he was testing the waters.

"C'mon in, lieutenant," Anita said. "The coast is clear."

Wall came in and settled in what PJ thought of as Schultz's chair, then put a folder on her desk. She pushed her emotions down and prepared herself to deal with whatever Wall was going to say.

"Well, surprise, Libby's gone," he said. "The Jeff City police checked out her house." Wall pointed his chin at the folder. "Here's a copy of Jeremiah's letter for you to go over. I think you're going to find it interesting reading. It fits with everything on that tape of yours."

PJ nodded. She knew Wall was saving the lecture about threatening Darla with a gun—a gun she wasn't even qualified to fire—for some other time, and she appreciated that.

"I could use a little time to myself to go over this," PJ said, tapping the folder. "Then I'd like to get out there and help."

Anita and Wall looked at each other. "There really isn't much for you to do at this point," Wall said.

"Why not?" PJ snapped. "I couldn't do any worse than you, letting Schultz get taken right out from under your nose."

"Do I have to remind you that watching Elijah was your idea? It's as close to certain as we can get without finding him in the act, you said." The sudden heat in Wall's voice could have cooked a steak.

"Since when do you rely exclusively on what I say, you patronizing—"

"Since you've been right," Wall said, leaning across the table, his face in hers. "Most of the time."

"All right, you guys," Anita said. "Save your energy for the chase. We're gonna find Schultz, and we're gonna find him in one piece."

Wall sat back and hunched down in his chair. PJ crossed her arms across her chest.

"Geez, grow up, will you?" Anita said to the room in general. "We've got a cop to save."

PJ let go of her anger. She knew it was based in fear, the fear that she'd never see Schultz alive again. She sucked in a deep breath, and saw Wall do the same.

"Let's be constructive about this," PJ said, using her best shrink voice. "What can I do to help?"

"Read the letter and we'll talk," Wall said.

Thirty-seven

"Ouch," Schultz said.

Brilliant comeback for being decked by an old woman.

Libby Ramsey told him to get up off the ground, and he did. The side of his face felt like a bus had hit it, but he hadn't lost consciousness. She took his gun, pulled his cell phone out of the pouch, turned it off, and tossed it into the bushes.

"You wired?"

He shook his head no, regretted it as bursts of color obscured his vision. Her hands ran over him like ants over a cake crumb, found the transmitter, and yanked it loose.

"Ouch. Damn."

"Walk," she said, and somehow he got to her car.

She made him drive. At first he said he couldn't. His head hurt and he couldn't see well enough. Then he found out an amazing thing: a gun held to his temple miraculously cleared his vision. He wondered if he should pass that along to the medical establishment.

She didn't blindfold him or put him in the trunk of the car, and he took that for a bad sign. It meant she didn't think it mattered that he saw where they were going. They drove southwest out of the city, on Interstate 44 toward Meramec Caverns. They didn't get that far, though. Libby had him take the St. Clair exit, and from there he got lost in all the twists and turns on country gravel roads.

At the farmhouse, he started to panic. It was so remote. He shouldn't have let things get so far. He'd have to take her out somehow, regardless of whether he had any proof of the other killings.

When he got out of the car he was poised to act, but she stood too far away to reach and calmly shot him in the foot. He bent over with the pain of it, his leg suddenly turned to jelly underneath him, and then he felt the impact of the butt of the gun behind his ear. After that he felt nothing.

Schultz came to with a stabbing pain behind his eyes. He had no idea how long he'd been out. His left foot throbbed. He experimented with opening his eyes. It took him several times before the world stopped reeling.

He was naked and tied to a chair. A bright lamp hung from the ceiling, casting a circle of light around him but obscuring the edges of the room so that he couldn't tell how large the space was. He leaned over as well as he could, bringing on dizziness but allowing him to glimpse a bloody rag tied around his left foot. At least the foot was still there. It hurt like hell.

He tried out his voice, found he could only croak. He swallowed a couple of times and tried again.

"Libby, you in here?"

There was no answer, which didn't mean she wasn't behind him at the moment with an ax the size of Texas. Reflexively, he drew his shoulders up around his neck, grateful at least that it was *Lizzy* Borden, not Libby.

Schultz tugged at the knots that held his wrists behind the chair, and found them disappointingly tight. Whatever else he thought of Libby, she deserved credit for tying a good knot.

He heard a small scrape behind him.

"Goddamn it, Libby, come on out. I know you're back there."

"Watch your language, you murdering son of a bitch. You're in the Lord's presence."

He heard the click of a light switch, then the wall in front of him was bathed in brilliant light. He blinked a few times until his eyes adjusted. On the wall were two stunning renderings. One was of the Four Riders of the Apocalypse. Pestilence, War, Famine, and Death galloped across the wall on their dreadful mounts. He stared at the other drawing for some time before he called up the names from distant memory: the Dragon with Seven Heads and Ten Horns and the Woman Clothed in the Sun. Both scenes were from Revelations, the book of the Bible dealing with judgment day. Done in black and white, they were line drawings, like intricate Renaissance woodcuts. He was certain they were copies of something famous he'd seen in art appreciation class, meticulously re-created with a patient and talented hand.

His eyes traveled over them, absorbed not only in their stark beauty but in their portent. Death, on his starving, skeletal horse, seemed to have a message meant directly for Schultz.

Libby appeared abruptly, blocking his view of the wall. She was holding a butcher knife.

"Oh, shit," he said.

Thirty-eight

Cut argued with the woman on the phone. She didn't want to send out one of her ladies without a credit card number in advance. He offered to double the fee for a cash payment in person. She was suddenly agreeable.

"Now we got that little business behind us," she crooned into the phone, "what kinda girl you lookin' for?"

"I want somebody over forty, tall and big, weighs about a hundred and seventy pounds. She needs to wear a long modest dress, flat shoes, and a shoulder-length blond wig."

The woman chuckled. "Hey, I got that. I got just what you lookin' for. You wantin' somebody to be your mama?"

"I guess I am."

"Anythin' else? Maybe you want your old granny, too? I got a special this time of night for two. It's gettin' late."

"Just the one," Cut said. "And tell her to pick up some burgers on her way. I'm hungry."

"That'll be—"

"Yeah, I know. I'll give her an extra twenty for the food. Just get her here quick. Room four oh six." He gave her the address of the hotel.

Forty minutes later, a car pulled into the front parking lot. By luck or by design on her part, she headed for a portion of the lot that was poorly illuminated and near a side entrance. Marking the position of the car in his mind, he watched the

woman cross the lot. A few minutes later, there was a knock
at his door. He let the woman in. The scent of hamburgers
and fries preceded her.

"Hi, I'm Marlene," she said. "Hope you like your burgers
with everything."

He looked her over at the same time she was appraising
the situation with a practiced eye. She was about his height
and a little heavier than he was, which was fine. Reaching
out, he tugged at her hair. The wig tilted sideways.

"I never was too good with these things," she said, straight-
ening the wig.

"That's okay," he said, opening the bag of food. "You're
not going to be wearing it for long."

"Where's the cash?" Marlene said. "I have to check in by
phone."

He showed her three hundred dollars and her eyes indicated
approval. She pulled a cellular phone out of her purse and
made a quick phone call.

"Now, then," she said, turning to him with a smile, "What
do you want to eat first?"

She never saw the blow coming, and Cut made sure to hit
where he wouldn't leave a visible bruise that might put her
out of business for a few days. He could be considerate when
he wanted to.

When he had the unconscious woman lying on the bed, he
stripped off her clothes and put them on over his own, rolling
his jeans up to the knees so that they wouldn't show beneath
the long skirt. Marlene was going to be hopping mad when
she woke up, and her only choice would be to wear the shirt
and slacks he left draped across the foot of the bed. Only the
shoes gave him a problem. He squeezed his feet in and ate
his dinner, wondering at what time a meal ceased to be called
dinner and became breakfast.

Emptying the food out of the bag, he put his own shoes
inside—he'd need them later—and slung the woman's purse

over his shoulder. He stood in front of the bathroom mirror and checked himself. He might pass for her, as long as the light was poor and the inspection was superficial. It was near the end of the shift for the officer out in the lot, and Cut was gambling that his attention wasn't what it should be. It was a risk, but he had to get out. The stay in the hotel had served its purpose, and now he had things to do.

He left two hundred dollars on the night stand. He didn't want to waste the extra hundred, seeing as he hadn't gotten full value from her visit. He didn't leave her any food, either.

Thirty-nine

It was nearly dawn when PJ got home. Overhead the sky was still dark, but in the east she could see the outlines of heavy clouds. She was keyed up, but intended to try to get a couple hours of sleep to help her work with a clear head. As it was, she didn't think she could drag herself up the back steps to the door. It had been an exhausting twenty-four hours.

She'd gone out to the abduction site because she felt compelled to be taking part in things. It gave her chills to stand in the spot where Schultz had last been. After milling around in the park for an hour or so, she gave up. There was nothing useful to be learned there, at least by her.

Helen had left the porch light on for her. On the top step, PJ noticed something odd on the door. She blinked her tired eyes. It was a small plastic bag, held onto the door with masking tape. A note was stuck next to it.

She pulled on the masking tape that held the bag to the door, and the bag dropped into her hands. It was cool and damp to the touch, and seemed to be filled with water. She held it up to the porch light.

The light shone through it, gleaming red as a ruby.

Red as blood.

She gasped and dropped the bag, which hit the floor of the porch with a wet thump and broke open.

Helen opened the back door, and light from the kitchen

flowed out onto the porch and fell on the spattered liquid. PJ was frozen in place, her mouth open, staring down.

"It's about time you got home," Helen said, in a good-natured teasing way. Then her mouth clamped shut as she got a good look at PJ. Her eyes followed PJ's.

"It appears to be blood," Helen said after a moment. "And I'm pretty sure that thing is a toe."

PJ sat at her kitchen table, all thoughts of sleep pushed from her head. Her body felt jangly, as if she'd had a huge dose of caffeine. Helen had called the police, and Anita was on her way over, to be followed shortly by the Evidence Technician Unit, or ETU. PJ was already convinced that tests on the blood and severed toe would show that both items had formerly been in Schultz's possession.

Helen had gone to keep a close watch on Thomas, to waylay him in case he woke up and make sure he stayed upstairs. PJ had the note from the door spread out in front of her. She knew she shouldn't have touched it, but stampeding rhinos couldn't have stopped her.

It had to be a message from the killer. It was handwritten in neat, large letters. As soon as PJ had gone through the first few words, she zipped through the rest because of their familiarity.

> *Little Bo-Peep has lost her sheep,*
> *And can't tell where to find them;*
> *Let them alone and they'll come home,*
> *And bring their tails behind them.*
> *Little Bo-Peep fell fast asleep,*
> *And dreamt she heard them bleating;*
> *But when she awoke she found it a joke,*
> *For still they all were fleeting.*
> *Then up she took her little crook,*

Determined for to find them;
She found them indeed,
But it made her heart bleed,
For they'd left all their tails behind them!
It happened one day as Bo-Peep did stray,
Unto a meadow hard by,
There she spied their tails; side by side,
All hung on a tree to dry.
Then she heaved a sigh and wiped her eye,
And ran o'er hill and dale-o.
She tried what she could,
As a shepherdess should,
To tack to each sheep its tail-o.

As far as she could tell, there were no changes in the rhyme from what she remembered from childhood. It was ghastly, that part about the tails cut off and draped on a tree. But a lot of nursery rhymes were horrible if taken seriously. Libby had been the owner of preschools, and would have a large store of nursery rhymes in her head to draw upon. But what was she trying to get across?

There was a grisly interpretation that PJ shied away from but eventually couldn't ignore. The severed tails referred to the severed toe that had been delivered to her back porch, and the fact that "tails" was plural might mean there were more parts of Schultz's body to come.

Libby was Bo-Peep, and her heart was bleeding for the loss of her son a year ago, and her daughter twelve years before that.

PJ had a feeling Libby wanted to taunt her with the knowledge that Schultz was going to die, maybe piece by piece.

Dead already? Probably not. If so, the body itself would be the message.

Then where was Schultz being held? PJ desperately needed

to find him, and she couldn't just go running over hill and dale-o.

Let them alone, and they'll come home . . .

Wall had said that Libby had left her home in Jefferson City. PJ phoned him and asked for an update, and was assured the house in Jefferson City was empty. She asked for a search anyway, and he said he'd arrange it. He didn't even put up his usual fuss. A nerve-wracking hour went by, during which Anita and the ETU came and went, before the answer came back that the home in Jefferson City was empty, of both the living and the dead.

PJ still thought that Elijah was responsible for the murders, but now it appeared that Libby had stepped in at the end and taken over while Elijah served as decoy in the hotel. The two worked exquisitely well together. She thought about the way she worked with Schultz. She was the logical element of the team and he was the intuitive part. She used her computer simulations to step through crimes and make logical extrapolations. He made leaps of faith.

Their roles were the reverse of Libby's and Elijah's. In the Ramsey working partnership, Elijah was the logical planner. Libby was the intuitive one. To go where Libby was leading her, PJ would have to set aside her logical impulses and think like Libby. She read through the nursery rhyme again, and tried to free her thoughts from the conventional paths they tried to fall into.

I'm Bo-Peep, she thought suddenly. *My heart is bleeding, and Libby knows it. "Home" should be my home.*

Apprehensively, she grabbed a flashlight from a kitchen drawer and began walking through the rooms of her house. She checked all the closets, the basement, even the storage areas in the attic. Nothing.

There were too many ways to interpret the clue. She balled her fists in frustration, and struck out at the door frame leading to the kitchen, once, then several times, then stopped and

an her fingers through her hair. How was she to know what
Libby's devious mind had cooked up?

Libby's connection was with Schultz. In her twisted thinking, it was Schultz who took her son away from her originally,
and Schultz was the one who'd had his symbolic tail whacked
off.

Schultz is the sheep. "Home" is his home!

The realization struck her like an arrow lodging in her heart.
The brilliant simplicity of it—Schultz was captive in his own
home. Who would think to look there?

PJ heard noises from upstairs. Thomas was waking up and
would be in the kitchen soon. She scrawled a note to Helen
and left it on the kitchen table, grabbed her purse with her
car keys and rushed outside. A few blocks away, when her
breathing had slowed a little, she fished around in her purse
looking for the cellular phone to call for backup.

It wasn't there.

She'd forgotten that she had given the phone to Schultz—
hours or days ago, she couldn't say. She cursed her thinking,
which was fuzzy with exhaustion.

All she knew was that she had to throw everything she had
at solving the puzzle, because the prize was the life of the
man she'd come to love.

"There. I said it. Love. Love, love, love."

She stomped her foot on the gas pedal. Maybe she could
find a pay phone.

Forty

Schultz's house looked down on her with golden eyes. The sun had finally made its appearance, a delayed showing caused by a bank of clouds. There was a light ground fog that gave the sunlight a thick syrupy quality, so that she seemed to walk through a jar of honey. The windows reflected the clear light above the fog, turning them into flat eyes as unfeeling as a spider's.

There had been no pay phone. Briefly she thought of pounding on a neighbor's door and asking someone to alert the police. But that might alert Libby also. She stared up at the windows, wondering if Libby was watching from one of them, unseen behind the brilliant reflection. Or perhaps she was holding a knife to some other part of Schultz's anatomy, something more crucial to life than a toe.

The house key was in her hand, then turning in the lock.

She slipped into the front hall. Subdued light was coming from the uncovered windows in the rear of the house. The hairs on her arms rose as she pressed herself against the wall and began moving toward the kitchen. There was a faint smell she couldn't recognize in the air, certainly not blood, not housecleaning liquids, not air freshener. Something.

In the kitchen there was indirect light from the rear windows. She moved first toward the drawers that looked likely to contain knives. She found the correct drawer on her second

try. Schultz had only a couple of short, dull paring knives and
a bent, serrated bread knife.

*Figures. Where are those Ginsu knives when you need
them?*

She chose one of the paring knives, clutched it tightly in
her right hand, and picked up the phone with her left hand.

It took her a moment to realize the line was dead.

Her heart thudding in her chest, she began to edge toward
the rear door, thinking that she'd better pound on the neighbor's door, after all—if she could get out.

She was nearly at the door when the faint smell suddenly
grew stronger, and she recognized it. Peppermint. Her brow
furrowed as she tried to work that bit of information into her
situation.

PJ felt someone close behind her and started to whirl
around. She didn't make it. She was shoved forward into the
door, with something that might have been a knee pressed
hard against her backside. Her arms, which had been raised
to ward off an attack, were caught at the wrists and so cruelly
twisted that she dropped the knife.

She struggled against the hands holding her wrists, and
found them to be like iron bands. Her attacker leaned the
length of his body against her, putting his mouth close to her
ear. Her nostrils flared, taking in peppermint and the rank
smell of her own fear.

"Thanks for coming by, Dr. Gray," the voice said in a harsh
whisper. "You're right on time."

Her voice was caught in her throat. The only thing that
escaped her was a squawk that sounded like the noise an animal might make when a predator struck.

She was spun around and pushed violently across the room.
Her left hip crashed into the kitchen table, and the momentum
carried the top half of her body over, bending over the table
so that she cracked her jaw hard against the tabletop. She
moaned and tasted blood.

PJ tried to straighten herself and found that the ribs on her left side hurt sharply when she moved or took a deep breath. Breathing in shallow pants, crouched to lessen the pain from her ribs, she turned around to face her attacker. The muzzle of a gun was pressed between her eyes. She froze, holding her breath.

"Come along, little lady," said the voice from above her head. "The show starts soon. You may not be the star, but you could win an Oscar for a supporting role."

The gun pulled away a couple of feet, and she exhaled. PJ stood at her full height, even though it was painful, bending her left arm and pressing it tightly against her ribs to immobilize them. She could see the face of her attacker, and recognized him as Elijah. PJ swiped at her bloody chin with her right hand and then wiped her hand clean on her jeans.

She knew Elijah to be a brutal killer, but what she didn't know was his state of mind. Was he unreachable—programmed to perform Libby's commands—or could he be reasoned with?

Before PJ had much time to think about it, Elijah grabbed her arm and shoved her face into the wall. Pain shot through her left side, and she gasped. He bound her wrists with cord, then turned her around again to face the gun.

He gestured toward the rear door. She didn't move fast enough. He placed his hand between her shoulder blades and pushed. Stumbling, she moved out of the door he had opened for her and into the backyard.

"Scream, and it'll be the last thing you do," he said softly.

She set her lips against the pain in her side and walked across the yard, keeping her eyes low.

Surely someone will see us. Surely the police will stop us before we go far.

There was a car parked in the alley behind Schultz's house. Elijah opened the front passenger door for her. When she hesitated, thinking that it might be her last chance to scream or to make a break, he roughly pushed her inside. She barely ducked her head in time to avoid colliding with the top of the door frame.

Inside, she struggled to sit up while he moved around the front of the car and got in on the driver's side.

The door slammed shut. She probably couldn't yell loud enough for neighbors to hear inside their homes. It had all happened so fast. The pain, the gun between her eyes, her wrists bound, and she was taken. Why hadn't she resisted more effectively?

As Elijah drove out of the alley, she angled herself sideways, bracing her back against the door. When she thought he was distracted with the task of driving, she tucked her knees up, ignoring the spasm in the left side of her chest, and extended them with as much force as she could, kicking his right thigh.

He grunted, and the car swerved over the center line, narrowly avoiding an oncoming vehicle. Before she could gather her legs for another kick, he brought his right forearm down sharply across her calves. The blow sent waves of pain into her spine, and her vision blackened around the edges.

"Don't try that again," he hissed, "or I'll blow your fucking head off." The gun, which had been tucked into his waistband, had reappeared impossibly fast. It was aimed at her face. She couldn't repeat the maneuver before he could fire at her, and as close as he was, he couldn't miss.

PJ wasn't sure she could move her legs, but she shifted them slowly until she was sitting up in the seat, facing forward. Her legs weren't broken, but it was miraculous they weren't. She was sure gigantic bruises were forming underneath the fabric of her jeans.

They drove in silence for a time, except for an occasional moan from PJ as bumps in the road shifted her ribs. She could feel two or three of them floating freely, ends grinding against each other with the motion of the car, and worried that the broken ends would puncture her lung. She wanted to press her left arm against her chest as a kind of splint, but couldn't because her wrists were tied behind her back.

Amazingly, exhaustion crept up on her, overcoming the pain and the flow of adrenaline, and her eyes slowly drifted shut. She awakened an unknown amount of time later, looked around and found that they were traveling on an interstate through open countryside.

Considering her situation, she realized that the Bo-Peep rhyme was a false clue, a trap, and she'd walked right into it. There was the note she'd left for Helen, so by now Lieutenant Wall knew she'd gone over to Schultz's house, and why.

A lot of good that did.

She watched the hills roll by outside. How was she going to save Schultz? She had to save herself first.

"Had a nice nap?" Elijah said. Some of the tension was gone from his voice since he'd captured her and things were definitely in his favor. She'd be a lot more confident, too, if things were reversed.

"Just fine, thanks," she said, keeping her voice even, betraying nothing of her fear and feeling of hopelessness. They might have been out for a Sunday drive. It was still Sunday, wasn't it?

She decided to play the only ace she had—knowledge of the contents of Jeremiah's death row letter. She thought for a few minutes, figuring out how to approach the sensitive subjects with Elijah, not knowing how much he already knew or how he was going to react. Finally she decided she would just have to feel her way along.

"I feel terrible about your son's execution," she said. "It's a hard thing when the justice system is fooled in a death sentence case. Trials are meant to uncover the truth."

He glanced at her. "What're you talking about? If you have to blabber, at least make some sense."

"I'm talking about Jeremiah being executed for a crime he didn't commit."

She saw uncertainty flutter across his face, like a quick rustling of the leaves of a tree in the winds before a storm. Then he shook his head and grinned at her. "You're trying to get under my skin, aren't you, Dr. Gray? You're a shrink, I remember reading that. You can save your breath. It won't work. Hell, I've been interrogated by a lot worse than you."

"I'm not trying anything on you, Elijah," she said calmly. "I'm just offering my sympathy. Your son didn't deserve to die."

"My son was a good boy," he said, keeping his eyes on the road. "He flipped out, is all. I've seen it before, in the field. It happens, and I'm not saying it's right, but he shouldn't have been punished like that. Taken away from me. From his Mama. That doesn't bring Eleanor back."

"The Lord would have dealt with Jeremiah in His own good time, is that it? He could have repented and left it all up to the Lord?"

Elijah turned toward her briefly, and she saw his eyes gleaming, from some inner light or simply from the sun's reflection. "Exactly. You got that exactly right. It's not anybody else's role to judge what he did."

"Except he didn't do it."

Elijah slapped the top of the steering wheel. "Damn, woman, what are you talking about? He confessed. The fool boy confessed. He took it all back later on, but he'd already done the damage."

"I want you to think about something," PJ said. She took a deep breath and regretted it as her ribs ground together. "Suppose he confessed to protect someone else. Someone he loved a great deal."

"That only happens in books and movies."

"Real life can be stranger than books. Can you at least open yourself up to the thought?"

"Her blood was on his hands. Sweet Eleanor's blood was on his hands. He did it, all right."

"You saw the scratches on Jeremiah's body, didn't you? Do you think Eleanor could have made those scratches without using her fingernails?"

"What the hell does that have to do with anything?"

"Just answer."

"No."

"Well then, why wasn't there any of Jeremiah's blood or skin under her nails?"

"Your precious Schultz explained that at the trial," he said bitterly. "Her nails were freshly clipped. Jeremiah saw what her hands looked like. He clipped her nails, cleaned underneath what was left of them, and took the clippings with him."

"All that careful action from a boy who 'flipped out,' your exact phrase? And if he was going to confess, why try to conceal any evidence?"

"A person flips out and realizes it right afterward. Can't undo the killing, but he can protect himself. That confession— I guess the guilt just swept over him. I wish to God he'd never confessed. That set the police on him like ticks on a dog."

"Has it occurred to you that maybe Eleanor's nails were clipped and cleaned to conceal the fact that there were no skin cells under them in the first place?"

"You're talking crazy. Can't say I blame you, in your position."

PJ didn't answer. She just looked out the window, refusing to meet his eyes when they darted in her direction, and waited him out.

"Who'd do a thing like that?" he asked after a while.

Hooked.

"From the way you're talking, I'm assuming you haven't heard Jeremiah's version of the story."

"Oh, and you have? What'd you do, go over to the cemetery and hook up earphones to his tombstone?"

"I didn't know you had a sense of humor, Elijah. I thought you just murdered people." She regretted her sarcasm, but the words were out.

He was quiet for so long that she thought she'd lost all chance with him.

"When you say Jeremiah's story," he said, as if nothing had happened between the two of them, "are you talking about his confession? I know all about that."

While he'd been quiet, Elijah had gotten off the interstate. He was turning the car onto progressively smaller roads. They weren't on gravel yet, but it was clear that they were heading for some isolated area. If she didn't speak up now, she might not get a chance to.

"Tell me something first. Is Schultz still alive?"

"Far as I know."

PJ closed her eyes in mixed relief and pain. "I'm not talking about the confession. Jeremiah wrote a letter just before he was executed. It was hand-carried to Darla."

"You talked to Darla?" She heard genuine interest in his voice. "I haven't seen her in . . . well, years."

"She didn't want to be found. By me or by you, either, I'm sure. She doesn't want anything to do with what's left of the Ramsey family."

"That's a hard thing for a father to hear."

PJ let the comment go by. There were even harder things for a father to hear coming up. "Darla never read the letter. It's been in a box in her closet since the execution."

"You aren't going to tell me he planned Eleanor's murder, are you? 'Cause all this time I believed he flipped out. It'd break my heart to hear that he went over there intent on killing her."

"Elijah, it's a lot worse than that." PJ had no idea how the man was going to take the news. She hoped he wouldn't run off the road. "Did you know Jeremiah and Libby were lovers for years, and that Eleanor was their daughter?"

"Christ Almighty, you're making this up. You're trying everything you can think of to throw me off track. Jesus motherfucking Christ."

"Keep your eyes on the road, please, or slow down. Don't get us both killed." They were on a two-lane road with a lot of twists and turns.

They rode in silence for a minute or two, the only noise Elijah's hard breathing.

"You're making it up," he said at last. "My son wouldn't do that."

"It was Libby who urged him on. Jeremiah genuinely thought he was in love with her. It tore him up, but he thought he loved her."

"When did this start? Or when do you say it started?"

"When Jeremiah was fifteen. It was Libby who went to him, not the other way around. But he must have felt some kind of attraction even then."

Elijah's hands were tight on the steering wheel and the muscles of his jaw and neck were clenched. She wondered if she should try pulling her legs up for another kick, maybe try to open the door and drop out on the shoulder of the road. Where would she go from there, if Elijah wasn't completely disabled?

"How could this have gone on and I didn't know about it?" His voice sharp as a switchblade, slicing through the thick fog of emotion around him.

"You were overseas a lot, weren't you? Eleanor found out who her true parents were. She never liked her mother much in the first place, and that knowledge clinched it. She did like Jeremiah, though. They had a good relationship. He writes lovingly of her in his letter."

"So that's what Jeremiah had to say from death row? If it's true, and I hope to God it isn't, he should have kept his mouth shut about the whole thing. He should have taken that to the grave with him. You'd think he'd be ashamed."

"He was. But he wanted Darla to know who the true murderer was. I guess he wanted someone to understand and for-give him. And I'm sure he meant for Darla to tell you, when she was ready. It turns out she was never ready."

"This letter still exists? Darla still has it?"

"No. The police have it now," she said. She saw a tremor go through Elijah's body. His family's shame, exposed to the people he hated the most, the ones who had deprived him of his son. "I have a copy. I have a copy with me, Elijah, right here in my pocket. You can read Jeremiah's words for your-self."

Color had risen in his face. "How do I know the whole thing isn't some trick you and Schultz cooked up?"

PJ tried to shrug, and was given a sharp reminder of the state of her ribs. "Because it's in his handwriting. And because Darla knows about the relationship between Libby and Jere-miah. She's known for a long time."

"Can you take me to Darla?"

"I doubt it. I talked to her in Dayton, Ohio, only a short time ago. She said she was going to disappear again, and she seemed serious about it."

"The true murderer, you said. Tell me about that. Tell me right now."

"Eleanor wanted to break up the sick relationship. She tried to get Jeremiah to move far away or just break it off, but he couldn't. So she went after Libby. When Eleanor got pregnant, she threatened to go public with a story that you molested her and were the father of her baby. And that you molested kids at the day care centers."

Elijah slammed the dashboard with his fist. "That's a lie! A fucking lie!"

"Eleanor knew that. But it was a lie that gave her power over Libby. Either Libby stopped seeing Jeremiah, or Eleanor's lie would crash her world. She'd lose the day care centers."

Elijah turned onto a gravel road. Agitated, he sped along, oblivious to the surroundings. Bouncing over the rough surface made PJ's ribs hurt more. She stopped talking and groaned. He slowed the car down, and that helped a little.

"Libby killed Eleanor," she said in between gasps. "She framed her own son for it. She let him go to the gas chamber for a murder she committed."

"The blood," Elijah said. "What about the blood?"

"The day of the murder, Libby went home with Jeremiah after the two of them went shopping together. They had sex, and Libby scratched Jeremiah's shoulder on purpose. Afterward, she cleaned him up with a handkerchief, then she put the handkerchief in a bag and took it with her. He wasn't supposed to see that part. She had sent him into the shower to scrub the scratches with soap, but he saw through the open bathroom door."

"Jesus Christ." Elijah shook his head.

"When he got out of the shower, she was gone. Presumably she took the baseball bat from his closet at that time. He didn't actually see that. Then she went back to her own home and beat Eleanor to death. She planned it, and she did it."

Elijah turned and looked at her. His eyes were dry, but an ocean of tears was held inside them.

"Jeremiah didn't know exactly what happened next, because he wasn't here. He assumed Libby carefully cleaned Eleanor's fingernails, then dampened the handkerchief and squeezed a few drops of Jeremiah's blood onto the dead girl's hands. She cleaned the fingernails to make it look like the killer tried to cover up but didn't get all the blood off."

"Why'd he confess then, if he didn't do it? How come he didn't tell me when I visited him on death row?"

"He confessed because his first impulse was to shield Libby. Later he changed his mind. He recanted, but couldn't bring himself to directly accuse her even at the cost of his life. At the end, he wanted someone to know how he'd been used, but he couldn't talk to you about it."

Elijah jerked the car sharply to the side of the road and

turned off the engine. PJ noticed that they were at a mailbox pulloff. There was a long driveway that wound away into the woods. No home was in sight.

When she turned to face him his eyes were unreadable, but the gun in his hand spoke plainly. She closed her eyes. He didn't believe her, and her effort was a failure. She was a failure, and Schultz was going to die along with her.

"Give me the letter," he said hoarsely. It sounded as though his voice were full of nails.

"I can't," she said. "My hands are tied."

He reached over and pushed her shoulder. He must have thought she was being flippant with him. "Which pocket?"

She gritted her teeth against the pain. "Left front."

Keeping the gun trained on her with his left hand, he dug into her pocket with his right, pulling out the letter.

He read slowly, with the sheets of paper draped over his right knee, raising his eyes frequently to check on PJ. She kept perfectly still, breathing shallowly.

She used the time to try visualization, imagining all the pain flowing into her hands, then balling it up and tossing it away from her like crumpled paper. She went through the process twice, and told herself it helped.

Forty-one

Cut unfolded the letter, pressing it down on his knee with a trembling hand. His gun hand was steady, though. Fortunately he had learned early on to be just as deadly with his left hand as with his right.

My dearest sister, the letter began. *I write this in hopes of your understanding and forgiveness.*

He choked back his emotions. If the letter was real, Jeremiah had written to Darla, not to him. Jeremiah didn't trust his own father with the terrible truth. The rejection hurt, even though he knew that was petty given the circumstances.

Well, shit, he thought. *It wasn't the kind of thing a boy could run to his dad with, was it?*

He read through the letter carefully, looking for flaws, inconsistencies, looking for things he could point at and say *it couldn't possibly be so.*

Jeremiah's words were powerful. He told his story from the time Libby first came onto him. She walked in on him in the shower, for God's sake. She ran her hands over his slick soapy skin, and his young body responded. He was scared and ashamed, but he couldn't push her away. Things didn't go far that first time, just touching, but he couldn't get the incident out of his mind. There was a next time, and a next, and he was buffeted in a storm of physical feelings and emotions he didn't understand. Things moved fast, and she gave the orders. It was the Libby show, one hundred percent.

How well Cut knew that feeling. Libby could run things like a military commander, and that was something Cut was comfortable with. He was good at following orders. The only thing that finally drove the two of them apart was quarelling over money. She could be so wasteful.

But Jeremiah didn't excuse himself on that account, that Libby handed out orders. He said in the letter that he was equally to blame.

Cut couldn't help thinking that if he'd been home more, been around while the boy was in his teenage years, it never would have happened. Cut and Libby didn't have any difficulties in the sex department. They could heat up the sheets and darn near set the bed on fire. He could have kept her satisfied, kept her from looking elsewhere. If only he'd realized what went on behind his back. How could he have been so stupid? He searched his memories, trying to find any times where doubts had intruded and he'd buried them. There weren't any. He felt his cheeks get hot with shame. He was such a blind fool.

Could he have prevented the whole thing if he hadn't taken himself off to all the corners of the earth looking for adventure? *Let's be blunt,* he thought. *Looking for chances to get that order to kill. What kind of father is that? A sorry excuse for one.*

Cut looked over at his captive frequently, but she wasn't causing any trouble. He could handle any kind of physical trouble she could raise, but she'd gone ahead and done what he'd laughed at earlier. She'd gotten under his skin, made him think maybe this load of garbage was true.

Cut put his finger on small spots on the right margin of the letter. It was only a copy he was holding, so he couldn't tell exactly what they were at first. His heart nearly burst when he touched them and recognized what they were. Tear-stains.

Jeremiah had cried when he wrote the letter.

It was too much. Elijah's mind snapped shut on it.

Forty-two

PJ noticed that it was getting hot in the car by the time Elijah finished reading. Her mind might be fuzzy on the big things, but all the little discomforts came through clearly.

She saw Elijah touching the paper gently with his fingertips, trying to connect with his son somehow. He ran his fingers over Jeremiah's signature as if hoping he could learn the truth by Braille. At one point, she knew he was touching the tearstains that were much clearer on the original than on the copy he held in his hands. Those stains were a large part of the credibility of the contents of the letter. She had felt the sincerity of Jeremiah's statement as she read it. And the letter explained things like Eleanor's clean fingernails, which had bothered PJ since her VR simulation of the killing.

"I don't believe it," he said, crumpling the letter awkwardly with his right hand. He tossed it into the backseat of the car. "It's a plot of some kind. I'm sticking to the plan." He shoved the gun back into his belt, started the car, jammed it into forward, and spun the wheels on the gravel as he started up the driveway.

His denial came as a shock to her. "Elijah—"

"I'm not listening to any more of your shrink lies."

"Ask Libby," she said, desperation plain in her face and voice. "Look her straight in the eyes and ask her."

"Shut up!" He brought his fist down hard on her thigh. "Shut the fuck up!"

PJ grunted with pain and doubled over. Tears sprang from her eyes at the sudden agony. Her left leg felt shattered inside. It was all she could do to keep from sobbing.

When the pain eased a little and she raised her head, she saw that they were approaching a house in a clearing. It was a nondescript white farmhouse, with none of the character of her own childhood home in Iowa. The grass in the clearing was too overgrown to be called a lawn, but too short to qualify as a meadow. Shades were pulled down on the windows. In spite of the lush greenery surrounding the place, it looked bleak.

This is the place I could die, she thought. *And Schultz, too, if he's not already gone.*

She hung her head in misery. Then she thought about Thomas, about what lay ahead for him. The thought of her son at her own funeral was too hard to bear. Her resolve re-kindled itself, running up and down her spine like flames following a trail of gasoline.

She wasn't giving up. She would never give up, not while there was a breath left in her body and strength for a single beat left in her heart.

Elijah opened the door on her side of the car. He'd gotten out and around the car while she had been consumed by hopeless thoughts.

"Out."

She swung one foot out, then the other, ignoring the stabbing pains in her calves and her left thigh. She was too slow for his satisfaction, so he grabbed her by the arm and dragged her out. She wasn't sure if her legs would hold her, but they did. The trip into the house was a blur.

She was taken to a door, and when Elijah opened it she saw a flight of stairs leading to the basement. She quailed at he thought of managing steep stairs with her aching leg. There was no doubt in her mind she would fall.

"I can't," she mumbled, and slumped to the floor.

"You'd be surprised what you can do with a gun to your head," he said. "Scoot your ass over to the top step, and bump your way down. I'll be right behind you."

She felt the pressure of the muzzle on the back of her head, and complied. It wasn't as bad as she had thought, although each bump down sent signals of distress from every part of her body, it seemed. She didn't pass out. At the bottom, he stepped around her and yanked her to her feet.

"Over here," he said, guiding her to an old swivel chair. From the startling surroundings, it seemed as if the office chair had strayed into some terrible hellish place. Her eyes were riveted on the apocalyptic biblical scenes painted on the wall, illuminated by spotlights.

PJ sank into the padded chair almost gratefully. She couldn't remember the last time she had put her head down on a pillow and gotten a good night's sleep. Or even a good hour's sleep. The time she'd drifted off in Elijah's car had seemed more like a blackout than a restful episode.

A light came on behind her, and suddenly her chair was swiveled so that she had her back to the brightly lit wall, with its nightmarish images. What she faced was an even worse nightmare for her personally.

Schultz sat naked, his arms and legs fastened with leather straps to a wooden chair. His mouth was covered with duct tape, and his head lolled to the side. A rag saturated with blood was wound around one of his feet, and there were bloody smears on the floor underneath. The chair stood inside sheets of plastic fastened to the ceiling, and the plastic was pulled back in the front like the flaps of a tent.

She had stopped breathing at her first sight of him. She was too late. He wasn't moving, and from where she sat, she couldn't tell if his chest was rising and falling. Her own breath rushed out, deflating her body.

"Leo," she whispered into the space between them, "oh, Leo."

Forty-three

Schultz heard his name, and not just in any voice, but her voice. It was like a knife in his gut. She was here, and that meant only one thing. He was going to see her die before the Ramseys were through with him.

Through the open flaps of his gas chamber, he saw her in a chair directly in front of him. For a second he was embarrassed to be naked in front of her, then dismissed the thought. He tried to catch and hold her eyes, but her gaze roamed anxiously over his body, lingering on his injured foot. He tried to shift it so she wouldn't have to see it.

He regretted his arrogance, thinking he could act as bait and bring out the killer. Elijah and Libby were a powerful team, more than he could handle on his own. He should have learned a little humility. With all his heart, Schultz wished he were back in Forest Park strolling along that path behind the art museum. He'd do something differently. What, he didn't know, but something to change this outcome, make it never happen. Like Scrooge weeping over his own tombstone, he wished for a second chance.

Elijah stepped into the cone of light around him. It was hard to believe the man was in his sixties. He was lean, with the kind of hard muscles Schultz hadn't had in fifteen years. There was a toughness to him that had been shaped by his military years followed by mercenary work, a toughness that

Schultz didn't think would be dented by two more killings in cold blood.

Elijah looked over at Libby, who was holding PJ at gunpoint. Schultz saw an enigmatic—hostile?—look on the man's face that vanished as soon as he made eye contact with Libby. He wondered if Libby had caught it. His cop's intuition latched onto that look, flipped it over on its belly, and examined the possibilities.

Trouble in the ranks?

A spark of hope ignited and streaked through him. But if there was trouble, how could he exploit it, sitting trussed like a Thanksgiving turkey, with his mouth taped?

It was all up to PJ. He was glad she was a shrink, and a woman to boot. That was a deadly combination in his estimation, and it gave them both half a chance. Well, maybe a quarter of a chance, but that was enough to put some fire in his eyes.

Forty-four

PJ was startled when Schultz raised his head. Then she couldn't meet his eyes anymore after a brief connection. She might get drawn too deeply into them and not be able to function. Instead, she checked him over, and didn't see any signs of serious injury besides the foot. One side of his face was bruised and his eye was puffy, but that didn't qualify. The foot looked bad, but if it came to that, he could do without a foot. Her mind wandered into a scenario of Schultz with a prosthetic foot, learning to walk again, with PJ at his side. Then she yanked her thoughts back to their situation. She had to get them both out of this horrible room before she could tack on the happy ending.

Her mouth wasn't taped like Schultz's, so at least she could talk. And talk she intended to do.

"No hidden tape recorder this time, is there, Miss Lakeland or Gray, or whatever your name is," Libby said. "I knew all along there was something phony about you." Her voice was soft and controlled, and all the more deadly for it.

"It's a good thing Darla got away from you in time," PJ said, turning her head toward Libby. "I think she suspected, but she just didn't want to know for sure."

"Elijah, get over there and cut that cord on her wrists. I want her arms tied down to the chair," Libby said. Then she turned her attention back to PJ. "Darla couldn't stand it when her sister was killed. She nearly had a breakdown. Or maybe she did have one, I don't know. You can't trust anything she says."

"Seemed perfectly rational to me." Out of the corner of her eye, PJ could see Elijah watching them with an almost morbid fascination, as he would a weasel about to attack a helpless snake. She reassured herself that, despite outward appearances, it was Libby who was the snake and she who was the calculating attacker. It felt good to tell herself that.

"You saw Darla? Tell me where she is," Libby commanded.

"Not a chance in hell," PJ said. "And you're going to know a lot about that. Hell, that is."

PJ darted a glance at Schultz. He was watching intently. There was something in his eyes she hadn't seen at first, something that said he hadn't given up. She licked her lips nervously. A verbal misstep on her part could cost them both their lives before she had a chance to worm her way out of it. Elijah came over and slit the cord on her wrists. Her hands fell limply to her side. Pin pricks from the numbness cascaded down from her wrists to her fingertips. Sitting in the swivel chair, she tried to loosen up and look more confident, but her ribs punished her for attempting to sit up straight.

Libby ignored PJ's remark and came over to her. She pointed the gun at PJ's head. "I said, I want to know where Darla is."

"I don't know where she is," PJ said.

Libby swung around and aimed the gun at Schultz. PJ saw him take a deep breath and fasten his eyes on Libby's. He didn't flinch. If he was going to meet death, he'd meet it straight on.

"Tell me, bitch," Libby said.

The sight of Schultz about to be gunned down nearly made PJ frantic. She strained not to show it. She wasn't going to let him die.

"I don't know where she is at this moment, but I do know

where she was," PJ said. "She was in Dayton. But you won't find her at home, especially if it's you at the door."

Libby spun and struck PJ across the side of her face with the gun. Blood filled PJ's mouth, and she coughed it out. She started to rise from her chair in pure reflexive anger at the woman, then realized that even if she could disable Libby, Elijah was armed and ready to take control. He was across the room where she didn't stand a chance of reaching him in time. Good teamwork.

"Don't get smart with me," Libby said. "I don't put up with that. Never have. 'Less you're under six years old. Then I figure God hasn't given you any sense yet, so it doesn't do any good to get mad."

PJ ran her tongue over her teeth and spat blood onto the floor.

"Let's get back to that hell part," PJ said. "When do you figure that Rider on the wall over there is coming for you?"

"You don't know what you're talking about. It isn't me who's going to hell. It's Schultz and all the others who killed my boy. I know all about the damnation of the wicked and the redemption of the just."

"Maybe you do," PJ said. "You just got the cast of characters mixed up. Why don't you ask her about that, Elijah?"

Elijah, who had been lingering at the edge of the room, started at the sound of his name.

"You got anything to say?" Libby said to him.

He shook his head. There was no defiance in him.

"Then get over there and tie her to that chair. I'm ready to get on with this."

"Jeremiah saw you take the bloody handkerchief," PJ said. Desperation had given her a cold calmness. She was running out of time. She had to skip to dead center.

Libby's eyes widened. PJ felt a twinge of satisfaction at the woman's reaction.

"Were you on top when you scratched him?" PJ taunted.

"Is that the way you liked it when you had sex with you
son, always in control?"

"Shut up!"

"Why should I shut up? What are you going to do to make
me stop? Kill me?"

Elijah was frozen in place. He'd started to walk toward PJ
Libby gripped her gun with both hands, uncertain whether to
choose Schultz or PJ as the first target.

"How many times did you hit Eleanor with that baseball
bat? Ten? Twenty? Then you clipped her nails like you used
to do when she was a child, and squeezed the blood onto her
hands. Your own son's blood."

Libby took a step toward her. "You don't know what you're
talking about. Everything you're saying is a lie." Her voice
was a low dangerous hiss.

"Jeremiah told me, Libby. In his own words, right before
he died for your crime. The blood's really on your hands, not
his. You killed your own daughter and son!"

Libby's face was livid. There was something out of control
in her eyes.

"What about it, Libby?" Elijah said, choking on his words
"I want to hear what you've got to say about it. I saw the
letter. I saw where my boy cried when he wrote it. I want to
know what that means, Libby. You tell me now, and you tell
me straight."

She rounded on him, her mouth in a deep frown. "You
ordering me around? That sure sounds like you're ordering
me, and you know that's not the way it is between us." She
pointed her chin toward some rope on the floor. "Get that
rope and fasten the bitch. Make it real tight. It's time to get
down to business here."

Elijah pulled himself up to his full height and met both her
frown and the stabbing light in her eyes. "You haven't an
swered my question," he said.

Libby shifted the gun and fired four shots in quick succession

Elijah's body jerked with the force of each one, and he was driven back against the brightly lit wall. He sagged to the floor, leaving a broad smear of blood across the hooves of the apocolypse riders' horses. His head fell forward on his ruined chest.

"There's your answer," Libby said.

PJ planted her feet and forced herself upright. Her left leg gave under her, but she dove for Elijah's gun, which had clattered to the floor. She got her hands on it, could barely hold onto it because of the numbness in her fingers. Then the rest of her hit the floor hard, and she crashed into Elijah's side. Twisting, she squeezed the trigger. Her first shot went wild, into the ceiling. She tried to get her wavering hands under control.

Libby fired in her direction, and she felt the thump of the bullet as it entered Elijah's body. A miss. PJ pulled the trigger and saw blood erupt from Libby's shoulder. Another shot, and Libby's face disappeared.

When the noise of the shots fell away, PJ dropped the gun. It clattered noisily in the stillness of the room.

A minute later, she scrambled to her feet and went to check on Schultz. He showed none of the shock of killing that she felt sure was visible on her own face. All she saw there was relief. She pulled the tape off his mouth. He took in a big gulp of air. Of life.

"Christ," he said, his chest heaving. She held his eyes as his breathing returned to normal.

Tentatively, she touched the bloody rag that enclosed his foot, uncertain if she wanted to get a better look.

"Better leave that for the medics," he said. "By the way, you should've aimed for the center of the chest with a two-handed stance. There's a high probability of missing when you go for the extremities."

She didn't know whether to slap him or hug him.

Epilogue

It was a beautiful morning for August. The night before, a storm had swept through in advance of a cold front that Canada had misplaced. Riding behind the storm were low humidity, blue skies, and a gentle breeze that stirred the flowers brought to the grave site.

It was eight days since PJ had killed someone.

She wasn't listening to the words spoken by the clergyman, although she assumed he had the usual things to say. Schultz had spoken earlier, at the funeral service in the chapel. Schultz had poured his heart into the words he'd said over his son's coffin. PJ saw that the gates were open and the grieving process was well under way, and for that she was relieved.

Schultz was in a wheelchair, and griped about it constantly. The bones of his left foot had been shattered by Libby's gunshot, but the damage was repairable. He wouldn't lose the foot, although he'd be a little off balance with it, the doctor said, because of the missing toe. He'd been unable to master getting around on crutches for anything more complicated than going to his refrigerator for a snack, so over his objections she'd insisted on a wheelchair.

Schultz fiddled with some lever on the wheelchair as the words that were meant to comfort floated up on the breeze. Julia stood next to him, in the same way she had psychologically stood next to the man who had been her husband for so many years, willing to lie to be his alibi and acting blindly on his word. Her face wore the same brave mask that had been held up to the public by countless millions of grieving mothers.

By her own choice, PJ stood apart and let the parents be together for the funeral of Rick Schultz. Thomas stood next to her, looking grand and solemn in his new suit. On her other side was Helen Boxwood, a loyal friend, one whom PJ had come to depend upon.

It hurt PJ to stand for any length of time, but she put aside her discomfort. Her cracked ribs were wrapped tightly with elastic bandages under her black dress, making her take shallow breaths. She didn't have any broken bones in her legs, just deep severe bruising. Emotionally she had bruising, too. She had taken quite a beating from Elijah Ramsey, but she'd been damaged even more when she shot and killed Libby. Even though it was a clear case of saving her own life and Schultz's, PJ regretted that she'd had to take a life in the process. Yet she knew she'd do so again if she had to. It was a hidden level of responsibility in her work.

Schultz had told her once that killing, even in a good cause, took away a little piece of your soul, and the more of it you did, the more your soul looked like Swiss cheese.

All Leo and I will need is a couple of pieces of rye bread to make a good cheese sandwich.

Anita was there, of course, and a large number of law enforcement officers, few of whom actually knew Rick. Dave was recovering from surgery to remove the bullet that had lodged near his spine. There had been some chance of it shifting, and so the risk of leaving it in place had outweighed the risk of removal. He'd come through the surgery like the tough young fighter he was. His girlfriend had pulled herself away from the hospital long enough to make a showing at the funeral. PJ saw her checking her watch as the graveside service came to a close.

The crowd broke up. Schultz talked quietly to Julia, who then left with her friend from Florida. Anita took Thomas home. That left PJ with Schultz. He rolled over to her.

"Hey, babe," he said, leering playfully at her. "You look sexy in black. How about you and I go back to my place and screw 'til the sun comes up?"

PJ burst out laughing. "Look at us. We're walking wounded—not even that, in your case. I hurt all over, you've got a cast on your foot, and now you've got sex on your mind? That reminds me. We need to talk about Helen, and where she fits in all this."

"I don't mind a threesome. I'm adaptable. I can do kinky."

"Really, Leo. You're supposed to be in mourning."

He gave her a mock frown. "Well, wanna get a pizza, then?"

"Sure," she said. "And besides, I might have two or three places that don't hurt."

A World of Eerie Suspense
Awaits in Novels by Noel Hynd

THRILLS AND CHILLS
The Mysteries of Mary Roberts Rinehart

_The After House	0-8217-4242-6	$3.99US/$4.99CAN
_The Album	1-57566-280-9	$5.99US/$7.50CAN
_The Case of Jennie Brice	1-57566-135-7	$5.50US/$7.00CAN
_The Circular Staircase	1-57566-180-2	$5.50US/$7.00CAN
_The Door	1-57566-367-8	$5.99US/$7.50CAN
_The Great Mistake	1-57566-198-5	$5.50US/$7.00CAN
_A Light in the Window	0-8217-4021-0	$3.99US/$4.99CAN
_Lost Ecstasy	1-57566-344-9	$5.99US/$7.50CAN
_Miss Pinkerton	1-57566-255-8	$5.99US/$7.50CAN
_The Red Lamp	1-57566-213-2	$5.99US/$7.50CAN
_The Swimming Pool	1-57566-157-8	$5.50US/$7.00CAN
_The Wall	1-57566-310-4	$5.99US/$7.50CAN
_The Yellow Room	1-57566-119-5	$5.50US/$7.00CAN

Call toll free **1-888-345-BOOK** to order by phone or use this coupon to order by mail.

Name _____

Address _____

City _____ State _____ Zip _____

Please send me the books I have checked above.

I am enclosing	$_____
Plus postage and handling*	$_____
Sales tax (in New York and Tennessee only)	$_____
Total amount enclosed	$_____

*Add $2.50 for the first book and $.50 for each additional book.

Send check or money order (no cash or CODs) to:

Kensington Publishing Corp., 850 Third Avenue, New York, NY 10022

Prices and Numbers subject to change without notice.

All orders subject to availability.

Check out our website at **www.kensingtonbooks.com**